Once again, the se_____ their evening meal was _____. Instead, Madeleine and Teeth made their way to the galley to fetch biscuits and salted cod. All eighteen mademoiselles and Elisabeth ate their meager repast seated on the floor of their sleeping quarters. At first, they made a game of the shifting of the boat. Teeth and Madeleine arranged a race with their clogs, seeing which one could slide from port to starboard fastest.

After some time, their good humor dissipated, replaced by fear as the rocking of the ship became so violent the girls began to slip along the floor, drawn from side to side like the clogs in Teeth and Madeleine's game. A sailor appeared and shouted at them to extinguish their lanterns. They did so, lying on the floor in the pitch dark, forming a net of sorts with their arms and legs splayed to brace against the undulation of the sea. The wind howled like an angry beast around them, and above the din, one of the younger girls began to cry and another screamed for her mother.

Teeth had to yell to be heard above the raging of the storm. "If I could see which one of you is whining, I'd get up and wallop you good. No one is to panic. No more crying for your ma!"

Praise for *A DAUGHTER OF THE KING*

"A captivating tale inspired by the author's ancestor, Jeanne Denot, one of 800 women shipped from France to the wilds of King Louis XIV's territory in the New World. Pettersson weaves this little-known chapter in history into a gripping story of betrayal and redemption. A must-read for lovers of historical fiction."

~Catharina Ingelman-Sundberg,
best-selling author of *The Viking Trilogy* and
The Little Old Lady Who Broke all the Rules

~*~

"A suspenseful and entertaining story of secrets and lies aboard a 17th-century ship carrying French brides to the New World. Grippingly told in two halves, we follow heroine Jeanne's picaresque adventures in Grand Siècle Paris alongside her escape, via the creaking, briny decks of the Saint Anne, to colonial New France. But who or what is she running from? Pettersson's cast of colorful characters and skillfully evoked settings bring this little-known episode of history vividly to life in this artful historical novel."

~Nikki Marmery, author of *On Wilder Seas*

A Daughter of the King

by

Catherine Pettersson

A Daughter of the King

Cover Art by *Jennifer Greeff*

The Wild Rose Press, Inc.
PO Box 708
Adams Basin, NY 14410-0708
Visit us at www.thewildrosepress.com

Publishing History
First Edition, 2021
Trade Paperback ISBN 978-1-5092-3801-9
Digital ISBN 978-1-5092-3802-6

Published in the United States of America

Dedication

To the best writers group in the world:
the Stockholm Writers Group.
And to the biggest fan of my book, Marti Parker.

Chapter One

"It is important in the establishment of a country to sow good seed."

~*Jean-Baptiste Colbert,*
Minister of State

The *Saint Anne, September 1668*

As many times as the young woman practiced the new name, it rang false. "I am Jeanne Davide." She uttered the words into the sea air, adding a curtsy for effect. As she did, the *Saint Anne* encountered a swell, and the roll of the vessel threw her off balance, sending her sprawling onto the deck. Jeanne glanced around to see if any of the crew had witnessed her indignity, then stood, smoothing the skirts of the rough-hewn dress pilfered from a laundry in Paris.

She tried again. "Allow me to present myself. I am Jeanne Davide."

"Jeanne," her name from birth, came easily enough, but the new surname continued to vex her. *Davide.* The word, as stiff as a new pair of boots, tripped her tongue, betraying the falsehood it covered. She spoke it rapidly, *Davide, Davide, Davide,* and a thought occurred to her: should one of the crew catch sight of her babbling to herself, they would think her mad. In her mind's eye she conjured the dormitory of the asylum at La Salpêtrière where the rats were as numerous as the inmates. She fell silent.

Jeanne gazed across the choppy waves. Her eyes, seeking the comfort of land, found only endless water. From this vantage on the highest deck of the *Saint Anne*, the sea met the bright morning sky without a seam, which struck her as both never-ending and finite, as if the ship were on a flat plane that could abruptly end. From a book on seafaring in her father's library at Mursay, she knew the world to be spherical. Yet looking out over the dark water, she understood why men of an earlier age had feared a ledge.

Her own fears caused her to startle awake each morning as she surfaced from dreams of the priest and into another kind of waking nightmare. Five days had passed aboard the ship, and with each sunrise her agitation showed no sign of abating. By now they would have discovered the body lying among the headstones, instead of under one. But would they pursue her as far as New France? They had set sail the first week of September under a tame sea. Madame La Plante, expert on all things, had told them the Atlantic could not be trusted past the summer months and this journey would be the last of its kind until spring. But would other ships chance the passage?

Her thoughts produced a queasiness the likes of which she had not experienced since acquiring her sea legs. To vanquish it, she began her walk, one hundred and twenty brisk steps on the starboard side of the ship. The impassable port side of the *Saint Anne* held a veritable farmyard of caged livestock: pigeons, ducks, three goats, and a litter of pigs. Over the course of the *Saint Anne's* two-month voyage, each creature would make its own journey from the top deck to the galley below only to reappear on the plates of the ship's passengers.

Arriving at the stern, Jeanne encountered a sailor, a boy too young to sprout full whiskers. He whistled as she passed. She wheeled around, and the boy smiled at first, then read the expression on her face and grew sober.

"Do you think I'm here for your amusement, boy?" she said.

The young sailor winked and said with a smirk, "You ladies are being shipped off to the other side of the world for someone's amusement. Why not mine?"

Jeanne stood as straight as she could manage given the sway of the ship. "We are here on the king's mission. Have you not heard what we're called? I am a Daughter of the King."

The young sailor bowed obsequiously. "Well then, I do humbly beg your pardon, my lady," he said before scampering off.

She continued her walk, anger accelerating her pace. The *Saint Anne* held a crew of a dozen men charged with delivering eight and twenty women to the New World. Both sexes had been warned of the dire consequences of association, and with a word to Madame La Plante, the boy would receive a lashing. But Jeanne refused to be the source of yet another human being's suffering.

As she headed back to the bow of the ship, she came across the captain who bade her good morning and added, "Mademoiselle, if I may be so bold, one could set a clock by your sunrise strolls on deck."

She hesitated before answering him, afraid that in

3

doing so she would be censored by Madame La Plante whose rules were absolute. Yet Madame, like the rest of the daughters, slumbered below deck. Surely the captain of the ship set the tone for comportment.

"I find it difficult to sleep," she said.

"Not to worry. You'll grow accustomed to it by and by. Most say sleeping is the one thing they do with ease under sail."

Up close, Jeanne confirmed what Madeleine had pronounced about him. The captain was not finely formed. While his chin lacked strength, his nose suffered from too much of it. Jeanne reckoned his age to be somewhere near four and twenty, only six years her senior and far too young to have reached so vaunted a station. Perhaps the cargo of the *Saint Anne* didn't warrant a more seasoned officer, the transport of fur being more valuable than the transport of women shipped off to market like any other commodity.

Jeanne spoke again. "It seems so precarious. To eat, sleep, and carry on living as if nothing is amiss, all the while skimming the depths of the ocean."

The captain smiled and gestured toward the endless expanse of waves. "Mademoiselle, I've voyaged to New France a dozen times without a single mishap."

"It relieves me to hear it. Every time the boat is captured in a gust of wind, and we lean, I fear we will continue to the floor of the ocean."

The captain wore a kind expression, one that reminded Jeanne of her father. "No need to worry. We will cling to the surface and reach terra firma in Quebec soon enough. You have my word on it, mademoiselle…" He hesitated. "Forgive me, what is your name?"

"Mademoiselle Davide." She smiled, pleased with how fluidly the name issued forth.

Chapter Two

"Modesty should be the lot of women. Your sex obliges you toward obedience. Suffer much before you complain about it."

~*Francoise D'Aubigné, Second Wife of King Louis XIV*

Mursay, May 1660

"Jeanne Denot! You will show your face this moment or I will tell your aunt what you're up to, I will."

From their hiding place crouched behind the garden wall, Jeanne and Francoise giggled as they watched the servant lumber across the lawn, an unwilling actor in their theatrics.

They weren't allowed to play outside of the chateau's neatly ringed park, but like Eve and the apple, Jeanne's nature pulled her toward the forbidden fruit, which on this day included a game of hide-and-seek with Henriette, the girls' minder when she wasn't minding pots in the kitchen.

Henriette changed tactics. "Please show yourselves or I'll get a good beating by the marquise for my neglect," she wailed. They watched as the girl fell to her knees and began to burrow like a mole in the dirt, which only made them snort with laughter.

"Does she think we're hiding under the plants?" Jeanne said. "She has the brains of a brick."

"Poor thing. It's no fault of her own," Francoise said. "Henriette's mother dropped her on her head as a baby, which is terribly tragic. Maman told me."

"What's tragic is how she always ruins our fun," Jeanne said, although she did feel a prick of conscience learning of the girl's early misfortune. Presently, Henriette gave up her digging and disappeared into the house.

"I have an idea," Francoise said. "We'll play Agnès and Marion." Francoise had invented the game, which involved playacting scenes with Jeanne's doll, Agnès, who had hair the same shade of brown as Jeanne's, and Francoise's doll, Marion, whose golden locks matched Francoise's own. The last time they played, Aunt Mimi scolded them for using a Turkey carpet to slide down the grand staircase. Francoise explained to her mother how Agnès and Marion had only narrowly escaped a villain by sledding down a mountaintop.

"Agnès and Marion is for children," Jeanne said.

Jeanne had passed her tenth year in April, only two months before her cousin, but she liked to remind Francoise of the wisdom of her advanced age. Papa had urged Jeanne to be kind to her cousin, who, after all, had no fortune. By allowing Francoise and Aunt Mimi to live at Mursay, Jeanne and her father had saved them from destitution. Jeanne had overheard snatches of conversation concerning her aunt's late husband, the Marquis de Vitré, but her father remained tight-lipped about the details of the marquis's demise. Beyond her promise to be kind to Francoise, a vow she often broke,

Jeanne understood the futility of clashing with her. Without Francoise, Jeanne had no diversions. More often than not, their truces arose out of necessity and lacked the spirit of true forgiveness.

"We will go into the woods and hunt toads to hide in Henriette's bed," Jeanne proclaimed.

In the full light of the late May sun, Francoise's hair was rendered a glorious shade of gold, an effect that made Jeanne wish her own locks were blonde instead of brown. "But Henriette will tattle to Maman, and I'll get a whipping," Francoise said. Her lip began to quiver.

"She will say nothing. I caught her stealing food from the dinner plates last night."

Francoise said, "The servants are allowed scraps. It is no crime."

"Not scraps. She smuggled an entire rabbit into her apron, and I caught her in the act. She'll keep her lips buttoned."

At first the girls stayed close to the wall separating the wilds of the forest from Mursay's manicured gardens. After some time, however, with the heat rising, they were drawn further into the cool shade of the woods. Jeanne lost sight of the wall entirely but said nothing of it. Instead, she scoured the ground for the greenish brown prey, wanting to best Francoise.

After fruitlessly hunting their quarry, Jeanne said, "Frogs favor water. We should go to the river."

They knotted their skirts to keep them from dragging on the forest floor as they hunted, at times on their hands and knees. Deeper into the thickness of the trees, Jeanne heard the murmur of the river, and as she drew closer to the sound, the hard earth became sodden.

She reached the river's edge at last and witnessed a tree branch as big as a ceiling beam born swiftly downstream by the engorged current.

When Francoise finally emerged from the tree line, her eyes widened. "Heavens! You look like a haystack!"

Jeanne's skirt was festooned with rents from the brambles on the forest floor and her boots appeared to be fashioned out of mud instead of leather.

Francoise screamed and pointed to the side of Jeanne's face. "You're gushing blood."

Jeanne touched her cheek and came away with a spot of red on her fingers. "It's a scratch. Don't be such a ninny." Francoise tended toward histrionics, which Jeanne attributed to her youth and lack of experience.

Miraculously, Francoise appeared no worse for the wear. Her blond locks were a bit askew, her color heightened. Otherwise, she appeared as neat and pristine as a spring bud. "My mother will throttle us both if she sees you in this state!" she said.

Jeanne told Francoise to help her tidy up. She peeled off her dress, leaving her wearing a thin cotton shift, and handed it to Francoise. "Shake off the dirt while I clean my shoes."

Jeanne found a flattish stone next to the rushing river. She knelt upon it, first dipping one shoe, then the other into the rapid waters which swept away the debris from the leather with a delightful efficiency. Still kneeling, she held up her shoes like shining trophies for her cousin to see. In doing so she lost her balance, wobbling momentarily before plunging forward into the water.

For the briefest of moments, she held fast to the

side of the muddy edge, her shoes still clutched one in each hand. Then the river fought to claim her, pulling her until it gathered her fully into its chill embrace, and bore her away as Francoise screamed her name.

The torrent was a liquid icicle. Jeanne managed to get her head above water, but the cold froze her lungs, making gasping for air impossible. She struggled to gain a foothold on the sandy river bottom and in doing so finally released her shoes, which bobbed up to the surface and ran merrily ahead of her.

The muscular current wrestled her down, plunging her head under water and dragging her to the middle of the stream. She surfaced and this time managed to gasp for air. Francoise ran along the riverbank shouting something Jeanne failed to hear over the roar of the deluge. She needed to break the water's terrible grip. Her legs performed a peculiar kind of dance, jigging and hopping to find purchase on the riverbed, until at last she stood, or rather slid upright, her feet carving a trough along the bottom.

At last her trajectory slowed, and Jeanne could see her cousin pointing frantically up ahead. Francoise had managed to heave a branch twice her size into the river, calling out to Jeanne, "Grab hold!"

Jeanne made to seize it. Although she nearly collided with the branch, the cold of the river had forged her flesh into iron, making it impossible to grip the limb. The tree snagged her clothing and disrupted her journey for a moment. With Jeanne temporarily fastened, Francoise tugged the giant branch, reeling Jeanne in like a fish.

But the river would have none of it. It unhooked her, setting her once again in motion with a mighty pull that caused Jeanne to slide further below the surface, so deeply, she felt the stones of the riverbed brush her back. Spent of energy, she no longer fought to stand.

Jeanne moved along underwater, an aurora of light looming above her. Then, like arrows hitting a mark, her legs met solid earth where the river widened and grew shallow. At last her awful progress slowed, and Francoise again threw out a branch. This time Jeanne folded her body around it and her cousin managed to haul her onto the riverbank. Francoise half carried her, barefoot and blue-lipped, through the forest to the safety of Mursay.

When they entered the house, Henriette screamed and kicked up a fuss, pronouncing Jeanne to be "on death's door." Aunt Mimi gave them a tongue lashing until she heard the story of Francoise's valor, whereupon she summoned her confessor, Father Dieudonné, to perform a special service in Francoise's honor to be held the following evening in Mursay's chapel.

****

Jeanne made it a habit to write daily missives of a line or two to her father when he was with the king's troops. After the service for Francoise, it took a full page for her to vent her frustrations. She concluded with:

Why was the mass not said for me? I was the beneficiary of a miracle, not Francoise. I do try to love my cousin and aunt as much as I know you want me to, but sometimes I wish them gone. It is sinful to say, but I wish the priest gone even more! Oh, how I miss you, Papa! As the others prayed for Francoise tonight, I prayed for you to return and never leave me again.

Chapter Three

"It would be good to strongly recommend that the girls destined for this country not be disgraced by Nature in any way. That they have nothing repulsive about their exterior, that they be healthy and strong for country work, or that they have at least some aptitude for household chores."

~*Jean Talon, Governor, New France*

The *Saint Anne*

Jeanne drew a breath and held it before descending the ladder leading to the realm of the mademoiselles. Below deck, the air held the stench of slop buckets filled with bile from those unaccustomed to the restlessness of the sea, and the ripe corporal odors of eighteen souls sleeping cheek by jowl. After a while she would grow accustomed to the foul air, her nostrils eventually so overwhelmed, they ceased to discern any smell at all.

On the first day of the voyage, Jeanne had caught a glimpse of the demoiselles' quarters on the deck above theirs. The ten women of higher birth enjoyed fine feather beds and wide portholes affording a view to the horizon. She thought bitterly of how fate had unjustly relegated her to the bowels of the ship. At times she wondered if it would be better to forego the light and open air of the top deck entirely and grow inured to the misery below. The hardship came in the transition between the two worlds.

Jeanne picked her way around the sleeping girls to find Madeleine, her hammock rocking with the cadence of the ship. Jeanne marveled at the girl's talent for sleep, recalling one night at the hellhole La Salpêtrière where they first met. In the dormitory, one of the girls had dropped a candle onto the straw mattress next to Madeleine's. Through the ensuing panic Madeleine slept on, insensible to the hysteria that had broken out around her.

Jeanne climbed into her own hammock next to Madeleine's and waited for her friend to rise. Fate was a slippery fish. If looks could be traded for lucre, Madeleine would be a queen. Despite her lowborn origins, she had the bearing of royalty. Presently her eyes fluttered, then opened. Even with the portholes ajar, the light in their quarters, three decks below the bridge of the ship, remained dim at best causing Madeleine to squint.

Madeleine whispered so as not to wake the others, "Poor Jeanne. Still rising before the sun. You remind me of the cuckoos in the asylum."

"I'm in awe of the serenity of your mind that allows you to sleep."

Madeleine yawned and stretched as best she could, given the confines of her hammock. "It's been how many days in this tub? Ten? Ten thousand? It feels like a lifetime. Two lifetimes."

"Exactly five today," Jeanne said. She knew this for certain, having carved a groove into the floorboards under her hammock to verify time as it passed in its desultory manner, one day mingling into another like so many waves on the sea.

"Nearly a week gone by and you're still fretting? We're safe now. Besides, rocked like a babe in a bassinette, the only thing I can do aboard this tub is slumber."

"What if they find us?"

"You worry too much, Jeanne."

"And you too little."

"Between us, we're perfect." Madeleine combed her fingers through her thick honey brown hair that came to a peak at her forehead, giving her face the shape of a heart. "If only we could be given a sleeping potion to be knocked out, then roused when we reach New France, and not a minute earlier."

Jeanne nudged Madeleine's hammock. "Stop your daydreaming and rise like the sun, which is, by the way, quite high and wonderfully bright. A welcome break from these putrid quarters."

Jeanne pushed her friend's hammock with a force that caused it to swing wildly. Madeleine shrieked and her outburst prompted the surly Parisian, Madeleine had christened Teeth, to growl, "Pipe down, slattern!"

"Who's calling who slattern, you louse-covered slut," Madeleine said. "Or did you not notice the deck you occupy? That would be the third, along with the rest of the lowlifes."

Teeth lacked any physical deformity and could be deemed pretty save for her most pronounced feature and the inspiration for her nickname: her teeth which were stained black, by what Jeanne couldn't divine and wouldn't dare ask.

Teeth snorted, saying, "I'll always be above the

likes of you."

"Rot in hell," Madeleine said.

"After you!"

Teeth and Madeleine's first clash came before either one of them had set foot on the *Saint Anne* in the port of La Rochelle. Each of the eight and twenty girls was obliged to show proof of baptism before gaining entrance to the ship, a tortuously slow process conducted under the brutishly hot August sun. Teeth made to cut in line and Madeleine would not allow it. An exchange of hair-tugging escalated to fisticuffs before an official separated the two.

Their fractiousness was understandable. Most of the mademoiselles had waited nearly a fortnight, finding refuge where they could in La Rochelle, before finally boarding the ship. Jeanne's own vexations had doubled with each passing day, and when the departure of the *Saint Anne* was finally announced, she felt certain they were being followed and would be caught before they could set sail. Her fears were such, that by the sweltering morning when the ship at last lifted anchor, Jeanne had chewed her fingernails down to the nubs.

After exchanging a few additional morning pleasantries with Teeth, Madeleine at last roused herself. "I have to piss like a horse. I'll meet you topside," she said to Jeanne. Then, for Teeth's benefit, she added, "The fetid wind coming from the port side is making me positively lightheaded." She pantomimed a fan with one hand and held her nose with the other.

"My farts is prettier smelling than your best perfume," Teeth rejoined.

"Can you please shut your beak!" one of the other

mademoiselles said to Teeth, which lit a flame of bickering that spread rapidly, kindled by close quarters and ill humor.

When Madeleine joined orbit on deck with Jeanne, the two made their way stern to bow and Madeleine shared her observations of the other girls in the group, with particular words devoted to her hatred of Teeth.

As they made their way back to the other side of the ship, someone called to them, interrupting their conversation: "Hello, lovelies." They looked around for its source, until the voice said, "Up here."

Madeleine spied him first, a deckhand perched on the foremast above them. He grinned. "You do know, my beauties, you won't be getting to New France any the faster by adding steps to the journey."

Jeanne looked away, pointedly ignoring his impertinence while Madeleine readily took the bait. "Is it so?" She blocked the glare of the sun with her hand.

"'Tis. Having made the journey myself thrice before, you have my word on it." With that he swung down from the rigging, as nimble as a spider on a web, and stood before them.

The male of the species aboard the *Saint Anne* fell into two categories: wizened old salts as natural a part of the vessel as the barnacles clinging to its hull, and whelps, young boys who swaggered like poor stage players acting the parts of men. This one fell into neither category.

Madeleine said, "I've never seen you before," which was a bold-faced lie, since the sailor's good looks had been the source of gossip among the mademoiselles.

"Well, I've seen you," he replied.

Jeanne guessed him to be near his twentieth year. He possessed a face at once beautiful in its features yet rugged. In truth, standing this close to him, Jeanne found it difficult to avert her gaze. Madeleine openly stared. From her limited experience, Jeanne had observed it was the nature of men to strut like peacocks, which this one did before them now, puffing his chest out to display the advantages of his physique. Madeleine, in turn, placed her hands on her hips, posing in a way that drew notice to her ample bosom, a maneuver Jeanne had witnessed before, but try as she might, could not satisfactorily reproduce.

"Can you suggest an alternative activity to speed the voyage?" Madeleine said.

Jeanne tugged her friend's elbow, urging her along, but the girl anchored herself before the strapping sailor.

"Aye, mademoiselle," he answered soberly. "I can usually think of one or two. But with you, I could imagine even more." His gaze swept over the two of them from the soles of their feet to the roots of their hair which produced in Jeanne a queer sensation of excitement mixed with shame. "How do you call yourselves, my ladies?"

Looking pointedly away from the man, Jeanne said stiffly, "It is forbidden to fraternize with the crew aboard this vessel."

Madeleine and the sailor exchanged glances then burst into peals of laughter while Jeanne blushed like a country rube. The two seemed to follow the rulebook to a game Jeanne had yet to play.

"Forgive me, dear lady, but the captain is below deck enjoying a nap," he said. "Surely no harm will come of knowing what name to put to the beauty that stands before me?"

Madeleine told him their names and the sailor bowed extravagantly. "I am called Laurent."

Madeleine curtseyed. "Laurent, we are enchanted to meet you. You improve the view on this deck considerably."

"As do you, mademoiselle," he said.

Jeanne tugged again at Madeleine's arm, this time more forcefully, and bid the sailor adieu.

As they walked away, Madeleine looked back and waved, then said, "You are a spoilsport. Flirting with that pudding is the only fun I've had in weeks."

"But you do know if Madame La Plante caught sight of you carrying on, you'd end up in her record book."

"I don't fear that old hag, La Plante. The king has gone to great lengths to see us chickens lay eggs for his new kingdom. 'Fraternization', as you call it, is the point of this entire venture."

"What then of the judgment of God Almighty?"

"Ha! At this point, I'll have to barge my way past the Pearly Gates or run through when no one's looking," she said, putting an arm across her friend's shoulders. "I'll try to fix a place for you if I get there first."

The truth of her words seized Jeanne with panic. She pictured the eternal flames of Hell raging far below the ocean floor, certain that damnation was both their fates. Jeanne began to cry at the thought of their eternal punishment, then at the knowledge she would never again see her father, or meet her mother, both of whom resided in Heaven above. Her tears led to an outburst of sobbing which Madeleine attempted to soothe. She sat down on the planks of the deck and pulled Jeanne into her arms, holding her like a mother would a child.

"Come now. Stop crying or your face will puff up, and you'll scare the crew," Madeleine said, swaying to and fro with the movement of the ship.

In the refuge of her friend's embrace, Jeanne quieted presently. Her melancholy, satiated by degrees, was replaced by a creeping dread: Regardless of the fate awaiting them in this life, they were surely doomed in the next one for what happened in the churchyard in Paris. Her thoughts wandered to Francoise, slumbering at this very moment in Mursay, tucked into her plump feather bed until Henriette arrived to awaken her by opening the heavy drapes and lighting a fire.

Jeanne would never again see her cousin or Mursay, of that she was certain. The thought made her despair until she reminded herself that in the bargain, she had gained her life. Her freedom. In fifty-some days, they would reach the shores of New France; a span of time that barely covered a season. Yet one to Jeanne seemed a lifetime away.

Chapter Four

"Life is a comedy to those who think, a tragedy to those who feel."

~ *Jean Racine*

Mursay

Father Dieudonné. His name meant, *God's gift.* Jeanne wondered if the priest was born to serve as a vessel of the Almighty, or had he been moved to do so given the happenstance of his surname? Staring was rude. Or so Jeanne had been told time and again by her aunt. She observed the holy man surreptitiously as he prayed, head bowed, blessing the meal from a seat at the table usually occupied by her father, on the rare occasion her father was home.

His face defied chronology, looking neither particularly young nor particularly old. Jeanne reckoned him to be close to her aunt's age. His blue eyes possessed a dreamy quality, an almost absent look, as if his thoughts dwelled elsewhere in a place free of the mundanity of the corporal world. In conversation, his voice barely registered above a whisper. After finishing grace, the priest muttered something.

"Pardon?" Aunt Mimi said. From her place at the far end of the table, she cupped an ear to catch what Father Dieudonné had said.

The priest cleared his throat and began again. "I noted how we are blessed to enjoy such a bounty of food," he said, gesturing toward a platter piled high with two hens and a half dozen pigeons. "Why, there's enough on this table to feed a parish."

"It would amaze you how much these two can eat," Aunt Mimi said, waving toward Francoise and Jeanne. "For all their demure looks, they have the appetites of farmhands."

Father Dieudonné coughed, or laughed, a sound too faint to identify with any certainty. "Well, this girl certainly has the strength of one." He lifted his chin toward Francoise who nodded in modest acknowledgement of her heroic abilities. "Tell me again how you came to retrieve your cousin, a girl considerably larger than yourself, from the clutches of the river?"

Jeanne arranged her face into a mask of placid attentiveness, but inside she seethed. Although taller than her cousin, Jeanne's figure was as slim. The priest made it sound as if Francoise had fished a whale from the water.

Francoise told the story again, adding new details: "Her lips were purple. She had only the faintest hold on the world of the living." As she spoke, Aunt Mimi hung on her daughter's every word, leaving a pigeon wing to dangle from her hand as if in lopsided flight. "Then a voice came to me from above. 'Francoise, God has chosen you to rescue this sad wretch. Be brave!' Which is when I found the strength to save her."

Father Dieudonné leaned forward and said in a voice filled with wonder, "Nothing short of divine intervention."

Francoise added a final flourish to her account. "If I had not been there, Jeanne would certainly be doomed."

The priest smiled beatifically. "Indeed."

After dinner, the girls made for the nursery where Jeanne proposed a game of "Lovely Princess," a diversion they had played as long as she could remember. They reenacted the narrative again and again with little variation. Jeanne always portrayed the princess, which required Francoise to perform a variety of roles from the evil witch who conspires to kill the young beauty, to the handsome prince who rides his steed—a wooden stick with ribbons as a harness—to a spectacular rescue.

Jeanne fastened a pale pink veil on her head, the costume of the princess. "Woe is me!" she said, clasping her hands together in mock prayer. "Who will deliver me from the evil hag who keeps me locked away in this prison?"

The words cued Francoise to respond as handsome prince, but instead she threw down the stick horse. "You're always princess. I want a turn."

"I invented the game. That means I play the princess. Those are the rules."

"Those are your rules. Why should I follow them?"

Jeanne wanted to tell her cousin that if it weren't for her, she wouldn't be here at all. She'd live on the streets, destitute with her mother. Instead, Jeanne tore the gossamer veil from her head and threw it at her cousin, who grabbed it as it floated toward the ground. "Fine. You can be princess." Then she muttered, "Baby."

If Francoise heard the insult, she ignored it. "Now,

I will lie here on the bed." She pointed to a divan. "You will come in and think I'm dead and weep and wail, but in a manly sort of way, and tell me how beautiful I am and how your world is destroyed." Francoise placed the veil over her face like a shroud. She held her breathe to stop the cloth from fluttering. Her face turned from pink to blue, and at last she sat up, gasping for air. "Why are you just standing there? Get on your horse. Rescue me!"

Jeanne kicked the wooden stick, sending it skittering across the stone floor. "I no longer wish to play. You've killed the pleasure of the game."

"Only because you can't get your way. You're a selfish little shit, Jeanne Denot."

"We are not to say that word. It is a sin!"

"Shit! Shit! Shit! Jeanne is a shit!"

If only her aunt and the priest knew the real Francoise. The thought spurred an idea, and Jeanne said, "I'm going to tell Father Dieudonné you cursed. He won't think so highly of you then."

Jeanne expected Francoise to protest. Instead she said, "Do it. See if I care. He won't believe you, anyway."

"I'm going to tell right this instant," she said.

"Then why are you still here?" Francoise said.

Jeanne could detect a tremor in her voice, a hint of nervousness lurking under her bravado. As if to appear nonchalant, Francoise retrieved the steed and pretended to feed him a carrot.

Jeanne skipped out of the room and made her way to her aunt's chambers to ask the whereabouts of Father Dieudonné but found it empty. She continued down the great hall and toward the main staircase. Rays of warm orange light from the setting sun spilled through the windows and bathed the portraits of Denot ancestors in its glow. When she came to the picture of her mother, she blew her a kiss and made the sign of the cross, a ritual she had performed as long as she could remember. She continued on, her leather boots tapping out a rhythm to which Jeanne added lyrics, "Going to tell! Going to tell! Going to tell!" On the staircase she met Henriette.

"And where might you be off to?" the girl asked impertinently.

"None of your business," Jeanne said.

Henriette, hands dug into her fleshy hips, moved to block Jeanne's passage. "The marquise wants you abed. Told me herself to make certain you were." Henriette was thirteen years of age, only three years Jeanne's senior, and neither old enough nor clever enough to command her respect.

"Be that as it may, I have something urgent to tell her."

"The marquise was very specific." The ponderous cadence of the girl's speech made Jeanne itch to push past her. "*Very specific* on those instructions."

"Yet, when she issued them, she could not have known I would require her counsel urgently, now could she?"

Henriette crossed her arms and stood her ground, until presently a spark of light flickered behind her gaze. She was thinking. "Well," she said, "I suppose it wouldn't hurt nobody if you had a brief word. It would be a brief word, now wouldn't it, mademoiselle? Otherwise, I'll feel her boot on my backside."

"Yes, yes. Tell me, where is she?"

"Headed to the chapel, last I saw," Henriette said. "Now promise you won't dawdle. You'll speak to her and go straight to bed?"

"I told you once. Now out of my way, girl."

Henriette said something under her breath, a word Jeanne could have sworn was *brat*. But she had no time to challenge the dimwit now. Aunt Mimi would be irritated with Jeanne for not doing as she was told, or rather, for not doing as Henriette was ordered to tell her, but the opportunity to correct the priest's impression of Saint Francoise would be worth any punishment.

Jeanne hoped to find the priest with her aunt so she could tell on Francoise to both of them. For as long as Jeanne could remember, Father Dieudonné acted as her aunt's personal confessor and spiritual counselor. Once, Jeanne had overhead Papa questioning his sister's devotion to the man and Aunt Mimi had said, "He cleanses my soul of the stains of my husband," which made Jeanne wonder what special holy powder the priest used for such a task.

Jeanne picked up her skirts and ran, a practice frowned upon by her aunt, especially indoors. *A lady is always busy yet never hurried.* She stood outside the entrance to the chapel and steadied her breathe. Carved into the imposing doors were figures representing the Denot lineage standing toe-to-toe with the Blessed Virgin and all of the apostles, each marked with a symbol: Peter with his keys to the Kingdom, Mathew wielding a sword, and Jeanne's favorite rendering, Judas, his purse bulging with the evidence of his betrayal.

She pushed mightily to open the towering portals,

and they moaned as if the effort taxed them as much as it taxed her. Once inside the chapel she shivered. With its walls of thick white stone, the chapel remained perpetually cold, and Jeanne hugged herself for warmth.

It took her a moment to adjust to the dim light cast by a single candle which adorned the altar. She passed a confessional. Empty. She called her aunt by name and moved down the center aisle toward the altar to extinguish the candle, and as she did so, she heard the rustling of skirts and the rapid exchange of whispers. As she cleared the last row of pews, she came upon her aunt kneeling at the side of the altar, the priest next to her, both with their heads bowed.

Aunt Mimi appeared surprised when Jeanne cleared her throat. She hissed, "What are you doing here?"

"Beg your pardon. It is just that—" The cut of her aunt's tone caused her words to jumble. "Francoise and I were in the nursery. She wanted to be princess, and I said she couldn't, then she said something wicked."

The priest raised his head and spoke. "Why do you bother your aunt with such petty concerns? Do you not see how she communes with a higher power?"

Jeanne blurted it out before her nerves failed her. "Francoise said, 'shit'!"

Father Dieudonné made the sign of the cross. "You came down here and disturbed this most holy form of prayer to tell tales about your cousin? The same person who not a week ago delivered you from certain death. For shame, Jeanne Denot!"

Jeanne ignored the priest and instead addressed her aunt. "A sin is a sin."

"Where is that silly cow, Henriette? She was to have seen you into bed. I'll cane that halfwit myself."

"Please, Aunt. It was no fault of Henriette's. It was my doing entirely."

The priest stood and adjusted his breeches. In the murky light she could make out sweat on his upper lip and in the ropey locks of his hair, as if he'd been exerting himself instead of praying.

He gently ran the tip of his finger over her cheek and as he did, a shiver crept down her spine and tiptoed its way back up her neck. "Very good, Jeanne. It is brave and right to own your transgressions. Now go. Forgive your cousin her sin and ask the Lord our God forgiveness of your own."

As she turned to leave, her aunt spoke in a voice now soft, almost meek. "Jeanne, I apologize for speaking so harshly before. But you startled me. Do as Father said and forgive Francoise. You must serve as an excellent example, a role model for her of righteous womanhood."

Jeanne walked with great composure back to the nursery, feeling the weight of her aunt's words: *righteous womanhood.* As she passed the portrait of her mother, she stopped for a moment to rest her gaze on the painting, making a silent vow to be a model of virtue and dignity henceforth.

As she reached the nursery, Henriette bustled out of it. "There you are," the girl said. "Now to bed straightaway. You promised."

"Henriette," Jeanne said. The girl narrowed her eyes and appeared to brace herself for an argument. "I apologize for speaking so harshly before."

"Oh, why—" Henriette's mouth hung open in

27

astonishment. Presently she recovered herself and said, "Why, thank you. Them words was most kind."

Chapter Five

"Great care was taken of the prospective wives during the voyage. They were put in the charge of a matron paid by the King for her services. It is estimated that in twenty years no less than a thousand young women were dispatched to New France."
                    ~*Mother Marie of the Ursuline Convent*

The *Saint Anne*

To while away the hours aboard the *Saint Anne*, the mademoiselles gambled, a pastime strictly forbidden by Madame La Plante, which only heightened the pleasure of it. Their wagers came in the form of pins, needles and the occasional ribbon, all precious bits of the trousseau each girl received in preparation for their lives in the New World.

They bet on most everything: breath holding, staring, upchucking, belching and breaking wind. Today's game involved placing pigeon bones at a starting line. Each undulation of the *Saint Anne* sent the game pieces skidding to and fro until the first gray-blue cartilage veered across a designated finish line.

When Teeth declared victory, they devised a new game out of who could stand longest on one leg, a feat made particularly difficult given the roughness of the sea. They played away, cheering as Teeth managed to withstand a roll of the ship that knocked down the rest of her competitors like pins on a bowling green. As Teeth at last fell over, Madame La Plante appeared in the passageway to their quarters and surveyed the room through the dim lighting. Jeanne, like the rest of the girls, had been lying on the floor, but she sat up, straightening her skirt.

Although the ship churned, Madame managed to stand stock still as if rooted to the planks beneath her feet, seemingly impervious to the forces of nature. "We have begun services in the captain's quarters." Her face registered her usual distaste with the lot before her. When no one moved, she added sharply, "You will come at once."

"You must be joking. We can barely stand upright," Madeleine said. "We can't even occupy our hammocks they swing so violently. How do you expect us to pray?"

Madame clutched a book to her bosom. Its dark leather cover was nearly lost against the color of her garb, which was black from bonnet to boot. In the early days aboard the *Saint Anne*, Jeanne assumed Madame's ubiquitous volume was the Bible, but later discovered it to be an account of the old woman's observations of the girls throughout the journey. As Madeleine spoke, Madame La Plante's fingers tapped on the book's cover as if impatient to record this most recent infraction.

Madame cleared her throat. "Girls, as lowborn as you are, you can still fight the baseness of your natures and conquer your laziness both corporal and spiritual. Now, if you can stand on one leg for your idle foolishness, you can stand on the two He gave you to give Him praise."

As soon as Madame departed, Teeth groaned. "You heard what hatchet face said. 'Conquer your laziness both corporal and spiritual.' Or as my own ma would say, 'Get off your arses.'"

Madeleine remained on the floor. "Look who's in charge now. Are we taking orders from you and from the old woman?"

Teeth stood with one hand on the hull for balance. "We all know the only one you obey. That randy sailor, Laurent. And when you do, the *Saint Anne* rocks and heaves mightily, for at least the few minutes of surge he has in him."

Jeanne gave a hand to Madeleine to help her stand. As she did, she whispered, "You started it. Say nothing in return and end it." To her surprise, Madeleine remained silent.

From this depth within the *Saint Anne*, the companionway leading to the upper deck was no more than a ladder, one that required climbing on all fours even on the mildest of days. The girls formed a line to make their ascent while Teeth oversaw their progress at the foot of the stairway.

When at last Jeanne and Madeleine were ready to climb, Teeth pushed in front of them and Madeleine said, "Better to look at your big backside than your ugly face." Teeth rewarded the comment with a kick that only narrowly missed Madeleine's head.

When they arrived at the captain's quarters, the demoiselles were already assembled. They formed a tight half circle around his desk which served as a makeshift altar. One demoiselle, Elisabeth, a plump girl of no more than fourteen, stood apart from the others, stationed close to a slop bucket. Unlike the rest of the demoiselles, her face wore a kind expression and on occasion, she even deigned to exchange pleasantries with the mademoiselles. At regular intervals throughout the service, Elisabeth rushed to the bucket to render the contents of her stomach, causing a few of the girls in her immediate vicinity to follow suit.

During a pause in the liturgy the captain spoke, raising his voice above the roar of the gaining storm. "Madame, seeing as so many of the maids are feeling poorly today, perhaps it would be more suitable to worship our Maker privately, in the comfort of our respective cabins."

Comfort was possible in the captain's room. Nearly as large as the mademoiselles' own quarters, the captain enjoyed the luxury of a generously proportioned berth built into one wall and ample room for a desk and small chaise.

Madame ignored his comment, although from the quiver of her nostrils, she had registered it clearly enough. Her voice competed with the howl of the storm and the groaning labor of the ship. "*Ave Maria, gratia plena, Dominus tecum.*"

After what seemed an eternity given the wretchedness surrounding them, Madame announced a merciful end to their worship and the girls staggered their separate ways, the mademoiselles to make the treacherous descent two decks below, while the demoiselles descended only one level to reach their quarters.

As Jeanne waited her turn at the companionway, Madame gestured for her to step aside. Out of earshot from the rest of the girls, Madame said, "You are not one of them."

"Beg your pardon?" Jeanne said.

Madame nodded as if Jeanne's response had confirmed a suspicion. "The mademoiselles. You are not of their ilk."

"Pray, Madame, what are you implying?"

"Pish!" Madame snorted. "Your carriage. Your diction. They paint a certain picture, girl. Now tell me your name again."

"My name is Jeanne Denot." She winced as soon as the family name escaped her lips. She added as mildly as she could, "Jeanne Davide."

Madame cocked an eyebrow. "Well, which is it? Denot or Davide? There can be only one answer."

"My given name is Jeanne Denot Davide. Denot is a name on my mother's side of the family."

"Denot, Denot." Madame's eyes were lively, calculating, as if Jeanne were an equation that defied reconciliation. Her thoughts at last appeared to settle. "There was one seigneur, Antoine Denot, a Maréchal de Camp for the king's army out of Perche. Do you know of him?"

Upon hearing her father's name, a wash of emotion swept through her very being causing her knees to buckle. To arrest her fall, Jeanne grabbed hold of a rope hanging on the hull, grateful for the turbulence of the ship which masked the turbulence of her heart.

After righting herself she said, "Yes, Madame. I believe him to be a distant relative, twice or thrice removed." She lowered her eyes. "Our side of the family was less favorably blessed."

"Still," Madame persisted, "how is it you came in with this lot? Creatures recruited from the warrens of La Salpêtrière. As common and numerous as jackrabbits and as fast in their ways, I dare say."

"Madame, decency prevents further explanation."

Madame La Plante knitted her brow then fell silent a moment before adding, "How very odd." Her perplexed state appeared to affect her balance, and in the next undulation of the ship, she nearly fell, but then tucked her book under one arm as counterbalance, regaining her usual implacable, stance. "Adieu," Madame said. "May the peace of the Lord be with you, Jeanne *Denot* Davide." Her words were tinged with a layer of irony Jeanne chose to ignore.

"And also with you, Madame La Plante."

By suggesting a sordid family history, Jeanne forced Madame to retire the shovel of her questioning. By the look on the old woman's face, she clearly longed to dig further. But the real story lay too deeply buried, known only to Madeleine and the people who would see Jeanne dead if only they could find her alive.

Chapter Six

"Good fortune will elevate even petty minds and give them the appearance of a certain greatness and stateliness, as from their high place they look down upon the world. But the truly noble and resolved spirit raises itself and becomes more conspicuous in times of disaster and ill fortune."

~*Plutarch*

Mursay

Each time Jeanne's father returned home he seemed a different version of himself. After a stretch at the court of the Palais Louvre, he came back rounder, a high shine in his complexion and mood. When he rode with the king's troops, he returned to Mursay thinner and capricious in his temperament.

One year, her father left on Jeanne's fourteenth birthday and didn't return until just before she turned fifteen. During his time away, he sent letters sharing light-hearted anecdotes about life in the king's military camps. But when he returned home, his face and figure told a more harrowing tale. His hair had turned gray, and his weight diminished, leaving him but a shadow of his former self. It took a few months' convalescence at Mursay to stoke the fire of his spirits. To celebrate her brother's return from the king's service, and Jeanne's fifteenth year, Aunt Mimi arranged a party.

Like a wallflower readied for a ball, Mursay endured every variety of primping: Dust-covered tapestries were beaten until fresh color bloomed from their threads, dull marble floors were made to shine like jewels, and silver chandeliers regained their sparkle, transforming Mursay into a radiant beauty prepared for her callers.

Every night leading up to the ball Aunt Mimi presented the latest developments concerning guests, food, and clothing as they sat at the dinner table. "Both the Duc D'Orléans and his wife are attending, which brings the number to just over one hundred. A small affair to be sure, but festive enough with the right accoutrement. Half that number will stay overnight."

Jeanne's father said, "If the affair is so small, why does it draw so large on the estate's coffers?"

"You know nothing, Antoine. The Fouquet's had a party with one thousand guests!"

"And now Fouquet is locked up at the fortress of Pignerol thanks to his extravagance. So, what will it be for us? The poorhouse or prison?"

Aunt Mimi ignored her brother. "The gamesman who gave me fits now says he can fulfil our order of quail. The man is an extortionist! Holding back his supply to inflate the cost."

"Quail tastes like rat!" Francoise, who would turn fifteen herself in two months' time with little fanfare, grew petulant when it came to the particulars of her cousin's celebration.

"Pray tell, on how many occasions have you dined on rat?" Aunt Mimi asked, and before Francoise could answer, her mother added, "Children are to be seen, not heard. Most of the time they shouldn't be seen either."

Francoise held up a pigeon carcass, which she dropped to her plate with a clatter. "I am not a child. I am nearly a woman of fifteen years, although no one cares to mark it." She leaned back in her chair, crossed her arms, and pouted like a spoiled brat.

As Francoise's temper boiled, Jeanne's own mien became more placid. She met her father's eyes and shrugged her shoulders prettily as if to say, "She is a trial, is she not?"

Her father said, "Come now. You shall have more than your fair share of parties in the future. With your beauty and wit, you'll be the toast of the Palais Louvre, and soon, I dare say. Besides, you can both oversee the festivities. Isn't that right, Jeanne?"

"Why, yes, Papa. Of course." She smiled magnanimously at her cousin and patted her hand. "It shall be both of our parties, even if it does happen to fall on the anniversary of my birth."

But when she found time alone with her father in his library, her thoughts turned sour. "Why must I share my party with Francoise?"

Her father lay sprawled on a divan, his head resting on her lap as they both read. It was their ritual, something Aunt Mimi and Francoise never shared nor asked to take part in as neither one of them cared much for books. More often than not, after several minutes in this repose, her father fell asleep until his book slipped off his chest, or until Jeanne tweaked his nose to stop his snoring.

"It is my birth date and mine alone," Jeanne said. She set aside her volume of Plutarch, a book she had read more times than she could count.

"What did you say?" Her father sat up. The disappointment on his face made Jeanne regret her words. "I can hardly believe my ears. You are the sweetest most generous creature in all the world, and these less-than-charitable thoughts shock me."

"It is only that it's unfair. I am, after all, the lady of Mursay. Not Francoise."

"Come now. Shall we speak of fairness? Is it fair that Francoise's own father died so untimely a death? Is it fair that my sister, and therefore her child, would be destitute if we refused to share our good fortune?"

"You confuse my point. I understand that without you, without us, they would have nothing, and of course I'm happy we can help. But why must Francoise take equal share of my party?"

Her father ran his fingers through his hair causing it to stand in spikes atop his head. "Francoise should not have to cower in the shadow so you can bask in the sun. There is ample light in the world to shine on both of you."

Jeanne knew it to be true, of course. If only the sun didn't turn Francoise's hair into an aurora of gold. After a moment, Jeanne asked her father, "Which one of us is prettier? Francoise or me?"

It took him so long to respond, Jeanne grew apprehensive of his answer. Finally, he said, "You are, in fact, exact equals when it comes to beauty. But in exactly opposite ways. You dark. She light. It's like thinking the sea is more beautiful than a field of flowers, or a mountain superior to the sky above it. Your two looks defy comparison. There is, however, one aspect where no one can be your rival. I love you most of anyone in the world."

With that he returned to his supine position and Jeanne leaned down to kiss his forehead. "I love you most, too. I only wish you were here more often. When you are here, everything is better."

"Is it?" he asked.

"Yes. To begin with, we do not see nearly as much of Father Dieudonné."

"Ah. Does his righteousness tire you as much as it does me?"

"He takes the fun out of everything. He once told Francoise and me not to laugh so much. He said opening your mouth too wide leaves room for the Devil to jump in."

"Nonsense. Advising children not to laugh!"

"Aunt Mimi consults with him on everything." Jeanne recalled that night years before when she came upon them praying together in the chapel.

"If your aunt finds comfort in his guidance, I'm happy for her. Your aunt is good to you otherwise, is she not?"

"Yes. She's wonderful and fun, except when Dieudonné is here, then she's rather dull and holy." Her father laughed even though she had not intended to jest. She said, "I do hope Aunt Mimi hasn't invited him to my party?"

"Rest assured, Father Dull and Holy will not attend. Nothing will spoil your fun, and you'll be the belle of the ball. And in two years' time, when you turn seventeen, you'll be presented at court."

As a child, two years had seemed an eternity. Now, with advancing age, Jeanne felt all too keenly the acceleration of time. "In the blink of an eye I will be presented, you will secure a husband for me, and I'll have children of my own. Am I to leave Mursay then, Papa?"

"That depends on the holdings of your husband. Worry not. Mursay is yours after I am gone."

As soon as he uttered the words, Jeanne was seized by a panic which set off a torrent of tears. As her father held her, in part comforting her, in part teasing her for her violent show of emotion, he said, "Come now. Dry your eyes. You shall have me forever."

Chapter Seven

"Charge the priests with the task of looking up country girls who are strong enough to bear the cold of New France, active enough to help with field work, good enough to make helpmates for decent young colonists, and adventurous enough to be willing to cross the sea."

~*Jean-Baptiste Colbert, Minister of State*

The *Saint Anne*

During a stretch of mild weather, the captain arranged for laundry to be done on the top deck. Sails remained slack as the crew stayed below for the better part of an afternoon to give the women ample room to work. Madame La Plante and three other demoiselles, including the young girl Elisabeth, washed their garments in a tub filled with sea water hot enough to produce a head of steam. The mademoiselles washed in a smaller barrel filled with tepid water.

Jeanne's arms were numb with the effort of scrubbing cloth against cloth, working the filth from a soiled hemline. She had learned the rigors of laundering in La Salpêtrière. Side-by-side, she and Madeleine had toiled, scrubbing the blood, excrement, and every other manifestation of wretchedness from the garments of the destitute.

Although the washtubs stood beside each other, the two groups worked without conversing until Madame La Plante straightened herself from the labor of wringing out a dress to proclaim, "The Denot family of Perche. A tragic story there. Most unfortunate circumstances were involved, although I struggle to recall the details."

Madame's words caused Jeanne's hands to cease moving but set her thoughts into turmoil. *The old lady knows!* Madeleine caught Jeanne's eyes and ever so slightly shook her head, her silent message received clearly enough: *stay calm.*

Jeanne continued her work. She replied to Madame in a tone she hoped passed for nonchalant. "I know not of what you speak. They were not close kin. Only distant cousins on my father's side."

"Your father's side?" Madame said it so sharply, Elisabeth startled, slopping water out of the tub and splashing it across her skirt.

"Yes, Madame. My father's side."

Madame's eyes narrowed. "You told me before your mother's people bore that name."

"What business is it of yours?" Madeleine slapped a sodden dress against the wooden tub to emphasize her words. "Are you taking a census? Good Lord, she knows the roots of her own tree!"

Under her bonnet, Madame's hair was matted from the steam of the water, her dress soaked through with the efforts of her labor. Even so, she assumed a regal bearing, puffing her chest out and training a sanctimonious finger toward Madeleine. "'Thou shall not take the Lord's name in vain!' This will go in my book. Of that you can be sure, mademoiselle."

After Madame's outburst, they fell silent again. After another few moments passed, Madame righted herself once again. "Now I recall it. Yes. There was some tragedy connected to the estate, Mursay. A drowning, as I recollect."

Jeanne fought to control the trembling in her legs, which threatened to give way. "I am certain you are correct, Madame," she said, fighting to control a waver in her voice. "But as I told you, I truly know nothing of the details of the extended family."

Madame stared at her. "Is that so?" she said, her words belying the quizzical look on her brow.

"Aye, you old crone!" Madeleine said, grunting between each word. She squeezed the water out of a garment with such vigor it looked as if she meant to kill it. "It is so!"

Madeleine's words seemed at first to blow the wind out of the old woman's sails, but she regained her composure and spluttered, "Sass pot!" Elisabeth covered her mouth as if to stifle a laugh. "As the moral compass guiding you to New France, I demand you speak to me in a tone reflecting my status."

"Moral compass, are you?" Madeleine squared her shoulders. "For days on end you've either ignored us or browbeat us depending on your mood. Your status is nothing to me or to any of our lot. Keep your comments and your compass pointed toward the demoiselles."

Madame raised her eyes heavenward and made an unsteady sign of the cross. "Lord! Please hear my prayer to show Your light to these heathens who have tasted the fruits of Eve. Those who have been lured into the darkness and the temptation of sin. Who refuse to walk toward Your eternal light!"

"Horse face," Madeleine muttered, turning back to her work.

"Hold your tongue," Jeanne whispered.

Madame La Plante announced she was going to fetch her book, but she stopped when Elisabeth began to shout, bobbing up and down like a sparrow: "Land! Land!"

Madame shushed the girl. "Stop your foolishness. We're in the middle of the sea."

Jeanne scanned the horizon. "She speaks the truth. It is land!" Jeanne said, and joined Elisabeth in a spontaneous jig, the two of them pulling Madeleine into their dance.

Madeleine shouted above the din of their merrymaking. "Could we have we already reached New France?"

"Stuff and nonsense! New France, indeed!" When Madame bade them to stop their cavorting and return to their duties, they took no notice of her.

"Well, what's all this?" It was the captain. "Your cries roused me out of an afternoon nap. Is this some form of mutiny, my dear ladies? Or a new way of laundering? If so, I would be most keen to learn."

Madeleine looped an arm through the captain's, swinging him around in a wild circle. "Land, captain! Land!"

"Captain! You will not encourage this nonsense!" Madame's words halted the captain in mid spin. Chastened, he straightened his hat and ducked his head, looking like a turtle drawing into its shell.

Arranging his face into a more sober mask, he said, "It's no more than an island, I'm afraid." His words halted their dance so suddenly the captain added,

"We'll dock there tomorrow and load supplies. If it's suitable, you'll be free to disembark for a stretch of your limbs."

"Sir," Madame retorted, "your responsibilities revolve around the care and management of this vessel. Mine around the care and management of my charges. It is for me to decide what is suitable and what is not. No girl shall disembark this boat until we reach Quebec."

****

The following day, the *Saint Anne* dropped anchor a short distance from the shore of the island and a group of men in a longboat ventured out.

"What supplies could be found on this Godforsaken hunk of dirt?" Madeleine asked as she leaned out over the rail of the top deck.

A half dozen hills formed the island, strung together like so many beads. But these beads were nothing pleasing to the eye, formed as they were by blackened stone and pitted with caves like the holes in rotting teeth. What little flora visible was devoid of color as if the island had been scrubbed clean of even the smallest of vanities. Jeanne imagined that with the addition of flowing rivers of fire, the island would perfectly match the Scripture's description of Hell itself.

"I saw a herd of goats and a house when we first approached," Jeanne said. "Smoke rose from the chimney. What would bring someone so far out into the sea just to herd goats?"

"I wonder what happens to the goats after enough time alone with a man," Madeleine said.

A thought seized hold of Jeanne's imagination.

"What do you suppose would happen if we were shipwrecked and had to live here?"

"I would cast myself off one of those yonder cliffs," Madeleine said.

A voice behind them answered. "And I would rush to catch you."

Laurent came to stand next to Madeleine in such proximity, Jeanne whispered a caution. "Take care. The watchful eyes of Madame are everywhere."

"I don't care if that old witch spies us," Madeleine said.

Jeanne said, "Oh! But you should. If she discovers your—" she hesitated, searching for a delicate enough word, "alliance with Laurent, she can withdraw your contract and the dowry attached to it. Then what will you have?"

Laurent stepped back and said wistfully, "I'll be off then. I look forward to tonight's 'alliance,'" he said with a wink.

They watched as the longboat reached the shores of the black island.

Madeleine said, "Your face is as clear as a pond, and I see every ripple on its surface. You don't like Laurent, do you?"

"Laurent is the most handsome man I've ever seen. He's clearly besotted with you."

"He is, isn't he?" she said with a smile.

"But he's not part of our plans."

"You speak of plans like they're forged from iron," Madeleine said. "They're more like clay and shaped as fortune sees fit."

"Do you mean to wed Laurent?"

"Wed him?" She laughed. "I haven't even decided

46

if I'll meet with him tonight."

****

They remained anchored off the black island for two days before continuing on to New France. Gossip had it that Teeth had offered the captain a special service to allow the mademoiselles a day on land, but he held to the orders of Madame La Plante, and they remained onboard.

The night they pulled anchor, Teeth said, "Nineteen days stuck on this soggy bucket." She carved a new notch onto the floor next to Jeanne's hammock.

"Twenty," Jeanne said. She shivered and pulled her blanket under her chin. Standing still, the air onboard had been stifling hot. Under sail again, a chill invaded their quarters, particularly after sundown. "Time moves with such alacrity on land and so very slowly on water."

"Alacrity!'" Teeth said. "Listen to her. Speaks like a duchess, this one. You're on the wrong deck, your majesty."

"Maybe she is a duchess," Madeleine rejoined. "We can't all be as lowborn as you."

"And where were you born? The Palais Louvre, I suppose?"

"Not far from it," Madeleine said and stuck out her tongue.

Teeth snorted. "In an alley behind the palace from the loins of a whore. Look who's putting on airs."

"Could you both please be quiet!" Jeanne sat up. "The captain says we have at least forty more days on this ship, and you will drive us all mad with your incessant bickering."

Jeanne expected a rebuff in answer to her outburst,

but instead Teeth whistled, "Forty days? If only we'd been allowed to pass one of them on dry land. I could kill La Plante, the old bitch."

"Your wiles weren't tempting enough for the captain to let us ashore, eh, Teeth? Or did he change his mind after you gave him the suck?" Madeleine laughed.

"Fuck off. As if you could have done any better."

"I didn't fancy going. Laurent says there's nothing out there but a pile of rocks and some goats."

"I would have made love to a bleating goat just to have me feet on solid ground." Teeth sighed. "Now snuff out that light and let's get some shuteye. If there's one thing I can do on this boat, it's sleep. With all this rocking, I slumber like a wee babe, I do."

Madeleine extinguished the lantern. "We took on a passenger from the black island," she said.

Teeth yawned. "How do you know? Did you see him?"

"He boarded in the dead of night. Laurent told me."

"What occupation could keep someone on that miserable island?" Jeanne asked.

"Laurent doesn't know. He barely laid eyes on him."

"Not surprised," Teeth grunted. "Your plaything doesn't know much, does he?"

"Oh, he knows a few things. More than a few, in fact." Her friend's voice held bait to hook a response from Teeth, but a moment passed, and presently Teeth's breathing fell into a rhythmic snore.

Long after her companions nodded off, Jeanne lay awake, wondering what circumstance would compel a person to live on such an uninhabitable wasteland in the middle of the sea. Perhaps they were not unlike the circumstances compelling her to voyage across it.

****

The following morning, weak rays of light made their way through the cracks outlining the portholes. Jeanne lay suspended in a state between sleep and wakefulness, feeling none of the usual desire to rise and seek out the fresh air above. Instead she marked the regular rocking of her hammock, which signaled calm seas. She surveyed the sleeping forms around her contemplating the myriad paths that brought them all to this one place.

More time passed and no one stirred. Jeanne closed her eyes, surrendering to her indolence, and fell into a dream. She was back in the asylum at La Salpêtrière. Francoise was there, as was Aunt Mimi. They beckoned her to one of the dormers lining the attic. Then Francoise began to scream, "Mercy! Please have pity on me."

Jeanne awoke, panting, the voice in her slumber carried over into her wakefulness.

"Please, Madame! I don't belong here!"

The cry came from the passageway connecting their cramped quarters to the decks above. One by one, the other girls awoke.

"God's nightshirt! What racket is this?" Madeleine asked.

Just then, Madame La Plante entered dragging the young girl Elisabeth behind her by the ear, compelling her into their cabin.

"You are to remain here for the duration of the voyage." Madame released the girl then bodily obstructed her from fleeing. "Make no attempt to return to the upper deck, do you understand me?"

Madeleine approached Madame La Plante and asked, "What's the meaning of this?"

"This—" Madame trained a lantern toward the girl who had collapsed onto the floor sobbing. "This person is not fit to reside with the girls of quality above. She has sinned before God Almighty!"

Teeth approached her, and said, "So, you discard her here like so much slop from a bucket?" She knelt by the girl. "What did you do? Pass wind at the supper table?"

Madame paused, making an effort to compose herself before, hand over heart, she whispered, "'Unto the woman He said, I will greatly multiply thy sorrow and thy conception; in sorrow thou shalt bring forth children,'" then turned abruptly and left.

Elisabeth's cries grew louder, as did the din inside the cabin.

"Shut your beaks, all of yous! Someone light a lantern," Teeth commanded, and the room fell silent save for the residual sniffling of the girl. "Now, what's with you, um, what's your name again?"

"It's Elisabeth," Madeleine said. "Out of all the fancy demoiselles, she's the only decent one."

"Well, Elisabeth, what got her holiness so hot today? Have you been caught giving favors to one of the crew?"

Elisabeth looked around as if to gauge the sympathies of her audience. "Marie-Louise de Grancey, she is a wicked girl, and I thought her my friend." She burst into a fresh round of sobs.

Madeleine said, "Aye, I know the one she speaks of. Miss My-Shit-Doesn't-Stink de Grancey."

"They're all like that," Teeth said.

Madeleine clarified by adding, "No tits, blonde hair, eyes too close together," upon which Teeth nodded.

"Well then," Teeth said, "What did Miss No Tits do to you?"

Elisabeth wiped her face on her skirt. "Oh, but she is treacherous. I despise her! I shared a confidence and she betrayed me so miserably. I shall never, ever forgive her. She's a snake in the grass!"

"All right then," Teeth said testily, "You are no longer on speaking terms. But how did you get thrown down here?"

The girl fell silent and as they awaited her response the sound of every creak and groan of the ship amplified then extinguished when she spoke. "I am with child."

All eighteen mademoiselles seemed to simultaneously gasp at the news, even Teeth, who added, "Fuck me standing! A little pansy like you has had your powder lit?"

Elisabeth nodded.

Madeleine asked, "How far along?"

"I'm not sure," she replied miserably.

"Have you felt the quickening?" Teeth asked, and the girl nodded slowly. "When did it begin?"

"Somewhere around early spring. At first I thought it a digestive ailment."

Teeth chuckled. "Something's eating away at you, that's for sure. Now pull up your skirt and let's have a look."

Elisabeth remonstrated, but nonetheless, Teeth compelled her to lie on the floor. "Enough with your modest airs," she said, and reached under the girl's dress. "Mine aren't the first hands under your skirt."

Jeanne and the other girls watched as Teeth pulled up Elisabeth's dress, revealing the girl's rotund form for all to see. "It is large, the baby. Near fully baked."

At Teeth's pronouncement, Elisabeth fell once again into a fit of emotion, gnashing her teeth and tearing at her hair. "It cannot be. What is to become of me? I shall die on this boat!"

While the girl carried on, Jeanne conferred with Madeleine and Teeth. "She cannot stay here in her condition. There are no places to sleep."

Teeth spat. "Birthing the babe on the floor, like a dog. These ladies who burn with the passion of Christ have ice in their veins."

Teeth's words caused Elisabeth to wail with renewed vigor. She knelt before the girl, her hand held aloft, and had to shout to be heard over the girl's keening. "Shut it, or you'll feel the backside of my hand, then you'll really have something to cry about."

Her words had the desired effect and the girl recovered herself.

She wiped her eyes and said pitifully, "It is only I'm so afraid. Neither my babe nor I stand a chance of surviving."

Teeth lifted Elisabeth's chin, forcing the girl to meet her eyes. "Listen, you dolt, as it so happens, my ma was a midwife. Delivered into this world countless infants, she did. I helped her on more than a few occasions and have delivered my own share all by my lonesome. This little loaf will give us no trouble popping out of your oven."

Elisabeth's spirits seemed to improve considerably. She even mustered a weak smile as Teeth helped her to her feet.

"Jeanne," Teeth said, "you need to talk with the captain. Tell him, until her blister pops, the girl can't sleep on the floor like a bitch."

"Me? Surely you know more about this than I?"

"Of course. But I lack your fancy manners and fine way of speech. You're bound to make a more favorable impression on him."

Madeleine said, "Her face will certainly make a more favorable impression than yours."

"I'll make an impression against your mouth if you say another word!" Teeth said, holding up a fist. Jeanne, tired of their bickering, hastened to leave.

As she made her way to the captain's quarters, Jeanne wondered how a vessel skimming over the sea could be so eternally soggy. Ribbons of water trickled down the walls and seeped through the planks, permeating everything aboard the ship. Even the hammocks, suspended well above ground, were perpetually damp. The wetness came as an unwelcome reminder: Life and death were divided by timber the breadth of four of her fingers.

She held up her hand then made a fist, knocking tentatively on the captain's door, but received no response. As Jeanne prepared to leave, the door swung open.

She turned, "Captain—" She began, then realized the person before her was a stranger, a wild-looking man with long black hair and a beard that hung midway down his chest.

He bowed his head and smiled, saying, "Sorry to disappoint. The captain is on deck. May I offer some assistance?"

"No thank you. My business is with the captain alone." In her own ears it sounded as if she sought the man for some overly intimate errand. In her mortification, she stumbled over her words: "There is a matter. I'm here concerning a demoiselle. Well, now it appears she is a mademoiselle. Anyway, it's about a maid who is, how shall I say this? She's not herself." She stopped then blurted out, "She's suffering from a most painful blister."

His affable expression changed to one of concern. "If this lady is in need, I possess some medical training."

"It is nothing requiring immediate tending."

The stranger held a quill in one ink-stained hand. He followed her gaze. "There is no writing desk in my quarters, so the captain generously loaned me his. Allow me to introduce myself: I am Jacques Suprenant."

Jeanne hesitated a moment, reminding herself to use her false name, "I am Jeanne Davide."

He answered her curtsey with a deep bow. Jeanne moved closer to the door, more directly into the path of light emanating from the captain's quarters. Monsieur Suprenant's expression took on a perplexed air, and he stared at her for a moment. Jeanne looked away.

"I will go now to seek the captain," she said. "Pleased to make your acquaintance Monsieur Suprenant."

"And yours, Mademoiselle Davide."

****

As Jeanne feared, the captain refused to countermand Madame's ruling but did allow the mademoiselles to make a bed of sorts for the girl.

Madeleine said, "Captain is a milksop who wouldn't dare disobey the almighty La Plante."

"In his defense," Jeanne said, "Madame outranks the captain, at least on this journey and in these matters. It is she who directly follows the king's orders. When I alluded to your predicament, Elisabeth, he was most sympathetic. He is a kind man."

"Kind man. Weak man. What's the difference?" Madeleine said, then asked Elisabeth to test her new accommodations, a burlap sack stuffed with straw, situated on the floor of the mademoiselles' quarters.

"It is rather nice." The young girl shifted her unwieldy form on the makeshift bed. "Thank you," she said. "I suppose it's better to sleep on the floor with people who are kind than to sleep in a down bed with people who despise you."

"Don't be silly," Jeanne said. "They don't despise you and by all rights you should be upstairs. I would trade my right arm for a down bed."

"By social ranking they're my people, perhaps, but their hearts are made of stone. Marie-Louise de Grancey would sooner see me and my babe dead than share quarters with me."

"So, she's the one who let the cat out of the bag?" Madeleine asked.

Elisabeth nodded, then sighed, looking so defeated that Jeanne sat next to her and presently Madeleine joined them.

"Why did you confide in her in the first place?" Jeanne asked.

"We are cousins once removed. It is her father who sired the baby. I told her as much. It does make us, or at least the babe and she, close kin. Does it not?"

Madeleine laughed. "You imagined her falling into your arms at the news you bore her father's bastard? You are a stupid little cow."

The girl's eyes filled with tears.

"She's not stupid. She's naïve. There is a difference." Jeanne gave Madeleine a look that silenced further commentary. She squeezed Elisabeth's shoulder and said, "What of your family? Do your parents know of your condition?"

"My parents are long dead, mademoiselle. The de Granceys took me in and raised me out of the kindness of their hearts." At that, Madeleine snorted, and Elisabeth added, "Monsieur knew of the child which is why he thought it best I go to New France."

Madeleine asked, "And what of Marie-Louise? Is she also carrying one of his brats?"

"Heavens no! Marie-Louise is to wed one of the king's highest-ranking officers. That match was made long before I can remember. With Marie-Louise journeying to the New World, and me in the family way, Monsieur de Grancey thought it a good idea for me to join her and meet my own fortune."

"Or hide his misfortune," Madeleine added. "He is surely a prince among men."

"No, mademoiselle. He only recently earned the title of duke," she said, which caused Madeleine to burst out laughing.

To change the subject, Jeanne said, "When I went to speak to the captain, I met the man who boarded the ship from the black island."

"Is that so? What was his business there?" Madeleine asked.

"I know not. Our conversation was brief."

Madeleine said, "Was he well-formed?"

"The passage was dimly lit, and his face was covered by a wild beard."

"'I need more to form a picture. Short? Tall? Fat? Thin?"

"Taller than I by a fair margin. Black hair. Light eyes, blue, I think. Not fat."

"How old?" Madeleine said.

"Older than the captain. Perhaps eight and twenty. Well-spoken. He was using the captain's writing desk. His name is Jacques Suprenant."

"Suprenant." Elisabeth said the name slowly. "It rings a bell. There was a family called Suprenant that had ties with the de Granceys. Although I can't recall exactly how."

"Lord!" Madeleine lay back on the straw. "You people with money and pedigree have both because you interbreed. Meanwhile the rest of us mongrels fight over the scraps."

"Speaking of pedigrees, may I ask you something, Jeanne?" the Elisabeth said. "How did you come to be on the *Saint Anne*? The other demoiselles and I often wondered."

Elisabeth's question was innocent enough, yet still it caused Jeanne's pulse to quicken. She formulated her response as truthfully as she could, replying, "Like you, I am orphaned. To say more pains me deeply."

"I'm sorry. It's only, well, you do not seem to quite—" Elisabeth glanced around at the girls in various stages of napping, chatting, and wagering, "fit in with this company. I mean no offense to you, Madeleine."

"None taken," Madeleine said.

"I'm not so sure," Jeanne said. Over the space of

months, she found herself feeling a greater kinship to the girls of the streets of Paris, than those from her former class. "With Madeleine I've found a connection stronger than blood."

"I guess you could say life made us sisters," Madeleine said, clutching her heart theatrically.

Although she jested, what Madeleine said was true: Fate had bound them together tighter than any consanguinity ever could. It was a queer thought, one that made Jeanne wonder yet again if she would ever see the people she used to call family.

Chapter Eight

"Of the duties of a wife and mother, the Frenchwoman was generally quite ignorant. A little fancy needlework and perhaps a smattering of Italian made up the sum of her accomplishments. A whole chapter could easily be written on the depth of the average woman's ignorance of the essentials of household management."

~The Splendid Century, W.H. Lewis

Mursay

To mark the importance of Jeanne's birthday, she and Francoise were allowed to have their hair properly dressed, something which took the better part of an afternoon and prompted a great deal of sighing and complaining from Henriette. Both girls wanted the hurluberlu, the latest style from Paris, one more suitable to thick hair. When Henriette had finished with the hot tongs, masses of curls framed Jeanne's face while Francoise's fine locks quickly lost their spring.

As they waited in an antechamber before entering the ball, Francoise stood on a footstool next to Jeanne and both the girls peered into a looking glass.

Francoise said, "I do wish we could join the party now. The longer we wait, the more my curls sag, while yours haven't dropped in the slightest."

"Papa will be here soon, then I will make my entrance and you can follow after me." Jeanne gazed at the perfection of her own extravagant mane. It was true Francoise's hair looked a mess, but it was not, after all, her party.

Aunt Mimi, who had been greeting guests, hadn't seen the girls since breakfast. Now, as she entered the room and laid eyes on her daughter, she seemed to deflate, losing the air of nervous excitement that had buoyed her in the days leading up to the party.

"Francoise, what have you done to your hair?"

"Nothing, Maman. I haven't touched it."

"Henriette, reheat the tongs." She snapped her fingers and gestured for Henriette to rise from her resting place on the floor. "Make haste, girl!"

Francoise turned from surveying her reflection to face her mother. "Is my hair not good enough, Maman?"

"Have you lost the power of sight? Look again in the glass. You cannot be debuted with that bird's nest perched on your head. I will not have it. Henriette will be beaten soundly for letting it fall."

Francoise burst into tears as did Henriette.

"But Aunt, it is not Francoise's debut. It is mine." Her words made Francoise sob all the more.

Jeanne made to apologize but was interrupted by the arrival of her father. "Is this a funeral or a party?" He gazed in wonder at the girls in various stages of upset. "You were all smiling and happy but a moment ago."

"Look at her hair, Antoine. I'd loan her one of my wigs, but she's too young to be wearing one. Instead she's left with," Aunt Mimi pointed at her daughter and sighed theatrically, "whatever one would call this."

"I'm a beast," Francoise wailed.

Jeanne could see the effort her father took to hide his amusement. "Nonsense. You're a vision of loveliness. Now dry your eyes and join the party."

"You and Jeanne go ahead." Aunt Mimi crossed her arms and took stock of her daughter. "She can't be seen like this! Now stop your blubbering, Francoise. Your face will be as fallen as your hair."

****

As the doors swung open to admit Jeanne and her father into the ballroom, the world fell silent save for the thrumming of Jeanne's heart which thundered in her ears so, she barely heard her own name announced: "Mademoiselle Jeanne Marie Marguerite Denot accompanied by her father, Monsieur Antoine Joseph Denot."

As they descended the steps into the pool of revelers, her father whispered, "Don't forget to smile."

Music recommenced as they waded through the crowd. More people than not seemed to know her, or at least pretended to know her, and they called out pleasantries as Jeanne and her father glided by. Guests praised various aspects of her anatomy: her teeth, skin, hair, bosom, so that after a while she felt like a prized horse at auction.

They had made a tour halfway around the room when Jeanne said under her breath, "Papa, I am at a loss for words beyond, 'Pleased to meet you,' and 'Thank you'."

"You require no words, my darling. Your beauty speaks volumes."

Although at first their trajectory through the party

seemed random, after a while her father began to scan the crowd until, at last, he appeared to spot a particular destination.

"Come, my dear. There is someone who very much wants to meet you."

Her father steered her toward a couple: an older man, slight of frame and his wife, as stout as her husband was thin. Beauty spots dotted her florid face like a constellation. The lady's wig was styled so precipitously, it added a foot of height to her otherwise stunted physique. Jeanne supposed the beauty spots were meant to camouflage some deformity of the woman's skin, and the dizzying coiffure compensated for a lack of stature. Instead, both served to underscore the woman's deficiencies.

"Jeanne, this is Madame and Monsieur Loret. I have spoken often of them, as you may recall."

"Pleased to meet you," she said and curtsied. "My father tells me so many nice things about you." In truth, she struggled to recall a single detail concerning the Lorets.

Monsieur Loret began to speak, but his wife interrupted. "In kind, we have received many reports of your character, modesty, wit and beauty. But there's one person in particular most interested in meeting you." Madame Loret took a step back and tugged at the arm of a gentleman behind her, compelling him to stand before Jeanne. "This is my son, August."

The young man appeared formed from the worst features of both his parents, possessing his mother's red-hued face and portly figure, and his father's thin, mouse-colored hair.

August bowed so deeply Jeanne wondered how the

buttons on his breeches held against the strain of his girth. "It is my greatest honor to make your acquaintance, mademoiselle," he said in a voice so theatrically humble, it sounded arrogant all the same.

"And you." Jeanne answered his bow with a curtsy.

She made to move away, but Monsieur Loret asked her father a question while Madame Loret stared pointedly at Jeanne's bosom.

"I do not particularly care for the new cut of dresses this year," madame said. "Much too vulgar. Then again, my tastes are too refined for most."

August Loret also gazed at Jeanne's décolletage. "Your dress is a delightful shade of purple. Or would one call it lilac?"

Madame Loret laughed. "It is puce, August."

She tapped her son playfully on the shoulder and he cried, "Ow. That hurt, Maman!"

"My son knows nothing of fashion and only concerns himself with finances. He's the smartest man I've ever known."

"Regardless, the color suits you perfectly!" August intoned. He had a stilted way of speaking, as if he were delivering lines in a play.

Jeanne thanked him again and made to move on. From the corner of her eye, she caught Madame Loret nudge her son. He responded by saying, "Felicitations on the anniversary of your birth! Today is the actual day, is it not?"

"It is, indeed," Jeanne said, looking around the room for Francoise and wondering if she had managed to salvage her fallen hair by now. She couldn't wait to tell her cousin about August. They would have a good laugh over him and his spotted mother.

"I inquire owing to the fact how many celebrate their birthdays on the days surrounding the actual date, based on the restrictions of other commitments."

"So true," his mother said vigorously, as if defending a point of contention. "August had his eighteenth birthday last year and we did not celebrate it on the day itself, but on the following Saturday. It was a grand party, I might add." Madame Loret took stock of the room. "Twice as many guests as are here presently."

Jeanne sought her father's attention, trying to catch his eye to signal they move on, but he remained engrossed in conversation with Monsieur Loret.

August's thickly formed lips were arranged in a preternaturally cheerful grin. "My party was good fun. All of France's finest families attended."

"What a shame we missed it. Our invitation must have gotten lost," Jeanne said to chide him, but her barb missed its aim.

He continued on, oblivious. "The Duc D'Orléans, who I note has condescended to attend your gathering, was there. Who else, Maman?"

"The Prince de Condé himself, a man who seldom attends any but the most exclusive of society's distractions," Madame Loret added. "You must visit us in Beziers, Mademoiselle Denot. You would be quite amazed by our estate, I'm sure. One needs a carriage to fully appreciate its vastness. August would happily show you the grounds."

"That sounds utterly charming," Jeanne said. "Excuse me. I must not neglect the rest of my guests. Such a delight to make your acquaintance."

Jeanne hooked her arm through her father's, interrupting him mid-sentence, not caring how rude she appeared. "Papa, our presence is requested elsewhere."

As they moved away from the Lorets, the crowd stirred. A buzzing noise like a swarm of bees filled the room and then, just as suddenly, it stopped. Jeanne followed the gaze of her guests toward the entrance to find Francoise, poised at the top of the stairway, her blonde hair fashioned in a sophisticated upsweep, not a girlish curl in sight. Her cheeks were flushed or painted. In lieu of the yellow dress, she wore a white silk gown, one Jeanne had never seen before, edged with blue cornflowers the same shade as Francoise's eyes. A ray of evening light bathed Francoise in a shimmering nimbus. Guests sighed or gasped at the sight of the angel before them, and the sound of their wonder rolled across the room in a wave broken only by the announcement: "Mademoiselle Francoise Josefine Antonia de Vitré."

Conversation resumed as Francoise descended into the crowd with Aunt Mimi in her wake. Even so, Jeanne overheard August clearly as he said, "Maman, can't I meet that one?"

****

Jeanne did not speak during dinner. Seated next to the young Monsieur Loret, she had no need. August had a dreary conversational style marked by the absence of actual exchange. Instead, he recited lists: the number and variety of apple trees on the Loret estate, the various breeds of livestock in their barns, the names and ages of his horses, and the species of game he had killed over the past season.

Jeanne's only obligation was to nod occasionally or say, "Oh really?" when all she wanted to do was flee his company. At last, she found the opportunity and

65

retreated with Francoise to her aunt's chamber where they refreshed themselves before dancing commenced. As Henriette helped Francoise out of her gown, Jeanne primped in the looking glass.

"Where did you get that dress, Cousin?" Jeanne asked. "Of all the choices we had before the party, that particular one was never on offer, or I would have taken it myself."

"God's nightgown, Henriette! Be careful with the buttons or they'll break!" Francoise regarded the dress as Henriette gently arranged it on a stand. "This dress is old. It's one mother had years ago. She remembered it and thought it a better choice than the yellow silk."

Jeanne examined it, running her hands over the needlework then sniffed the garment. "You lie like a tooth drawer, Francoise de Vitré. It smells of newly loomed silk."

"I'm not lying. Maman told me so herself. Yellow dress or white dress? What does it signify?"

"This is my birthday party, Francoise, not yours. You had no right to make a formal entrance as if you owned the day, floating down the stairs in a dress better suited for a princess."

"One day, I'll be a marquise and you will not. You're jealous."

"Jealous?" Jeanne turned to face her. If Jeanne were a few years younger, and not a refined lady, she would have delivered a physical slap. Instead she delivered a verbal one: "I am the mistress of this house, cousin. Mursay belongs to my father, and therefore to me. You are nothing more than a guest here. You would be wise to guard your tone!"

Jeanne became aware of her aunt standing at the

door behind her. She didn't know how much she'd heard until Aunt Mimi whispered, "A guest? Jeanne, how can you speak to Francoise that way?" Upon seeing the look on her aunt's face, Jeanne wished she could take back her words.

As if on cue, Francoise dissolved into tears. "You are wicked, Jeanne!"

She had been wicked, yet she refused to bend to the force of her cousin's hysterics. "No, I'm not. You are! You could not let me have this day for myself, could you? You are a selfish brat!"

"Fine." Francoise began to tear at her hair. "I'll take my hair down and burn the stupid dress if that's what you want."

Aunt Mimi ran to her daughter and grabbed her hands, holding them tight. "Stop this. Both of you. Screaming like banshees. Every guest in the house will hear!"

Jeanne herself began to cry at the familiar feeling of being outnumbered by her aunt and cousin. She needed to discuss this with her father. She made to leave the room. "Let them hear. This party is ruined for me. Francoise spoiled it with her grand entrance!"

"Come now," her aunt said, "none of this is Francoise's fault."

"No. Nothing ever is," Jeanne retorted.

"I suggest you and I speak in private," her aunt said.

"What of me, then?" Francoise wailed.

"Henriette, repair Mademoiselle Francoise's hair. And stop crying. I cannot tolerate the excesses of your emotions on a day like today."

Outside the room, Aunt Mimi took Jeanne by the

hand. "Darling girl, please don't be cross with Francoise. We had to fix her hair and in doing so, Henriette dropped the hot tongs onto the skirt of her gown and burned a hole in it. Francoise was positively unhinged until I remembered my old white silk."

"What of her entrance? Only I should have been formally announced." In her own ears she sounded vainglorious, yet she felt too wronged by Francoise to care.

"The footman is to blame. We did not request it ourselves. You see how this was all just a series of misunderstandings? Surely you know how much we love you, Jeanne."

Jeanne nodded, mortified at having made so much out of nothing and for being so cruel to her cousin.

Aunt Mimi embraced her, and Jeanne breathed in the lavender scent of her aunt's perfume. "Your mother would be so proud of you today," she said. "Her little girl finally a woman."

At the mention of her mother, Jeanne's petty jealousy transformed into melancholy. Tears came unbidden. Her aunt continued to hold her, comforting her until presently she drew back. "Why do you cry so, my dearest Jeanne?"

It took her several moments before she could formulate the words, so overwhelming were her emotions. "It is queer to long for someone you never knew. Yet I miss Maman more with each passing day."

Francoise appeared in the hallway. "What is this? Why is it Jeanne is comforted when I am the one offended?"

"Never mind, Francoise. All is well," Aunt Mimi said, wiping the tears from Jeanne's cheeks. "I'm but a poor substitute for her, but you are like a daughter to me. Now into my arms both of you."

Francoise hesitated, then relented and Aunt Mimi gathered the girls into her embrace. As she did Jeanne whispered, "I am sorry, Francoise. Truly I am."

And Francoise whispered back, "So am I."

****

Francoise and Jeanne entered the ballroom hand-in-hand on Jeanne's insistence. Young Monsieur Loret soon appeared by Jeanne's side seeking a dance. Stung by what he had said to his mother upon Francoise's entrance, and bored beyond redemption by his lists, Jeanne declined.

His expression took on a puzzled air. "But mademoiselle, are your shoes pinching your feet?"

"No. They are fine."

"Is there some other physical impediment preventing you from taking a turn on the dance floor?"

"No. I just don't want to dance," she said, and before he could remonstrate further, she curtsied and pulled Francoise into the crowd of partygoers. They held their hands over their mouths to stifle their laughter.

"Why does he continue to plague me? I've shown him no interest. During dinner, I yawned in his face," Jeanne said.

"He is in love with you, of course."

"Love. He has only just met me. He is a pig. He resembles one in face and manner."

Francoise held her nose and giggled. "And he smells of one, too."

Jeanne spotted her father and aunt on the far side of the dancefloor. "There is Papa. He is the only man I will dance with tonight." They had taken a turn around the floor when he suggested she find a more suitable partner for the next dance.

"You are the most suitable partner here and the finest dancer."

"What about August Loret?" Her father nodded toward the edge of the room where August hovered, regarding her peevishly. "His eyes are positively fixed on you."

"He asked. I declined."

"Not too rudely, I trust. You know, I had hoped you would like the boy. There have been discussions with his parents about the two of you—"

Jeanne stopped dancing and took a step back. "You meant to make a match between us?"

"Only if you were warm to the idea. Come now. We can't stand here in the middle of the dance floor," he said, and began a box step.

"I am not at all warm. In fact, I'm stone cold to it. August Loret is stupid and pompous and ugly. How could you think of him for me?"

"Don't get your feathers too ruffled. His father is a good man. Their estate is one of the most lucrative in the country. If he holds no charm for you and fails to inspire even a modicum of affection, I won't force the issue."

For the rest of the party, Jeanne avoided August Loret. As the evening ended, the Loret family came to bid their adieu and Papa compelled Jeanne to accompany them to their carriage. Madame Loret was in her cups. Her wig itself seemed drunk as it listed to one side, giving her the appearance of a bent ladle. She shifted it in an attempt to stand it upright, but overreached the mark, causing the wig to tilt precariously in the opposite direction.

Madame Loret took hold of her husband's hand and prepared to be bundled into the carriage but then released his grasp, turning abruptly to face Jeanne.

"My dear girl, the Loret name and fortune cannot be underestimated." Madame Loret placed a heavy hand on Jeanne's shoulder and for a moment, she looked as if she would fall over.

"Come now, Victoria, it is time we leave." Her husband took hold of her elbow and attempted to propel his wife into the carriage.

Madame Loret's eyes went crossed for a moment, and then, after wandering from Jeanne's chin to her nose, finally fixed somewhere in the vicinity of Jeanne's eyes. "I have friends in high places at the Palais Louvre. Family members. When you are ready to be presented, we shall talk my dear girl." She patted Jeanne's cheek. "Adieu until our next meeting." She grasped her husband's hand and nearly fell into the carriage.

Jeanne watched as they rumbled down the long allé and into the night. She shivered against the chill evening air, and her father placed an arm around her shoulders.

"At last they are gone," he said. "Goodbye and good riddance, eh?"

"August and his mother are horrible people." Jeanne yawned, the sort of gape-mouthed yawns Aunt Mimi forbade, pronouncing those who did as "common." Perhaps that was her problem. Jeanne preferred the ordinary pleasures of life over the extraordinary ones.

She stood with her head tipped up and gazed at the night sky. Only in the silence did she realize the cacophony of the ball still rang in her ears.

"So now I've been to a ball," she said.

"Yes? And what did you think?"

"I like the silence better."

Her father laughed. "As do I. Or to look at the stars in the night sky. There's the Great Bear, the beautiful Callisto." He drew lines in the air, tracing the shape although he didn't need to. He had taught Jeanne all the star signs. "If you need to get your bearings, just follow the Bear and you'll find Polaris." He pointed north. "Do you see it there, Jeanne?"

"Oh, Papa. The funny things you say! Why would I ever need to navigate? My north and south, east and west are here at Mursay. I shan't ever go too far from it, or you."

Days later, after Papa had once again acquitted Mursay for more pressing matters with the king's army, Jeanne came upon the yellow dress, rolled up and stuffed under her cousin's bedstead. She unfurled it, examining every inch of the fabric. It was pristine. Not a burn mark in sight. Jeanne returned it to its hiding place. She would speak to her father about this. Until then, she would not trust her cousin a whit.

Chapter Nine

"Along with the honest people comes a great deal of rabble of both sexes who cause a great deal of scandal."

~Mother Marie of the Ursuline Convent

The *Saint Anne*

Like the workings of a clock, the women on the ship moved round and round in the same grooves, their petty diversions slowly and steadily ticking off the minutes, the hours, the days of their captivity. At first light, the mademoiselles arose and waited for the signal from Madame which marked their turn to take a breakfast of gruel in the galley after the demoiselles had eaten.

On good weather days they enjoyed a constitutional around the top deck after the demoiselles had finished their own stroll. Back in their quarters, they chatted, wagered, quarreled, braided and dressed each other's hair, whiling away time until their lunch repast at which time the process repeated: eat, walk, lie about until an evening supper of stew. After-supper distractions included more wagering until Teeth called for lights out. On the Sabbath, they gathered in the captain's quarters and Madame recited the liturgy.

According to Jeanne's calendar carved under her

hammock, they had completed just over a third of the journey: twenty-two days at sea. In the monotony of the passing time, Jeanne often thought of the library at Mursay and the stacks of leather-bound volumes that filled the shelves from floor to ceiling. Inside the pages of a book Jeanne's thoughts would be free to escape the drudgery and confinement of the *Saint Anne*, but she had not so much as touched one since before La Salpêtrière. She made it a game to envision one of her favorite tomes, holding her hands out before her and reciting passages from memory.

It had been two days since Jeanne's encounter with the passenger from the black island and since then there had been no further sightings of him. Jeanne half wondered if he had been a figment of her imaginings.

Then one morning, as the other girls slumbered, she went topside for her walk. Given the list of the ship, and the need to clutch a blanket around her shoulders for warmth, Jeanne paced the deck with an awkward gait, charting her usual path from aft to stern and back again. She feared the captain would close the deck as he did on rough weather days, but no one arrested her progress. Upon reaching the stern a second time, she heard her name called out above the wind.

Jeanne failed to identify the source of the sound until the voice came again, this time more clearly. "Mademoiselle Davide."

Monsieur Suprenant stood on the quarterdeck above her. He gestured for her to join him. After climbing the short ladder leading to the raised deck, Jeanne nearly toppled over, and he rushed forward to lend a hand. This close, she saw that he had trimmed his hair and shorn his unkempt beard.

"Hold onto the mast. It will steady you," he said.

She did and the two of them stood a while without speaking, each with a hand holding the lines of the mast, the wind at their backs. Jeanne contemplated opening a conversation but wondered if it would appear unseemly. In her old life at Mursay, social intercourse was governed by clear conventions dictating how, what, and when to eat, speak, dance and dress. In her new life, no such guidance existed. Perhaps she could ask why he lived on the black island? Then again, it could present an affront to his privacy. Or she could inquire as to the comfort of his quarters, but that could appear overly intimate.

Jeanne remained silent, casting about for appropriate topics but was saved when Monsieur Suprenant spoke. "I observed you walking and debated whether I should call attention to myself. Wrapped up the way you are from head to toe, I wasn't even sure it was you."

"Oh," she said. Then, so he wouldn't think her simple, she added, "I walk here most mornings unless the weather won't allow for it."

"Yes. I marked you here day before last." He went quiet for a moment, then added, "It's preferable to be out in the open air, even if it is cold. I loathe being cooped up inside."

In the early morning sunlight, Jeanne confirmed his eyes to be a shade somewhere between blue and green. She looked away and watched as two helmsmen maneuvered the massive wheel that steered the *Saint Anne*.

He cleared his throat. "You are quite far along in the journey, I suppose."

"Twenty-two days and thrice as many to go."

He laughed. "I almost said, 'But it's difficult to measure time precisely,' but not, it seems, for you."

"Every day I carve a mark on the floor under my hammock to count the passing days, although the captain informed me it's difficult to determine an exact day of arrival."

"I see." He nodded, then after another long pause added, "A voyage of this length leaves a harrowing amount of time to pass with precious little to occupy oneself."

"It would be tolerable if only there were books."

Monsieur Suprenant's face registered surprise. He hesitated before saying, "Do you read, Mademoiselle Davide? I mean, are you able to?"

He had not intended to be rude, but the question stung, nonetheless. Then again, why would he think her lettered? None of the other girls on the lowest deck could so much as write their own name, signing the papers for entry onto the *Saint Anne* with an "X". Few of the high-born demoiselles had learned more than the letters of the alphabet.

"Yes. Reading is a passion. Although I have not so much as held a book in quite some time."

"Which works are your favorites?"

Jeanne said, "Plutarch, 'Parallel Lives.' I've read it too many times to count."

His eyes widened. "It's a favorite of mine. Which of the stories do you most enjoy?"

"Lysander and Sulla or Themistocles, but not Camillus."

"Camillus is rather dull with all of his posturing about the love of one's homeland," he said.

"Although I understand him better now. To imagine I will never see France again—" Caught off guard by a sudden rush of emotion, Jeanne turned away, wiping her eyes surreptitiously with the edge of her blanket.

"Mademoiselle, forgive my impertinence, but how is it you came to be on this vessel? Why are you not with the demoiselles? I share my meals with them and have not seen you in their company. Yet clearly you belong among them."

His observations prompted a new welling of tears.

Monsieur Suprenant clutched his hair and then made a show of knocking his head against the mast. "I'm an idiot. Forgive me. I've always had a talent for saying the wrong thing, or the right thing but at the wrong time."

"Pardon me, Monsieur Suprenant." Before he could respond, she climbed down from the quarterdeck and returned to the very deepest depths of the ship where the Fates had decided she belonged.

****

The following morning, the sea lay flat, making her walk less arduous. Jeanne surveyed the deck for signs of Monsieur Suprenant, anxious to avoid encountering him after her outburst the day before, yet, in equal part, worried she would miss him. As she made yet another round on deck, she became aware of steps echoing behind her own and turned to encounter Monsieur Suprenant.

"Mademoiselle Davide. I had hoped to find you here."

Flustered by her conflicting emotions, Jeanne smiled in an overzealous fashion. "It would have been remarkable if I could have hidden from you on a vessel of this size," she said, then regretted her words when she saw they had offended him.

"Forgive me if I am too familiar, it's just, I have something for you." He held up a book. "Plutarch. Perhaps you will pass the hours more easily now."

He handed it to her, and Jeanne held it the way one would hold a precious jewel. She carefully turned the pages. "Oh my! What fine printing. Monsieur, I could not possibly take this! It is far too precious."

He grinned and seemed pleased by her reaction. "Do not take it then. Borrow it for the remainder of the voyage."

"Are you certain?"

"Entirely. It is why I came looking for you this morning."

Jeanne experienced a thrill at his words and grinned herself, then sobered to impart how solemnly she took her custodianship of the book. "I shall treasure it and treat it with the utmost care. Thank you. You are most kind. But now you must close your eyes," she said.

Monsieur Suprenant seemed completely taken aback at her request. "Why? Are you planning to abscond with my Plutarch?"

"Just close them for a moment," she said, and when he did, she opened the book to its center and pressed her face to the pages. She filled her nose with its scent.

"Dear girl, what are you doing?" he asked, squinting comically through one eye.

"The worst thing about being aboard this ship besides the boredom is the complete lack of any pleasant scent."

Monsieur Suprenant nodded his head seriously, but his eyes sparkled. "Give me the book," he said, and then performed the same ritual as Jeanne. "Hmmm. It is a wonderful smell. Not unlike a wine cellar." He handed the book back to her.

"Or a cedar chest," she said.

"Or a cedar chest in a wine cellar. I only hope you enjoy reading it as much as you enjoy smelling it. It's meant as a peace offering. I upset you yesterday and have been cursing myself ever since. I hope you can forgive me."

"It is I who should apologize for storming off. My story is this, monsieur: Both of my parents departed this world long ago." She sketched her account with broad enough strokes for the truth to hide within its vagaries. "What was left of the family estate is lost to me and lacking any prospects, I had no alternative but to leave France for the New World."

"I'm sorry to hear it and hope you find everything you wish for in New France."

"May I ask what brings you onboard the *Saint Anne*?"

"I could make myself sound important and tell you I'm on the king's business," he said, smiling. "But the truth of the matter is, I am but a cog in the wheel of his army and have been tasked with helping to settle the territory."

"How did you find yourself on the black island?"

"I sailed there on another of the king's ships to establish it as an outpost for trade until the *Saint Anne* arrived and I could make my way to the new territories. I'll be in Quebec a short time, then I'll ship out again to Martinique, then sail back to Quebec."

"Changing ships like someone changing carriages," she said. "What a remarkable life you lead."

"I don't know about that. But this voyage has been remarkable."

"How so?"

"Under normal circumstances, I journey on ships surrounded by men and livestock. The environment of the *Saint Anne* is considerably more pleasant."

"I'm happy you think so," Jeanne said, finding it difficult to meet his gaze and impossible to look away. "I should have finished my walk by now and will be soon missed at the breakfast table."

"Adieu, mademoiselle."

"Thank you once again for the book, monsieur. I shall return it to you in the condition I've received it."

She made her way quickly across the deck and at the top of the stairway she turned: Monsieur Suprenant regarded her progress. Up close, his face had been cheerful. From a distance, however, he wore a look of utter sadness. His eyes met hers and he nodded his head in acknowledgement. Jeanne turned away and without hazarding another backward glance, descended into the darkness below.

****

Once again, the seas became rough, so much so their evening meal was cancelled. Instead, Madeleine and Teeth made their way to the galley to fetch biscuits and salted cod. All eighteen mademoiselles and Elisabeth ate their meager repast seated on the floor of their sleeping quarters. At first, they made a game of the shifting of the boat. Teeth and Madeleine arranged a race with their clogs, seeing which one could slide from port to starboard fastest.

After some time, their good humor dissipated, replaced by fear as the rocking of the ship became so violent the girls began to slip along the floor, drawn from side to side like the clogs in Teeth and Madeleine's game. A sailor appeared and shouted at them to extinguish their lanterns. They did so, lying on the floor in the pitch dark, forming a net of sorts with their arms and legs splayed to brace against the undulation of the sea. The wind howled like an angry beast around them, and above the din, one of the younger girls began to cry and another screamed for her mother.

Teeth had to yell to be heard above the raging of the storm. "If I could see which one of you is whining, I'd get up and wallop you good. No one is to panic. No more crying for your ma!"

Jeanne held hands with Madeleine on one side, and Elisabeth on the other and prayed once again to be united with her mother and father in Heaven. Surely the boat could not withstand this violent lurching to and fro and would upend, plunging their souls to the murky depths. Jeanne anticipated the moment when the thin wood of the *Saint Anne* gave way to the water outside, swallowing all of them whole.

Given her sizeable girth, Elisabeth lay on her side. "Oh Jeanne. I am wet all over."

"Yes. The water rushes through every nook and cranny of the ship."

"No. Between my legs. I have wet myself."

"When the storm passes, we'll attend to it. There is nothing to be done now."

Jeanne squeezed the young girl's hand and Elisabeth returned it with a grip so strong, Jeanne's bones ached. Elisabeth moaned, and in the next moment the moan turned into a scream.

Teeth growled from the darkness, "What did I say? Don't make me light the lantern to come find you."

Elisabeth cried out, "I am dying. Oh, merciful Jesus, help me!"

Her cries of agony inspired several of the other girls to begin screaming and moaning and even Teeth's threats could not quell the storm raging within their own quarters.

Jeanne propped herself up as best she could and began to stroke Elisabeth's brow, urging her to hush to no avail. Then a light appeared. Teeth had made good on her threat. She stood, bracing herself by placing the palms of her hands against the low ceiling.

"Now, listen you lot! You will stop this caterwauling this minute or, by God, I will choke the noise out of you with my bare hands."

The lantern in its hook on the ceiling swung violently with the movement of the ship, causing arcs of light to flash across Teeth's face. She looked like the Devil himself. Fear of the monster looming above them silenced the girls for a few moments, but then Elisabeth let out another scream and a cry for mercy. Teeth began to climb over the netting of girls toward Elisabeth, stepping now and again on an arm or leg, producing fresh cries of agony.

Jeanne spread her arms awkwardly over Elisabeth to block Teeth from getting too close. "I won't let you hurt her!" she said.

Teeth paused for a moment then laughed. "As if you could stop me. I mean to aid her with the baby."

Dumbstruck, Jeanne managed to say, "The sea is

raging. She cannot have her baby now."

"The sea in her belly rages even more and will spit the babe out, storm or not. Now be of real use and let her rest against you like a pillow."

Jeanne did as Teeth ordered. She sat up and Elisabeth lay with her back against Jeanne's bosom. Upon Teeth's instruction, another girl sat back-to-back against Jeanne, bracing her. Teeth propped up Elisabeth's legs and drew her skirt fully over her belly, causing Jeanne a moment of mortification on the young girl's behalf, yet Elisabeth seemed unaware of her nakedness, or of the howling of the wind or of anything but her torment.

"Please, God, get it out! Get it out!" she cried.

"It is coming out on its own, girl. Your passage is open three fingers. When it has opened a fist, you will push. Not until then."

Elisabeth writhed in agony. "No. Now. It is killing me!"

"Listen to me." Although the howling storm around them caused her to shout, Teeth remained calm. "You will wait. Push now and you'll damage yourself and the babe."

They waited, Jeanne comforting Elisabeth as best she could. The chaos outside worsened. As the ship listed to its greatest angle, Jeanne had the sensation of dangling in mid-air before it rolled back, causing her stomach to drop, calling to mind the tree swing at Mursay. She shut her eyes tightly and wished herself home, back in the downy folds of her bed.

Jeanne opened her eyes again to take in the pandemonium before her: the terror in the faces of the young women struggling for a purchase as they shifted with the movement of the boat across the floor, each reciting prayers for salvation silently and occasionally shouting them aloud. Jeanne's dress was soaked through with the co-mingling of Elisabeth's sweat and a mist of seawater that sprayed through the cracks of the hull. After some time, gullies of water gathered, sloshing to and fro with the rocking of the ship. Even if the water rose to the point of drowning them, nothing could be done. No one was able to stand long enough to bail out the relentless sea. Jeanne herself sat captive like an animal in the jaws of a trap: Elisabeth pressing deeper into the front of her as her agonies mounted, and the girl behind her counterbalancing by pushing forcefully against her back. Jeanne gasped for breath as if she too were in the throes of childbirth.

Hour after hour crept by. How many, Jeanne could only guess. Each minute elongated, distorted by torments beyond any idea of Hell she could have imagined. The knowledge that Elisabeth's anguish exceeded her own by a thousand-fold kept Jeanne steadfast.

Finally, Teeth pronounced the baby ready to be sprung. "I can see the top of its head. It's time to spit the seed out of the apple."

Teeth instructed two girls to hold fast Elisabeth's ankles giving her leverage to push. Jeanne had once witnessed a colt being born. The mare endured the process with serenity. Elisabeth shrieked at each mighty surge of labor as if her innards were being ripped out, and Jeanne feared the poor girl would die from her efforts.

"Its head is out now. You need only to pass the shoulders and the hard part is done." Teeth yelled,

"Now push with all your might!"

Miraculously, a moment later, Teeth held a mewling infant in her arms.

Elisabeth only barely clung to consciousness. "What is it? Boy or girl?"

Teeth smiled like an angel, if an angel could have blackened teeth. "'Tis a girl, of course. We couldn't have any menfolk living in these quarters."

****

Shortly after the birth of the baby, the storm seemed to have spent its energy and the seas returned to placid. The girls made a great fuss over the baby, taking turns holding her as Elisabeth fell into a deep sleep.

Night turned into day, and still the young girl slumbered on. Teeth approached the bed of straw she had been removed to, and said, "Wake up sleepy head. Your child is in want of the breast."

Jeanne cradled the baby in her arms and Teeth beckoned for her to bring the child to her mother.

"Enough sleep now." Teeth began to pinch Elisabeth's cheeks and the young girl groaned but would not awaken. Teeth shouted the girl's name several times.

"She is exhausted after last night's efforts. Should we not let her rest?" Jeanne said.

"I've never seen a woman who hasn't been wrung out from birthing. Yet Mother Nature has a way of keeping her alert. There's something amiss." As if to prove it to Jeanne, Teeth pulled back one of Elisabeth's eyelids. "See? Her eyes roll back into her head. She is not, in fact, sleeping. She's knocked out."

Teeth pulled up Elisabeth's skirts and Jeanne stifled a scream. Blood puddled between the girl's legs.

Teeth sucked in a breath. "This is bad."

"You birthed the baby. Can you not help with this, too?"

"Fixing this is beyond my ken. If it continues, she will bleed to death. I've seen it many a time helping my ma."

Jeanne fought a rising panic. How could it be that the act of producing new life claimed so many existing ones in the process? There had to be something they could do for the poor girl. Then the words came to her, and she calmed as she said them: "Take the baby. I will fetch Monsieur Suprenant."

****

Jeanne did not know the location of monsieur's cabin, so she made haste to the captain's quarters, and before knocking, had to steady the trembling in her hand.

The captain opened, a look of surprise on his face. "Hello, Mademoiselle Davide. I understand you have a new addition to your company. Word has it the child is a girl and a healthy one."

"Yes, yes," she said. "Her mother, however, is doing very poorly, indeed. I'm looking for Monsieur Suprenant to provide medical assistance. It is of the greatest urgency."

"I will take you to him directly."

Jeanne watched as Monsieur Suprenant examined poor Elisabeth and marked the grave look on his face. "We need to make her more comfortable. In this condition she can't be on the floor. Captain, give me a hand, and together we can transport her to my quarters."

Jeanne followed as the two men delicately carried

Elisabeth to the upper deck where they rested her gently on Monsieur Suprenant's more ample berth.

The girl moaned piteously. "Jeanne, where is my baby?"

"She is being looked after. Teeth fed her goat's milk and will mind her until you have mended."

"I want to hold her. Oh please, Jeanne, get her for me!"

Jeanne hastened to fetch the baby, bringing Teeth with her.

Elisabeth, who could barely produce a sound above a whisper, said, "Pardon, Mademoiselle Teeth, may I ask your given name?"

"It is Anne."

Elisabeth smiled weakly. "Like the ship. Surely you too are a saint."

Teeth beamed. "Well, I've never been accused of that before."

"It's a fine name for my baby," Elisabeth said faintly. "She shall be called Anne after her savior."

Outside the cabin, Monsieur Suprenant conferred with Jeanne, Teeth, and the captain. He paused a moment as if weighing how much to say, then began. "She has lost a prodigious amount of blood. There were small traces of the womb evident which leads me to believe that it has not adequately contracted."

"I rubbed her belly after the babe popped out, but I reckon it weren't enough," Teeth said.

"Mademoiselle, you delivered a healthy baby under horrific circumstances. You are to be commended." Teeth's usual hard-edged expression softened at Monsieur Suprenant's words. "Complications of this nature are not uncommon, as surely you know."

Teeth nodded.

"Do you expect her to recover?" the captain asked.

Monsieur Suprenant glanced at Jeanne and spoke reluctantly. "There is a chance she will not. I staunched the blood flow as best I could, but she needs to be watched around the clock for the foreseeable future."

Chapter Ten

"I wish that someone had taught me something when I was a girl."

~Madeleine de Scudéry, Writer

Mursay

Like most other demoiselles of wealthy families, Jeanne and Francoise were starved of formal education. Over their fifteen years of existence, they had been treated to nibbles of grammar and writing when tutors on the subject came through town seeking temporary employment, and even had a small brush with figures so that both girls could add and subtract. Although Jeanne's passion for reading was fed by the volumes from her father's library, Francoise's skills were limited. The girl's lips moved, and her finger tracked the rows of text when she did venture to open a book. They could both sew—Jeanne with a coarse style, Francoise with a fine one—and could hold a tune.

More important than academic schooling was the tutelage they received throughout their lives from Aunt Mimi concerning social comportment. How to gracefully enter and withdraw from a room: "Make your bodies light. You must float! Never clomp from place to place." "Neither rush, nor move too sluggishly. The former makes one appear highly strung. The latter, dull." On dress: "Day to day, if no one remembers what you wore, you are well dressed." "The bosom and waist are the points of keenest interest on a woman's figure. Be sure to flatter both to the fullest." Concerning conversation: "Avoid being too eager to make your own point or witticism." "Do not ask questions in conversation concerning unfamiliar vocabulary. People will judge you a bumpkin."

As the time drew closer for Jeanne's introduction at court, efforts for instructing the girls intensified. Like life's most important lessons, the curriculum lacked books, requiring only a capable guide to steer them around the many ditches on the road to acceptance among people of quality. Many years had passed since Aunt Mimi had been a star in the firmament of the court of King Louis. Her best connections had been burned by the exploits of her husband, the late Marquis de Vitré. Madame Loret, claiming to be "a favorite" of the king, stepped in to show Jeanne the way. Jeanne suspected her aunt wished to continue relations with the Lorets so a match could be made between Francoise and August.

Madame Loret arrived one mild April morning, on the anniversary of Jeanne's seventeenth year, to deliver her tutelage and stayed through the end of May. When Jeanne and Francoise complained about the lady's extended presence, Aunt Mimi called them ungrateful. Madame Loret would provide them entrée to society through her cousin, Françoise-Athénaïs de Rochechouart de Montespan, King Louis' favorite mistress, a name Madame Loret peppered throughout her interminable lessons.

"My cousin, Athénaïs, threw a grand entertainment

to mark the newest play by Molière. This particular performance took place at Versailles. Given Versailles is considerably smaller than the Palais Louvre there were only 2,000 intimates at the celebration, and I was among them, naturally. In Paris, one would expect double the audience." They sat in the drawing room, the shutters drawn against the sun's rays. Despite the coolness in the room, Madame Loret perspired profusely, causing her faux beauty spots to regularly lose their hold on her face and go flying. "Picture it, girls: The courtyard filled with an infinite number of sparkling chandeliers so that you would think the night sky had landed on Earth. Canons fired. Fountains sprouted. Orange trees scented the air. To be part of it was like glimpsing Heaven!"

Madame Loret ended her story by staring into the distance, as if she could see the spectacle of that night before her. Jeanne and Francoise had heard the florid description so many times over the duration of Madame Loret's stay, they too could see it. The lady never recounted any other experience, making Jeanne wonder if the night of Heaven-on-Earth was the only bow in the lady's quiver of anecdotes.

"Apparently, the event has impressed you deeply, madame," Jeanne remarked, "as it does us. With the intricate way you've weaved the story, I feel as if it happened to me."

Her words broke Madame Loret's reverie, and the lady responded sharply. "I'm not impressed in the least. As one accustomed to such things, I remain unperturbed by splendor. No. I merely paint a picture for you girls so that you are not too amazed when you are exposed to this level of grandeur."

"You have rendered the picture of that evening using every hue in the palette," Aunt Mimi said. "It is vivid to the point of haunting for all of us, I'm sure."

Madame Loret appeared momentarily at a loss for words, unsure how to interpret Aunt Mimi's wry comment. As was her predilection, the lady chose praise over umbrage. "Why thank you, marquise. I am considered a skilled raconteur. Let us now turn to the business of my cousin's letter that arrived today, although Athénaïs is more sister than cousin to me, in actual fact."

Aunt Mimi said, "We understand your bond is extraordinary."

"Well put. Her mother is my father's sister, after all. Very close by blood ties and ties of the heart."

"What does your cousin convey?" Aunt Mimi stifled a yawn.

"As soon as I wrote to her of our desire to codify the rules of court, she promptly responded with this dispatch. Of course, I am well-versed myself with every manner of etiquette. Though I would never presume to know more than my dear cousin!"

Seeing her aunt yawn, and given the closeness of the room, Jeanne followed suit and a moment later, Francoise yawned as well, although less discreetly.

"Yawning is strictly forbidden in the court. It is considered, in the king's own words, *fort mauvais*. The very height of bad manners." Madame shook her head so violently another beauty spot popped off and landed on the table, at which the lady nonchalantly picked it up, wet it with her tongue and reapplied it to her cheek.

She held the letter at arm's length to adjust her vision. After an eternity she cleared her throat and began to read. *"The lack of adherence to the following rules are considered fort mauvais by our dear king: Do not knock upon entering a room. Scratching on the door with one's little finger from the left hand is the correct way to gain attention. You'll observe how most courtiers have grown the nail on that hand long and pointed for this express purpose. Upon receiving a message from a personage of superior social ranking, one must stand and show obeisance to the lackey delivering the message. You asked specifically for points concerning the consumption of meals at the palace: If the king's dinner is carried past, one must curtsey before it and men are obliged to bow and remove their hats. Under no circumstance can one consume a dish before the king himself begins his portion. At the table, ensure you are not seated above or below your station. Do not rinse your hands from the water bowl before a person of higher rank first cleans their own hands. Rank is as important in the drawing room as it is in the dining room. Courtiers with the highest rank have first rights to any armed chair. Those of humbler rank should use armless chairs or even three-legged stools."*

Francoise interrupted Madame Loret with a question: "But how does one know who is higher and who is lower ranked?"

Madame patted her arm. "Not to worry, my dear girl, most everyone you encounter will be your superior."

At Madame Loret's words, Aunt Mimi rose abruptly. Clapping her hands, she said, "Lessons are concluded for the day, girls."

Madame Loret still held the letter out before her.

"Concluded? I have shared but half of my cousin's counsel. There are many more pearls of wisdom she condescends to caste before us."

"Nonetheless, the girls have grown weary, and I too could use a rest after all of your generous condescension."

Madame Loret seemed oblivious to the sharpness of Aunt Mimi's tone. She carefully folded the letter and observed brightly, "I suppose the mind can only absorb what the rump can bear.'"

****

"I do despise Madame Loret," Francoise said.

She and Jeanne sought refuge from the heat under the branches of a willow. As children, the tree served as any number of backdrops, from pirate's cove to tower prison, depending on the nature of their play. As women, it offered a hideaway to share their thoughts and dreams away from the eyes and ears of Aunt Mimi and the servants. They each sat on a cushion, their backs against the trunk of the tree, completely obscured by a veil of flowing branches.

"Did you hear what she said to me? 'Everyone is your superior.' She is a fat, spotted cow! Mother should have slapped her!"

"It looked like she wanted to," Jeanne laughed.

"Madame Loret isn't even titled."

"She is truly a dreadful person," Jeanne said, and shuddered. "And August is even worse. I just don't understand why your mother bears her and why we're made to do likewise?"

"Maman knows more about the court than that old sow. She was lady-in-waiting to Queen Anne while Madame Loret attended one party she's stretched into a lifetime of intimacy."

"Why inflict her upon us then?"

Francoise sighed. "Mother says Madame Loret can gain favor for us through her connections. You know, 'I'm a special favorite of the king!'" Francoise said, aping Madame Loret's pompous tone causing Jeanne to laugh again. "Besides, Maman still hopes you'll reconsider August. Or she wishes me to marry him."

"He is repulsive and conceited with his endless lists of possessions and accomplishments."

"Imagine the poor woman who marries him?" Francoise said. "For her sake, I hope she is both blind and deaf. She will certainly be dumb."

As they speculated on the wretched soul who would one day have the title of Madame August Loret, they became aware of someone calling Jeanne's name.

"It's only Henriette," Francoise said, closing her eyes. "She's such a numbskull. Mother caught her using the hair tongs, and when she yelled at her, Henriette said she was sacrificing her own locks to perfect her technique for us."

"What an answer. That girl has become quite the minx."

Presently, Henriette's cries became louder and tinged with panic. "Please, Mademoiselle Denot! Do make your presence known!"

With that Jeanne stood. "That silly girl. She's positively hysterical!" Jeanne parted the willow boughs and reminded herself it was unseemly for a lady to shout, so she waved her arms to gain the girl's attention. Henriette darted about the park like a headless chicken crying, "Mademoiselle Denot! Where are you? It is most urgent!"

Francoise stood next to Jeanne. "God's nightgown! What has gotten into her?"

Jeanne finally broke with decorum and bellowed, "Over here, Henriette!"

Henriette, whose normal state of being ranged from mild to extreme disarray, resembled a sweaty lump by the time she reached the girls. Without warning, the servant broke out into pitiful sobs, crying, "Mademoiselle Denot! Oh please! You must return to the house at once."

Jeanne took hold of Henriette's shoulders. "What is it? Tell me now!" Despite the heat, a chill of fear began to make its way through Jeanne's person.

Henriette bawled even louder, her words coming out as gibberish.

Jeanne said, "Spit it out, girl. Is my aunt not well?"

Henriette's cries only intensified at the question.

Francoise grabbed Henriette and slapped her across the face. Henriette calmed in an instant, her face returning to its usual docile expression. "It is your father, Mademoiselle Denot. He is dead."

****

Before his passing, Jeanne's father rarely figured in her dreams. Now he came to her nightly, spoke with her, held her in his arms so that Jeanne longed to sleep, yet dreaded it all the same. Each day, rising to consciousness, he was stolen from her yet again and the wounds of mourning reopened.

She took to visiting the family burial ground and tended to the chalk-white headstones for Charles-Louis, the brother she never knew, born and died March 30, 1650, and Agnés née Leduc Denot, Jeanne's mother, whose date of passing out of the physical world coincided with Jeanne's entry into it: April 25, 1652. A fresh mound of earth marked her father's final resting place. His headstone read, "Antoine Denot, Born July 19, 1628, Died, May 6, 1667. Loyal Servant of God and King."

Jeanne wondered over the brevity of his epitaph. The words imparted nothing of her father's essence: His open spirit and the way he could engage in lively discourse with everyone from a stable hand to the king himself. His fine intellect, balanced by his love for art, music, and dance. All his qualities, both definitive and ineffable, now gone forever.

The headstone also failed to capture the heroism of his final moments on earth. He had ridden out with the king's troops. Upon receiving word that a group of soldiers, not much older than boys, were stranded behind enemy lines, he led the cavalry to save their lives, losing his own in the bargain.

As summer turned to fall, Jeanne removed the leaves littering the family cemetery. She did so with tireless devotion, keeping the ground pristine. Aunt Mimi sent one of the servants to lend a hand, but Jeanne chased him away, saying it was her duty to care for her family.

On occasion, Francoise would join her vigils. One day, when Jeanne had whispered, "My entire family— gone. I am so dreadfully alone!" Francoise cried and kissed Jeanne's hand.

"How can you say that? What about me? Or Maman? We'll never leave you."

Jeanne's fugue persisted throughout the winter, her grief shrouding her so entirely, she lost interest in the corporal pleasures of life: eating, singing, even reading, save for her father's letters, particularly the last one he'd sent to be opened on her birthday:

My Dearest Darling,

Although you have bloomed like the rarest of roses into womanhood, I trust some things shall never change: That you will continue to work your way through the tomes in the library. Have you reached the 300 mark yet? Upon my return, there will be new additions including the five missing volumes of Madame de Scudéry. You will doubtless be in seclusion until Christmas! You became upset last we discussed it, but you must know that upon your sixteenth birthday, the ownership of Mursay will be held by law in both of our names equally.

She read the next lines through a blur of tears.

I have had the papers drawn and finalized so in the event of my passing (don't worry yourself now, my dearest angel, I am as stout and hearty as a farm horse!) there will be no discussion as to the rightful ownership of Mursay. Your future must be guarded above all else and it eases my mind (although it troubles yours, I know) to have these matters squared. If I am not home by the anniversary of your birth, know that you're in my heart.

Chapter Eleven

"The scars of the body—what are they, compared to the hidden ones of the heart?"

~*Francoise D'Aubigné, Second Wife of King Louis XIV*

Mursay

After her father's death, the priest visited Mursay with such frequency, Aunt Mimi arranged rooms for him in the house. On one bright spring day, a year after her father's passing, she asked Jeanne and Francoise to help her make vestments for Father Dieudonné in preparation for Easter services. The three women sewed in the brightest drawing room so that Aunt Mimi had an easier time seeing the fine needlework.

Jeanne sighed as she regarded her work. Her stitching, meant to be a tulip, more closely resembled a haystack. Her hands simply lacked the ability to translate the visions of her mind onto the cloth. Francoise possessed a dexterity that made it possible for her to artfully reproduce any variety of form or figure onto cloth or canvas.

"What do you think?" Jeanne held up the lilac-colored vestment for inspection and Francoise burst into peals of laughter.

"Jeanne, you are hopeless!" she said.

"Don't be cruel, Francoise. Apologize to your cousin," her aunt said. Since her father's passing, she had been solicitous in the extreme when it came to Jeanne's feelings.

Jeanne made a sad face, pretending to be wounded by Francoise's fit of mirth until she could no longer contain her own laughter.

"Well, it's a wonder to see you smiling, my dear," her aunt said.

Jeanne examined her creation. "Yes. At least my work inspires laughter if not admiration."

"Father Dieudonné will appreciate the effort, I'm sure," her aunt said.

At length, Jeanne set aside her needlework. "The good priest has scarcely left the grounds of Mursay since Christmas." She had meant to ask her aunt when the man planned to leave but wasn't sure how to broach the topic. "It's soon Passiontide."

"His sacrifice to the family is admirable," her aunt said. "Father Dieudonné devotes his life to the service of others, foregoing all creature comforts and securities."

Jeanne wanted to ask, *What, exactly, has the good father sacrificed?* He dined on the choicest meats. Drank the best wines. Now he enjoyed the luxury of a three-room suite, as well.

A knock on the door interrupted the discussion. Father Dieudonné asked if he could enter, which vexed Jeanne immensely since, while asking, he had already situated himself well into the room.

"I was most anxious to see the fruit of your labor, my ladies," he said.

Francoise held up her own creation, a vestment

featuring an intricate vine of morning glories rendered in pink against the purple backdrop of the fabric.

Father Dieudonné handled the vestment with great reverence, placing it around his shoulders. "Dear girl, it is divine! As if inspired by God Himself."

As the priest continued to extol the virtues of Francoise's artistry in his unctuous manner, Jeanne surreptitiously hid her own, stuffing it into her sewing basket. Then she changed her mind and retrieved it, spreading the vestment out across her lap.

"Is mine equally inspired, Father?" Jeanne kept her expression neutral and observed how the light in the priest's face dimmed when examining her less-than-divine creation.

"Well, your vestment is, indeed, what words to describe it?" He paused. "That shade of lilac is most fitting for the season. As for the motif, well," he hesitated again, then said, "I've never seen the likes of it before."

"Can you recognize the flower?" Jeanne asked innocently.

"Well, Francoise's is a lovely climbing morning glory, and yours is, clearly, another species entirely."

While Aunt Mimi's expression hardened at Jeanne's questioning, Francoise's face began to convulse.

"Which species exactly?" Jeanne asked.

Aunt Mimi interrupted. "What does it signify if Father Dieudonné can identify the flower or not?"

"Thank you for intervening on my behalf, Marquise, but I do believe I know the answer," the priest said brightly. "It is the thistle!"

"A weed, father? You have offended me deeply,"

Jeanne said, causing Francoise to fall into convulsions of glee.

The priest observed the girls as they doubled over. Befuddlement turned to consternation and transformed his fair skin to a shade not far off the color of his new vestments.

"I find this sort of levity most inappropriate during Lent. Most inappropriate, indeed, Marquise."

Aunt Mimi stood. "As do I. Girls, you will stop this nonsense immediately!" After a while, her words had their desired effect, and the two girls fell silent. "Now Jeanne, you will ask forgiveness of Father Dieudonné for your impudence."

"Aunt, I was merely jesting. It was a joke based on my own lack of abilities, and no indictment of the good and holy father."

Aunt Mimi weighed Jeanne's comment and would have perhaps relented, until Father Dieudonné added, "All parties must find the humor to qualify as a jest. Yours fell well short of the mark."

"Agreed, Father." Aunt Mimi stood behind Jeanne's chair and beckoned for her to stand. "Apologize."

Jeanne remained seated, her playfulness gone, replaced in an instant by a roiling anger. "No," she said quietly, but firmly, "I will not."

"Maman, please." Francoise's face grew pale. "It was not entirely Jeanne's doing!"

Aunt Mimi's voice filled the room. "Quiet, Francoise!" She turned her attention back to Jeanne. "Rise this instant and offer your sincerest apology to Father Dieudonné!"

Jeanne clasped the arms of her chair so tightly her

hands appeared bloodless. She stood slowly, and as she did, her emotions rose with her: sorrow at her father's passing, gratefulness that Francoise had at least tried to defend her, hatred for the sanctimonious priest, and outrage at her aunt for humiliating her under her own roof.

She wanted to scream, to tear up the vestment and toss it in the fire. Instead she willed herself to speak steadily. "You forget your place, Aunt. I'm the lady of Mursay now. I will not be ordered to apologize to anyone. Particularly to the person who has entered my house without my permission."

With that, she crossed to the door, brushing past the astonished priest, and exited without commotion, displaying the comportment of a lady, just as her aunt had instructed on so many occasions.

****

On Easter Sunday, Father Dieudonné wore the vestment Francoise had rendered so beautifully. Seeing it brought back the sting of her aunt's words. A handful of days had passed since then and Jeanne ordered her meals to be taken in her room, moving in wide circles around her aunt and the priest. Francoise had begged her at one point to relent and dine en famille, but Jeanne refused.

Jeanne, Francoise, and Aunt Mimi occupied the front pew. Every available seat was filled with servants and their respective kin in a hierarchical order, front to back, with household servants seated immediately behind them, followed by a strata of groomsmen and gardeners, ending at the farthest reaches of the church with lackeys who had no fixed position at Mursay.

Easter had fallen late in the calendar and the light

air of spring had already gained the heft of summer. The thick stone walls offered a respite from heat most days, but today the chapel felt swollen with the tumid air, trapping the smell of incense and the corporeal odors of the residents of Mursay inside, baking them like an oven.

Father Dieudonné's face bore the effects. His usually mild complexion heightened. Beads of perspiration hung on his forehead, and he used Francoise's vestment to delicately dab at the perspiration dotting his brow.

He began his homily. "Today all of our souls can be saved thanks to the magnanimous actions of our Lord Jesus Christ who was crucified and rose to join his Heavenly Father so our sins could be forgiven. Today is then a day of great celebration for all true believers." Father again mopped his forehead. "Does this mean our work as Christians is complete? Jesus has saved me, therefore I am safe. Free to live my life in any fashion."

His voice, which had been measured, took a turn, rising in pitch and cadence. "No, no, no! Remember your scriptures and Jesus's words: 'Behold, I come like a thief! Blessed is he who stays awake and keeps his clothes with him, so that he may not go naked and be shamefully exposed!' Some of us drape ourselves in our arrogance. Protect ourselves with pride and worldly goods. Wrapped in our selfishness, we stroll through life without a care in the world or a thought for others. Yet we have been warned. We shall be taken, whisked away to the fiery pits of Hell should we let drop our humility before Him!"

Not once did he look at Jeanne, but the sharp point of his words met their mark.

"Celebrate, doing so moderately. Be joyful. Yet hold your happiness in check. For the day of reckoning can come at any moment. The mild. The obedient. The humble. These are the souls who will find eternal life with God in Heaven. As for the rest," he said, fixing his gaze on Jeanne, "they are without redemption."

****

Back in her bedroom, Jeanne read the letters she had preserved from her father. She stored them in a wooden box tucked under a loose floorboard beneath her bed. She sat at her desk and reread the last one she'd received, looking for a mention of the priest she only half-remembered:

Give my regards to Mimi and Francoise. Is Father Dieudonné still vexing you? If he is, remember my advice: Ignore him or at least pretend to give him your attention. He is tiresome and not nearly as spiritually minded as he would have us believe. More on that when I arrive home. I count the days until I see your sweet face again!

All my love,

Papa

There came a knock on the door and although Jeanne did not bid enter, it opened to reveal her aunt.

"Jeanne, Henriette tells me you plan to take your repast alone in your room yet again." Her aunt made to cross the threshold into the room, but then hesitated. "Is it true?"

Jeanne folded the letter gently, saying nothing.

"My dear girl, about this scene with the vestments: a fly has been made into an elephant. I am in part to blame." Aunt Mimi took a few steps toward Jeanne. "In the spirit of the holiday, and Jesus' dying for our sins, can we not put this peccadillo behind us?" Aunt Mimi's dark brown eyes shone as if she were about to cry or had just finished crying, and Jeanne nearly relented.

"That's not why I wish to be alone," Jeanne said. "I simply don't have an appetite for much food or conversation with Papa gone."

"Then do it because you are a Christian. By avoiding our company, you cause grievous injury to our feelings. Father Dieudonné is particularly mortified by your behavior."

"My father did not care for Father Dieudonné and advised me in so many words not to trust him."

Aunt Mimi narrowed her eyes. "My brother advised no such thing."

Jeanne held up the letter, her heart pounding. "It says so here in his handwriting. I assure you it's true."

Aunt Mimi went to grab the letter, but Jeanne held it behind her back. "This is private correspondence."

"Really, Jeanne. The way you speak to me. You're like a stranger to me."

"I have changed. Grown. And am a woman in my majority. As such Mursay is mine and mine alone. Which means I decide who resides under this roof. I don't recall you asking me if Father Dieudonné could have rooms here. If I had been consulted, I would have resolutely declined."

Her words seemed to fall like a slap, and her aunt even raised her hands to her face as if warding off their sting. Jeanne braced herself for a show of tears. When at last her aunt spoke, her eyes were dry.

"It is odd to have this conversation with you, here, in particular." Aunt Mimi crossed the enormous room and stood by the marble fireplace. "For this room, and the two others comprising the suite, were once mine. I see you're surprised."

"You've never mentioned it before," Jeanne said in as callous a tone as she could muster.

"No. Nor would I have for fear of injuring you. Many years ago, I graciously accepted my small place in the dark northern rooms of Mursay, the ones my brother assigned me because fate dictated that my rank in the household descend. I remain in those rooms after all these years, although I could have easily convinced your father to have me returned to more desirable accommodations. But I embraced my humility. Accepted it as punishment for marrying my husband, the marquis. You see, both my father and I were impressed with his title. I would win the family such prestige! But the grand marquis was in reality a drunkard and a brute. The fortune I brought to the union only served as tinder for his vices. He burned through my money like that." She snapped her fingers.

Jeanne had never heard so frank an admission from her aunt, or from anyone else for that matter. Her heart filled with equal parts horror and pity.

"But he wasn't all bad." She ran a hand over the marble mantelpiece, pushing dust from its surface. "He had a soft spot for his hunting dogs. Two lackeys slept in a room designated for the beasts and attended to them at all times. The lackeys slept on the floor while the dogs occupied feather beds." She laughed in a humorless fashion. "He never laid a hand on his animals yet beat me quite severely. On one occasion, he nearly killed me. I was so miserable with him, for a time I contemplated taking my own life."

"Oh, Aunt, I don't know what to say!"

She shrugged. "What is there to say? This is ancient history. Now that you're a woman, I trust you can bear hearing it. Although I ask for your discretion with Francoise. She is ignorant of the details concerning her father and I would like for it to remain that way." Aunt Mimi crossed the room to sit on Jeanne's bed. "During my time with the marquis, I met a young priest who showed me God was my salvation. He gave me hope and strength and a new hold on life. It was he who convinced me life was worth living."

"Father Dieudonné," she said, and her aunt nodded.

"He alone is responsible for my deliverance from the lowest rings of Hell. Without him I'd be dead."

Jeanne put an arm around her aunt. "I feel wretched for how I've behaved. You must forgive me." She took hold of her aunt's beautifully formed hands and kissed them.

"It is as you say. You are now the mistress of this place. Regardless of what Father Dieudonné signifies to me, it is well within your right to decide who shall and shall not inhabit Mursay. I will ask him to leave tonight. Only let me deliver the news to him so that he receives it gently."

"No. He must stay. And you mustn't share what I told you tonight, I beg of you!"

"Of course not, my darling." She drew Jeanne into her arms and over her shoulder she said, "Will you join us for Easter repast then?"

"Gladly."

"Good." Aunt Mimi squeezed her, then kissed both her cheeks. "We shall put this behind us and never look back."

How could she have been so beastly? Life had

delivered such pain to her aunt. Jeanne vowed to shield her from any suffering henceforth.

Chapter Twelve

"Our French colonists have very large families; eight, ten, twelve, and occasionally fifteen and sixteen children. The Indians, on the contrary, have as a rule but two or three and very seldom above five."

~*Francois de Laval de Montmorency, Bishop of Quebec*

The *Saint Anne*

The fever that held Elisabeth in its grasp seemed to toy with her, on one morning releasing her long enough so she could sit up and take a bowl of gruel, then, hours later, returning so ferociously, the girl thrashed and convulsed. Jeanne slept on the floor next to the berth in the cabin supplied by Monsieur Suprenant. In the middle of one interminable night, Elisabeth cried out in terror and could not be soothed. Jeanne lit a candle and held the girl's hand assuring her all was well. Elisabeth stared at her, eyes vacant, her face as white as the bed linens, and whispered, "I trust you will care for me, Uncle."

Madeleine and Teeth tended to the baby in their quarters below, bringing her up when Elisabeth, in her delirium, called her by name. On most occasions the girl was too addled by fever to do more than look at the infant and sigh or stroke one of her tiny hands. As for Madame La Plante and the demoiselles, not a single one of them deigned to call on her.

Monsieur Suprenant remarked upon the lack of visitors one day as Elisabeth slept. Standing at the foot of the berth, he said in a low tone, "Why hasn't Madame La Plante visited the girl? I haven't seen her so much as stop by to inquire about poor Elisabeth's health. Surely it's her duty as chaperone."

Seated on a low stool next to Elisabeth's bed, Jeanne dipped a cloth into a bowl of water and gently dabbed at the girl's forehead. "Madame has washed her hands of Elisabeth, I am afraid. She made it clear she is no longer a Daughter of the King."

"Is it within her power to make such decisions?"

"Yes. She marks every infraction, down to the smallest one, in the black book of judgment she totes around day and night. Certainly, what happened to Elisabeth is no peccadillo, although she was powerless to do anything to prevent it, poor girl."

"I wonder what will become of her and her child."

All fell silent save for the creaking of the boat, a sound so omnipresent, Jeanne failed on most days to register it. Now it seemed as if the *Saint Anne* itself bemoaned the bleak future awaiting Elisabeth.

Monsieur Suprenant interrupted her thoughts. "Forgive me if I speak too plainly, mademoiselle, I do not wish to offend, but I can't help but think it." He hesitated before continuing. "Will it not be strange to disembark and be, well, assigned a husband?"

"I take no offense and have thought the same myself. I've decided it's not so different a fate than what confronts most young women." She thought of

111

August Loret. "My own father considered making a match for me. He allowed me the right of refusal, thankfully, a right we can exercise in New France."

"Your father?" he said, raising an eyebrow. "Did you not tell me you were long orphaned?"

Monsieur Suprenant's cabin was considerably brighter than the mademoiselles' dark quarters, and Jeanne turned her face away so he couldn't see as she blushed. "Yes. I had forgotten." She stood, and in the confines of his cabin, found herself uncomfortably close to him, so sat again.

He said wryly, "You know, my mother always said, 'Those who speak only truths can afford poor memories.'"

"Are you calling me a liar, monsieur?"

"Everything about you tells me you should be with the demoiselles. Then again, having gotten to know you, I believe if you were lying, it must be for a good reason."

"Rest assured if I could say more, I would. I prefer to let leave the matter there." She swallowed to quell an impulse to cry.

He crossed the divide between them and sat on the floor beside her. Looking up at her, he said, "It is clear, once again, I've upset you. It's the last thing I wanted."

Jeanne found his gaze unnerving. He seemed to lack any artifice, which only made her wish to be more honest. Yet she could not. To cover her growing consternation, she placed a hand on Elisabeth's forehead. "Her condition seems to be improving."

He nodded. "Her fever has calmed since yesterday. A sure sign the tides are turning in her favor."

A heaviness weighing on Jeanne lifted. "She's a

good girl. A sweet girl despite her predicament."

"Your lack of judgment is admirable. Instead of casting stones, you tend to the poor girl tirelessly and your friends look after the babe. All the demoiselles seemed to have abandoned her completely."

Madeleine and her lot had been called, "trash from the streets of Paris," by Madame. Jeanne would have held the same view herself before she learned better. Yet Madeleine, and even Teeth, had proved to be cut from the finest of fabrics, and served as kind, fiercely protective allies to Elisabeth, a virtual stranger.

"I've learned so much about what separates mademoiselles from demoiselles." She spoke the words bitterly.

Monsieur Suprenant smiled. "Indeed. Enlighten me."

"Two things. The letter 'm' and the letter 'a'."

Monsieur laughed. "That is an opinion some would call jaded, but I would call wise. Wisdom at odds with your youth."

"I am eighteen, monsieur. At fifteen I was young. These past years have aged me so, at times I feel I've become an old crone."

From his vantage below her, he studied her a moment before saying, "As an ancient man of five and twenty, my vision still works tolerably well and informs me you are the furthest thing from a crone. And when you smile as you do now, you transform these quarters."

"Thank you. You are kind, monsieur."

"Kindness has nothing to do with it. I report the facts before my eyes."

Jeanne stood again, and as she did, the ship rolled,

causing her to stumble and land in Monsieur Suprenant's arms. Later that day, and for many days after, Jeanne recalled the warmth of his body as he braced her fall, wondering how it was possible to be filled with a moment of such pure joy amidst so much suffering.

****

As Elisabeth's fever loosened its grip, she regained strength until at last she could eat and nurse her baby. Jeanne kept the mother and child company.

"Oh, but she is a sleepy head, my little angel." Elisabeth lay next to Anne and kissed the fuzzy down of her hair.

"Just like her maman," Jeanne said. "It warms my heart to see you with your eyes open now. You gave us all a scare."

"Thank you for caring for my little one and for me. I hope one day to repay your kindness."

"You have repaid it. You're sitting up and smiling. Who could want more?"

Elisabeth held her face next to that of her sleeping infant and said, "Does she take after me?"

Jeanne could see no clear resemblance, but considering the story of the baby's father, she answered, "She is an exact replica of you."

Elisabeth laughed. "Poor girl. Cursed with her mother's looks. Her father is quite handsome."

"You mean blessed by them. She is a fortunate girl," Jeanne said.

It was true that Elisabeth, at first glance, was rather plain. But with her flawless skin and eyes the color of a clear summer sky, Jeanne thought she possessed a singular beauty.

"Now that I'm better, can you read the story of Romulus and Remus to us again?"

It was Elisabeth's favorite. In it, the heroine's uncle forces himself upon her and she bears twin sons. To hide his misdeeds, the evil uncle calls for her death and the death of his offspring. A servant, tasked with the murders, takes pity on the infants and instead of killing them, puts them in a basket and floats them down a river.

"Is it not remarkable the parallel in the story and what has transpired between myself and my uncle?" she said. To baby Anne she whispered, "Instead of a basket on the Tiber, we're banished on a ship and out of his life. Your father is not a very good man, I am afraid. I begin to see that now." Tears welled in her eyes as she turned to Jeanne. "He professed his love for me, and I for him. How is it he abandoned us?"

Jeanne thought of her aunt. "Love is not a fixed star by which to navigate. It is inconstant for some. Changing."

"My love for this little cherub will never change." She rained kisses onto little Anne's chubby cheeks and the baby stretched and mewled before falling back to sleep. "You are stuck with me forever, my sweet pea, and I with you."

A knock on the cabin door sounded and Monsieur Suprenant entered. Jeanne had not seen him since the morning before, and her heart surged with happiness until she noticed Madame La Plante close on his heels, her book clutched to her chest. Madame brushed past him and stood at the foot of Elisabeth's sickbed. Jeanne had been seated by the bed but stood to face the lady.

"I see you have had the brat," Madame said. She

looked down on the baby. "Boy or girl?"

"Girl," Elisabeth said.

"Such a pity. Boys are more highly sought after. There are orphanages of a sort in New France. I have connections there who will see to it the child finds a worthy home."

Elisabeth cried out, "No! I won't give away my Anne." Her distress caused the baby to wail.

Madame snorted. "Pish! No convent will accept you burdened with a child. With the lack of French citizenry in New France, I grant that with a word to the right authorities, we can arrange a new family for it."

"Anne is no burden to unload," she said, hushing the baby. "She is mine and mine alone to care for."

"Madame, you are frightening her." Jeanne knelt and put an arm around the girl's trembling shoulders.

Monsieur Suprenant stepped forward. "Madame, the girl is not yet fully recovered from the shock of the delivery. A conversation this fraught should wait until the demoiselle is stronger. Had I known of your intentions, I would have forbidden you from visiting."

"Forbidden me?" Madame's eyes grew as did the pitch of her voice. "Who are you to forbid me of anything, monsieur? On this ship, I am the commander. I follow the bidding of the king himself. You will forbid me nothing!"

Monsieur Suprenant bowed his head a moment, then said, "Madame, I only suggest you be reasonable. You gain nothing by tormenting the girl in her fragile state. If you would like to continue to discuss the matter, I advise we depart to the captain's quarters and leave the young mother to rest."

As they made to leave, Madame La Plante wheeled

around. "Mademoiselle Davide, you will join us as well."

When Madame departed, Elisabeth clutched at Jeanne's hand and whispered, "Dear Jeanne, I have caused you much trouble and for that I am sorry. But do not let her take my Anne!"

"Not to worry. Madame is full of her own importance, but she can be reasoned with," Jeanne said calmly, although she knew the fate of Elisabeth and her baby dangled on the sword of Madame's righteousness. "Now curl up under the blanket and follow your daughter's example. See how she sleeps again."

When she opened the door to the captain's quarters, Madame La Plante turned and pointed at her. "And this one presents yet another problem."

Jeanne stopped short. "Forgive me, Madame, but what problem do I cause?"

"You have been tending to that fornicator alongside Monsieur Suprenant in an overly intimate fashion. It is most unseemly. My eyes cannot always stay trained on you. But do not forget the One who sees all." Madame pointed Heavenward. "He knows the truth. Even the truth about you, Mademoiselle Davide? Or is it Mademoiselle Denot?"

Like Elisabeth, Jeanne's fate was bound to the capriciousness of Madame La Plante, and until now, Jeanne had tread lightly around her. But hearing the lady's words against Elisabeth unleashed her anger. "If only life were as black-and-white as the pages of your book, Madame."

"Oh, but it is for the righteous," Madame retorted.

Jacques held up his hands as if in surrender. "Madame La Plante, your standing on this ship as administrator of the king's wishes is irrefutable. I question, however, the same status as administrator of the Almighty's wishes."

Madame La Plante recoiled. "The audacity! You have overstepped your bounds, monsieur! Captain, you must order this man to move back into his cabin. To have them carry on in this fashion goes beyond the boundaries of decency."

The captain shrugged his shoulders. "Monsieur Suprenant's accommodations are his to offer. If he wishes to bunk with the crew, it is entirely his prerogative."

Madame held her black book up high. "I'm drafting a report to be sent directly to the offices of the king." She pointed a crooked finger toward the captain. "You will figure prominently in it and in a most unflattering light! As for you, Mademoiselle Denot Davide," she put a special emphasis on the two surnames, "your own reputation is on very thin ice. Very thin, indeed."

Madame exited the room with the flourish of a stage actor, slamming the door behind her. The captain put his hat on with a determined air and made to leave.

"My good man, you're not going to pursue her, are you?" Monsieur Suprenant asked.

"She has flown the coop and it is my duty to smooth her ruffled feathers or risk having my own plucked."

After the captain hurried off, Monsieur Suprenant ran his fingers through his hair in a way that reminded Jeanne of her father. She smiled at the thought of it.

"You look the picture of serenity right now, mademoiselle. Another girl would be reduced to tears hearing the pronouncements of Madame and all of her dire predictions concerning the Almighty and thin ice."

As a child, she had understood her future to be ineluctable, determined by God and her father's fortune. Now she knew otherwise. Fate was brutally mutable and could shift as frequently and violently as the wind. The trick lay in bending the current to one's own advantage in the same way the *Saint Anne*'s sails sped or slowed progress, according to the captain's maneuvering.

"Madame is no deity. You said so yourself. She's weak and fears losing control of her charges because of how it will reflect on her."

Monsieur looked at her appraisingly and shook his head. "You are a mystery, mademoiselle. You possess the face and figure of a young lady, yet you contain the wisdom of Solomon. I am befuddled by you and amazed with you in equal parts."

Having never received so extravagant a compliment, Jeanne was confused as to the proper response. "I was not fishing for compliments, Monsieur Suprenant," she said.

"No. You do not try to impress which makes you all the more impressive. What did Madame mean when she called you, 'Denot Davide'?"

Her trust of this man had grown with every passing moment in his company. He had proved, in so many ways, to have a kind and generous heart. Yet she hesitated before answering. "Denot is a family name," she said finally, and paused again before continuing, wishing she could open her heart to him fully. "At one point it was my surname, but I was forced to change it for reasons I cannot say."

Monsieur's expression changed upon hearing her words. "Denot? There was one Antoine Denot, a Maréchal de Camp for the king's army. Mademoiselle, the thought occurs to me that you bear a resemblance to him."

For months she had denied her blood lines, eschewed any connection to the person dearest to her, but now she found herself blurting out, "Antoine Denot was my father."

His expression held a look of utter amazement. "Jeanne Denot. Can it be? Why then give the name Davide? Why are you here at all? Your family's estate is in Perche, is it not? Your revelation has set a multitude of questions running through my brain. My mouth cannot keep up with the task of posing them."

"If only I could explain, monsieur." She thought of the complicated web of deceit which had forced her aboard this ship. "Revealing the full truth would put my life in grave danger."

"You are trembling and the terror in your eyes is clear." He took hold of her hands. "Mademoiselle, it seems every other time we meet I upset you. It's nothing I plan to do, yet here we are again."

"Cloaking my identity, I've escaped death only narrowly. You and one other person are the only souls to whom I've confided the truth. More than that, I dare not say. Now I beg of you, please pursue this subject no further."

"I'll respect your wishes, but I must tell you something almost too amazing to believe. I knew your father. Not only that, I counted him as a counsellor and a friend."

His words had a most remarkable effect. Her brain

buzzed with alternating feelings of shock at the coincidence, and pure happiness. "Dear monsieur, you bring such great joy to me. It's been so difficult denying his existence. I loved him so dearly."

"That's not the half of it." Monsieur's voice broke with emotion. "If it weren't for your father, I wouldn't be standing here holding your small hands that, despite their coolness, warm my heart."

The door flew open, marking the return of the captain, and Jeanne stepped back and released Monsieur Suprenant's hands.

The captain cleared his throat. "Well, her anger has waned a bit." He removed his hat and mopped sweat from his brow. "She acknowledged your right to do with your cabin as you see fit. I would advise, however, discretion when it comes to attending to the young girl in the presence of Mademoiselle Davide."

Monsieur Suprenant said, "There has been nothing untoward about my dealings with the mademoiselle."

The captain raised an eyebrow. "Did I not just see you holding hands?" Monsieur made to protest but the captain cut him off. "It signifies nothing to me, Jacques, but you may want to consider the reputation of the young mademoiselle if she is to have any future in the New World."

****

With Elisabeth so greatly improved, Jeanne fell into her normal routines, including, when weather permitted, her morning walks in the open air. She longed to discuss in full Monsieur Suprenant's revelation about her father, but their paths did not cross. As each day passed with no sight of him, her corporal being became more at odds with her intellect.

Though she told herself it was no use wasting time recalling how Monsieur Suprenant's eyes seemed to give off light when he laughed, or how his skin felt against hers when they had held hands, she could not will herself to stop recalling every minute detail of his physical being, nor could she cease reconstructing their conversations, searching for nuances, hints to other, deeper, sentiments.

On one particularly fine morning, a footfall echoed behind her as she paced the deck. She turned, expecting to find monsieur, but instead came face-to-face with Madeleine.

"Did I startle you? You look as if you've seen a ghost," Madeleine said.

"Yes. I thought you were sleeping. It's so unlike you to rise with the sun."

Madeleine rubbed her eyes and squinted up at the sky. "In truth, I feel as though I may be sick. I thought the fresh air would help."

Jeanne's thoughts had been preoccupied of late. Now, examining her friend's countenance, she saw dark circles around her eyes and her skin lacked its usual luster.

"You don't look particularly well. Why don't we rest."

They sat huddled under their shawls on the edge of the quarter deck. Jeanne spotted Laurent, who regarded the two of them from a respectable distance. Madeleine blew him a kiss, which the sailor pantomimed catching and putting to his lips.

"My, but the two of you are bolder and bolder. Do you not fear getting caught by Madame?"

"Not especially. In fact, I'm meeting Laurent

tonight if the weather holds. He has something important to tell me."

"Who does?" Jeanne said distractedly.

"Laurent," Madeleine said. "You make a poor listener these days."

"Forgive me. I'm not feeling quite myself either."

"Aye. You're beyond distracted. It's like your mind has journeyed to a place your body can't follow."

"Have I?" Jeanne said.

"Or perhaps your thoughts have simply climbed the ladder to the deck above ours?"

"Yes. Elisabeth. By the grace of God, she and Anne are well."

"Come now." Madeleine rolled her eyes to the heavens. "You can't be that thick? I mean Monsieur Suprenant. By the look on your face, I see I'm right."

Jeanne sighed. "In truth, it's been nearly impossible for me not to think of him. The more I tell myself I cannot, or should not, the more he occupies my thoughts."

"Your head doesn't rule your heart. It's the other way around." Madeleine slumped against the hull of the ship and shivered. "It's getting so cold."

"I haven't even told you the most extraordinary thing of all. Monsieur Suprenant knew my father."

"Wait. You told him who your father was?"

"Yes. I didn't mean to," Jeanne said. "It just came out."

Madeleine sat up straight. "You didn't tell him about Paris?"

"No. Of course not."

"Jeanne, you're too trusting. It's too late to tell you to harden your heart against the man. Anyone could see you're head over heels. But you have to hold some distance."

"The way you hold distance toward Laurent?"

Madeleine shivered again and put her head on Jeanne's shoulder. "How could this have happened?"

"What?"

"That we'd both find love on this godforsaken ship."

"You're right. I do love him." Just saying the words aloud filled her with a desperate desire to see him, to hold him. "Now I know why people say, 'lovesick.' It is an illness. A fever burning in my head so brightly it pains me with its intensity."

"It's more like madness. Not to worry." Madeleine took hold of Jeanne's hand. "From my experience it doesn't last."

"My dear Madeleine, your hand is hot to the touch." Jeanne felt Madeleine's cheek. "You're burning up. Come now, you must rest a while."

Jeanne made to leave, but Madeleine didn't move. Jeanne helped her rise.

"Oh, but I'm tired, Jeanne," she said listlessly. "I fear I won't manage the stairs." And with that she collapsed.

Chapter Thirteen

"If my father had loved me as well as I loved him, he would never have sent me into a country so dangerous as this, to which I came through pure obedience and against my own inclination. Here duplicity passes for wit, and frankness is looked upon as folly."

~Madame Elizabeth-Charlotte of Bavaria,
Sister-in-Law to King Louis XIV

Mursay

My dearest Marquise,
I have news of a most extraordinary nature. Its source: my close relative, Athénaïs, the king's most treasured consort. The king will appear in a new ballet by Lully to be performed at the Palais Louvre at the end of June and tout le monde will be in attendance. I have asked special favor that yourself and your girls gain admittance to the performance that will be an intimate, exclusive diversion.
I understand the great loss that has befallen your family with the death of your excellent brother. Between that time and now, four seasons have passed. What's done is done and Mademoiselle Denot's age advances, as does all of ours. It is time we move swiftly before the bloom is off the rose!

Do impress upon the girls, and to Mademoiselle Denot in particular, since I gather it is she who hesitates; court is a flock of the rarest and most beautiful birds. Flying in their company means achieving heights impossible to gain solo. If your niece seeks to achieve rara avis status she must be pushed out of the nest. Acceptance there, to stretch my colorful phraseology further, leads to a pleasantly feathered nest and newer horizons of fortune.

Your truest friend,

Madame Victoria Loret

"There you have it! Another letter from Madame Loret entreating us to consider introduction at court. How many has she sent now? A half dozen?"

Aunt Mimi fanned her face with the letter. On days such as this one, when the sun beat against the stone walls of Mursay, they spent their afternoons in the cool, easterly facing salon with the shutters drawn.

Jeanne took the letter from her aunt's hand. "She writes, 'What's done is done.' As if father's death were insignificant. A trifling mishap. How I despise her!"

Aunt Mimi seemed to measure her words carefully. "Despise her all you want. Madame Loret has a point." Jeanne made to protest, but Aunt Mimi held up a hand. "One year has passed since my brother's death. A year of great darkness for all of us. As much as we may desire it, we cannot stay hidden under this shadow. My brother expressly desired you to be betrothed by this, your eighteenth year. Which means you and Francoise must go forth into the light of society, and soon, before you're both too long in the tooth."

"Introduce Francoise, then." Jeanne crushed the letter and threw it to the floor.

Aunt Mimi frowned at Jeanne's childish gesture and recovered Madame Loret's letter, carefully smoothing out the wrinkles. "I grow weary of explaining this, my dear girl. Please do try to get it through your obstinate head. As the lady of Mursay, it would not be proper for Francoise to be introduced before you. Only alongside you. And Madame Loret is positioning her family favorably with ours by helping."

Francoise put her latest needlework aside and loosened the neck of her gown. "Madame hopes you'll marry her little son, August."

The stifling heat coupled with the odiousness of the conversation made Jeanne peevish. In her own ears she sounded like a child when she said, "Never! I don't care how many advantages he lists. I will never ever, ever accept August Loret."

Henriette entered the room bearing a bowl of cool water. Her face was as red as a ripened tomato and she moved slowly, struggling to carry the bowl without sloshing its contents.

"You are the slowest creature on God's Earth, girl!" Aunt Mimi administered a swift kick to Henriette's leg, which made the girl cry out and spill some of the water. "You dawdle as we melt in this heat. Where are the cloths?"

Rivulets of sweat plastered Henriette's already unfortunate hair to her face. "I must fetch them, madame. It weren't easy to manage the bowl, let alone the bowl and the cloths."

Aunt Mimi said, "Cloth weighs as much as air, and you couldn't manage?" Jeanne and Francoise laughed at the girl's ability to make even the simplest requests complicated. "You continually confound me with your lack of inventiveness. Make haste! Or we'll be puddles by the time you return!"

Aunt Mimi rolled up the sleeves of her gown and dipped her wrists into the water and the girls followed her example. Jeanne wished she could plunge her head into the bowl and stay there, skirting the current topic of conversation and escaping the discomfort of the heat.

"August Loret or no August Loret, you must find a suitable match, and soon. I myself was introduced at court by my fourteenth year and betrothed to the Marquis at fifteen. Time is wasting. Besides, madame's latest suggestion sounds like the perfect forum for your debut."

Henriette came back with the cloths and Jeanne dipped one into the cool water, pressing it against her neck. "I do hope to meet a kind man. A man of letters like Papa."

Francoise had covered her face with a cloth, but when Jeanne spoke, she tore it off. "Do you mean we shall go, Jeanne? Please say, yes! Please, please!"

"It appears we must." As soon as Jeanne said the words, Francoise bounded out of her chair and hugged her.

Francoise, who, not a moment before, wilted from the heat, now pirouetted in the center of the room. "At last! To court." Only then did Jeanne understand how much this meant to her cousin. "And what gowns shall we wear?" Before Jeanne could reply Francoise said, "I know, the pink silk for the night of the ballet."

Jeanne, infected by Francoise's enthusiasm, joined her in her impromptu dance, twirling around the room. "We'll be flying high with the royal flock!" She spread her arms wide, pretending they were wings. "If

Madame Loret was a bird, which would she be?" Jeanne called out.

"A cuckoo," Francoise answered. "No, with all her beauty spots, she'd be a speckled hen." Francoise grabbed her cousin's hands and began to spin, just as they did when they were children, until dizzied, they fell into a heap on the floor.

Aunt Mimi laughed at their antics, then pulled a serious face. "Enough of that. You're too old for this nonsense. Now, we need to review gowns for the big night. Francoise, your silk slippers need repairing. Henriette needs to arrange the portmanteaux." She looked around the room. "Where did Henriette go? Why is she never here when I need her?" She got up to search for the girl, and at the doorway she stopped. "Oh, and I will ask Father Dieudonné to join us as chaperone on the journey to Paris." Her aunt paused. "If, that is, you allow it, Jeanne."

Jeanne said, "Of course!" then regretted acquiescing so quickly. She loathed the sanctimonious father. Yet, seeing her aunt humble herself, asking Jeanne for permission, filled her with shame. She recalled her father's favorite quote from Plutarch, "To find fault is easy; to do better may be difficult." She vowed to do better in matters concerning the priest.

****

Given the magnitude of preparations, it seemed they were not merely visiting Paris, but rather launching an attack on it. Half a dozen portmanteaux held a trove of supplies to secure victory in the upcoming siege: silk gowns, corsets, rouge pots, taffeta handkerchiefs, shoe ribbons, ear bobs, stockings, gloves, enough shoes to outfit an army and a retinue of pins and headdresses.

On the morning before their departure, Jeanne awoke to the sound of shrieking from Francoise's room. She dressed hurriedly and arrived at her cousin's threshold, followed by her aunt. Francoise sat at her dressing table, her back to Jeanne; at first, Jeanne could not see the source of the girl's torment.

"I am a monster!" Francoise shouted, and turned to face Jeanne.

"Heaven help us," Jeanne cried.

Her cousin's face was transformed by scarlet bumps rising angrily from her skin, disfiguring Francoise's lovely features so that her cheeks appeared to be stuffed. Her eyes were swollen to slits. Even so, tears managed their escape and poured down her tortured visage.

Aunt Mimi drew back Francoise's hair to reveal similar welts crisscrossing along her back and shoulders. "Bedbugs. They have eaten you alive. It's a wonder you slept through it."

Francoise began to tear at her face, screaming, "It itches like the Devil!"

Aunt Mimi grabbed her hands, forcing them to her sides. "You mustn't touch them, or you'll be pocked for life. This is disaster enough. We must fumigate this room. Burn the bedding and the drapery. Henriette!" Mimi bellowed. "Where is that stupid girl?"

Francoise turned back to the mirror and, catching sight of her reflection, let out another pitiful cry. "What shall we do about my face, Maman? Shall we burn it too?"

In truth, her face looked as if it had been through a fire. Where Francoise had scratched, pinpoints of blood arose, dotting the hilly landscape of her once creamy skin.

"Calm yourself," Aunt Mimi said. "All traces will be gone in a matter of days."

"Days?" Francoise covered her eyes. "How many days?"

"Ten. Perhaps fourteen. By month's end no one will be the wiser if you don't scratch and make it worse."

"But that isn't time enough," Francoise cried.

Aunt Mimi stood behind her daughter, studying her distorted features. After a moment she spoke: "No. Not nearly enough time. We cannot delay the trip. We are expected. You must stay behind."

"No, Aunt, please!" Jeanne took Francoise in her arms. "If Francoise isn't able to go, I myself will stay back."

Aunt Mimi smiled. "A very pretty gesture, Jeanne, but folly all the same. The king himself expects us. Expects you."

Having only recently established a truce with her aunt, Jeanne didn't wish to argue. "I suppose you're right," she said.

Francoise peered into the mirror, her nose nearly touching the glass. "Perhaps I can accompany you and hope it clears? Or paint myself and hide the worst of it?"

Aunt Mimi shook her head. "For what purpose? To develop the reputation of 'that blotchy-faced marquise?' I think not. You have one chance to make a first impression, my love. Memories are long at court. I won't have you a laughingstock at your debut."

****

Old people did not fare well in carriages. Father Dieudonné groaned and sighed each time the horse and five met with an impediment on the road to Paris. Jeanne felt no discomfort, although she did her own amount of sighing at the memory of Francoise who had rushed out at the last moment, still in her dressing gown, to bid her a tearful adieu. The salt of Francoise's tears seemed to aggravate the welts, making them more pronounced. Aunt Mimi scolded her daughter for charging outside half-dressed. Something a child would do, not a full-grown woman. Francoise ignored her mother's pleas to return to the house and instead threw her arms around Jeanne before she could climb into the carriage.

Francoise clung to Jeanne, weeping, and Aunt Mimi snapped, "Dear God, what nonsense!"

Francoise's theatrics filled Jeanne with a sense of dread, one she sought to assuage by comforting her cousin. She pulled away, her hands on her cousin's shoulders: "Now you're being silly. I'll be back soon, full of stories of the royal flock with their high manners. You'll hear who sat on what stool and how many times I made a perfect fool of myself."

Francoise smiled and sniffed then scratched at her face like a dog scratches at fleas until her mother shouted, "How many times have I told you? No scratching! Henriette, I want you to sit on Mademoiselle Francoise if you see her scratching her bites during our absence."

Henriette, who had been loading cases onto the carriage, stopped and looked from Aunt Mimi to Francoise and back again. She took a few steps toward Francoise then paused.

"Do you want that I start now, madame? It will be awful rough on the girl to be sat on what with the hardness of the pavestones."

Francoise darted behind Jeanne for protection, hiding her hands behind her back.

Aunt Mimi rolled her eyes heavenward. "No, you great oaf. Finish the packing!"

As the carriage lumbered along, the day lengthened and gained heat. Aunt Mimi wore a gown of yellow silk. She loosened the stays of the bodice saying something about melting in the carriage. From his seat opposite them, Father Dieudonné's eyes were drawn every moment or so to Aunt Mimi's bosom, lighting on her flesh like a fly on a horse. After a while, he caught Jeanne staring at him and cleared his throat and officiously consulted his gold pocket watch, a recent gift from Aunt Mimi the priest had a habit of fondling during lulls in conversation. Jeanne thought it an ostentatious bauble for a man of the cloth, but Father Dieudonné appeared to hold no scruples about fine possessions. He announced they had been travelling a full three hours then rapped on the side of the carriage signaling the driver to stop after declaring his need to attend to "certain natural demands."

They arranged a picnic at the side of the road in a clearing by a wood. As the priest and Aunt Mimi discussed the route to Paris, Jeanne's head became heavy with the weight of the heat and a satiated appetite. She lay back, resting her head against the palms of her hands and in a moment fell into a slumber. She dreamed of sitting by the river behind Mursay with Francoise. Dark brown water lapped at her feet, and she smiled at her cousin who sat next to her on the riverbank. Francoise called out: "Whatever you do, Jeanne, you mustn't fall in!" And with that, Francoise grabbed her shoulders and pushed. Jeanne broke to the surface of consciousness with a gasp. She sat up to find herself alone.

When she asked the driver the whereabouts of her aunt and the priest, he pointed toward the forest. "They went looking for a spring. Said not to disturb you, mademoiselle."

Jeanne expected to find them within the nearest perimeter of the trees. But as she picked her way through the brush covering the forest floor, she detected no sign of them. The trees thickened, their shade tempering the oppressive heat. She paused a moment, listening intently for the sound of water. Standing stock still, she heard a foreign sound, a noise she could not readily assign to any bird or other woodland creature. It drew her eyes to a distance, and through the trees she caught a glimpse of yellow, the same canary shade of her aunt's silk gown. She nearly called out but as she continued to advance, Jeanne could make out her aunt more clearly and the sight rendered her dumbstruck.

Her aunt stood with her back against a tree, her corset gaped open, revealing her breasts. Father Dieudonné knelt before her, his head buried under her skirts. Jeanne knew she should run back to the carriage, she even took a step backward, but her eyes stayed trained on the spectacle before her. Aunt Mimi's back arched, and her hands clasped the back of the priest's head, pressing him deeper inside the folds of her gown. Then her aunt let out a cry and shuddered and as she did so, the priest stood and hastily dropped his britches, then plunged into her, rocking back and forth on his heels.

The sight before her caused her knees to buckle and Jeanne sat down abruptly before her legs failed her entirely. She half crawled back toward the carriage, thankful her gown, the color of spring leaves, helped her to hide in plain sight. A burning shame consumed her and by the time she reached the carriage, rivulets of perspiration coursed down her back and dampened her hair. She remembered coming upon her aunt and the priest in the chapel all those years before. How could her aunt engage in such wickedness? And the priest. Jeanne had understood men of the cloth to be like eunuchs. Immune to the lure of carnal sin. Knowing the extent of their duplicity, their degeneracy, how could she face either of them? Arranging herself in the same spot they left her, Jeanne feigned sleep. Presently she heard footsteps.

"Rise sleepy head! We've had enough rest for the day." Aunt Mimi poked her playfully with a stick.

Jeanne made a show of waking. "Oh. You're back. Did you find your spring?"

Aunt Mimi appeared momentarily flustered, then recovered her usual composure. "I thought you were asleep?"

Jeanne yawned theatrically. "I woke momentarily. You were gone. The driver informed me of your whereabouts." Jeanne stared at the priest whose pale blond complexion bloomed a shade of pink. He kept his gaze averted and made his way toward the carriage.

Her aunt tilted her head and regarded Jeanne for a moment. "Really? You seem out of sorts. As if you've been out galloping, not in a slumber. And you have pine needles stuck to the hem of your dress. Did you come searching for us, Jeanne? You weren't snooping, were you? You've always been such a terribly curious little kitten."

Jeanne rose. Turning to escape her aunt's scrutiny, she brushed her skirts. "I made a small attempt to find you, but the underbrush got the better of me, so I returned and fell asleep again."

Aunt Mimi picked a leaf out of Jeanne's hair. "You look tired just the same."

Back in the carriage, Father Dieudonné slumped into his seat and began snoring. Aunt Mimi was in high spirits, which threw Jeanne's consternation into greater relief. Her aunt seemed to mark her strained mood.

"Are you well, my dear? You look rather pale."

Jeanne shrugged. "Nerves, I suppose," she said.

"When I had my debut, I was terrified. You may find this difficult to imagine, but as a girl, I was quite a little country mouse. Afraid of my own shadow. My first week at the palace the king threw a masquerade." Aunt Mimi glanced at the priest who continued to snore. She lowered her voice. "As it so happened, I experienced a most urgent need for the privy, having had more than my fair share of wine. I became hopelessly lost in the labyrinth of hallways and passages. After endless wandering, I came across a gentleman dressed like a rooster. He was making water in one of the darker stairwells." She laughed.

"What did you do?"

"I hid until he finished his business, then relieved myself in the same spot!"

Jeanne had known her aunt to be the quintessence of elegance and virtue. This stranger sitting next to her, hair slightly unkempt, bodice disheveled, fornicating in the forest like an animal, bore no resemblance to the fine lady Jeanne had come to know these past eighteen years. It was as if a gilded surface had been scraped away to reveal a baser metal beneath.

"I don't think I could ever do that," Jeanne said.

"My dear, you'd be surprised by what you're capable of, if pushed." They were quiet a while and when her aunt seemed to nod off, Jeanne closed her eyes. But then her aunt spoke, "You know, spying can win you advantages, but most of the time, it is best not to pry."

"I would not know, I'm sure."

Her aunt's gaze sought out the truth lying under Jeanne's artfully composed features. Jeanne turned her head toward the window to study the landscape as it rolled by. A moment later, a gentle rain began to fall, and Jeanne made a silent prayer it would not impede their journey. They were due to reach the Seine before nightfall and would continue their journey to the Palais Louvre by water. There would be more room on the boat, or so she imagined, and more possibilities to escape her aunt and the priest.

Chapter Fourteen

"Send me wives! With wives I will anchor the roving *coureurs de bois* to the soil of New France and make of them the farmers that I need."

~*Pierre Le Moyne d'Iberville, Adventurer*

The *Saint Anne*

A new passenger had embarked on the *Saint Anne,* a gruesome presence which made itself known when Madeleine fell ill. The dreadful visitor wracked her being with such spasms of pain, she could not rest securely in her hammock but instead was placed on the floor. There she writhed in agony, wrestling with the twin demons of pestilence and fever. Within the space of two sunrises, half of the mademoiselles joined Madeleine in her misery. Jeanne, Teeth, and the other healthy girls tended to them as best they could, cooling their feverish brows and cleaning the detritus of disease. Jeanne sought out the advice of Monsieur Suprenant, who visited their quarters accompanied by Madame La Plante.

Madame La Plante held her record book in one hand and a lavender-scented handkerchief in the other, clutching it over her nose to cover the odor permeating the lower deck.

Monsieur Suprenant knelt beside Madeleine. "At

first it had the markings of the grippe. Now I fear it is a pox. Those who contracted it earliest are showing signs of pustules at the back of the neck." Monsieur Suprenant gently pulled back the blanket from Madeleine's shoulders and turned her head slightly, causing her to cry out. "For reasons unknown to us, the mademoiselles appear to be especially vulnerable. Those on the upper decks have yet to manifest it."

Madame La Plante recoiled at the sight of Madeleine's tortured flesh and held the handkerchief so tightly over her face, her words came out muffled and she was obliged to repeat them. "I said, monsieur, I know exactly why these girls suffer. It is because they are heathens! Sinners before God. In His wisdom, He has spared the girls above from His almighty wrath. Not one of them attended services this week. Nor have you, for that matter, Monsieur Suprenant. Shameful!"

At Madame's words, Teeth clenched her hand into a fist and Jeanne touched her arm, whispering, "Stay calm."

Jeanne turned to Madame, gesturing toward the girls who lay side-by-side in various stages of torment. "Attending services is out of the question. You can see for yourself, Madame. Those of us not stricken with the disease are obliged to care for those who are suffering."

Madame La Plante surveyed the wretches who lay at her feet. "Just be sure you're not exploiting the situation. Using it as pretense to have a lark."

"Did you say, 'lark'?" Teeth changed her stance, squaring her shoulders for a fight. "Take that hanky from your face, you old cow! It's affecting your vision!" Teeth lunged toward Madame La Plante, but Monsieur Suprenant stepped in front of her, protecting the old lady from any physical violence.

"Mademoiselle, please," he said. "Madame, surely it is as worthy an effort in the eyes of the Lord to attend to the suffering members of His flock as it is to attend services?"

"Sir, it is not my place to judge." Madame pointed upward. "It is His and His alone. As for you, mademoiselle." She brandished her book. "You should consider yourself officially notified. One more misstep and you no longer qualify for the king's program and will be stripped of your trousseau and dowry."

With her pronouncement made, Madame hurriedly departed for the upper deck and Teeth muttered after her, "Dried up old hag!"

"Indeed," Monsieur Suprenant said, "and one who carries the authority of the king and, it appears, God himself. If only she had the Almighty's healing powers."

"Teeth!" Jeanne said, "Go after her. Apologize."

Teeth shook her head. "I was in the right. It is she who should say sorry."

Jeanne chose her words carefully: "Your will is formidable. Your integrity unquestionable. Yet both could work against you."

"I suppose I'll live to see another day." Teeth smiled in her tight-lipped fashion.

"Are you not frightened of her?" Jeanne asked.

"Frightened? Ha! I've faced worse things than that old turd. My own dad for one. My brothers for two, three and four. Besides, there are more terrifying forces at work right here at our feet. Madame She Monkey I can handle."

Madeleine cried out piteously then, and Jeanne

returned to her side. Her friend's eyes were unfocused, as if blinded by pain.

"Jeanne," she whispered. "Please. Make it stop."

"I will fetch you more wine," Jeanne said. Try as she might, she found it impossible to keep a note of panic from her voice, but Madeleine was too adrift in her own torment to notice. "You are to continue with the quinine as well. Monsieur Suprenant says it will tame the fever."

Jeanne made to leave but Madeleine caught hold of her skirt and tugged on it weakly. "Send Teeth for it, will you? Don't leave me."

Teeth went to fetch the wine and Jeanne began to read Plutarch, the story of Theseus, Madeleine's favorite because of the young hero's devotion to Ariadne.

Madeleine's pitiful moans broke the narrative until at last she fell into a troubled slumber. Jeanne replaced the mustard plaster on her friend's neck and felt the beat of her heart by pressing firmly on her wrist, something Monsieur Suprenant had taught her.

"You make a capable doctor, mademoiselle," Monsieur Suprenant said, kneeling beside her. "How is she doing?"

Jeanne stood and beckoned Monsieur Suprenant to join her in the passageway leading to the upper decks. She spoke in a low voice. "She is increasingly plagued by pain in her limbs and the beating of her heart is at times wild, then slows."

He nodded. "Her body is at war with the disease."

"There is something I must ask you, out of earshot of the other girls. I beg you to be honest in your response. Will she survive it?"

Monsieur Suprenant put a hand lightly on Jeanne's shoulder. "I don't know. I've witnessed battle wounds that appeared fatal, yet their victims lived to tell the story of their scars. Likewise, I once treated a man who had foot rot who died as a result. The course of disease is too unpredictable to say."

Jeanne covered her face with her hands and Monsieur Suprenant drew her against his chest. "Fear not. We shall tend to her the best we can."

"Madeleine is the reason I'm alive. I cannot go on if she passes." She thought of the sacrifice Madeleine had made for her in Paris and prayed silently for her friend's salvation.

Monsieur Suprenant held her a moment longer, then stood back to meet her gaze. "You are stronger than you know, mademoiselle. Brave like your father."

At the mention of him, Jeanne began to cry anew. "Sometimes it feels like my heart will break apart from the sadness of his loss."

He took her into his arms again. "I'm sorry to have awakened it."

"No. I want to speak of him. To keep him alive if only in my words." She stepped back and dried her eyes. "Can you tell me the story of how you knew him?"

He paused and seemed to consider his words.

"What is it? You look frightened to tell me," Jeanne said.

"Only because I am frightened of how you'll receive the story. You see, my past, like yours, isn't typical. I didn't stay the course the circumstances of my birth ordained for me. I am the last of four sons so had no rights to my father's fortune. Instead, I sought a career as an officer in the military."

He paused again before continuing, his face so close to hers in the narrow passage, she could feel the warmth of his breath as he spoke.

"My parents had hopes of making an advantageous match for me and had even chosen the prospective bride. Yet I was in love with someone else and refused the arrangement."

Monsieur Suprenant's words had a queer effect on Jeanne. Her pulse quickened and she felt light-headed. He seemed to mark the change in her. "Is my story overly familiar?" he asked.

"Pray, monsieur, continue. I am not a child."

"No. Your nature is open, not prone to prejudice. Although my story may test even your generous spirit. You see, Adelaide, the object of my affection, was our stable master's daughter. To say my parents were opposed to the union is to put it mildly. But after a time, the subject was, you could say, forced rather unexpectedly."

Jeanne held her breath praying the words she anticipated would not materialize.

He continued: "Adelaide, as fate would have it, carried our child. Given the strength of my conviction, and her condition, we were at last given blessings to marry." A wife and child. She willed herself to ignore the sting of new tears and encouraged him to go on.

"After we married, I joined the king's army and became acquainted with your father. It is there I received my medical training."

She said quietly, "I see. Where are they now, monsieur? Your family?"

He bowed his head. "They are in Heaven. I was

away when the child came. The baby, a girl, entered this world without mishap, but Adelaide died shortly thereafter, and the girl followed her mother within the space of a few days. Both were gone by the time I returned home." His voice broke and he struggled to regain composure. "We never named her. We were waiting, you see. Sometimes it's as if she never existed."

"How long ago did they pass?"

"It's been four years. I would have followed them out of this world myself. When I rejoined the regiment after burying my girls, I took greater and greater risks, rushing headlong into the most dangerous of battlefields. Your father marked my recklessness. One day he took me aside and told me sacrificing myself wouldn't bring my family back and would do even less for my fellow soldiers. His words had an effect on me. I began to comport myself more cautiously. To this day, I can only speculate how he discerned my motives."

Jeanne wiped her eyes. "He understood. His own wife, my mother, was taken too soon. As was a brother who came before me and died at birth."

"You were all he had."

"And he was all I had," Jeanne said and thought of her aunt and Francoise. Her father had loved them too and had entrusted Aunt Mimi with Jeanne's upbringing. "Sometimes I wish I could join him. There's so much I want to tell him." She let herself cry without attempting to hide her tears, knowing he would not think the worse of her for it.

He gathered her into his arms again and presently asked, "Mademoiselle, can you now tell me how it is you ended here on this ship?"

"I want to, I really do, but it's simply too dangerous," she said. In truth, she feared her narrative would repulse him.

"Dear Mademoiselle Denot. Jeanne." He took one of her hands and held it up to his chest. "When I consider what your father told me that day so many years ago, I think he must have known our paths would cross. But that's not possible, is it?"

"I no longer consider myself a judge of the possible, monsieur. So many strange and impossible things have come to pass. Things I could not have foreseen in my most terrible nightmares." Standing so close to him, feeling the beat of his heart beneath her hand she added, "Or in my most wonderous dreams."

He bowed his head and softly touched her hand with his lips. "I have now called you by your given name, daring to believe our connection strong enough to justify the intimacy. Could I ask you to do the same?"

She hesitated the way one pauses at the threshold of a forbidden room.

"Jacques."

As soon as she uttered his name, she found herself wanting to repeat it again and again.

****

As sunset turned to sunrise, three more girls from the lower deck were taken ill and one of the demoiselles was in the throes of fever. The crew was no longer outside the reach of disease. Two sailors were stricken during the night. The ship's dreadful visitor carried Madeleine further and further away. She remained insensible, occasionally mumbling unintelligibly or crying out.

Jeanne tried to speak to Madeleine, to throw her a lifeline connecting her to the living. She recounted the first time Madeleine rescued her outside the gates of La Salpêtrière.

"You were so fierce that night. I had never met so powerful a person before. So strong. You must continue to be strong, my dearest Madeleine. I need you to be my champion when we reach New France." Jeanne thought she saw the shadow of a smile on Madeleine's parched lips but couldn't be sure. "What can I do for you? Anything. Tell me."

Madeleine's eyelids fluttered as if in response, then she spoke a single word: "Laurent."

"Shall I fetch Laurent? Would you like to see him?"

Madeleine answered her question with the slightest of nods.

Jeanne felt a keen stab of guilt at her friend's request. All these weeks she had dismissed Laurent as Madeleine's plaything. Madeleine herself had proclaimed love was for ninnies. Yet Jeanne should have seen past her friend's usual bravado to the truth.

The churlish sea made it difficult to climb the steep companionway to the top deck. Jeanne made her way from bow to stern, fighting to maintain her balance against the roll of the ship. Finally, she located the sailor and urged him to follow her to the lower deck.

As they passed the middle deck where the demoiselles had gathered for their morning repast, Madame La Plante called out to her, "Mademoiselle Davide. What is the meaning of this?"

Madame stepped out into the passageway, blocking their progress down the stairs.

Jeanne made a quick calculation: Whatever lie Jeanne could formulate would be as unsatisfactory to Madame as the truth, so she spoke the latter. "I am taking this man to see my friend. She has asked to see him and—"

Madame shook her head before Jeanne finished speaking. "Outrageous! Crew members are forbidden to enter the sleeping quarters of the female passengers unless to deliver urgent information."

"Madame, she is gravely ill and has been incoherent. When she gained a moment of lucidity, she called for him. Surely you understand why we must respond to her request."

"I see no such logic." Madame looked at Laurent with the same disdain one has inspecting muck on the bottom of one's shoes. "Young man, why do you suppose she has requested you of all the shipmates on the *Saint Anne*?"

Laurent stuttered a bit before answering. "We are in love, Madame."

Laurent stood a head taller than Madame La Plante, yet as she interrogated him, she seemed to grow and he to shrink. "How could this so-called love come to pass while fraternizing is expressly forbidden?"

"I do not wish to answer, for doing so could harm the reputation of the lady," he said nervously.

"Her reputation, indeed! Your lack of an answer is answer enough. Now return to the upper deck, rascal, or I shall report you to the captain!"

Jeanne thought of poor Madeleine locked in the embrace of an illness instead of in the arms of her one true love. She recalled the time Laurent presented Madeleine with an exquisite rose he'd carved from a block of wood. How could she have doubted that the man was besotted with her friend, and likewise Madeleine with him?

"Do so," Jeanne moved pass her, "but for now you will give way and let us through!"

Madame called after them, "If you're not careful, mademoiselle, you will find yourself out of my favor and the king's favor. Thin ice, Mademoiselle Davide! Thin ice!"

When they reached Madeleine's side, she was again insensible, occasionally muttering or crying out in pain.

Laurent knelt beside her, gently stroking her face. "Poor, poor rose." He began to cry so extravagantly, Jeanne urged him to quiet or risk upsetting the other girls.

"But what shall we do to make her better, mademoiselle?" he asked pitifully.

Jeanne knelt beside him, handing him a cloth to wipe Madeleine's brow. "We are doing all we can. She is in God's hands now."

"Will my lovely rose die?"

At the mention of death, a fear gripped Jeanne, but she pushed it aside, answering resolutely, "Madeleine is young and strong. Monsieur Suprenant says the pox runs its course within five days. Madeleine has been ill for four. She will be better. I will see to it."

Laurent hung his head. "I'm most grateful for everything you've done. And for seeking me out."

"I did it for her," Jeanne said, her voice breaking. "I'd do anything for her."

After Laurent took leave of Madeleine, Jeanne made her rounds among the wretched occupants of the lower deck, pondering yet again how the chasm of the future gaped before her with no definition, no milestones by which to navigate passage. She prayed wherever it took her, she would land safely.

Chapter Fifteen

"I know nothing in the world so noble and so beautiful as the holy fervor of genuine piety. So, there is nothing, I think, so odious as the whitewashed outside of a specious zeal; as those downright imposters, those bigots whose sacrilegious and deceitful grimaces impose on others with impunity."

~*Tartuffe, Molière*

Paris

Jeanne had never been on a boat. She decided within the first few minutes of their journey down the Seine she would never again step foot on one. She had fancied that travelling by water would be like floating on air, the boat skimming the surface without the bumping and jolting of a carriage journey. In reality, the Seine seemed to hold as many impediments as the road, and the small barge jostled and heaved over the watery thoroughfare now engorged by rain.

Through the dim lighting of the passenger compartment, Jeanne marked the anxiety on her aunt's features. "Is it not dangerous to travel this way?" Aunt Mimi asked the priest. Although the rain had ceased, the wind continued to howl, causing her to raise her voice to be heard. "Should we not instruct the crew to dock and wait out the weather?"

Father Dieudonné said, "At times the river is so thirsty for water, passage on the Seine is slower than passage on the roads. But now it is swift. God, in His providence has sent us this deluge." Although the priest smiled, Jeanne detected an anxiety beneath his reassuring exterior. He took out his gold pocket watch and tapped the crystal face. "I dare say, thanks to these turgid conditions, the journey will be halved. We should reach our destination within the passing of an hour."

Jeanne tried to listen as the priest and her aunt made small talk, but she became increasingly aware of a turbulence in her stomach which matched the turbulence of the boat. She swallowed hard to combat the sensation of her insides riding up to her throat. At last she stood, fighting to maintain her balance.

"I think I'm going to be sick," she gasped.

"Heaven help us," her aunt shouted above the din. "Father, can you accompany Jeanne outside?"

Jeanne followed as Father Dieudonné climbed the short ladder leading to the back of the boat. As soon as the priest cracked open the hatch, it blew back from the force of the wind. He shouted to make himself heard above the storm. "Follow me."

Outside, Jeanne could see no sign of the two men who guided the craft. She staggered, then fell in the few steps it took to reach the boat's side rail. The priest helped her to stand. She clutched the rail, and the priest placed his hands on the back of her head as she began to retch. Her body hung precipitously over the churning water of the Seine as her stomach raged like the swollen river, offering a seemingly endless amount of bile. At last the heaving ceased and Jeanne made to rise, but the priest still maintained his hold on her and, in her weakened state, she found she could not escape his grasp.

"It has passed. Release me," she yelled above the wind.

But the priest only tightened his hold. "This river is holy, my dear girl. It's the burial ground of another Jeanne, Saint Jeanne of Arc, who was instructed by our Lord to mount a holy war, leading France to victory."

Jeanne waited for him to come to the point of his impromptu sermon. "For all the good she did, they burned her and threw her ashes into the Seine. It is easy, you see, to be misunderstood. To be judged and then disregarded." His hands dropped to his sides and Jeanne stood, wheeling around to face him.

"Spare me your sanctimony, monsieur! You claim to be a man of God, yet I saw with my own eyes your idea of holy communing with my aunt in the woods. Or will you tell me it's a special form of prayer with your head under her skirts?"

At her words, the priest's features were transformed by fear, then rage. "It is not your place to judge," he cried out, holding a fist up to the blustery sky. "Only God himself can pass judgment on our earthly comportment."

Jeanne made to push past him, but the priest gripped her shoulders.

"Unhand me!" Jeanne screamed to alert her aunt or the crew, but the raging wind vanquished her cries.

The priest released his hold for a moment, then grabbed her again and shoved her backward. At first her back met the resistance of the railing behind her, but he pushed her again, and Jeanne fell overboard, her body sinking like a stone into the depths of the water. It took a few moments to grasp her predicament. She had cried out as she fell, so held little air in her lungs. She kicked furiously to propel herself upward, but her legs, tangled in her skirts, were trapped. By holding her arms above her head and pushing down with all her might, she at last began to ascend until she finally broke the surface of the ice-cold water. In the short time she had been submerged, the barge had travelled a remarkable distance down the river. She thought she heard her aunt call her name and she tried to respond, but instead found herself plunged yet again under the surface, deeper this time.

The current propelled her. Her copious outer skirt billowed over her head and her underskirt again wrapped around her legs, making it impossible to kick against the water. She floated like some mythical sea creature, carried along until she managed to propel herself yet again to the surface. She tried to call out to the boat which was by now no more than a speck in the distance but couldn't summon enough breathe. Then she remembered what Papa had told her after her fall in the river at Mursay. By lying on one's back and filling the lungs with air, the body becomes buoyant, like a dumpling in soup.

Marshaling her fear, Jeanne drew a mighty breath and lay prostrate, managing to remain afloat until the current carried her to the edge of the Seine where she was able at last to drag herself out of the water. Although it was June, soaked to the bone as she was, it could have been a January night.

I must move, find shelter, keep my blood from freezing. She began to climb a steep embankment but slipped and fell, nearly tumbling back into the river. She made her way upward more carefully this time, digging her hands into the muddy slope. When she reached the top, she looked around to gain her bearings. She needed to follow the flow of the current. Eventually it would lead her to the palace and to her aunt who would surely be searching frantically for her, undoubtedly fearing the worst.

Her progress along the riverbank proved tortuously slow. No star or moonlight guided her, and she stumbled and fell as she made her way. After what seemed an eternity of this inching progress, Jeanne rested under the ledge of a boulder, hugging herself for warmth. She clenched her jaw to stop her teeth from chattering and imagined Francoise at home, cozy and comfortable and plagued only by the occasional itch. Jeanne wished more than anything she could be by her side, laughing, reading, even sewing. *I would give anything to be embroidering right now,* she thought. She grew warmer. In her mind's eye she recalled the look on the priest's face as he pushed her into the water, and she began to shake anew.

A plaintive howl sounded in the distance and Jeanne recalled the stories of wolves that attacked travelers, tearing them from limb to limb. Wearily, she climbed to the top of the boulder and out of harm's way. If she could only survive this dreadful night, she would find the palace and her aunt by sundown tomorrow. She prayed, making promises to God to be a better, kinder person should she be delivered from her predicament. Presently, exhaustion trumped fear and Jeanne slept.

When she awoke, the sky was lit with the first pink

hues of dawn. She sat up and stretched, stiff from her stony bed. A chill had burrowed deep within her bones, and she shivered as she looked for signs of civilization, only to find woods on one side of the rock and the turbid river on the other. Her complete desolation inspired great gulping sobs which, after some time, turned into a mournful wail over the vagaries of life: that she never knew her mother, her father was gone, and the woman she counted as a replacement for both loved the man who had tried to kill her. She touched the nape of her neck gingerly, still sore from the grip of the priest's hands. Her aunt would hear about this, and Father Dieudonné would be made to suffer. Jeanne would see to it.

The Seine's waters, still swollen from yesterday's storm, roared beside her. Because of the din, it took her some time to notice the man who stood at the base of her high encampment throwing pebbles at her from below.

"Girl! You there! What is your business on my roof?"

Jeanne peered over the side of the rock to find the source of the voice: an odd-looking man, old, perhaps fifty years in age, wearing what looked to be a monk's robe and sandals. His hair resembled a bird's nest and even had twigs and leaves residing within it, not unlike a woodland creature or a character in the fables she and Francoise read as children.

He called to her again: "Come down and tell me what force of nature blew you to the top of my abode."

Jeanne began her descent and the old man hunched over and offered for her to step on his back to ease her landing.

She hesitated. "It is a kind gesture, monsieur, but I cannot. It will cause injury."

He braced his hands on his knees. "I'm stronger than I look and you're just a wisp of a thing. Climb aboard."

She did as he instructed, and back on solid ground, she thanked him. The man bowed, "Michel du Petit Thouars, mademoiselle. Pleasure making your acquaintance."

"Jeanne Denot," she curtsied, a strangely formal exchange given the circumstances.

"Mademoiselle, may I invite you for a morning repast where you can share with me the narrative of how you came to find yourself on my roof?"

Jeanne stood back and examined the boulder which she half expected to have transmogrified into a cottage. "This is a very peculiar sort of house, monsieur."

The hermit laughed and gestured toward the rock. "Yes, indeed, but I still call it home. It's the greatest castle a man could have, with no need for servants or the trappings of our modern times."

They arranged themselves in a spot Monsieur Du Petit Thoaurs indicated was his dining room, but was, in actual fact, a crevice under the stone where the gnome-like man lived.

As Monsieur Du Petit Thoaurs sparked a fire and prepared a meal on it, Jeanne related the turn of events that brought her to his stony home. He eagerly absorbed her story, shaking his head now and again or clucking sympathetically.

"Now you must find your auntie and tell her of the evil deeds of the sinister minister," the hermit said.

Jeanne nodded and helped herself to more of the

pan-fried fish her host had expertly prepared. She tried to show some delicacy while consuming it but could not contain herself and gulped her food like a dog.

Presently she said, "I must make my way to the Palais Louvre and ease my aunt's mind that I did not perish on the boat. I'm sure Father Dieudonné concocted some story of me falling overboard." The hermit nodded vigorously, sending bits of food flying off his beard.

"How close am I to Paris, monsieur?" Jeanne had yet to see a single house and although she had never been there, she understood Paris to be stuffed with grand houses and grand people to occupy them. Here there were only woods and this odd little man with his feral exterior and courtly manners.

"Not far." He picked his teeth with a fishbone. "A day's walk following the bend of the river. Is it wise, however, to leave?"

"Why yes! I must find my aunt."

He rubbed his chin in a contemplative fashion. "There is one major flaw in your plan, mademoiselle. I feel I must point it out."

Jeanne sucked her fingers so as not to miss the last morsels of food stuck to them. She looked around to ensure no other soul could see her appalling manners, but her only witness was the hermit, and he did the same.

"If you have lived in the wilds as long as I have," he continued, "you know the golden rule of rescue: 'Never leave the place you were last witnessed to be.'"

"But that was in the river. I had no choice but to leave it."

"Consider this. When your beloved auntie comes

searching for you, where do you think the effort will begin?"

Jeanne recalled how swiftly the swollen water had carried the barge and the distance it had gained after she surfaced. "It would be a struggle to fight the current. Perhaps it's wisest to return by land and launch a boat upriver, retracing the journey."

"Precisely! You are a very clever girl. I understand how you've survived so harsh an ordeal so well. What does this tell you of your plans to leave this place and journey on to Paris? A city of countless souls, not all of them righteous ones, to which I can attest having lived there myself."

"I must stay here, by the river, and flag the passing rescue boat!" The thought cheered her considerably.

The hermit nodded. Soon her aunt would find her, and this terrible misfortune would be in her past. She stood, restored by the breakfast and the heat of dawn, and bounded down the riverbank to await her rescue.

After a while, the hermit joined her. The carcasses of two jackrabbits were slung over his back. "Have you caught sight of any boats yet, mademoiselle?"

"Yes. I have even shouted and waved, but it appears they're on other errands."

"Do not lose hope. The day is young. As soon as I joint these carcasses, we'll have a feast of rabbit stew!" He turned to show her his score then added, "If you do not meet your rescuers first, of course."

As the hours passed, and with the sun directly overhead, Monsieur Du Petit Thoaurs returned to the river's edge and beckoned her to eat. Jeanne eagerly accepted his invitation but insisted they dine within sight of the river. He fetched his pan as Jeanne continued to pace the water's edge looking for signs of rescue.

When he returned, they sat down and the hermit said, "Pardon me, mademoiselle. I have no spoons for the stew. You must think me a dreadful host."

"Not at all, monsieur. I am indebted to your kindness." Jeanne followed the hermit's example, picking out chunks of the moist rabbit meat from the top of the stew where they were coolest, then blowing on the morsels before popping them in her mouth. The two of them made short work of finishing the meal. Jeanne tried to lighten her spirits by imaging what she would tell Francoise of this al fresco experience with her hermit friend.

The hermit let out a mighty belch. "Was the stew to your liking?"

"It was delicious, monsieur. I wonder how one can manage such a flavorful dish in the wild? This could have come from the kitchen of Mursay, my home."

Monsieur Du Petit Thouars bowed his head modestly. "Baked goods are a challenge, mademoiselle. I will not lie. We do not enjoy bread or buns or cakes of any kind."

"'We' monsieur? Are there more in your company? I have seen only you."

Monsieur laughed. "No, no, no. It is only me. Sometimes I say 'we' to give myself the feeling of association. I have lived alone in these woods for many beards."

"Many years, monsieur?"

"Many beards. It is how I mark time. I grow them to where they cover my most private parts, and in spring I shear myself like a sheep." He ran a hand over the growth on his face. "I use the hair for pillow stuffing."

With that he grabbed the pan and began licking it nonchalantly and Jeanne, for the first time since their short acquaintance, began to feel uneasy by the frankness of his language.

"Monsieur, if I can be so forward as to inquire, why do you live outdoors? Have you no family?"

"Why of course I do. No one springs fully formed from the ground. I'm not a turnip, after all!" He chuckled at his joke then sighed. "I was born and raised a half day's walk from here in a fine chateau to a fine family. A place stuffed with breeches, and bedpans, tapestries, and tobacco and all the spoils of the rich. Everything covered with silk and silver and gold. What do you think lay beneath all that finery?" He scowled, the remembrance of his people transforming his expression from mild to fierce.

Jeanne responded evenly so as not to further pique his emotions. "I cannot venture to guess, monsieur."

"Putrefied flesh, wicked notions, veiled motives, willful ignorance, and artful deception. So many lies tripping off so many silken tongues."

A shiver made its way up her spine and Jeanne prayed the hermit would reveal no more. Yet he continued, "Out here, in communion with nature like Saint Francis, I found my freedom." He seemed particularly pleased with his phraseology and repeated it. "Yes. I found my freedom."

He resumed the business of licking his pan. A queasiness arose from the pit of her stomach, born in small part by the sight of the hermit's eager tongue foraging for every particle of food, and in greater part by the unsettling thought the man was mad. She must break free of his company but had to do so in a manner that would not fan the flames of his addled mind.

"If only I myself could say the same. Here I am in the open air, and I may as well be in prison." Struck by a profound sense of desolation, Jeanne began to cry. What had Father Dieudonné said last night? Paris was a few hours distance as the crow flies. "If only I could sprout wings."

"You need no wings to escape the bounds of society. Throw off the shackles of conventionality and decide your own fate." Monsieur Du Petit Thoaurs gesticulated vigorously as he spoke, acting out the binding, then freeing of his hands from imaginary restraints. "Can you not see it? The horizon has not closed, but rather broken wide open, dear Jeanne!" The hermit's enthusiasm only served as a weight to her spirits.

"I can no longer hope for rescue. I must make my way to Paris and to my aunt as soon as possible. Monsieur, can you be good enough to show me the way?"

"Of course. I'll even take you there myself." He extended a hand and helped her to rise.

"You are too kind, but that won't be necessary."

He took a step back and searched her face, for what, she could not fathom. Then he muttered to himself, "This one has not been sufficiently schooled in the lessons of artifice." Addressing Jeanne, he said, "I have rung an alarm within you and now you find me abhorrent. It is clear from your gaze which you avert even now."

Jeanne began to protest, but the little man cut her

off. "I take no offense, mademoiselle, and hardly blame you. I am exceedingly peculiar, I suppose. Follow me. I will set you on your path."

The hermit accompanied her a short distance down the river and as they walked, Jeanne kept her sights on the water, still hoping for rescue to materialize.

Presently, the hermit stopped. "Continue this way," he pointed, "and you will reach Paris by nightfall."

"How, monsieur, will I know where the palace is?"

"Do you question where your heart lies within your body? It is the center. The drumbeat setting the measure for all other motion, thought, word. You will find it without problem. Remember: Always keep the river to your right."

She bid the hermit adieu, thanking him for his care and guidance, and as she turned to walk away, he grabbed hold of her hand.

"I am no longer adept with all things silken and gold. My uncouth persona may have caused you unease, but I would never harm you. I am a lamb in wolf's clothing, mademoiselle. Beware, Jeanne Denot. More often the reverse is true."

Chapter Sixteen

"The utmost care was exercised in the selection of colonists for New France. When girls were sent over to be married, their conduct was rigidly examined, their stories and their circumstances were well known."

~Jean-Baptiste Colbert, Minister of State

The *Saint Anne*

Of the eighteen mademoiselles onboard, Jeanne shared her suppertime with half that number. The others lay in the quarters below in various stages of contagion and misery. Their nightly repast consisted of a thin sauce poured over an oatcake. Between the lackluster food and her own exhaustion, Jeanne barely possessed the wherewithal to lift her hand to her mouth but forced herself to do so. Jacques had insisted she go to the galley, reminding her she would do no one any good if she failed to tend to her own sustenance.

As she ate, she fretted as to why Madeleine's illness had yet to turn. One of the girls who fell ill shortly after her now showed signs of improvement. Yet Madeleine remained insensible, her body wracked with fever.

As she pondered Madeleine's condition, her dinner companions complained about the victuals. One girl said, "The closer we get to New France, the more we get oatcakes. I would give anything to bite into a juicy flank of meat."

"There's one goat left in the pens topside," said another girl. "It looks old, but I'll take tough meat over this slop any day. I'd eat a rat if it was cooked through."

Her companion howled in laughter and Jeanne nearly chided them for making merry while the rest of their company suffered, but the girls stopped cold on their own. It was then Jeanne became aware of a presence behind her: Madame La Plante in the company of the demoiselles.

Madame clutched her black book to her breast and wore a look of righteous indignation. "What a dreadful lack of humanity on display. Cavorting at the dinner table! Particularly unconscionable given the suffering around us. For shame, girls! For shame!"

Madame was right, of course, but the validity of her outrage made Jeanne's dislike the old crone even more.

"We shall return to our quarters. Let us depart, girls," Jeanne said quietly, standing to leave.

"Spare me your airs, Mademoiselle Davide."

"Pardon me, Madame?" Jeanne said.

"You fancy yourself the leader of this group. It is I who decide on this ship." She pounded her fist against the leather cover of her book. "Me! Not you or your ruffian companion, Mademoiselle Tooth."

Madame's mangling of Teeth's name caused a few of the mademoiselles to titter, further exciting the lady's captious nature. She wagged a finger at them and spluttered, "You girls!" Her face turned a variety of colors before settling on a vivid shade of purple. "None of you are worthy of the king's honor. You are trash!

Vermin! Nothing but worthless—"

Her tirade ended abruptly as, without warning, the old woman collapsed. The demoiselles screamed and clutched at each other. Jeanne rushed to her side. Madame La Plante convulsed, her back arching upward, bucking against some invisible force.

"Fetch Monsieur Suprenant at once. He is in the lower quarters," Jeanne ordered the demoiselles.

"We are forbidden to go there. Madame has said so expressly."

Jeanne raised her fist. "Get him and make haste, you dolts! Or I will beat you black and blue."

Madame's fit had transformed her face into a grotesque mask: her eyes, open yet fixed, stared vacantly while her jaw spasmed, opening and shutting so violently, Jeanne could hear her teeth gnash. After a few moments the palsy grew more subdued, yet Madame's body twitched like a fish hauled to dry land still attempting to swim.

At a loss for anything useful to do, Jeanne simply held the woman's hand and spoke to her in a low voice, assuring her help had been summoned.

Presently the old woman asked, "Why have you put me on the floor?"

"It was not I who put you here, Madame. You suffered a fit and fell to the floor."

She whispered a response, more confirmation than question: "I have."

Presently, she tried to stand and transport herself, but ultimately Madame had to be carried to her accommodations by Jacques. Jeanne followed him to the demoiselles' quarters, a cabin with the luxury of beds instead of hammocks. As Jeanne prepared to leave, Madame La Plante said weakly, "Mademoiselle Davide, won't you stay here a moment?"

Jeanne paused at the doorway. "I must return to the girls below."

"Please, Jeanne," the old woman said.

Jeanne registered the surprise written on Jacques' face. Madame had addressed her by her first name.

"Teeth is below with the girls," Jeanne said. "Perhaps I can spare a moment." She drew closer to the old woman's bed.

Madame La Plante beckoned for Jeanne to sit beside her, and when Jeanne did, Madame whispered, "I am so frightened. Could you do me the service of once again holding my hand as Monsieur Suprenant conducts his examination?"

She answered levelly, "Of course, Madame."

As Jacques touched her forehead, felt her wrist for her heart's rhythm and looked for signs of pox, Madame's gaze remained fixed on Jeanne.

"Madame," he said, "you are burning with fever. Did you fail to mark it?"

"Heat and cold run through my veins in a most mercurial manner," Madame replied weakly.

"You are gravely ill with the pox. The fit you experienced was prompted by burning heat which excites the body's temperament."

His talk of things corporal mortified the old woman, and she covered her eyes with her hands, as if by doing so she could make him disappear. After a moment, her gaze sought his and she asked, "Am I to meet my Maker?"

"You are firmly in the realm of the living. Rest and let the heat burn its course."

****

With Madame confined to her bed, Jeanne and Jacques could meet more freely without fear of reprisal. They were topside on the quarterdeck watching the setting sun. Now, in the late days of September, it vanished earlier and earlier as the *Saint Anne* drew closer to New France.

Jeanne stood so close to him that if she'd tilted her head to the side, it would have rested against his shoulder. Standing here, she felt perfectly safe, Jacques' body serving as a barrier from the wind and chill and everything else wrong with the world.

If only we could stay on this ship forever. Jeanne smiled at the queerness of the thought. To wish to stay on this cramped, fetid vessel stuffed full of every known human misery. Jeanne amended the thought. *If only I could stay with him forever.*

"There is something on your mind, tonight. A moment ago, you seemed on the verge of laughter and now your brow is wrinkled."

Jeanne said, "It is Madame."

"I admire your concern," he said. He seemed inclined to always interpret her behavior in the best of lights. "Although I wish her no harm, my own thoughts are not overly occupied with her recovery."

Jeanne considered not correcting his perception, then said, "It's not that, monsieur."

"Jacques," he reminded her.

"Jacques," she said. "Madame continues to threaten me with all her talk of thin ice. If I am no longer a Daughter of the King, what will become of me? I would be destitute. Lost."

Jacques fell silent for a moment, seeming to weigh

his words. Then he spoke softly. "Not lost. After my wife and child were taken from me, every course charting my future vanished. Yet here I stand next to you. Now it seems fate has forged a new way." He brushed aside a wisp of hair from her forehead. "A way we could travel together."

All elements of cold and wind, any sensation of the noisy labors of the boat, all thoughts of the misery of the journey were diminished by the touch of his hand. Jeanne raised her lips to meet his. At first the kiss was shy, glancing. But after a while it grew bold, consuming them, so that presently the world disappeared entirely.

****

Outside the *Saint Anne*, dawn broke revealing a bright sky which held an unusual warmth for an autumn day. Inside the ship lurked darkness and despair.

One of the demoiselles, Therese, felled by the pox more recently than Madeleine, passed away during the night. Jeanne comforted the demoiselle, not much older than a child, who had discovered the corpse. The young girl was so distraught, Jeanne had to usher her out of the demoiselle's quarters to the open air on the main deck.

"At first I thought her to be asleep." The girl bowed her head and sobbed before continuing. "I recall thinking, 'She must be better now.' She was calm, you see. Last night she was agitated, thrashing around as if the pain were animating her arms and legs. Then she grew so very still." Her narrative inspired a fresh outpouring of tears.

To help the girl marshal her emotions, Jeanne asked her, "What is your name?"

Presently, she managed to answer, "Mademoiselle

Marie Jeanette de Valois. I am known as Nettie."

"My name is Jeanne. Nettie, your friend—" Jeanne failed to remember the poor soul's name although she had just been informed of it.

Nettie said, "Therese."

"Therese is with our Heavenly Father now. Her earthly trials have passed. As for the others, there are three of you in good enough health to attend to your ailing companions and Madame La Plante."

At the mention of Madame, Nettie cried out pitifully, "How are we to manage without her? These past weeks she has directed our every waking moment. It is she who tells us when to pray, to eat, to sleep. She even instructs us as to when to make use of the privy. Why, she is the sun rising and setting on all we do."

Jeanne took hold of the girl's dimpled hands. "It is for that reason you must be strong. Monsieur Suprenant spends his days running between the two quarters but cannot tend to those who suffer alone. You and I will be his best helpers, won't we?"

Nettie nodded miserably.

"Now dry your eyes. Tears are a luxury we can ill afford."

With help from the captain, Jeanne and Nettie removed Therese's lifeless form to his quarters where they washed her, dressing her in her finest garb. All her remaining clothes were burned; her blanket would be used as a shroud for her burial at sea.

Within hours of tending to Therese, two mademoiselles drew their final breaths. Nettie, Teeth, and Jeanne tended to their burials. At sunset a small assembly gathered on deck: The captain, Jacques, Jeanne, Nettie, and Elisabeth who held baby Anne in her arms. Elisabeth had been no use to them when it came to tending to the sick. Although she had offered aid on more than one occasion, Jacques forbade it, urging her to sequester herself as best she could for the sake of her child.

The three girls were arranged side-by-side, the mademoiselles distinguishable from the demoiselle even in death: Jeanne's cabinmates would meet their Maker sewn into the rough burlap of their hammocks while Therese's body was shrouded in fine wool cloth.

As the captain recited a psalm, Jeanne became aware of Laurent standing next to her.

"Why are you not with Madeleine?" she said under her breathe. He had agreed to stay with Teeth, tending to Madeleine and the others during the service.

"She is resting easily now," he whispered. "It is what I came to tell you and Monsieur Suprenant."

She held a finger before her lips to silence him. "We shall speak after the service."

After the captain concluded the makeshift ceremony, the crewmen loaded each girl onto the tipping plank and one-by-one their bodies, so light and insubstantial, disappeared into the vastness of the sea. The oldest of them had been eighteen, the same age as Jeanne. She wondered why God had taken these girls in full bloom of their youth. Would it not have been better to let them live and serve the purpose of their King and country? How could He have so great a need for youthful occupants in Heaven when so many died before their first year of life? Jeanne pictured the girls in a great celestial nursery, tending to the scores of baby angels gathered in Heaven, including her infant brother. The thought comforted and terrified her in equal parts.

The captain spoke and she emerged from her reverie. "There are increasing signs of approaching land." He pointed overhead. Birds. It had been weeks since they had seen any other animal save for those in captivity on deck. "We should reach New France within two weeks' time by my best reckoning. I pray to God that when we arrive it is with all our remaining souls accounted for. It is confounding that only two of my men have fallen ill yet so great a number of our female passengers have been stricken."

Jacques nodded. "It could be that the men are out in the open air and not as vulnerable."

The captain said, "How many remain invalid?"

Upon hearing the captain's question, Laurent stepped forward. "Sir, the tide has turned!"

They regarded the sailor, whose eyes shone brightly in his careworn face. "You stare at me as if I were mad. I swear I speak the truth! I have only just left Madeleine. Her fever has vanished. She's resting ever so peacefully."

****

After hearing Laurent's pronouncement, Jeanne and the others made haste to the lower deck. Madeleine had been tossed on the tempestuous sea of illness for more than a week, the first to fall ill but the last to arrive safely on the shores of recovery. When Jeanne arrived at the mademoiselles' quarters, Teeth blocked the entrance.

"Where are you rushing off to, then?" Teeth grabbed hold of Jeanne's arm, arresting her progress. Their quarters were, as always, murky, and it took a moment for Jeanne to adjust to the darkness. As she did, she noted the strange look on Teeth's face.

"We are here to see Madeleine. Laurent shared the good news." Jeanne glanced at the floor behind Teeth. Madeleine lay there, in perfect repose, her hands folded across her chest.

Upon hearing Jeanne's words, Teeth began to moan, a sound more animal than human. She sank to her knees whispering, "No, no, no!"

"What is the matter with you? Rise. You will frighten Madeleine and the other girls with this display. You're frightening me," Jeanne said.

Her words further ignited Teeth's lamentations and she began to rock back and forth, tearing at her hair as if she meant to pull it out a fistful at a time.

Jacques moved with alacrity around Teeth to attend to Madeleine, pressing his fingers to the girl's wrist. Jeanne knelt beside him as he lay his head on Madeleine's chest then lifted the lids of her eyes, his face taking on an increasingly pained expression.

Her father often said knowledge lit the dank caves of ignorance, flooding the mind with the enlightenment of truth. Yet the understanding that took hold within Jeanne bloomed darkly, blackening out all hope, enveloping all happiness in a mantle of gloom.

Jeanne spoke the words slowly, softly, terrified of the answer she already knew in her heart. "Is she gone?"

Jacques touched Jeanne's cheek. "I am so sorry."

Chapter Seventeen

"All latrines in the city must be emptied by the municipal scavengers before six in summer and before seven in winter.' The edict was reluctantly obeyed for a few days, then tacitly ignored, and household filth was still being disposed of by being flung out of the windows."

~The Splendid Century, W.H. Lewis

Paris

A path ran next to the river, hewn, Jeanne suspected, by travelers such as herself, following the Seine to Paris. Keeping the river to her right, as the hermit advised, Jeanne walked for a good stretch of time. Gradually, the landscape changed. The forest thinned. In the place of trees stood the products of their making: sheds, shacks, barns, cottages.

After a while, she encountered a gathering of boys not much younger than herself huddled at the edge of the river laughing and cheering, at what amusement, Jeanne could not fathom. As she drew closer, she saw the boys had in their possession a litter of kittens. One lad, the biggest of the group, with mangey red hair, dangled a kitten by its paws over the water and shouted, "Let's see if this one sails as far as the last!"

Standing this close, she could hear their chanting:

"Throw it in! Throw it in! Throw it in!"

A note of alarm sounded within her. This had to stop. Without hesitation, Jeanne called out, "For shame, boys! What are you doing to these defenseless creatures?"

Her words had an instant effect on the group, causing them to fall dumbfounded, which gave Jeanne confidence to carry on her lecture with more vigor.

"These are God's creatures." The boys regarded her slack jawed as she clambered down a small hill and to the riverbank in righteous fury. "They live and breathe and are not meant to be treated as playthings." She made to take the mewling creature from the big lad's hands, but as she did, he dropped the animal and grabbed her wrists in the same hold he'd used with the kitten a moment before. His action excited the pack of boys. They began to shout their approval to their leader: "You got her good, Red." "Hold her tight!" "Let's throw her in next. See how far she sails!"

She screamed wildly, a feral howling that came from the depths of her being, a protest to the twisting of her flesh under the ruffian's hands and to a fear so complete, it invaded every part of her being. They meant to kill her for sport, and she was no better equipped than a kitten to stop them. She kicked the boy, but her legs tangled in her skirts and the sight of her struggles only amused the gang.

One boy at the edge of the mob began to chant, "Throw it in," and the rest of them joined in. "Throw it in! Throw it in!"

Jeanne dropped to her knees so that the heaviness of her body would cause the boy to lose his grip, but to no avail. On the contrary, it made her easier to handle for now he more handily dragged her to the water's edge.

She redoubled her effort to escape, twisting and turning and screaming so violently she became unaware of any other sound save for her own wailing agony.

Then she heard a voice powerful enough to override her own. "What are you pack of bastards up to now?"

A moment later, the young brute released her so suddenly she nearly tumbled into the Seine. A man stood on the hill above the riverbank, appearing from her perspective as formidable as a benevolent wizard in a fairytale. His words certainly held magic, for the boys scrambled up the hill then vanished.

Jeanne stood, more grateful than she had ever been for the simple luxury of moving on her own volition. She examined the flesh of her wrists, which had been rubbed raw by the great oaf's manacle-like grip.

"Monsieur, thank you for coming to my aid. I am most indebted to your kindness."

The man said nothing in response, and only stood at his vantage examining her in a brazen manner, occasionally tipping his head from one side then to another so that Jeanne began to feel like goods for sale at a market.

His gaze made her acutely aware of her own dishevelment. Her dress, once the loveliest shade of green, was now mud brown, the selfsame mud that lined the Seine. Her hair hung about her face with only a few ineffectual pins buried deep within her locks.

Presently he said, "Follow me."

The man had been her savior, but still, Jeanne did not appreciate his tone or his lack of manners. She made to disobey his order then remembered the gang of blackguards and thought better of it. Jeanne followed him to a lane, keeping a distance of a few paces, something that required an effort, for the man walked with a limp and moved slowly.

Presently Jeanne said, "Monsieur, this is where we shall part company. I am most grateful for your help. However, I must continue to follow the river and make my way to Paris." As she spoke, her savior turned to regard her again in his queer appraising manner, and when she said, "I am expected at the Palais Louvre," he smiled or rather grimaced, then performed an exaggerated bow.

"My lady. Pardon me, what is your name? Princess Dirt Face? Lady Drowned Rat?" He continued to limp along, any vestige of good humor come and gone in the blink of an eye. "Shut your trap and follow me if you know what's good for you," he grunted.

It occurred to Jeanne: happiness, satisfaction and other pleasant emotions manifested corporally in a predictable fashion, while the physical consequences of fear were inconstant, in one instant, animating arms and legs and kindling the spark of survival. In other moments such as this, fear filled Jeanne's limbs with clay, and even as her mind ordered her legs to run, they remained maddeningly immobile.

When the man noticed she'd stopped, he cursed under his breath then backtracked, grabbing her roughly by the arm and propelling her forward. At his touch, Jeanne's body caught up to the plan her brain had hatched. She twisted out of his grip, elevated her skirts to a most unacceptable height, and ran as fast as she had ever run in her life.

Instead of following the river where there were fewer signs of civilization, she raced down the dirt lane dotted with people and houses. No one took notice of her as she sped by. Even if someone had called to her by name, she would have continued to flee, putting more distance between herself and the limping man.

She tripped, and her flight halted. Moving at so great a speed, her body continued its trajectory on the cobblestones. She was propelled forward, arms outstretched, like an arrow shot from a bow. She skinned her hands and tasted blood in her mouth. Jeanne stood and looked back but could see no sign of the brutish man. She slowly dusted herself off and continued down the road. On occasion her slovenly appearance drew glances, but no one molested her as she made her way.

In a short time, the village became a town, then the town became a city. On countless occasions her father had regaled her with stories about the wonders of Paris. Six hundred thousand souls inhabited it, an impossibly grand number, one that defied comprehension. Walking through the city, witnessing the frenetic activity of its denizens as they ran to and fro like ants on a hill, she began to grasp the sheer magnitude and potency of the place.

She had imagined Paris as beautiful, an enchanted city filled with gilded castles inhabited by a gentry as polished as silver. The city before her was fashioned of muck, rubble, and waste, and stunk like the depths of a privy. Or perhaps she had yet to reach the golden environs. Another oddity: Paris was a veritable lazarette. Its people suffered from every form of physical malady including limps, like her riverside savior, to missing eyes, limbs, and the most dreadful skin afflictions. Beggars dotted the streets.

A woman propped against a building suckling a newborn babe cried out to Jeanne, "Have pity on us, mademoiselle!"

Jeanne slowed her pace and responded, "I do pity you!"

"Got any coins then?"

"No. I am on my way to the palace. Don't worry, I'll get money from my aunt and make sure it reaches you and your infant."

The woman scowled and pulled the baby away from her teat so abruptly, its mouth made a popping sound. It began to cry wretchedly. "Move along before I set this lump down and deliver you a good beating!"

Jeanne, bewildered by the woman's response, continued down the lane, sympathy for everyone save herself draining with each step. It was now early evening in the longest day of her existence. Only this morning she had awoken atop the hermit's roof. Only yesterday she had worn silk finery. Only the day before she had lived in Mursay where every one of her needs were met, if not anticipated.

Her existence had become a perverse fairytale, one that had transformed her from princess to peasant. Worse than a peasant, for even the lowliest wretch possessed some bodily comfort, whereas Jeanne starved, her last meal with the hermit a distant memory. Her feet were raw from having walked in delicate kidskin boots fashioned to tread daintily on parquet and marble, not mud and cobblestone. Her lips split from lack of water. Although she passed any number of public fountains, she took only a few sips and no more, for on top of her other discomforts, Jeanne urgently needed a privy.

Church bells sounded and Jeanne counted them. Seven. Soon it would be nightfall. The thought made her accelerate her pace. If Parisians were this unsavory in the full light of day, she did not wish to encounter the creatures emerging under the cover of night.

She continued in a near-run until the delicate stitching in one of her boots at last protested, giving way so that the sole hung to the rest of the shoe by a few threads. This last injustice, in addition to her other physical trials, proved to be the straw that broke the camel's back and caused Jeanne to stop entirely. She sat against a building, like any other street urchin, and removed the offending shoe. As she did, the voice of an angel came to her.

"My child, do you require assistance?" The sound, gentle and mellifluous as a lullaby, came from somewhere above her. Jeanne looked up. From an open window, a kindly face peered down. "I have never seen you in this quarter before. Are you lost?"

Jeanne stood. "Dreadfully so!"

"Wait there a moment, I shall come round and collect you." With those words, her angel disappeared only to reappear a moment later at a side gate.

"Come in." She beckoned Jeanne to follow her and for an instant Jeanne hesitated. The day had taught her that evil lurked under many guises. Jeanne searched the neat features of the old woman's face, observed the grace in her movement and speech and the tidiness of her dress. Presently, Jeanne stepped through the wrought iron gates and the woman secured the lock behind her, barring the rest of Paris from entry.

Chapter Eighteen

"When a boatload of girls came to port, the few recalcitrant—and there were very few—were told to choose a wife within a reasonable time or forfeit the right to hunt and fish in the woods."

~Mother Marie of the Ursuline Convent

The *Saint Anne*

Teeth and one of the other mademoiselles sewed Madeleine's body into her hammock. Those able-bodied enough gathered topside to hold yet another service. All save for Laurent, who sought comfort at the bottom of a bottle.

A full moon lit the early evening sky. With Madame La Plante ill, the captain again led the short service. Jeanne had yet to cry since learning of her friend's death. Not for lack of grief. On the contrary. Her sense of loss so filled her brain, her heart, her very being, it rendered her paralyzed when it came to manifesting it. Until, that is, two crewmen lifted Madeleine's shrouded corpse to the tipping plank. Jeanne's wretchedness unleashed itself at last in a great torrent of tears. Crying unabatedly, her head resting against Jacques' shoulder, it took Jeanne a moment to become unaware of a commotion on deck.

"My rose!" It was Laurent, staggering wild-eyed

toward Madeleine's lifeless body. "You mustn't put her in the sea. I won't have it."

Before the other sailors could stop him, he grabbed hold of the shroud and lifted Madeleine's body off the plank, resting her on the ship's deck.

"Gain hold of yourself, man," Jacques said. "Out of respect for the girl, let us not turn her passing into a spectacle."

Laurent, oblivious to Jacques' plea, or to any other protestation, began to untie the binds holding Madeleine within her shroud.

"This is beyond grotesque," the captain said. "You will stop this immediately!" Two sailors advanced on him, and Laurent turned, brandishing a knife.

"Back! Back! You will come no further! I will let no one near my rose."

He had loosened the shroud freeing the upper half of Madeleine's body from its casing. As he tenderly cradled her head, he shouted, "Murderers! Why would you cast her overboard? See for yourselves! She is beautiful and as alive as any of us!"

The captain said, "If you do not surrender the girl's body, and lay down your weapon, you will spend the next week in lockup."

"Why does no one see?" Laurent cried. He stroked Madeleine's hair and rained kisses upon her face.

Jacques took a half step closer. "Your vision is impaired by spirits and grief, monsieur. Please. You are upsetting others who also cared for the lady."

Laurent waved the knife again. "Not a step closer, if you know what's good for you!"

Jacques retreated and Jeanne said, "I will go to him."

"No, Jeanne. He is mad with grief. Who knows what he's capable of?"

"He will not hurt me," Jeanne said. Despite her reassurances, she approached him tentatively. "Laurent," she said softly, "may I see her? I'd like to say my goodbyes."

He nodded but kept his knife at the ready. Jeanne knelt beside him, wiping the tears from her face. "I loved her too. She saved my life on more than one occasion. I know not how I will continue without her."

Laurent lowered the knife. "Nor I, mademoiselle. Nor I!" He wept great gulping sobs, and Jeanne gathered him in her arms.

As she did, Jeanne saw something that made her question her sanity. A nearly imperceptible movement had passed over Madeleine's features. Impossible. Laurent's madness had infected her somehow. Yet, as Jeanne continued to stare, Madeleine's eyelids fluttered, then presently, they opened.

Chapter Nineteen

"The colonists of New France are vigorous men, well-made, nimble, and self-reliant. They are always ready for war, and capable of enduring great fatigue. They are born in a good climate, are sufficiently nourished and accustomed from childhood to physical exercise, hunting, fishing, and canoeing."

~ *François Dollier de Casson, Priest*

The *Saint Anne*

Boundaries separating mademoiselle from demoiselle no longer existed on the *Saint Anne*. The only lines of distinction drawn were ill or not ill. Although, miraculously, Madeleine was alive, she remained in a weakened state and stayed with the rest of the suffering in the more spacious, although dank, mademoiselles' quarters on the bottom deck.

Those in the earliest stages of the grim malady lay furthest back from the entrance in beds fashioned from straw. Those convalescing, like Madeleine, lay closer in. Anyone of sound body slept in the demoiselles' quarters one deck above. Eight and twenty girls began this voyage. Disease had claimed three.

Madame La Plante, at first insensible when Jacques carried her to the quarters below, was now coherent. When she awoke to find herself "alongside the riffraff," she attempted to move. Between the roll of the ship and her weakened state, she resigned to remain among her inferiors, but not without a good deal of complaint.

Madame's thin fingers gripped the edges of a blanket. Her face, so white from illness, glowed in the dim light. "I must be returned to my quarters this moment! It is not fitting for me to lie on the floor." She paused, overtaken for a moment by a spasm of coughing. "It diminishes my station. Undermines my authority."

Jeanne formulated her first response silently. *How is it you can worry about such trivial matters as station in a time such as this? While three of your charges resting forever at the bottom of the ocean?* She fought the urge to shake the vainglorious woman. Jeanne, as she often did with Madame, passed over her first response, formulating a second, milder alternate. "You will be well again soon, Madame. The captain tells me that in a matter of days, we will once again step foot on solid earth."

Jeanne pressed a cool cloth to Madame's forehead. She was the only one who would tend to the old woman. Teeth and the other mademoiselles refused, so great their hatred toward her, while the demoiselles were simply too frightened to do so.

Madame La Plante moaned, then added softly, "Solid earth. Oh, how I look forward to the end of this infernal rocking."

"I will not so much as look at a glass of water after this voyage." Jeanne said, causing Madame to muster a smile.

A fit of coughing once again overcame the old woman. When it calmed, she said, "I shall be forced to endure yet one more trip back to France, and then I shall resign my post. I will be the ancient age of fifty in one short year. Too old for this sort of business."

Jeanne resisted exploring any personal topics with the lady, but her curiosity got the better of her and she asked, "How did you first decide to work in the king's service?"

Madame smiled wryly. "Decide? Decisions are luxuries too rich for my means. I was engaged into service by circumstance. I'm one of eight children, all girls, of a noble home with lucre too thin to plumb the depths of my birth order. My dearest sister, Geneviève, died of consumption when I was but a child. Three of my sisters took the veil. Three were matched with suitable husbands. I became a governess for one of the king's ministers. When my wards outgrew me, I was recommended for this post. When I return to France, I suppose I'll follow my sisters into the convent."

Jeanne said nothing in response. She hoped Madame would continue with her history, which was the lengthiest and most pleasant exchange she had ever held with the woman, but she fell into silence, closing her eyes and sighing as Jeanne applied a cold cloth to her forehead. After a while Jeanne spoke. "Shall I fetch the pan again, Madame? It has been some time since you relieved yourself."

Madame's eyes filled with tears. She nodded ever so slightly in acknowledgment of her corporal needs.

Teeth stopped Jeanne on her return to Madame La Plante. "How can you tend to that old she monkey? I'll tell you right now, she'd never return the favor. With the shoe on the other foot, well, she'd take your shoe and whack you with it."

"Perhaps you're right. Even so, no one is all bad. Not even Madame." As she spoke, the thought occurred to her: there was one person with a truly black heart, someone who at this moment resided in luxury in Mursay, her birthright, having their needs attended to down to the smallest comfort as Jeanne lived in watery squalor.

Jeanne visited Madeleine next. She appeared stronger today. A blush of pink bloomed in her cheeks and the clarity of coherent thought shone through her eyes.

"I'm getting up." Madeleine made to rise from her sickbed. "I can't lie here like a slug for another moment." As soon as she stood, her legs gave way, and Jeanne caught her before she fell.

Jeanne helped her back into the makeshift bed and tucked the covers under her chin. "You're not well enough by a good measure." Jeanne shuddered at the image of Madeleine poised to be thrown overboard, a thought so terrible, she kissed her friend's temperate forehead to banish the sight from her mind's eye. "Good. The fever is gone."

"Laurent told me what happened between you and old lady La Plante. You're a hero, my friend," she said. "But don't go getting yourself tossed out on my account."

"Madame's bark is worse than her bite. Besides, her illness has softened her stance toward me somewhat."

"How can you have such faith in humankind, Jeanne? It's one of your only faults." Madeleine glanced toward the far end of the room where Madame lay. "I myself don't have any worries when it comes to

Madame La Plante. Laurent has asked me to become his wife and I have said yes."

If Jeanne had heard Madeleine's news before almost losing her friend forever, she would have been disconsolate. Now Madeleine's words settled gently in her heart. Tears came to Jeanne's eyes, and she blinked them away.

Madeleine said, "You are unhappy. I've ruined our plans."

"These are tears of joy. Without you, dear friend, I wouldn't have a life to plan. And without Laurent, I wouldn't have you. I'm very happy, indeed."

Madeleine lowered her voice to a whisper, and Jeanne nearly asked her to speak up. "You too have found your love." Madeleine's eyes were trained behind her. Jeanne turned to find Jacques making his rounds.

"Mademoiselle, what a wonder to see roses back in your cheeks!" Jacques said.

"I nearly feel my old self, monsieur. And am completely unworthy of any fussing or tending."

"You are more worthy than anyone I can think of, my darling friend, and you must let us fuss over you," Jeanne said.

"I'd give anything to breathe the fresh air." Madeleine said.

Jacques smiled. "Soon enough. You will be of no use to anyone if you hasten your recovery. In the meanwhile, you must allow Mademoiselle Davide and I to tend to you."

Madeleine sighed. "I'll try to behave meekly, but you know it's not exactly in my nature."

****

Jeanne and Jacques had formed the habit of

meeting on the quarterdeck after evening repast, like two homing birds migrating to the same point as twilight fell. Jacques took a blanket with him on one such evening to ward off the blustery air on deck, and they sat huddled under it, the prow of the ship serving as a barrier to the wind blowing at their backs.

Presently Jeanne's hands and feet began to thaw, and she stopped shivering. She rested her head against Jacques' shoulder, and he kissed it.

"Strange, isn't it?" he said.

He had a habit of thinking aloud. Jeanne waited for him to continue, although she already sensed his unspoken sentiments: strange how the two of them could be seated like this on a ship in the middle of the ocean, thrown together by the Fates, to find such perfect happiness.

"There should be a new word invented just for us," he said. "A word that captures when wonder and joy takes root in the midst of something utterly dreadful."

"Yes. But what would the word be?"

He laughed. "Good question. 'Dreadjoy,' perhaps?"

"Or, 'happible' for happy and horrible?"

He considered her word. "Happible. Yes. It has a ring to it. I am so verily happible at this moment." He pulled her even closer. "There is another word I've come upon since meeting you. One I feared had vanished from my heart's lexicon."

Jeanne's own heart began to race in anticipation of his words. "To utter it unnerves me for it must be reciprocated to blossom. But to keep it locked inside me will kill it and me, I fear. So, say it, I must: I love you, Jeanne Denot."

His lips sought hers and they joined in a manner which by now had become both more practiced and increasingly improvised and urgent. When they broke for a moment, he whispered with a mock formality, "May I inquire, are your feelings in kind, mademoiselle?"

She laughed, copying his stiff tone: "Yes, monsieur. I fear they are."

"Fear?" He pulled a wounded face. "Is loving me a fearful thing?"

"Terribly so," she said in jest only to be struck a moment later by the truth of it. Love was moored inexorably to loss. To dare to love was a blind wager on the vagaries of changing circumstance and sentiment too often leading to the greatest depths of sorrow. "If one never loves, one never knows the pain of its loss. In that way, I am very much afraid."

"You possess the wisdom of a person thrice your age. It is one of many things to be admired about you, my lady." He lifted her hand and kissed it. "Yet I must take issue. Does having feasted worsen the effects of starvation? An empty belly is just as hollow for having been, at one time, satiated. What's more, the memory of a fully laden table may comfort those who dine on dirt."

"Does knowing pleasure magnify one's pain?" she added.

"Exactly my point! If anything, while one suffers, one can envision a state of non-suffering and grab hold of the stays of hope."

They kissed again.

"When I am by your side, I think it impossible I will ever suffer again," Jeanne said.

"Then stay by my side. Do not take a husband in

New France."

"I have been given funds for passage. One must repay a great sum to break the obligation."

He fell silent, the lightness in his voice now gone. "What happens at the marriage market?"

"From my understanding, we gather in a meeting place where we are introduced to the men. Some sort of preference is decided, and the pairings happen under the space of a fortnight."

"Bid on like livestock," he said, his voice edged with bitterness.

"No. We have the rights to refuse as many suitors as we please. After the decision is made, we are given fifty livres for provisions."

"Fifty livres! All your needs cared for!" He gave a hollow laugh.

"Are you angry with me?"

"Forgive me. No. I am angry at the thought of another man having you."

Jacques shivered under the blanket and Jeanne wrapped her arms around him. "The man I want is beside me now."

"Then we will extract you from your obligation," he said.

"But how?"

"Give me time. I will have the means shortly and will come up with a plan. Until then, give me a kiss."

Chapter Twenty

"Truly, the destinies of some are strange in this world."

~Françoise-Athénaïs de Rochechouart de Montespan, Mistress of King Louis XIV

Paris

Jeanne dined on a bowl of broth and a loaf of bread, and as she did, it took every bit of discipline to consume it gracefully, although at times Jeanne slurped from her bowl in a most unseemly fashion. Madame Couret, the kindly old woman, nay, the saint, who had invited her off the street, seemed to take no notice of her lapse in manners, listening intently as Jeanne related the story of being pushed off the boat.

"It is a most remarkable tale, mademoiselle. Most remarkable!" Her small features shone with concern throughout Jeanne's narrative. "Although I myself have never read one, I imagine a narrative such as yours could be found in a novel."

"The rest of my life has been quite unremarkable. It is only these past two days that stand apart."

Madame Couret cleared Jeanne's bowl from the plain oak table in the kitchen of the presbytery where she worked as housekeeper for the parish priest, a man Jeanne had yet to encounter.

"Why don't I prepare a wash basin so you can tidy yourself? I suppose we should have done that first, but when I mentioned food, you seemed so keen, I didn't have the heart to suggest it."

With all the abuse she had experienced over the day, Jeanne had yet to cry. How strange that kindness and a safe harbor would unmoor the emotions inside her, causing her to weep profusely at the woman's words.

"Madame, you are the kindest person I have met thus far in all of Paris!"

Madame Couret patted Jeanne's hand. "There are many kinder than I, many wiser you will find, mademoiselle. Now wash away your tears and the grime of the city and you will find your spirits much improved."

Catching sight of herself in the mirror above the washstand flooded Jeanne with shame. She resembled a wild beast. Her matted hair hung in clumps. Her face and neck were crusted with so much dirt, the water in the washbowl turned as brown as the Seine. Yet cleaning herself caused her spirits to lift just as Madame Couret presaged.

"Madame, do you know the distance to the Palais Louvre? I feel I've been walking an eternity and must be nearly there."

The old woman turned from her tidying. "Why, yes. At a brisk pace you could gain the Pont Neuf in little time. Minutes. Cross it and you will find the palace."

"So close? Oh, I must make haste. My aunt will be beside herself by now!"

At Jeanne's words, Madame Couret's mild features

transformed, taking on a look of alarm. "My dear girl, the nine bells struck some time ago. It is dark outside, and these labyrinthine streets are confusing to navigate. They shelter all manner of undesirables in their darker corners. Stay overnight. Rest and recover yourself and journey forth in the broad light of day."

Jeanne considered her new friend's counsel and contemplated the ruffians at the river and their lame ringmaster. She recalled the brutish beggar and her threats and shuddered at the specter of encountering the crepuscular denizens of Paris who could use the night as a shield to hide their darkest deeds. She had waited this far. What would one more night signify?

****

Sleep came to her at once, mercifully wrapping her weary body and troubled thoughts in a blanket of oblivion. When she awoke the next morning in the small chamber off the kitchen where Madame Couret had so graciously settled her into a straw bed, she became aware of a noise just outside the door. Whispering. She listened. Madame spoke with a man. The kind lady had mentioned the parish priest was away. Perhaps he had returned and out of consideration for her slumber, they spoke now in hushed tones.

Jeanne swung her legs over the side of the bed. Doing so brought a sharp reminder of yesterday's hardships. Her feet were covered in blisters, some of which were now open sores. She wondered how she would manage the remaining journey on foot, and upon arriving, how she would bear dancing at the palace ball.

Before opening the door, she tidied herself as best she could but could not find her broken shoes. Although the prospect mortified her, she decided at last to present herself barefoot. Opening the chamber door to the kitchen, Jeanne found Madame Couret seated at the table in hushed consultation with a man dressed in rough clothing. At the sight of her, their conversation came to an abrupt halt.

Madame Couret said, "Ah! Here she is. This is Mademoiselle Denot. Mademoiselle, this is my brother, Monsieur Couret. He has use of a carriage and can transport you the last bit of the journey."

Monsieur Couret nodded his head and mumbled a greeting, although he did not stand, a faux pas Jeanne overlooked considering the man's generous offer.

"Your largess shall be rewarded, monsieur, when we reach the palace."

Jeanne's mention of the palace and reminder of her own elevated status seemed to overwhelm their modest sensibilities: Madame Couret smiled sadly and shook her head ever so slightly. Neither met her gaze and Monsieur Couret coughed rather theatrically while Madame Couret brushed crumbs off the table. Their modest reaction touched Jeanne. These people were the veritable salt of the earth. Jeanne vowed to reward them handsomely.

****

Monsieur Couret's carriage was nothing more than a chaise drawn by a single horse, and Jeanne had to sit in uncomfortably close proximity to the man. Monsieur's only words were the occasional scold he directed toward his horse. After several failed attempts to engage him in conversation, Jeanne abandoned the effort and regarded the myriad dramas small and large playing out on the streets of Paris as they plodded along. A young girl, with a face painted so brightly it was difficult to tell where nature began and artifice left off, argued with a gentleman old enough to be her father or even her grandfather.

"I don't do nothin' for free, you great louse! Now hand over the money!"

Jeanne pondered the business that could have transacted between such an odd pair and decided the girl must have performed a household service of some sort.

"Perhaps she sharpens knives," Jeanne said aloud, causing Monsieur Couret grunt.

"Huh?"

"The girl we passed exchanging angry words with the gentleman there. It appears he owes her money. I only wondered what sort of service was rendered."

A moment passed before Monsieur Couret let out a mirthless chuckle. "Sharpened his knife good, I'll wager." He laughed again at his joke, occasionally punctuating the silence with, "Knife sharpened is right," causing Jeanne to wonder how the cretinous Monsieur Couret could be cut from the same fine cloth as his gentle sister.

They continued their excruciatingly slow progress as the horse navigated around the capricious streets teeming with obstacles: foot travelers, animals, other carriages, and holes that appeared without warning, causing the current of traffic to circumvent around them like a river around a stone. Jeanne would bolt from the chaise now and run to the palace, sore feet and all, if only she knew the way. How she longed for her aunt to hold her in her arms! She imagined their reunion and the image in her mind's eye inspired tears she hastily wiped away lest the strange Monsieur Couret notice.

Although she resembled a haystack, she would make a heroic impression. By the strength of her wits, she had survived an ordeal that would have broken someone of a less substantial character. Scenes of her triumphant reception flooded her imagination. Why, she would be the talk of the court. Perhaps the king himself would hear tell of her Homeric journey and personally order the evil priest locked up.

Presently the chaise turned down a lane at the end of which stood an imposing structure so massive, Jeanne reckoned it could comfortably house the entire village of Perche and the neighboring village as well.

"Is this the palace?" Jeanne asked.

Her question was greeted by another chortle. "That's right, my lady. King's in there and all. Dying to meet you, he is!"

"Why have we not crossed the bridge? I was informed the palace is situated on the other side of the Pont Neuf."

"You was informed, was you?" Monsieur Couret said, offering no further explanation.

How could such a sweet soul as Madame Couret be consanguine with this taciturn troll? Although he had been kind enough offering her transport, Jeanne decided to substantially decrease his reward to teach him a lesson.

Having arrived at last at her destination, Jeanne felt a curious mix of excitement and dread. She would soon be reunited with her aunt, but such humiliation to plod up to the gates of the palace in a rig fit for a pauper seated next to the thoroughly uncouth Monsieur Couret! And what of Father Dieudonné? There were no witnesses to their tangle on the barge. She was sure he'd deny her version of what had transpired.

As they pulled up to a great arched entrance, Jeanne searched the endless rows of windows stretching along the horizon as far as the eye could see, hoping that, by chance, her aunt would be leaning out one of them, holding vigil for Jeanne's return.

An attendant with a scruffy uniform approached them. He stared for a moment at Jeanne and nodded his head. He addressed Monsieur Couret: "Got another one, eh? You'll clean out the king's treasury at this rate."

At the man's words, Monsieur Couret smiled and for a moment his countenance lost its usual malevolence. "Funny you mentioned the king. This one's come here to meet him."

Monsieur's acquaintance rolled his eyes and grinned, revealing a single tooth on his upper gums. "Is that right? Here to meet his majesty are you, princess?"

"Yes," Jeanne answered. "But I am not a princess. My aunt, however, is the Marquise de Vitré, and I'm most anxious to see her."

Jeanne waited for the toothless attendant to offer his assistance before alighting from the chaise, but he seemed disinclined to do so.

The attendant said, "Ah. But of course. She awaits you eagerly," he said with a gummy grin.

At his words, Jeanne clambered out of the rig herself. "She does? Who announced my arrival?"

"Why you are the talk of the entire palace, mademoiselle." He winked at Monsieur Couret, who laughed.

Jeanne could not tolerate a moment more of these two buffoons. She snapped, "You will take me at once to my aunt."

"Yes, my lady." The attendant bowed obsequiously. "Right this way."

Before following the attendant, Jeanne turned to address Monsieur Couret. "Sir, I know not why you laugh so gleefully. I suppose you are happy to be rid of me. Although I am grateful for your generosity, you have behaved in a most insolent manner. Trust, however, that a reward will be delivered to the presbytery to your sister." She placed particular emphasis on the final word. She had decided not to give this man a sou.

Monsieur Couret nodded toward his unsavory friend. "Hear that? I'll get paid by the king and paid by the princess." He flicked the reigns of his rig and rode off shouting, "I'm rich! I'm rich!" which inspired a fresh spasm of snickering in his friend.

Aunt Mimi had told her thousands of souls inhabited the Palais Louvre, from legions of footmen and ladies-in-waiting all the way up to the Sun King himself. Yet the palace courtyard was desolate. Jeanne supposed the courtiers slept late, an idea she shared with the attendant who only grunted in response, causing Jeanne to vow not to address him again. She would lodge a report to her aunt about his behavior as well. They passed a chapel, one unadorned by gilding of any kind. In fact, although the various buildings were grandiloquent in size, they were lacking in surface embellishment. At last, they arrived at a door after passing through yet another courtyard.

"Here we are," the attendant said. "The queen's apartments."

Jeanne drew back. "No, no! You mustn't take me to the queen! It is my aunt, the marquise, I seek."

"No need for alarm, mademoiselle. I was merely sporting with you. Now follow me nice and easy, okay? No foolery."

"The only foolery I have seen evidence of comes from your direction, monsieur!" Jeanne swept past the man brusquely and found herself in a small antechamber that held a wall of bookshelves, two chairs and a desk. Not a single Turkey carpet, chandelier or tapestry adorned the room.

"What is this place?" Jeanne demanded, but her odious guide had remained outside and firmly shut the door behind her. She called out for her aunt and then wandered around the room, reading the titles of the books, *The Reformation of Mendicants*, *Hysteria in the Feminine Form*, *Anatomy of Melancholia*.

As Jeanne contemplated the owner of this curious array of volumes, a door opened behind her and a voice Jeanne mistook for that of a man commanded, "Keep your hands away from the books. Those who touch books anywhere on the premises will be subject to censure."

Jeanne turned to find the speaker, a woman, or so she appeared by her garments. Standing two heads above Jeanne, she wore a set of keys fastened to her dress that jangled with her every move. Her gangly frame lacked any feminine curvature or softness of flesh. Her hair, thin and lank, only barely concealed bald spots that dotted her scalp.

"Pardon me, madame. My name is Jeanne Denot. I have no interest in your books, but only seek to locate my aunt, the Marquise de Vitré."

The woman nodded as if she expected Jeanne's response. She took a seat behind the desk.

"Mademoiselle Denot, was it? Be seated." She gestured toward a plainly hewn chair situated on the other side of the desk. "How long have you searched for this aunt of yours?"

"I have only just arrived at the palace."

An eyebrow rose on the woman's angular face. "The palace? What exactly do you mean by that?"

Since her arrival Jeanne had the sensations of moving through a dreamscape. Her interactions with Monsieur Couret, the toothless attendant, and now this odd woman were mundane yet also remarkable, leaving her with a growing sense of unease. Jeanne smoothed her tattered skirt and sat up straight to remind the woman, and herself, of her fine upbringing.

"Here. The Palais Louvre, of course. I am fully aware my looks belie my station, but I am to have my introduction to court at the Lully ballet. On the journey here I was pushed into the Seine by a black-hearted priest and became hopelessly lost for a time. With some assistance from a kindly hermit who helped me in the woods and an angel who rescued me from the streets of Paris, I have at last found my way."

The woman drew out a paper, sharpening a quill as Jeanne spoke and began to make notations. "Were you pushed into the river, mademoiselle, or did you, in fact, jump?"

"Jump? Only a fool would jump into the river!"

"Of course. And you are no fool! Now returning to this aunt of yours, does she figure in your dreams, too? Or does she occupy your waking hours? Does the angel resemble her? Or is the angel another figure entirely?"

"Madame, I am not here to be interrogated. Your questions are wearing at my already frayed patience.

Now please, I ask you to consult with the necessary parties and take me to my aunt. We have been separated for nearly three full days. I also require a hot bath if you would arrange it."

Her interviewer responded obliquely, "Fascinating!" which further tested Jeanne's patience.

"I insist you take me to my aunt's quarters, madame. Pardon me, I do not know your name."

"It is Madame Pelletier."

"Madame Pelletier. This place is vast, and I fear I would get lost all over again attempting to navigate myself."

Madame Pelletier seemed to weigh Jeanne's words a moment, then she stood briskly. "Well then, we would not want you lost again, mademoiselle. No, no. That would not do. Follow me and I will lead you to where you belong."

Jeanne followed Madame Pelletier up a staircase, and across a vast corridor until at last they came to a massive iron gate beyond which Jeanne could hear a distant cacophony that flooded her with a sense of dread. While the woman rifled through her set of keys, Jeanne began to back away slowly from the portal.

"Mademoiselle, if you know what is good for you, you will remain where you are." Madame Pelletier had not so much as turned her head as she spoke the words. At last, she selected a key and unlocked the gate.

"I am confused, madame. This is not the palace."

"Ah ha! At last you come to your senses. No. It is not. You are a visitor at La Salpêtrière. While it is not the Palais Louvre, like that place, this one is of the king's own making. It serves as a holding, shall we say, for the rabble: the licentious, the slothful, the destitute, the mad. This section," Madame pointed to beyond the gate, "is the special domain of the latter. It is, I believe after our little chat, your rightful destination."

At that moment a cry rang out above the din, a sound so otherworldly, it could have emanated from the mouth of Hell. What had been a kindling of fear now raged through Jeanne's veins, burning so brightly she feared she would collapse against its all-consuming heat.

"Madame Pelletier," Jeanne said unsteadily, struggling to command her faculties, "I do not wish to follow you."

Madame bared her teeth in a cunning smile. "You will follow me calmly or you will be bound and dragged inside. The choice, mademoiselle, is yours."

Chapter Twenty-One

"La Salpêtrière's purpose: clear the streets of vice whilst providing shelter for this wretched portion of humanity and put an end to beggary and idleness, as being the source of all disorder."

~*From King Louis the XIV's royal edict*

La Salpêtrière

The inmates of La Salpêtrière spent their nights in an attic dormitory that at one time contained proper beds. Nothing was left of those now save for a scattering of broken bedframes. Instead, the women slept on straw mattresses so poorly stuffed, Jeanne could feel the surface of the floorboards against her bones. They were left to sleep as late as they wished. Yet on most mornings, Jeanne rose by first light, woken by the torments let loose from the fantasies of her fellow captives, or by the noise of rats which far outnumbered the human occupants.

During those bleak hours, Jeanne gazed out the dormers lining the length of the room, none of which were barred, and contemplated her escape. A single ledge no wider than her hand edged the building. Even if she dared climb outside, the four-story drop to the ground below would mean certain death. Yet, should she remain here, confined in this madhouse, she would surely die anyway, if not in body, then in spirit.

When the pacing, shrieking, cackling, singing and other manifestations of delusion reached a crescendo each morning, Madame Pelletier's assistants would arrive, throwing the door open, screaming, "Shut your crazy mouths!" or a similarly unpleasant tiding. They were then herded to the level below, another great open space where they would spend the next hours as indolent as a rout of snails. Gruel, doled out for lunch and dinner, was eaten by hand so that it plastered every surface in the place.

When the sun set, they were shepherded back to the dormitory where Jeanne awaited the merciful escape of slumber. Candles were too hazardous a luxury to risk on the madwomen of La Salpêtrière. Thankfully, the days of summer grew longer and longer. Jeanne wondered what it would be like here in the short days of winter and vowed to never to find out.

From the ramblings of one of the more coherent inmates, Jeanne had come to learn the provenance of this hellhole. La Salpêtrière had been a factory designed to manufacture and store gunpowder for the king's army and now warehoused the incendiary denizens of Paris.

On the third day of her incarceration, during the midday repast, a girl came through the ward delivering laundry. She asked Jeanne her name. "You're not one of these cuckoos. I can see it plain as day. How is it you got thrown in with this lot?"

After being berated and bullied for three days as she pleaded for her release, the girl's civility brought tears to Jeanne's eyes. She shared her story, adding, "It has been a week since I've seen my aunt. She must think me dead by now. I have explained to Madame Pelletier a dozen times or more that I must be allowed to go to the palace."

"Madame Monsieur is what we call her. She's a heartless baboon. You're wasting your time playing to her reason or her sympathies. Listen up. Quit this story of yours."

"It is no story. It's the truth!"

"You think truth matters here? Look around you."

Jeanne surveyed the scene before them. Most of the inmates were seated on the floor, listlessly stuffing fistfuls of gruel into their mouths. An older woman, who heard the voices of God, the Devil, and King Louis in her head, and at times all three at once, had been wrestled to the ground by Madame Pelletier and her two attendants.

"Recant. Or stay locked in this hellhole with the rest of them," Madeleine said, nodding toward Madame Pelletier who sat with her knees dug into the chest of the troublesome inmate.

"If I lie, claim my account to be a falsehood, will she not judge me to be even more unstable?"

Madeleine asked, "Do you wish to be sprung from this cage?"

Jeanne nodded.

"Then tell Madame that you did, in fact, fall into the Seine and you must have bumped your head on a rock."

"I fell into the water. There are no rocks."

Madeleine dismissed her comment with a wave of her hand. "Then tell her the water soaked the sense out of your brain. Now your noggin has healed, and you realize you are not a lady after all."

"Why will Madame be inclined to believe me?"

Madeleine pointed at Madame Pelletier who had stuffed the howling inmate's mouth with wads of soiled cloth as her assistants, both as big as bulls, bound the woman's hands and feet. "There are dozens of lunatics in this ward attended by Madame Monsieur and her toadies. Three against a mob. Losing odds. If you play nice, and make like you're sane, she'll transfer you to the alms ward."

"Is that where you reside?"

She nodded. "It's not so bad. It beats life on the street. And it beats life in here."

"Why do you not live with your family?"

Madeleine smiled at her the way one smiles at a child. "You don't know much, do you? I never had one. Sometimes I wonder if I weren't hatched like a chick from an egg."

"But how have you survived?"

"With what's upstairs. My wits." Madeleine patted Jeanne's head. "You best start using yours."

Chapter Twenty-Two

"The mind is not a vessel to be filled, but a fire to be kindled."

~Plutarch

The *Saint Anne*

Jeanne read Plutarch each night to the girls as they slowly recovered from the torment of the pox. She had reached the story of Cato the Younger, championing the rights of the weak.

One of the mademoiselles said, "What worlds open up through them letters. It is nothing short of magic how you can conjure Rome hundreds of years ago as if it were here on this leaky tub."

Despite their privilege, most of the demoiselles were, in kind, unlettered, or could manage only the forming of their names.

One of them added, "We are only allowed to know the Bible at home. Is it blasphemy to prefer Plutarch?"

Jeanne had heard such opinions before and repeated her father's own feelings on the matter. "There is no need to ascribe to one at the exclusion of the other. Both offer their own enlightened views on humankind."

"Nonsense!" Madame La Plante had entered their quarters without Jeanne noticing. The lady had only just recovered from her own illness two days previously. Her form, petite before her bout with the pox, was even more so. Yet her voice and spirit were as indomitable as ever. "There is only one true word! His word. Not this Plutarch."

"Madame," Jeanne said, "the greatest politicians, writers and philosophers of history lean on Plutarch's work." A strong swell momentarily lifted the *Saint Anne*, causing Madame to lose her footing.

"Those same politicians, writers and philosophers would do better to stick with the Holy Scriptures. If they did, we would avoid most of mankind's suffering."

Instead of objecting, Jeanne sighed and closed the book. "Madame, it appears, has concluded our session."

"Mademoiselle Davide, I require a word with you in private. Gather your cloak. We shall meet up top."

Although the sun shone brightly in the sky, a biting wind swept across the deck. Madame motioned for Jeanne to follow her to the shelter of the quarter deck, the same spot Jacques and Jeanne used for their own rendezvous.

Madame began, "Now that I have, by the grace of God, recovered my faculties, I have reviewed my records in anticipation of our landing."

Jeanne waited for the old woman to continue, afraid she would ask yet again about her true connection to the Denot name. Madame's penetrating gaze shifted from Jeanne's face to the horizon.

For a moment she studied the sea as if buying time as she formulated her words. "I have discovered an uncomfortable—" she paused, "—or rather an inconvenient lack of balance."

"Lack of balance?"

"A shortage in the form of eligible brides. As you know, one of our demoiselles was taken by the pox and we now need an additional bride."

During her convalescence, when Madame had confided certain particulars of her past, Jeanne's heart had thawed toward her. Now, speaking of the women on the ship as if they were lines in a ledger, it once again hardened.

"How does this concern me, Madame?"

Madame's gaze shifted back to Jeanne. "There are a number of more junior officers, men who may be less discerning yet still expect a certain standard when it comes to a match. Now, with one candidate gone, our stock is woefully lacking. You, Mademoiselle Davide are cut from a finer cloth than the others." Jeanne made to protest but Madame spoke over her. "Save your arguments! Your tale may blind those whose sight into such matters is not as acute. I, however, cannot be so easily hoodwinked. Although you do not possess a bona fide pedigree, you can certainly pass muster well enough for the lower ranks."

"You speak of me as if I am a particular breed of horse, Madame. I find it thoroughly insulting!"

"Stuff and nonsense!" Madame waved a hand. "You are of the weaker sex, which makes you no more consequential than any other chattel and perhaps only slightly more significant than a horse." Madame managed to smile and for a moment her face appeared to be nearly kind. "My offer solves a problem on both our sides. You will be rewarded with a husband of a higher station. I will offer a worthy bride. You should be flattered."

"Thank you, Madame, but I must rescind your

offer."

"Rescind? Rescind! I am offering you a chance to elevate your station. To raise yourself to a higher plateau."

"I have been on a higher plateau before and found it caused a great deal of grief. In fact, I'm much happier now in my lower station."

"Does your reluctance have something to do with Monsieur Suprenant? Are you harboring fantasies of a match, mademoiselle? Because it would be no more than that. A fantasy. Monsieur Suprenant is certainly out of your reach."

Jeanne felt nearly sorry for Madame La Plante. Distracted by the surface of things—titles, rank, and social standing—she understood next to nothing about what dwelled in the depths of the human heart.

Jeanne said, "My answer is final, Madame. No."

"You are a fool, mademoiselle. What I offer is a greatly improved circumstance. To reject it would be madness."

"I have been called mad before, you know. I was even locked up. Imprisoned with the cuckoos at La Salpêtrière."

Rendered dumbstruck by Jeanne's words, Madame opened her mouth then shut it with such force, Jeanne could hear her teeth as they bit into the emptiness of her response.

"So, you see, Madame, my sullied pedigree is far too base to be suitable. Even for a junior officer."

Madame recovered the power of speech. "No one has to know the particulars of your history. You are a fallen woman, Jeanne Davide. Like Christ with Mary Magdalene, I am giving you a chance at redemption."

At the old woman's words, she made to leave but Madame grabbed hold of Jeanne's hand, arresting her progress. "I know I am a figure of scorn amongst the mademoiselles. It is only because I care for the welfare of each and every one of the young lambs for which I am the shepherdess. Perhaps I am too stern. But the eye of the needle is thin, Mademoiselle Davide. To pass through requires the very straightest of paths!"

Jeanne weighed the directness of her response. "You are not loved by the mademoiselles, it is true, but only because you harangue them with talk of the straight and narrow when most of them, thanks to the circumstances of their birth, have already traveled down a twisted path."

"They've been on the road of sin, which leads to eternal suffering in the beyond. I have done my best to save them. To save you. Take this chance. It may be your last."

Madame's judgement of the mademoiselles was as narrow, as damning as Jeanne's own had been. The course of her life before Paris had been as circumscribed, as predictable as the hedge labyrinth in Mursay's park. Choosing one direction over another at the entrance still led swiftly to the center. Girls like Madeleine were not afforded the luxury of neat paths, of predetermined end points, something Madame would never understand.

****

She sought out Jacques, wishing to relay the encounter with Madame and finally reveal the true narrative behind taking the name Davide. By the position of the sun, it was nearly noon, a time by which Jacques usually made his rounds on the lower deck.

211

Making her way into the depths of the ship, Jeanne came upon Elisabeth with baby Anne heading in the same direction.

Jeanne kissed the top of Anne's head. "How is our little angel today?" Jeanne said.

Elisabeth's face held a quizzical expression. "Can it be? Have you not heard, Jeanne?"

"Heard what? Is something wrong with the baby?"

"Not with the baby. We have only just vacated Monsieur Suprenant's quarters so that he can again occupy them. He is there now. The captain discovered him this morning ailing quite badly." The faintest of light shone from the hatch above, enough to illuminate the glint of tears in Elisabeth's eyes. "I am sorry to be the bearer of bad news. Surely he'll regain his health soon enough."

Jeanne raced to the upper deck and threw open the door to Jacques' quarters without announcing her presence.

The captain knelt by Jacques' bedstead. "Hello, mademoiselle. It did not take you long to hear the news. We only just settled him a moment ago."

"How does he fare?" Jeanne asked, but the answer appeared in Jacques' ghostly visage. He shivered violently, occasionally muttering unintelligibly.

"Not at all well, I fear. We had to carry him here, he was so insensible." The captain stood, and Jeanne claimed his spot, taking hold of Jacques' hands.

"Jacques. It is me, Jeanne. Can you hear me?"

Jacques' eyes fluttered and Jeanne sensed the smallest of pressure to her hand in response.

"We were together at sunset, and he seemed—" Jeanne meant to complete her thoughts with the word, "fine," until she recalled how he had shivered. He had been ailing even then. Still, it seemed impossible for him to have been this diminished in so short a time.

"Mademoiselle, take comfort in this: in a matter of days, we'll reach Quebec. If he hasn't recovered by then, we'll get the regiment's physician to call on him."

Jeanne stood, formulating a plan. "Until then, I will tend to him. I will not leave his side." She needed to fetch a supply of saltwater to cool Jacques' fever and fresh water to make him drink. There were mustard seeds in the storeroom for a poultice. She would enlist Teeth's help in making one.

The captain said, "It will set Madame's tongue wagging, I'm afraid."

"So be it. Madame has no hold on me anymore, captain."

He smiled kindly. "Unlike this man before you, who appears to have captured you entirely. Let the old woman's tongue wag out of her skull! I for one will be the happiest man alive when Madame La Plante departs the *Saint Anne* once and for all."

Rumor spread faster than illness on the ship so that before Jeanne had concluded her conversation with the captain, Teeth stood at the door offering her assistance.

Teeth set about preparing a plaster of Jesuit's bark while Jeanne held Jacques' hand and spoke to him. Kissing his forehead revealed the fever had increased. She repeated his name to raise a response, but his fugue state had deepened so that he no longer mumbled or flailed. Instead, he lay deathly quiet, his breathing slow and labored.

Jeanne recited the Lord's Prayer, concluding it with, "Father, I beg you to protect him," addressing both her heavenly and earthly fathers. Thinking of her papa, she began to sob. "Please, please do not take him from me!"

"Rise up. Clear out of here," Teeth said.

She was so lost in her own torment she had momentarily forgotten Teeth's presence. "You want me to leave?"

"Go take one of your walks. Or tend to the girls below."

"No. He needs me now."

Teeth gestured for her to come closer, then whispered in her ear: "Stop gnashing your teeth and pleading for his life as if he's already as good as gone. He may be insensible, but the sick, they take in words around them, tucking them away deep like a squirrel does nuts in winter."

"I am so desperately afraid." Her despair caused the words to ring out through the cabin.

Teeth held a finger before her lips and made a shushing sound. "Go," she said softly. "Take some air." Jeanne began to protest, but Teeth cut her off. "I will not leave his side. Now collect yourself and return only when you've regained your bearings."

****

On the top deck, Jeanne came across Madeleine and told her the news. With the telling came a fresh issue of tears.

"Come now," she said. "He's young and as strong as an ox. We'll get him back on his feet in no time."

Jeanne cried even more pitifully. "Please don't be kind or sympathetic," she said through her tears. "I was much stronger with Teeth barking at me."

Madeleine laughed. "I can't promise to be as nasty

214

as Teeth, that's a tall order, but I'll try. Now let's go and get something to eat."

Jeanne shook her head and Madeleine insisted she eat at least a few scraps of food to bolster her strength and saw to it that Jeanne complied. When they returned to Jacques' cabin, they found the door locked.

"How odd. Why would Teeth lock it?" Madeleine knocked on the door to gain entrance.

"One minute!" Teeth called out. They heard a sound, like a heavy object being dragged across the floor. Another moment passed and Teeth's voice came to them from just behind the door. "I'll unlatch it but count to five before opening."

"What kind of game is this?" Madeleine asked, but did as Teeth ordered. They counted then opened the door to encounter Elisabeth hurrying to leave. The girl's eyes were red and swollen and there was a welt across her cheek.

Jeanne asked, "What's this, Elisabeth. Are you not well?"

Elisabeth pushed past them and when Madeleine made to follow her, Teeth called out, "Leave her. We had a disagreement and exchanged choice words."

"She had a mark on her cheek. Did you strike her?" Jeanne asked.

"I did not strike her," Teeth said with special emphasis on the first word.

"Is there anyone on this ship who has not exchanged choice words with you?" Madeleine said.

Teeth knelt by Jacques' bedside. "Stuff it or there will be more. We don't need the distraction."

"How is he?" Jeanne knelt beside her. "Any signs of improvement?"

Teeth kept her eyes on her patient. "No. Then again, there's been scarcely time for change. In him at least."

After a while, Madeleine left to check the hold for more mustard seed, while Jeanne fetched a supply of fresh water.

Upon returning, Jeanne again found the door locked. "Do you not fear an unexpected visit by Madame La Plante?" she asked when Teeth again opened the door. "Barring the door will only raise her dander."

"I fear nothing from that old crow. I guess you could say to me she's dead."

Jeanne sat at Jacques' bedside and put her hand on his wrist. When she did, she felt the strength of his life's blood coursing through his veins and made a silent prayer for his speedy recovery. She leaned forward, her mouth next to his ear, and whispered, "Captain says we will reach the shores of New France in the space of four days. Hang on, my love. Everything will be better then."

Chapter Twenty-Three

"I am told that the great hospitals in Paris and the one in Lyon have proposed to send some girls at their expense provided we give them land and grants in exchange."

~*Archives de Québec*

La Salpêtrière

Jeanne stopped pleading for her release and instead avoided Madame Pelletier for the next few days after talking with the laundress. One afternoon she found an occasion to engage her. "Madame, I wonder if I could have a short word with you?"

Madame and her cronies were seated at the only table in the ward, supping on loaves of bread and cheese. Jeanne forced her eyes to stay trained on Madame and ignore the food although her hollow stomach ached at the thought of even a morsel.

"Let me guess," Madame Pelletier said, her tongue sliding over her hairy upper lip to catch an errant cheese crumb. "You demand to see the king?"

Her comment set off howls of laughter from her cronies as mad as any of the inmates.

Jeanne smiled. "No, Madame. That has passed. You see, I fear I suffered some concussion of the brain. My thoughts were jumbled. As I awoke this morning, I felt right again. My old self. I no longer wish to see my aunt. Although I have an actual aunt, she is a housekeeper for a priest, not a marquise."

Madame Pelletier narrowed her eyes and sucked on her fingers to clean them. "Is that so? Pray tell, now that you are recovered, in which parish does your actual aunt work?"

Madame Couret had mentioned the name of the local parish. Was it Saint Stephan or Saint Sebastian? "Saint Sebastian," Jeanne answered.

"You were not born in Perche as you first claimed?"

"No, no, Madame. I was born here. In Paris."

Madame stabbed the wedge of cheese savagely, sawing off a great chunk. "Where did you reside?"

She recalled the name of a street she'd passed on her journey with Madame Couret's brother. "On the Rue de Reims."

"The Rue De Reims? A street trafficked by whores and whoremongers. Is that your occupation, Jeanne?"

One of madame's sycophants, the smaller one called Ella, laughed so hard wine bubbled out of her nostrils, causing her friend to fall into a fit of giggles.

Jeanne's blood rose. If she moved fast enough, she would have just enough time to slap each of these impudent gargoyles and then turn on her heel to run. But where? They would find her and do God knows what to her when they did.

"Of course not, Madame," Jeanne said levelly.

Gabby, the larger and crueler of madame's aids, threw her powerful shoulders back. "Look at Miss High and Mighty. Me own mum was a whore and a fine one at that! It's a line of work like any other. You got something against whoring?"

Three pairs of eyes stared at her with deadly intent, awaiting her response. "I am sure your mother was a good woman," Jeanne finally managed.

"Not at all. She was a right surly bitch, that one."

Gabby's comment sparked more guffaws from her bulbous sidekick. Madame allowed herself a smile then trained her unblinking gaze back to Jeanne.

"The girls are having a bit of fun with you, Jeanne. Like a country rube, you fell into their clumsy trap. I do not for a moment believe you to be Parisian. Your dialect, your manner of speech and everything about you points in a southerly direction. They may be simpletons. I am not."

Madame's insults seemed to have no effect on her brawny companions who grinned and nodded their heads in league with their superior. Jeanne had witnessed the way the cats in the barn at Mursay played with the field mice. Slashing at them with their claws, allowing them to limp away, only to drag their defenseless bodies back for more sparring. Jeanne was a diversion, a mouse to be toyed with. In the end, however, the cat always won.

"I wish to be released, Madame. I do not belong here with the rest of these women."

Madame shook her head slowly. "I decide who stays here, Jeanne. But I have no say as to who is fit to leave."

****

On the afternoon following her encounter with Madame, as Jeanne queued for the day's repast, she watched as Gabby picked her nose with her grubby hand, flicking the gooey yield into the gruel pot as her friend laughed and cheered her on.

After each addition, Gabby stirred the pot, saying, "Yum! Yum! Come, you idiots. I've added a special spice today. Special Gabby spice!"

For more than a week, hunger had been Jeanne's constant companion. Today was no exception. Yet no amount of starvation could inspire her to eat the food ladled with a wink by Gabby into her bowl.

"You hungry, your highness? I made sure you got extra Gabby spice in yours! Don't you think princess deserves it, Ella?" Her comment provoked an appreciative guffaw from her friend.

Jeanne had learned in her new life how invisibility provided security. Averting eyes, ducking at the right moment, escaping notice meant surviving another day. Yet, in staring at the beast before her, Jeanne forgot the rule governing her new, miserable existence.

"How dare you conduct yourself in this manner?" Jeanne said. "We are human beings. All equal before the eyes of God. Yet you treat us like animals. You! You gargantuan dolt! You are the animal. Nothing better than a hog. A big, stinking hog!"

Gabby slowly lowered her ladle, looking for a moment as if she were about to cry.

"Did you say hog?" Gabby asked. She turned to her friend. "Did she call me a hog?"

Excited anticipation marked her friend's face as she nodded enthusiastically. "She did, Gabrielle. She called you a big stinking one. Something about you being a dummy, too, I recall."

Gabrielle dropped the ladle, and it sank slowly into the kettle, like a stone into quicksand. As addled as most of the inmates at La Salpêtrière were, they sensed the approaching storm and cleared back from the food line.

Gabby placed her hands on her hips, lowered her head, and charged. The blow catapulted Jeanne backward, crashing her to the floor. In no time, Gabby had pinned her and sat on her chest.

She fought back, but starved for food and given Gabby outweighed her, she lay helpless as one of the kittens the ruffian boys had tossed into the Seine. Now, with this bull on top of her, she would die. Her chest struggled to rise against the force of Gabby's knees. Jeanne had the sense of drowning on dry land. She thought of her father, not for the first time since she'd arrived here. They would be reunited in Heaven in the space of a few painful moments. Jeanne ceased to struggle. Her mind began to lose its grip on consciousness.

The jangling of keys announced Madame Pelletier's presence. "Ella, Gabby! What's this?" Gabby shifted her weight ever so slightly to address Madame.

"This one's giving us quite a time of it."

"Is she? From the shade of purple on her face, she looks very near to expiring," Madame said.

"I'm just teaching her a lesson, is all." Gabby smiled and winked playfully.

"Just see that you don't kill another one," Madame said, and clucked her tongue. "You remember where that got us last time."

"That were an accident," Gabby said and looked again as if she might burst into tears. She slumped back on her heels, and Jeanne filled her lungs. When she did, Ella kicked her in the ribs with one of her wooden clogs and whispered, "Bitch. We'll see to you later."

Although Jeanne could at last breath, she could scarcely move. All her faculties strained for air as she panted and coughed. Struggling back to life, she had one clear thought: She was going to die here.

****

Between the almshouse, hospital, and asylum, La Salpêtrière held two thousand human occupants and ten times as many rats. Vermin were so ubiquitous, Jeanne no longer startled or screamed upon seeing them scurry boldly across the floor of the main room. Yet at night, her terror of the little beasts rekindled. Jeanne slept inside the burlap sack that covered her mattress straw to prevent being bitten by the rats that scurried so brazenly over their sleeping bodies.

One night, Jeanne awoke suddenly, conscious of a noise. Not the sounds produced by the chimeras running through the heads of her fellow inmates after sundown, or the bold traffic of rats, but something else. Footsteps. A few moments of silence. A giggle. More footsteps and laughter, a pattern that began at the far end of the dormitory and repeated, coming nearer to where Jeanne lay. A dawning realization filled her with terror. Now she could clearly make out the voices of Gabby and Ella. She covered her face and crouched inside the burlap. Hidden within her sack, it took them longer to identify her, but at last they did and tore back her rough cover. Gabby tilted a candle so close to Jeanne's face, Jeanne felt the heat of the flame.

"Got her!" Gabby seized Jeanne by her arm and hauled her up as if she were lifting a child. Equal parts of fear and pain caused Jeanne to cry out and Gabby whispered, "Another sound, princess, and I'll toss you out yonder window."

They dragged her through the length of the dormitory, past the tormented dreamers, and as they did, Jeanne fell into her own waking nightmare. They could kill her for what she had done and who would know or care? The two oafs shoved her into a passage and down a staircase leading to the hall below where the women spent their days. Instead of entering, they approached the iron gate, the selfsame portal through which Jeanne had been delivered into this Hell.

Ella struggled to fit the key into the lock. "Have I got the right one?" She hiccupped, then belched.

"Course you do, mutton brain! We used it to get in, remember?"

"Mutton brain? Who's the mutton brain? Bring the candle closer. I can't see a thing."

With the flame in one hand, and Jeanne clutched in the other, Gabby drew nearer and after a moment, the lock tumbled, and the gate swung open. Jeanne's heart bounded at the thought of stepping outside the confines of the ward. Perhaps she could twist free and make a run for it.

"Don't even think of trying to escape," Gabby said, digging her fingers deeper into the flesh of Jeanne's upper arm.

They continued down two more flights of stairs and at last came to their destination. Gabby commanded Jeanne to sit still and shut up as she and Ella lit candles. As the room slowly illuminated, Jeanne could see they were in a vast kitchen. Shelving from floor to ceiling held enormous sacks of provisions, including the horrible gruel that constituted the diet at La Salpêtrière.

"I'll get the glasses." Gabby disappeared into the darkness beyond the weak pools of candlelight. She returned with three glasses which she lined up on the table.

"Large or largest?" Gabby asked Ella and giggled.

"Largest," Ella said.

Gabby filled all three glasses from a cask and the smell of red wine permeated the air.

The two great oafs lifted their glasses. "A toast to you, your royal highness. To the pretty princess who thinks she's better than all the cuckoos. Now raise your glass," Gabby said.

Jeanne did as commanded.

"To her highness," Ella said. To Jeanne's astonishment, both women drained their glasses in one go. Jeanne merely sipped hers.

"Look at this one. Quite the refined manners, I would say, Ella. A hog such as myself don't know nothing about such delicate ways. But you aren't in the palace now. And we order you drop your airs and slop like us pigs."

Jeanne lifted her glass tentatively and took a gulp. Her body immediately revolted at the sudden deluge of strong drink, and she feared she would be sick.

"No, no, no," Gabby said. "You need to finish it."

"I couldn't possibly."

Ella threw her voice into a falsetto. "'I couldn't possibly! I couldn't possibly!' So refined, this one is!"

Gabby's leaned closer to Jeanne, and she could smell the sour reek of wine on her breathe. "You'll either drain the glass or I'll stick your head in the cask and have you drain the cask instead. Now which one will it be?"

Jeanne raised the glass and held her nose, then emptied it in a few choking gulps. She slammed the glass onto the table just as Gabby and Ella had done. This delighted her companions.

"Good job! We'll see you stuffed full of grape and raving drunk in no time," Gabby said, refilling their glasses. "Then you won't be so high and mighty."

This time all three of them drank in unison, the second round going down easier than the first. Jeanne stopped wondering why they had taken her here or how she could escape. Her thoughts fell into jumbled musings: how Ella could almost be pretty if it weren't for the unfortunate wart on her chin, and Gabby resembled someone. Who was it? Then it came to her: August Loret. She could have been August's brother or sister. Which one? Her confusion caused her to giggle.

"Having a good time, are you?" Gabby asked placing the third round on the table. "We're you're pals, Jeanne, ain't it so?"

"Yes," she said sincerely. In fact, as she contemplated it, she could not recall the reason why she ever disliked these two rough-hewn, yet amiable souls. "At first it didn't seem possible. We are so different. Not the two of you. You two are very similar. But I am quite different. As different as someone can be really and still be part of the same fundamental species."

Gabby scratched her head. "So, I'm no hog?"

Somewhere in the clearer recesses of her mind, Jeanne remembered a significance associated with the word "hog" but couldn't grasp its importance.

Jeanne said, "Of course not! You are a lovely person with a delightful wit!"

Gabby narrowed her eyes. "Are you making fun?" she asked. Jeanne solemnly shook her head no and Gabby raised her glass. "Why thank you. Them's the kindest words anyone has ever spoken concerning me."

"I think you're delightful, too!" Ella said. She smacked her glass against theirs and drank the wine as if it were water. Although they had not demanded she do so, Jeanne followed suit, draining the third, or perhaps the fourth glass, she couldn't be sure.

Gabby raised her glass yet again. "I know I'm as drunk as a bell ringer, but this isn't the wine, speaking. You two are my best friends."

After another prodigious gulp of wine, Gabby wiped the back of her mouth with her meaty hand. "You know, Jeanne, we was going to have some sport with you tonight."

Ella laughed and even in the dim candlelight Jeanne noticed her teeth were tinted with a patina of purple from the wine. Aunt Mimi advised a surreptitious gargle between each glass to avoid such a social disaster, but no water flowed here, only a veritable river of grape.

Ella said, "We was going to carry you out to the street, strip you naked and tie you to a post." She giggled. "What a riot!"

Among her warm drunken musings came a cold sobering thought. She said, "I would not have cared for that one bit."

"Well, our appetite for it is waning now," Gabby said.

"What would Madame have said when I went missing?"

"Well, we would have brought you back and made sure you was tucked in before anyone was the wiser," Gabby said. "Then the ugly baboon couldn't complain. It's always 'Gabby and Ella, this' and 'Gabby and Ella, that.' She's always plaguing us for something or another. Making herself look all perfect in the eyes of the boss."

"Madame is the boss, is she not?" Jeanne asked.

"She can dream of it! No. Doctor Villette runs this place and he who decides who is released," Ella added. "She's sweet on him. But he don't take no notice of her because of her face. Doctor Villette has a fine wife, he does. Saw her once waiting for him in a carriage with a pair of pretty children, too."

Sensible thoughts pushed their way through Jeanne's wine-addled brain. "Why have I not seen Doctor Villette?"

Gabby poured yet another round of drinks, "for the voyage home," and presently answered Jeanne's question. "The good doctor is here every day, I reckon. He rarely condescends to visit the ward. When he does, he makes a face like he's smelling something bad." She aped the doctor, holding her nose comically.

Ella guffawed then added, "It is awful smelly up there."

Gabby said, "Mostly works down in his office. He don't care for seeing the cuckoos."

"I would very much like to meet this doctor," Jeanne said. As drunk as she was, she tucked the thought away to be retrieved later. *It is the doctor who decides.*

Chapter Twenty-Four

"If God strikes us with one hand, he consoles us with another."

~Mother Marie of the Ursulines

La Salpêtrière

Jeanne awoke the next morning to find the dormitory empty except for the rats that scurried about on their frantic errands. She rose slowly, the pain in her head escalating as she gained an upright position. How had she managed to get back here? She had no memory. The throbbing in her head made it impossible to retrieve even a scrap of coherent thought. She shuffled to the washstand and prepared to join the others.

She found Madame, Gabby and Ella enjoying a breakfast of tea and cake in the day room. The sight of the food made Jeanne's stomach rise in revolt, and for a moment, she feared she would be sick.

"Not feeling well this morning, mademoiselle?" Madame asked, slathering a layer of clotted cream on her cake.

Jeanne grabbed her stomach as if to physically hold down its contents. "No, Madame."

Gabby winked at her slyly.

"You were quite impossible to rouse this morning. Gabby and Ella reported you to be ill."

"Yes." Then a sliver of last night's conversation pushed through her muddled consciousness, the mention of a doctor at La Salpêtrière. Someone who was, in fact, Madame's superior. What had they called him?

"I believe I need a doctor, Madame."

Madame ruminated her food and Jeanne's request and presently responded by saying, "We will see if the good doctor can be entreated to pay us a visit."

Jeanne lay curled on the floor for the remainder of the day, her pose not entirely theatrical. Her insides rioted against last night's grape. Toward suppertime, when Jeanne refused her portion of gruel, Madame approached her: "I have spoken with Doctor Villette, and he will see you tomorrow. Make sure you are still ailing. The doctor is a busy man."

****

The following morning, Madame herself came to rouse Jeanne from her slumber. Looming over her, she clapped her hands. "Quickly! Dr. Villette awaits us downstairs."

Jeanne rushed through a semblance of her morning toilet and hurried to keep pace with Madame Pelletier.

"Why are you trotting in that manner? You must be slow and infirm. If the doctor fails to find you ill, he will be cross with me. We must not make Dr. Villette cross!"

They made their way to the day room, Jeanne clutching her stomach for show, and approached a finely dressed gentlemen ensconced at Madame's dining table. He wore breeches cut from an expensive cloth and, from the scent of it, a freshly powdered wig.

"Doctor Villette, this is the patient who requires

your ministrations."

Doctor Villette gazed languidly across a distance of a few yards toward Jeanne. He sat ever so carefully on the chair, legs crossed, hands on his lap, perched the way a finely dressed person would sit on a small picnic blanket. In the surroundings of the ward, Dr. Villette looked like a glorious blossom rising in an onion patch.

"How long has she been ill?" He pressed a handkerchief to his nose.

Jeanne made to respond to the question, but Madame answered instead. "A number of days. Weeks perhaps." An interesting response considering Jeanne had only been in captivity for just short of twelve days.

"Is she with child?"

The question caused Jeanne's face to flush, and she answered herself, saying, "Most certainly not, Monsieur Doctor."

"We could take her to the hospital ward and bleed her," the doctor said, stroking his chin as Madame stroked her mustache. Both regarded her as if she were a painting that defied placement on a wall.

"Is she hysterical? Prone to imaginings or fits?"

"No, Doctor," Madame said quickly. "She is docile and quite well-behaved."

Again, Madame's answer surprised Jeanne. No mention of delusions or her desire to be taken to the palace.

"Good. I will not tolerate a repetition of March's episode." The doctor touched his arm. "My forearm still carries the scar of that villain's teeth."

Madame shook her head. "No, no. There will be no fits, Doctor. I will take it upon myself to personally chaperone her during the treatment."

He drew a gold watch from his pocket. "Let us begin at once. I have an appointment at the opera tonight with my wife."

At the mention of his wife, Madame grimaced as if she'd been pinched.

****

To reach the hospital ward at La Salpêtrière, Jeanne and Madame followed the doctor out of the building and across the same unending courtyard Jeanne travelled her first day here, which now seemed an eternity ago. Madame kept a grip on Jeanne's arm so tight, Jeanne feared she would leave a mark.

As they walked, Madame occasionally called out reports to the doctor, who strode several paces ahead of them: "She seems capable of the journey, but still weak. Not too weak to get the wrong idea. I have her in a tight hold, doctor."

They arrived at the hospital which consisted of a long ward filled with bedsteads, only half of which were occupied with patients.

"You have so few patients, Doctor. It speaks volumes about your work," Madame Pelletier said, nodding toward the empty beds.

"Not at all. It is no reflection of any skill on my part. The grippe normally passes by this time of year, Madame."

"Oh, but you are modest," Madame Pelletier said, whereupon she produced what was meant, Jeanne supposed, to be a coquettish grin. It caused the doctor to look away. Madame was one of the few people Jeanne had encountered whose face appeared comelier without the flourish of a smile.

****

Although Jeanne had been playacting on the way to the hospital, after the bloodletting, she could barely lift her head off the mattress and teetered on the edge of unconsciousness.

"Madame, you may leave now. The girl can stay here overnight." Doctor Villette neatly wiped his lancet clean with a white cloth leaving behind a streak of Jeanne's blood.

Madame's smile, a constant feature in the doctor's presence, faded. "Perhaps I should stay to guard her. She could pose a threat."

"This girl is as menacing as a newborn babe. Return to your ward, Madame." To prove his point, the doctor lifted one of Jeanne's arms and released it. It flopped to her side like a dead fish. Madame offered yet another entreaty to be allowed to stay, but Jeanne fell blissfully into the abyss of unconsciousness before the doctor could respond.

She awoke to a late afternoon sky visible through the hospital windows and rolled weakly to her side. Her empty stomach cried out to be filled, and Jeanne found herself longing for her daily gruel as if it were the finest cut of meat.

Rising slowly from her bedstead, blood rushed like wind through her head, and she nearly fainted. She shuffled past a long row of beds, viewing an assortment of humanity as she made her way: A woman bound by ropes at her hands and feet tossed and turned in the throes of some hidden torment, an old man without teeth waved to her with a hand that lacked fingers while another, quite a bit younger, propped himself up on his elbow as she passed and called out, "Looking for company, lovely?" causing Jeanne to quicken her pace.

She came upon an elderly ward sister and asked to see the doctor. Following the sister to the office where she first met Madame Pelletier, Jeanne contemplated escape. If she were only stronger, not this depleted version of her normal self, she could have easily outrun the woman. Yet the bleeding, and days of poor nutrition left her body in no condition to fulfill the desires of her mind.

Doctor Villette sat behind his desk writing when they entered the room. He arched an eyebrow in surprise at the interruption and bade her to sit.

"How is it that you are ambulatory? We bled you quite thoroughly. Most patients require at least a day of convalescence."

She smiled and straightened her posture. "You have cured me completely, Doctor. I thank you."

The doctor waved off her compliment, but his face beamed with pride. "Although medicine holds many mysteries, we know bleeding is one treatment that cures most ailments."

"On the subject of cures, I have not only achieved an extraordinary physical recovery, I have also quite recovered from a malady of the mind I suffered of late."

Jeanne considered telling Doctor Villette the truth, yet if he found her story too incredible, as everyone else had, she would be locked up again with no chance of release. The doctor listened as Jeanne related her fall into the river and the fabricated story of her life in Paris on the Rue De Reims.

His eyes never left her face. "Extraordinary. I gather from your diction and powers of speech you were educated while living with the priest?"

Jeanne said, "You have extraordinary powers of

observation. You are correct, monsieur."

The doctor nodded and smiled as if pleased with his own powers of deduction. "It is certainly unusual to find someone as well-spoken as you within the walls of La Salpêtrière. Consider yourself released then, mademoiselle. Free to return to the presbytery."

The doctor returned to his writing.

Jeanne remained in the chair as if rooted to it. She should bolt to her feet and flee this place, yet she sat like a dolt, too stunned to move. "As readily as that? I may simply walk away from this place?"

He regarded her, a shadow of impatience crossing his otherwise placid features. He snapped his fingers and said, "Just like that."

Jeanne could not fathom this sudden and glorious turn of fortune. "If Madame Pelletier chances to see me, how shall I prove I am, in fact, released?"

The doctor sighed. He scratched a note on a piece of paper. "You will show her this. Madame is lettered enough to recognize my signature. If I encounter her," he appeared to shudder at the thought, "I will mention it myself. Good day, mademoiselle."

****

With La Salpêtrière at her back, Jeanne contemplated the streets before her. She knew the Seine was nearby. If she could locate it, she could again use it to divine a course to the palace. Jeanne surveyed her broken shoes. Her feet were barely contained within the leather and spilled out from gaping holes on the sides. After days of indolence, the sores covering them had healed but would return soon enough. In her trunk, she had packed three sets of shoes more suitable for dancing than walking. At this instance she would give anything to possess even her most frivolous pair for the journey ahead.

A woman pushing a cart trudged toward the entrance of La Salpêtrière where Jeanne stood. Jeanne deemed it safe to ask her directions to the river. The woman pointed and Jeanne started out. Her shoes flopped and caught in the crevices of the cobblestones, causing Jeanne to limp. Hunger and the loss of blood made her dizzy, and she found it necessary to stop every few feet or so to catch her breath.

The sun had retreated, its milder rays washing the filth of Paris in a pink glow. She needed to reach the palace before nightfall when the riffraff emerged to perform deeds best done under the cover of darkness.

Jeanne stopped yet again to catch her breath, panting with the effort of her tortuously slow pace when she became aware of someone calling out. "Hello, my beauty." She looked around to locate the source of the voice, a man's, coming from within a fine carriage. She glanced backward. Surely, he could not be addressing her. "You look weary. Need some food?"

A gentleman leaned out through the window of the carriage.

"Are you addressing me, monsieur?" Jeanne said.

"Yes." He smiled kindly, revealing perfect teeth. Even in the failing light Jeanne noted the richness of his clothing and the gleam of a gold ring on his little finger. She could not be sure of his age, only that he was older than her.

He opened the door of the carriage. "Climb in, dear girl. Climb in! You look as if you haven't had a proper meal in ages. My city residence is close by. Cook is preparing a fine dinner of goose. You shall join me."

At the thought of food, Jeanne's knees gave way and she righted herself before falling to the ground.

"Dear, dear. You haven't eaten in quite some time," he said smiling. "You're barely holding up. You shall have extra helpings of apple tart then."

"Monsieur, you are too kind. But in actual fact I would much rather trouble you for the use of your carriage. Could you take me to the Palais Louvre?"

He sank back into the recesses of the carriage so that Jeanne could only see his hand and its gleaming ring. He leaned forward once again, grinning. "I had not planned to cross the river. For a beauty like you, however, I will reconsider my route."

If she had possessed the strength, Jeanne would have laughed at his words. Beauty, indeed! Covered from head to toe in dirt and grime, she had last bathed in the Seine when the priest pushed her in. She had seen finer clothes and shoes on a pauper.

She took a step forward and her shoe lodged in the cobblestones. As she grappled to free it, she could feel the man's eyes on her. That so fine a gentleman could see her in this state of mortification would have caused her to die of shame in her old life. In this new one, her sense of pride was as starved as her stomach and produced only the faintest pang of humiliation.

As she stood again, the door opened wider, and the gentleman hopped out and in no time took hold of her elbow to escort her into the carriage. He tightened his grip on her arm as one ill-clad foot landed on the step to the carriage, and in a motion, he made to stuff her inside like so much baggage. She drew back, one foot on the street.

He said sharply, "What are you doing?" He nudged

her forward. "Get in, girl. Make haste. Make haste."

"Monsieur, I have reconsidered. I no longer require your generous offer."

He smiled. This close, his face took on a sly look. "My, don't you talk like a lady! Now get in, slut, or I'll cuff you, I swear it!"

When he shoved her forward Jeanne resisted, and fell backward onto the street. The gentleman dragged her back up and propelled her toward the carriage. Jeanne willed herself to scream, but the forces of hunger and blood loss made it so she could barely muster a growl, like that of a wounded animal. After a few moments struggle she became aware of someone standing nearby, watching the commotion.

"Get off of her, villain!" A woman wearing a hooded cloak stepped toward them.

The gentleman's wig went askew during their scuffle, and he adjusted it primly. "Who are you to command me? Mind your own business, whore."

The woman pulled back her hood. It was Madeleine, the girl who had counseled her at the madhouse in La Salpêtrière. "The girl is defenseless. Weak. I assure you I am not." She produced a sizeable knife from beneath her cloak.

The man waved her away. "Be gone. If you had any sense, you would see I am helping this urchin."

"That's a funny kind of help. I know others you've given aid to, and they didn't feel any the better for it after. Let go of her or I'll rake your handsome face with my blade so your fine surface matches your rotten core."

The man maintained his hold on Jeanne's arm. Madeleine took another step forward and brandished her weapon. The false gentleman unhanded Jeanne, causing her to fall back once again with even more force onto the cobblestones. He retreated hurriedly into the dark recesses of his roaming lair and sped off into the tortuous streets of Paris.

Madeleine knelt by her side. "Are you all right, Jeanne? That is your name, isn't it?"

"Yes," Jeanne said, meaning it as a response to the latter question only. As to the former, she was not at all well. Terror, hunger, inadequate clothing, loss of blood: these conditions conspired to keep her from her aunt and her salvation.

"Come now. Get up. I'm afraid that devil will come back for you."

Jeanne sat up slowly and with Madeleine's help presently managed to stand. As she did, the sound of a carriage could be heard and terror, newly drained from her person, flooded back with redoubled force.

Jeanne clutched Madeleine's arm. "He has returned! What are we to do?"

She never heard Madeleine's reply, for a moment later she fainted.

Chapter Twenty-Five

"Occupation is the best safeguard for women under all circumstances—mental or physical, or both. Cupid extinguishes his torch in the atmosphere of industry."

~ *Madame de Sévigné, Writer*

La Salpêtrière

When Jeanne awoke, she found herself lying in a bed, Madeleine by her side. In the darkness she struggled to make out her surroundings.

"Where am I?" She sat up. "That awful man. He will find me!"

"Hush. You are safe. Rest. You have nothing to fear," Madeleine replied.

With those words Jeanne sank back beneath a new wave of oblivion until the sound of her own cries carried her back to consciousness. She dreamt she had escaped the hellhole La Salpêtrière only to find herself back in it again. Opening her eyes, she realized the dream was, in fact, reality. The early dawn lit an endless dormer, not unlike the one that housed the mad, except this place had a row of proper bedsteads with homely mattresses instead of piles of straw. Madeleine lay beside her in one of dozens of beds wedged so tightly together, one had to crawl to the foot of the bedstead to enter or take leave of it.

Impossible! She found herself caught in some Sisyphean madness. She had to escape. Find her aunt. Run through the streets of Paris to the palace while daylight shone. Jeanne bit her hand to stifle a sob.

Madeleine awoke. "Quiet now. You've had a nightmare is all. The other girls are still asleep and there'll be hell to pay if you wake them."

I did not have a nightmare," Jeanne whispered. "I am living one. My only desire was to escape this place. How did I get back here?"

"I hauled you back myself like a sack of potatoes."

A picture of the terrible gentleman came back to her. She ran her fingers over a tender spot on her arm, a souvenir of last night's struggle. "Who was the gentleman in the carriage?"

A figure on the other side of Jeanne's bed stirred and growled. "Shut your traps, chatterboxes, or I'll shut them for ye."

Madeleine lowered her voice. "No gentleman. A monster in the guise of one. He hunts the young girls of the neighborhood. I know maids who have entered his carriage whole and emerged broken."

Jeanne shivered as she recalled how close she had come to the same fate. She recalled his panting breath on her face as he attempted to drag her into the darkness of his carriage.

"Why is he not locked away?"

Madeleine dismissed her comment with a short laugh. "There's a lot you don't know. Why would anyone lift a finger to help the likes of us against a man in a shining carriage? They say he's connected to the king himself."

"Because it is simply not right. We are all God's

creatures!"

Madeleine regarded her as if she were mad. "It's the girls' word against his. Who do you think the law believes?"

Jeanne did not hazard an answer. In the space of little more than a fortnight she had witnessed it for herself how the invisible bonds of justice, truth, and dignity—ones she had thought of as unifying all of humanity into a code of behavior—were, in fact, reserved for a privileged few.

"I'm so grateful for your kindness and courage. You have saved my life. Or at least my virtue, which is one and the same thing. I don't know how to thank you."

Madeleine studied Jeanne, shutting one eye and then the other in a comic fashion that made Jeanne want to laugh, but also made her feel queer, self-conscious, like a bug on a pin under a particularly keen glass. "You said you're from Perche, is that right? Where is Perche? How far from Paris?"

"It is a days' journey from here."

Madeleine said, "In which direction? Show me."

"The sun rises in the east which is there." Jeanne tracked the dawning light through the window. "Which means Perche must be there." She pointed in the direction of the wall behind them. "To the south."

"Is it a very nice place, this Perche? Better than Paris?"

Jeanne had never thought to qualify it before. Questioning Perche, weighing its particulars, was like questioning her own skin. How would she know differently? She considered Paris: vile, rotten, corrupt, filthy, sly, dangerous, Paris. Measured against this yardstick, she delivered her answer with great conviction. "Yes. A far, far better place than Paris. Perche is quite probably the nicest place in all the world."

Madeleine nodded. "I thought so. Anyone as thick as you must have been raised up in a fairytale, swaddled in silk and fine manners."

Although Madeleine said the words without rancor, Jeanne felt their sting. She said, "I know a good deal about the world. My father's library is one of the best in the land. I myself have read dozens of the volumes, more if you consider that some were collections."

With that, the snarling girl from the bedstead next to her sat up, glaring. "If you'd like to stay in this world, you had better seal your lips or I'll seal them for you!"

Madeleine whispered, "Come. It is a fine summer day. We will go out to the yard."

"You mean, we can come and go as we please?"

"Of course, silly. This isn't a prison."

****

La Salpêtrière was only in part a jail. The insane were confined to the wretched ward from which Jeanne had only newly found release. A tide of Paris' destitute citizens drifted in and out of La Salpêtrière, their ebb and flow dictated by the weather and the vagaries of their individual fates.

Jeanne and Madeleine walked through a series of courtyards laid out one after the other like a giant's lattice.

Madeleine pointed. "You see that there?" A chapel was under construction in the middle of an open space, one Jeanne remembered seeing after being dropped off by the duplicitous Monsieur Couret. "This is a place of prayer ordered by King Louis himself. If that sounds nice, it's not. You see, this way we don't have to mix with the general population of Paris when we want to worship. One of the old knitters at the laundry told me La Salpêtrière was like a royal carpet. Underneath it, the king sweeps the dirt of humanity. The unwanted. The poor. The cuckoos. That lady knew what she was talking about."

"Yet you can leave when you wish? And enter on your own volition?" After being locked up, the notion was unfathomable.

Madeleine nodded. "Knitters and jewels can and do. Angels are more or less stuck here until they're ripe enough. After all, they have nowhere else to go." Madeleine read the question on Jeanne's face and explained: "Knitters are the old ladies still capable of work. Angels are the child orphans and jewels are like us. Although why they call us jewels, I don't know. We're only treasured for our ability to toil at the laundry or the bakehouse, a condition for getting our daily rations at this great house of alms."

"When I was brought here, why did they incarcerate me? Why was I not placed with the rest of the jewels?"

"You came with a wild story, and they thought you were a cuckoo. There are rewards for bringing cuckoos to La Salpêtrière, you know." Jeanne recalled the gentle face of Madame Couret, and the wound of the lady's betrayal opened again in her heart.

"In the infirmary there were men."

"There is a section for men in the same categories as the women. The mad, the orphaned. Some young men our age, but not as many."

Jeanne said, "How is it that you came here?"

"I told you. I don't have a family."

"Everyone has a family."

"Well then, mine sure was rotten. Or I was a bad apple, because I was dumped on a trash heap outside the churchyard of Saint Madeleine, which is how I got my name. It could have been worse," she said. "I could have been dumped outside Saint Eustache. I can't picture being called that."

"I never knew my own mother. She died after I was born. Yet I have seen her face in a painting and feel I know her from my father's stories."

"There are times when I'm at Les Halles, when the market is crowded, and I search the faces, looking to see if one looks like mine. When I was little, I followed a beautiful lady, dreaming she could be my mother. At first she thought I was cute, and she laughed and called me a funny little monkey. Then I followed her home and told her in front of her husband that I belonged to her. The husband threw me off the premises so hard, I landed face down on the cobblestones, so I didn't think he could be my father. At least I hoped not. Anyway, I've lived here in this dump on and off for a few seasons."

"How do you manage?"

"I'm like a cat. I purr when it serves me but keep my claws sharp." With that, Madeleine drew her blade from underneath her skirt. "You would be smart to get one yourself."

"I have no need for protection, only to reunite with my aunt." Jeanne stopped, stooping to adjust a strap she had tied around her broken shoe. "If I can leave when I wish, then I must make haste." She stood and put one hand on Madeleine's shoulder. "You have already done me the greatest service one person can do for another. Yet I must ask you for one more. Take me to the palace."

"Now? The sun is only just over the horizon."

"It is late by another measure." In the chaos of her confinement, she had lost track of the exact count, but reckoned it to be close to twenty days since the night she plunged into the Seine.

"We can't just march up to the gates and say, 'Let us in.'"

"Perhaps not. But I have to try. Please, I beg you, just take me there."

"If we leave now, I'll be late to the bakehouse and won't receive my rations."

"I will remunerate you tenfold if you help me." Madeleine appeared confused by her choice of words. "Pay you. I will pay you handsomely." She placed her hand over her heart. "I swear to it."

"You don't speak like a cuckoo. You don't act like one. But you are a queer little bird anyway. Come. If we walk quickly, I can still make it back here for an afternoon shift and be," she said the word clumsily, "'remunerated' with supper."

****

Even at a distance, as they walked across the Pont Neuf, the profile of the Palais Louvre could be seen clearly, so grand were its features. If La Salpêtrière could swallow ten Mursays in its girth, the palace could consume another twenty.

Jeanne stopped on the bridge and stared. "It is magnificent. Zeus's Olympia! Like the temple of all the gods in one! Have you ever seen anything so glorious? Are you not awestruck?"

"Awestruck?" Madeleine barely glanced at the wonder that lay before them. "Never really thought about it. It's just always been there."

As they approached the palace, Jeanne replayed in her mind's eye the reunion with her aunt. There would be astonishment, tears, but above all unbridled joy at her safe recovery. Before the gilded palace gates stood two sentries with more soldiers milling about the perimeter.

Jeanne approached them, addressing the one with the kinder-looking face. "Excuse me. My name is Mademoiselle Jeanne Denot, daughter of Antoine Denot, a Maréchal de Camp for the king's army."

Jeanne waited for some acknowledgement. A short bow would have sufficed but given her slovenly appearance, none came. Instead, the sentries gazed at them in a manner most insolent and provocative. She braced herself for their disbelief.

The one with the more forbidding expression spoke. "What's your business?"

"I'm here to see the Marquise de Vitré. I am her niece. I believe her to be in residence at the palace."

The sentry, not much older than Jeanne, and puffed up with his own importance said, "And I'm the king's bastard son!"

Madeleine said, "That explains your plumb position."

His cohort burst forth with a great guffaw, slapping his thigh and calling out, "Touché, mademoiselle! She stung you there, André."

This had the effect of infuriating the pompous

guard who turned a shade of red that rivaled the color of his coat. "You would be wise to keep your smart comments to yourself, mademoiselle. We have the authority to arrest anyone affronting His Majesty on these premises!"

Jeanne held up her hands to beseech the guard. "Please, we do not seek trouble. I only wish to see my aunt."

The friendlier of the two men said, "Understand, mademoiselle, we cannot very well escort you two lovelies into the palace without so much as an invitation, or proof of your claim. If we did, every ragtag miscreant, no offence, could do so." The man cupped a hand to the side of his face as if sharing a great confidence. "It has happened before that the public got inside, all the way to the king's bedroom. That is why the gates are higher, the protocol stricter. King Louis loves his subjects with all his heart but prefers a cordial distance and a girding of iron between him and them."

Jeanne tried a new approach. "Could you pass a note to someone inside asking them to consider my plight?"

André, the humorless guard, shook his head no. "I won't stick my neck out for the likes of these two."

The more companionable one winked. "Step inside the guardhouse, ladies."

Jeanne considered any number of messages to compose, but in the end, she kept the note short:

"I am Jeanne Denot, niece of the Marquise de Vitré. Through a series of unfortunate occurrences, I have been separated from her and held at La Salpêtrière. Only now have I been at liberty to seek her.

If she is in residence, please summon her to the gate with the greatest possible speed!"

Jeanne handed the note to the guard whose eyes trained on Madeleine. He said, "I'll deliver this to a footman who can then seek out one of the ladies in waiting. You won't disappear now, will you?" He directed the question toward Madeleine.

"Of course not!" Jeanne said curtly, then softened her tone. Best to keep their new friend buttered up. "What is your name, monsieur?"

His gaze fleetingly lit on Jeanne then returned greedily to Madeleine, like a bee seeking the sweetest nectar. "Tristan, like the skillful lover from the story."

Jeanne colored but Madeleine laughed in delight, which seemed to please Tristan. "I shall return!" he said with a courtly bow, as if his mission required crossing a mountain pass instead of a courtyard.

Madeleine clasped her hands over her breast. "My hero!" she called out.

They watched through the window of the guardhouse as Tristan strutted like a peacock toward the palace, his pompous gait performed for an audience of one.

Out of earshot from the guards, Madeleine sighed, "Why are men such buffoons?"

"Buffoons? I thought he pleased you to the fullest. You seemed entirely captivated by his silliness."

"Hardly! Pluck the right string, tickle a few keys and you can play them for your own purposes. To be pleased by one? Not likely!"

Tristan made good on his word and returned to the guardhouse within a quarter of an hour.

"My lovelies," he said to Madeleine. "I have

successfully delivered the note. Now we await the next move."

Upon arriving at the palace, the bells of Saint-Germain L'Auxerrois had struck seven times. At the stroke of nine bells, Jeanne and Madeleine remained captive outside the guardhouse, watching Tristan perform for Madeleine. As romantic protagonist, he regularly tossed out a bon mot or an amorous look. In his role of fearless hero, he made a great show of berating a hapless vagrant who wandered too close to the gates.

To think of her aunt only yards away after all these days made Jeanne nearly mad with frustration. She wanted to charge the gates and rush to one of the great portals demanding for her Aunt Mimi to be summoned.

"Steady now," Madeleine said, taking hold of one of Jeanne's hands. Jeanne had been wringing her plain-hewn dress so tightly a hole had formed in the cloth.

Tears formed in Jeanne's eyes. "Why do they take so long? How can we trust this fool isn't playing a charade? Pretending he delivered the note to keep you captive? I shall ask him!" They sat on a patch of grass in sight of the gates. Jeanne made to stand, but Madeleine stayed her with a gesture.

"He did deliver the note."

"How can you be so certain?"

"He fancies himself to be a white knight and he doesn't want to disappoint," Madeleine said. "Hold tight. I do hope something happens soon though. I could eat a horse. Are you not hungry?"

Locked away in the cuckoo ward, her hunger had manifested in visions of sumptuous banquets laden with meats, pies, and cakes. The visions produced a searing pain emanating from her stomach and radiating outward, invading every part of her body. Yet after weeks of near starvation, the frenetic desire quieted. Now hunger made itself known through a few muted pangs, weak chords barely registering on her consciousness. When had she last eaten? A day ago? Longer? She was so starved she was no longer hungry.

"I suppose I should eat," she said more to herself than to Madeleine.

A moment later Tristan appeared. "I could not help but overhear you. Take this bread and I shall fetch a little cheese and wine."

They consumed every morsel of food Tristan offered and Jeanne found herself restored in spirit, although anxious for some sign of acknowledgement from the palace. As the clock struck ten, it arrived in the form of a pageboy who seemed confused as to which guard to deliver the note. Tristan made the choice clear by jumping up and snatching it out of the boy's hands.

"For you, mademoiselle." Tristan handed the note to Jeanne.

It read, "The Marquise de Vitré has not been separated from her kin. Furthermore, she fails to see the humor in this mischief." The handwriting was not her aunt's.

Madeleine said, "What does it say?"

Jeanne gave it to Madeleine who shook her head. "I am not lettered."

Jeanne read it aloud. "It's not possible. Whoever wrote this has not spoken with my aunt."

"How do you know? Why would they lie?"

Jeanne paced before the gates. "Maybe the priest

has something to do with it. Perhaps he intercepted the note."

"Who did you give the note to, handsome?" Madeleine asked the guard.

Tristan said, "To the very same page who just left."

"That boy still wet behind the ears?" Jeanne asked. "He has misdirected my communiqué. Summon him back."

"My, but the lady has a regal way of commanding servitude." Tristan performed a mocking bow. "May I remind you, Mademoiselle Rags, who is in charge here? Me! That's who. It is I who let you loiter here when it is expressly forbidden to do so. I was the one what arranged the supplies for your note, those supplies belonging to King Louis himself. Furthermore, I shared my food rations even though I got five mouths to feed in addition to my own! I issue the commands here!"

Madeleine said, "Tristan, we are only too aware and too impressed by your authority." She reached out to take one of his hands and placed it against her bosom. "Can you feel how my heart pounds in fear and excitement at your power? Why, we're as defenseless as baby chicks."

Tristan tipped his head back and closed his eyes. "Yes. I feel it."

"The sensation would be even more clearly felt if it weren't for the barrier of my dress." Madeleine stepped away from the guard. His arm remained erect. "Shall I meet you after your watch so you can feel yourself my true emotions?"

Tristan nodded, answering in the affirmative with a groan. Jeanne fought the desire to upbraid him for taking advantage, but with the way her new friend was behaving, she felt uncertain as to who took advantage of whom.

Jeanne spoke softly, slowly. "For now, we must make another try. The first note has gone astray. Fallen into the wrong hands through no fault of your own, of course, good sir."

Jeanne quieted the tremor in her hand before composing a fresh missive:

"There is no mischief played by these words. I am Jeanne Denot, the same person who was pushed off the side of a vessel while journeying to the palace. After reaching Paris, I found myself incarcerated, mistaken for mad. My story defies belief but is factual. Please summon the Marquise de Vitré to the gate. I can prove beyond any shadow of doubt the veracity of my statements. Signed, Jeanne Denot."

The new note was dispatched. Within the space of an hour, a remarkable-looking young woman materialized at one of the portals and began making her way toward the gates. She had the appearance of a walking confection, a sugar stick the likes of which Jeanne ate as a child. She wore a frothy white wig as tall as a footstool and a dress in a garish shade of pink. She teetered across the courtyard in heeled shoes so high they left a considerable gap between the hem of her gown and the cobblestones below.

It took the young woman some time to reach them. When she did, she panted with the effort. Up close, her face could almost be considered pretty, except her eyes were too close together. She squinted toward Jeanne and Madeleine which did nothing to improve her looks. "Which one of these claims to be family to the Marquise de Vitré?" she addressed Tristan.

Before he could answer, Jeanne stepped forward. "It is I."

The lady drew nearer to Jeanne cautiously, the way one would a mongrel on the street. "You look like a haystack! Yet we are to believe you are the daughter of a marquise?"

Jeanne contemplated slapping the preposterous-looking ninny. Instead she straightened her posture, hoping her bearing would speak louder than her disreputable appearance. "I do not claim to be her daughter. I am her niece!"

"Oh." The girl frowned. "I understood it to be the daughter. One Francoise. With blonde locks and eyes the color of the sky above. A description that does not match you in the least."

"Francoise de Vitré is my cousin. Your words draw a clear picture of her. I am Jeanne Denot."

"Yet you are not Francoise."

Madeleine said, "No. Are you thick?" Then murmured to Jeanne, "Talking to this idiot is like talking to a parrot."

The parrot got its fine feathers ruffled at Madeleine's words. She turned abruptly and began to hobble away. Jeanne called out, "Please, my lady, where is the note I've written? If you read it, you will see yourself I do not claim to be Francoise, who is, in actual fact, my cousin!"

The girl turned with a sigh. "I know nothing of a note. The marquise herself asked me to come to the gate to verify this foolishness."

"The Marquise de Vitré? She is here? In the palace?"

"Yes, you dolt. If she were not, how could she have

sent me?"

Impossible. If her aunt had seen the note, she would be here herself. "It cannot be her. What shade of hair has she?"

"A reddish brown. That is more than I should reveal to the likes of you. If you are who you claim, you would have known that particular fact."

"I do know it. I am only testing that it is really she."

"Outrageous! You question her authenticity when you are the fake! It is wicked of you to pretend and play on her nerves so."

"I know the king recently had a ball to celebrate the newest ballet of Lully. A ball I should have attended."

"Everyone knows the King favors the artistry of Lully. I have had enough of this charade."

"Wait," Jeanne called out. "Before you take leave, tell my aunt to reconsider the truth of my words. She will find me at La Salpêtrière."

The girl laughed. "The king's madhouse? Asylum for whores and orphans?"

Madeleine clenched her fists and made to advance on the girl, but Jeanne stayed her.

"I beg of you. Relate the message. What harm could it bring you? Please."

The girl squinted again as if to sharpen the focus of both her gaze and her thoughts. At last she said, "So be it. I will tell her. Only to add the last ridiculous brushstroke to the absurdity of this scene." With that she teetered back to the palace. They watched her retreat until her bright pink form disappeared inside.

Jeanne hung on the gates until the surly guard

ordered her to step back. She scanned the endless rows of windows hoping to catch a glimpse of her aunt in one of them. Thousands of souls occupied the palace. Not one was visible.

Chapter Twenty-Six

"Bachelors were especially persecuted in an attempt to induce them to marry early. They were forbidden to hunt, fish, trade with the Indians or go into the woods under any pretext for fear they would take up the life of a coureur de bois."

~*King's Daughters and Founding Mothers,*
Peter Gagné

The *Saint Anne*

Jeanne tended to Jacques from first light to sundown, noting the dreadful symptoms that came in an all too familiar pattern: High fever announced the arrival of the disease, followed by pustules that formed around his neck and across his back. With the help of Madeleine and Teeth, Jeanne applied poultices to absorb the infestation, holding the weeping wounds at bay.

Toward suppertime, Madeleine urged Jeanne to take her meal and rest a while. "You can't help him if you're wrung out like a dishrag. Besides, he won't mark the difference."

Jeanne knelt at Jacques' bedside, holding his hand. As listless as he was, every few moments she could detect just the slightest movement, an almost imperceptible pressure as if he tried to squeeze her hand. "No. He is aware of my presence. What will he think if I take leave of him now?"

Teeth knelt beside Jeanne. "I'll hold his hand while you're away. My own is as rough as a cat's tongue, but it'll do in a pinch. Now go. Madeleine, accompany her. Be sure she gets some eats."

When both Madeleine and Jeanne hesitated, Teeth nearly shouted, "Look at him! He's as insensible as a sleeping babe. Off with you. I will see to him."

Outside the cabin door, Madeleine said, "She's a funny one, Teeth is. Tough as leather outside. Soft as a feather inside." After supper, making their way back to Jacques' cabin, they were stopped as they passed the demoiselles' quarters by Nettie.

"Mademoiselle Davide, may I have a word?" From within the demoiselles' quarters, Jeanne heard someone wailing and feared a new girl had been called to their Maker.

"Good Lord, now what?" Madeleine said.

"You must help us!" Nettie took Jeanne's hand to draw her into the room where Marie-Louise de Grancey had collapsed on her bedstead, sobbing with abandon. Her friends tried to comfort her to no avail. Nettie said, "We are at sixes and sevens. We know not the whereabouts of Madame La Plante."

"What do you mean, you dolt?" Madeleine quipped. "This is a ship. Do you imagine she's on a carriage ride in the forest?"

"We have not seen her since morning repast!" Nettie said. Jeanne had been too preoccupied to notice, but now realized it to be true. Madame's ubiquitous presence had been absent all day. "Throughout the voyage, she has been separated from us only when stricken by the pox."

"There must be an explanation," Jeanne said.

Overhearing Jeanne's words, Marie-Louise sat up. "Oh, but there is one! And such a terrible explanation it is, mademoiselle!" She then commenced wailing and moaning with renewed vigor.

"God's nightgown! Can one of you shut her up?" Madeleine said.

"We have tried, mademoiselle," Nettie said. "She is beyond comfort. You see, she claims that Madame La Plante has passed to the other side."

Eager to return to Jacques, Jeanne fought her impatience with the bubble-headed demoiselles. "The other side of the ship?" she asked.

Nettie dropped her voice to a whisper. "No. Marie-Louise believes Madame La Plante is a ghost."

Nettie's words inspired a hoot of laughter from Madeleine. "You ladies have fertile imaginations. Or maybe it's indigestion. Madame is a ghoul, but she's no ghost."

Marie-Louise brushed tears off her mottled face and hiccupped out the words: "This is no flight of fancy, I assure you. No jest. I saw her with my own eyes as real as you are to me."

"What of it?" Madeleine said. "You saw Madame. Tell us where and we will locate her and put an end to your theatrics."

"There," Marie-Louise pointed toward an open porthole. "That is where I saw her. Her face as white as flour! Oh, how horrible to behold!"

Jeanne addressed Marie-Louise calmly, hoping to assuage her agitation. "Before then, when did you last see Madame?"

"This morning. She led us in prayers, accompanied us to breakfast then mentioned she had business with the captain." Louise managed to deliver this information calmly enough but was presently overcome and began quivering anew. "I swear it is the truth. She hung upside down. Her eyes staring. They bored into my own. Her mouth gaped as if in mid-scream. I myself cried out and a moment later she vanished."

Madeleine snorted. "Now you claim she hung upside down like a bat? What nonsense is this?"

Madeleine's consternation excited a fresh outpouring of tears from Louise.

Jeanne said, "We will inform the captain of Madame La Plante's—" she hesitated, at a loss for how to characterize this turn of events, "—absence. In the meantime, you are upsetting your companions." Jeanne placed her hands on the girl's shoulders. "You must marshal your faculties. You've been strong enough to endure this wretched trip day in and day out all these weeks? You can be strong now, can't you?"

The comment appeared to make a change in the girl. She drew back her shoulders. After a while her breathe became even.

"Good girl," Jeanne said.

As she turned to leave, Nettie said pitifully, "Mademoiselle, can you not sleep in our quarters tonight? We are afraid of the dark without Madame La Plante and even more frightened should the good lady turn up at the porthole again."

They were such ninnies, these girls. Yet it was futile to chastise them. Jeanne had to return to Jacques. "It is not possible. There are more important matters I must attend to. I shall send Teeth. There is nothing in this world or the next that frightens her."

****

The captain called for a thorough search of the ship beginning in the deepest supply holds and progressing upward until every cabin and hold of the *Saint Anne* was examined for signs of Madame La Plante.

Jacques' condition had improved over the last hours. He remained insensible but appeared to be struggling to the surface of consciousness. His body moved the way one does under the spell of a dream: his arms and legs twitched and flailed like a marionette on strings that are pulled too roughly. As late afternoon turned to night, Jeanne fashioned a bed of sorts on the floor so she could stay by his side. A knock on the door sounded as Madeleine prepared to take leave. Upon opening it, they were met with the captain and two of his men.

"You have come to search Monsieur Suprenant's quarters?" Madeleine said. "There is not much to see. Only Mademoiselle Davide and I tending to Monsieur Suprenant." She gestured toward the bedstead.

"Beg your pardon. Of course. For the sake of scrupulousness, I felt it proper to at least stop by. Are there signs of improvement?"

"Yes." Jeanne said. "The fever has cooled."

The captain nodded. "With the winds as they are now, we will drop anchor in New France the day after tomorrow. If all goes well, Monsieur Suprenant will depart this vessel of his own volition."

Madeleine asked, "Have you found Madame La Plante?"

"It is the queerest thing. She appears to have vanished entirely. We have only my quarters and the upper deck to search, and we've found no sign of her beyond her personal effects which are quite unmolested. Did either of you notice anything amiss about her? Did she say anything of any significance that could explain her disappearance?"

Jeanne recalled her conversation with Madame about leaving the king's service. "She did intimate this would be her final voyage. She intended to join a convent upon returning to France."

"Could she have been so despondent over her future as to have cast herself overboard?" The captain asked the question aloud in the manner of someone weighing any and all possibilities. Then added, "With the strength of her faith, it is difficult to believe she would have taken her own life. Well, I bid you adieu, mademoiselles. There are a few more nooks and crannies to search."

****

The next morning, Madeleine came to Jacques' quarters and woke Jeanne with news. "At breakfast the captain confirmed it: There are no signs of Madame La Plante. She has vanished."

"Not vanished. She went overboard."

Madeleine raised an eyebrow. "What? What of her great devotion to God?"

"No. It is monstrous to say but say it I must. I believe she was thrown overboard."

"Who would do that?" Madeleine asked, then answered her own question a moment later in a whisper. "Teeth."

"Consider it: Marie-Louise said she saw Madame hanging upside down, hovering. The porthole to this cabin is directly over that of the demoiselles' quarters."

"Teeth hated the old hag, God rest her soul, but enough to kill her?"

"I've been thinking about it: What if there were some violent altercation while we were out? He would have been unaware of it." She gestured toward the unconscious form of Jacques. "Remember the handprint on Elisabeth's face?" Madeleine nodded. "Perhaps the girl tried to intercede."

"If word gets out about this, they will hang Teeth as soon as we reach New France."

"If she did what we think, she should be punished."

"But we don't know what happened. Maybe the old lady provoked her. It could have been justified."

"Murder? Justified?"

"Why do you take that tone with me, my friend? Have you forgotten the churchyard already?"

At that moment Jacques called out weakly, "Jeanne."

Jeanne rushed to his side. His eyes fluttered open. "Is it you, my beautiful Jeanne?"

"Yes." She said through tears. "I am here."

"Stay with me," he said weakly. "Do not leave."

She kissed his forehead. "Your fever is gone."

He brushed his hand against hers, as if wanting to grasp it. He whispered something and Jeanne leaned closer to catch his words. "Stay with me forever," he said.

Chapter Twenty-Seven

"Hope says to us constantly, 'Go on, go on…'"
~*Francoise D'Aubigné, Second Wife
of King Louis XIV*

La Salpêtrière

Back at La Salpêtrière, Jeanne lamented the day's events. "What sort of chicanery is this? I am prevented from seeing my aunt? She is in the palace, yet upon seeing my own lettering, seeing the account of true events, she refuses to acknowledge me? I can't believe it. And all this while I have imagined her searching desperately for me."

Madeleine had managed to get servings of bread and cheese for both of them, how, Jeanne didn't dare ask. She made an effort to eat slowly, with decorum, even as the women around them dug into their food like spring pigs at a trough.

"Wha if iis trah?" Madeleine spoke with so much food in her mouth, Jeanne couldn't distinguish a word. Madeleine took a swig of water, wiped the back of her mouth with her skirt and said more clearly. 'What if it is the truth?'"

"What if what is the truth?"

"Your aunt is in the palace and read the note."

Jeanne found herself void of a response. It simply

could not be so.

Madeleine again spoke through her chewing, "My question is this: Does your aunt have anything to gain by your disappearance?"

Before Jeanne could arrest the word, it issued forth. "Yes."

"Ah ha!" Madeleine said. "Now we have found a more fruitful path than circling round and round the *how*. The *why* is the more interesting question."

A commotion broke out on the other end of the dining hall, a squabble over portions from the sound of it. Shrieking accusations of, "It's mine, you ape!" could be heard echoing over the heads of the hundred or so women crowded into a hall built for half that number.

Noise of the fight grew so loud Jeanne had to raise her voice to a near shout. "Without me, my aunt would inherit my father's land, his funds." The cacophony subsided as quickly as it broke out and Jeanne found herself yelling, "She stands to gain his entire fortune!" She lowered her voice to a near whisper. "Everything. Without me, my Aunt Mimi inherits everything."

Madeleine arched an eyebrow. "Everything? Is that all? In short, she has more than enough reason to claim you're not who you say. Maybe she told everyone that you, and what was the name of your cousin? The one who had her face eaten?"

"Francoise."

"Maybe she told them you and Francoise both suffered a condition that prevented you from coming to the palace. But she decided to carry through on the visit anyway accompanied by the no-good priest. A tidy little tale no one would question."

As much as Jeanne's mind rebelled against

Madeleine's reckoning, it followed a reasonable path. Why else would her aunt refuse to see her?

"What of Francoise? The servants? They will surely note my absence."

"Easy. She cooks up another story for them. You fell out of the boat. Drowned in the Seine. She searched desperately. Came back from Paris alone to grieve your loss, healing her wounded heart with the help of your father's fortune. She would only need the priest to back up her tale."

Jeanne stared dumbfounded at her friend's perspicacity. "I happened upon them in the woods on the journey to Paris. They were—" Jeanne struggled to put into words the licentious tableau she witnessed not more than a month ago.

"You caught them in a tumble?" Madeleine suggested.

Jeanne nodded.

"God's nightgown! More than reason enough to lie."

Jeanne cried, silent tears at first, leaking out from twin springs of betrayal and despair. After a moment her sobs gained momentum, pouring forth in torrents so strong, Madeleine hustled her away from the curious glances of their dining companions.

****

The bakehouse at La Salpêtrière was the size of the grand ballroom at Mursay and held an oven as big as a giant's. It belched out an aroma of yeast that permeated every courtyard, stairwell and dormitory, exciting the appetites of the already half-starved denizens of the wards. Upon entering it, one confronted a heat so ferocious it took on a near-solid presence. On her first day working there, Jeanne hesitated at the threshold: She stretched out her hand to be sure her flesh could withstand the hellishness inside. Each shift, at least one of the women became overcome by the heat and had to be dragged out and revived, only to be sent back in.

Despite the sweltering conditions, Jeanne thought the bakehouse preferable to the laundry. There they scrubbed every manner of human filth from the linens of La Salpêtrière and its environs. The only clean work involved the dying vats. Those who worked the vats were easy to spot. Their flesh was mottled with hues of black, green or blue that took weeks to fade away. One poor soul, a knitter who had worked for untold years, had arms the color of a frog.

Madeleine and Jeanne stood side by side next to a line of girls kneading dough on a table twice the length of the dining table at Mursay. Jeanne had never had to touch food before, except to deliver it to her mouth and imagined the sensation would not be entirely unpleasant if done on a much smaller scale. One loaf, perhaps two. By sunrise she had already formed countless loaves of bread. As she and the other angels and knitters worked the dough, rolling it and pounding it until it reached a satisfactory consistency, her body felt as if it had suffered from a similar process, but instead of becoming more malleable, she stiffened from the pain that travelled from her arms up to her shoulders, spreading down her back and legs.

She perspired so heavily, flecks of her own sweat mixed with the dough. Aunt Mimi had scolded her and Francoise more times than she could count, "Ladies do not mist. That's for servants and animals." Mortified at her body's betrayal, she wiped dew from her brow but failed to keep pace with the prodigious quantities her body produced. Presently she noticed that the other girls perspired just as heavily, if not more, wetting the dough liberally with the liquid yield of their bodies.

Madeleine appeared unaffected by the drudgery of the bakehouse and prattled away on a variety of concerns: from the merits of other girls working the line, to the specific advantages of markets around the city, and finally to news that had provoked considerable gossip among the angels.

Madeleine said, "The official who set up camp here is looking for girls to be married."

"He has come here to find a wife?" Jeanne, distracted by her own thoughts, found it difficult to care about a man looking to marry. It had been two days since their attempt to get word to her aunt. Although no longer held under lock and key, Jeanne was nevertheless imprisoned. Her only other recourse was to make her way back to Perche, which required transport.

"He is not looking for a wife. The king is."

"The king seeks a bride in La Salpêtrière? He is already married."

Jeanne's question caused the girls nearby to break out into fits of laughter.

"Yes. He has found Queen Maria Theresa quite lacking and will return her to Spain." Madeleine replied. "No! Have you not followed a word? The king seeks women who will go to the new territory and marry soldiers there and settle the land. The women will be paid fifty livres. A fortune! More money than everyone in this bakery put together has ever held."

One of the girls on the line asked Madeleine a question while Jeanne's own thoughts returned to puzzling out how to get transport to Perche.

Madeleine had asked her something and awaited a response. She snapped her fingers before Jeanne's eyes. "Will you answer, or shall I ask someone else?"

"Pardon. What should I ask?"

"Your body is here, but your brain has packed up and left. Still considering how to get through to your treacherous auntie?"

Jeanne shook her head. "No. It is of no use. She either will not or cannot see me."

Madeleine scoffed at Jeanne's suggestion and pounded at the doughy lump beneath her hands. "You think the priest is somehow steering her hand? Forcing her to act this way?"

Jeanne said nothing. She knew Madeleine believed both Father Dieudonné and her aunt to be in commerce with the Devil. But Jeanne refused to believe it.

"I must go to Perche. To Mursay. My cousin Francoise, the servants, the people of the village, they will vouch for me. The question is how to get there. Do you know of anyone who could provide me transport?"

"I may. There's a certain young man, a braggart to be sure, who told me tales of a four-in-hand he drives on the king's business. He may be mounting his station on a pin, but I can ask him."

A wave of hope filled Jeanne, causing her momentarily to forget her physical agony. "Where would I find him? I need to speak with him! If he could take me there with the promise of payment when we reached Mursay, I would offer him double his usual fee."

Madeleine held up her flour-coated hands. "Whoa. You have already galloped halfway to Perche, and I don't know if he has the means to take you past the Seine."

"You must bring him to me directly! Today. Now."

"Your highness." Madeleine performed an obsequious curtsy. "Your every wish is my command." When Jeanne failed to laugh at her little joke, Madeleine added testily, "All of this running around on your errands is costing me my daily bread."

"Forgive me. You have my deepest gratitude for all you have done for me." They returned to their work, yet it took some time for Madeleine's icy temperament to thaw in the heat of the workroom.

Finally, Madeleine said, "There is a market in La Vau tomorrow. If he is not there, we can leave word for him."

****

Unlike the madhouse, where the routines of the day were regimented to the minute, the dormitories housing the angels, jewels and knitters ran more liberally. The strength of the sun in the sky dictated bedtime. Madeleine taught Jeanne that it was wiser to head to the dormitory well before sunset to claim a bedstead. Arriving too late meant sleeping on the floor in the company of rats.

Settled into bedsteads furthest from the door, most removed from the disturbances of late-night arrivals, they discussed in more detail their plan to strike out for La Vau the following morning. They were deep in their discussion when a faint voice from the far end of the room arose above the din. "Jeanne Denot! Is there someone here by that name? Jeanne Denot! I seek Jeanne Denot!"

Jeanne sat up. The call came from a young girl who

stood at the door on the other side of the attic, her hands cupped around her mouth. "Jeanne Denot! Please make yourself known."

Madeleine's brow knitted. "It is you she calls for. How odd."

In the crawling anthill of activity, the girl now stood on her tiptoes to listen for a responding cry. Jeanne stood on the bed, waving her arms to be noticed over the chaos around her. "Here! Over here!" Something about the urgency of the girl's efforts made Jeanne's heart bound forth. Her legs trembled as she scrambled out of the bedstead to make her way across the length of the room. As Jeanne wove through the crowd of girls, she could hear her name again and again above the chatter. Some of them began to harass the young messenger.

"Your Jeanne Denot doesn't exist." They sneered at her. "Stop your caterwauling, you idiot."

The girl, no older than twelve years of age by the looks of her round face, had turned reluctantly as if to leave when Jeanne rushed toward her. "I am Jeanne Denot."

She rolled her eyes theatrically. "I thought I would never find you in this lot." Sweat stood on her brow, evidence of the temperature in the attic dormitory and of her great exertion.

"Why do you call for me? Have you been sent to find me?"

The girl lifted her skirts to mop her face. "Aye. I was minding my own business, selling wares outside the gates of this place, when the funny-looking man bade me to fetch you. I told him you were unknown to me and that I did not live here. Then he says, 'I cannot very likely barge up there and fetch her myself.' I took him to mean he was of the wrong sex. Then he offered me a tidy sum to venture forth and promised even more coin to return with you in tow."

"A man? To what purpose does he seek me? Is he a priest?"

The girl laughed, revealing a set of teeth so incomplete, Jeanne wondered how she could chew. "I don't think so. Please, mademoiselle. Do follow me so I can collect my reward. I have a number of mouths to feed besides my own."

Jeanne thought of turning back to notify Madeleine. Would Madeleine wish to accompany her? Then they would lose both their beds. Jeanne followed the girl out.

Gloaming had fallen over La Salpêtrière, a sign the race for beds was already lost. Even so, two girls scampered past them, a blur in the fading light, hurrying toward the entrance of the dormitory. In their absence, the courtyard stood completely still, devoid of any other occupants, or so Jeanne thought at first.

She began to ask, "Where is this man?" when she spied someone leaning against a tree in the middle of the courtyard.

The girl rushed toward him, pointing toward Jeanne. "This is her! I did it! I'll take my payment now."

Jeanne heard the noise of at least a few coins falling into the girl's hands. A handsome reward for so small a chore. Without so much as an adieu, the girl disappeared, and Jeanne found herself alone with the stranger.

As Jeanne drew closer, she could make out his

face. The skin on one side, scarred and lumpy, looked like the melted paraffin of a wind-blown candle. The other half of his face was unblemished, handsome even. Like the masks of tragedy and comedy fused together into a single form. As if to compensate for his disfigurement, the man held himself with a studied insouciance.

Jeanne mustered the courage to ask, "Who are you? Why have you gone to such great lengths to summon me here under nightfall?"

The man held up his hands. "Patience, my dear girl. All will be revealed in a moment. But first, I've been instructed to confirm your identity."

"Confirm my identity? I have no idea who you are."

The man straightened, delivering a short bow. "Mademoiselle Denot. I am Monsieur Arnold, your humble servant, or rather the humble servant of your aunt, the marquise."

At the connection of her own name with that of her aunt's, at the recognition of their consanguinity by any soul, even this stranger, Jeanne's heart bounded, bumping against her breast like a bird attempting to escape a cage.

She struggled to contain her emotions. "My aunt? Where is she? Has she sent you to collect me?"

"Shush." He put a finger to his divided mouth. "You must first pass the test. Tell me, what was the name of your most treasured childhood doll?"

"Agnes," she said. Her answer seemed to satisfy the man because he nodded. "Take me to my aunt at once."

"Calm yourself. We mustn't draw unwelcome

attention." He produced a letter from inside his coat and before he had even fully extended his arm, Jeanne grabbed it.

Dearest Jeanne,

For reasons I am too fearful to explain in writing, I could not own my connection to you when you presented yourself at the palace. Fear not. We will be reunited soon enough, darling girl. At that moment all will be made right again. I have arranged passage for both of us in secret to Perche. You must not breathe a word of this to another soul. Trust in Monsieur Arnold. He is a faithful servant who will help see you to a safe delivery home. As you have now divined, forces are at work that would prevent you from ever returning to Mursay. Signed, your loving aunt.

Monsieur Arnold studied her as she read, as if she were an object to be painted at some later point in time. If they were in polite company, she would have chastised him for his overly familiar gaze. She held her tongue and wondered why fate continued to pair her with such remarkable rescuers: the Hermit, Gabby and Ella, Madeleine, and now this disfigured soul.

"This letter is written in my aunt's hand. Monsieur Arnold, you must take me to her at once!"

Monsieur let out a short giggle. "All in good time, mademoiselle." He composed himself, arranging his uneven countenance into a mask of sobriety. "This is a sensitive matter. Your aunt impressed that upon me. Gave me clear instructions. Said, 'Arnold, tell her to hold her water.' Them were her exact words."

Jeanne doubted her aunt would ever utter such a coarse phrase. She fought the urge to slap the little toad to put him in his place, but instead asked with all the calm she could muster, "Did my aunt offer further instruction beyond this note?"

He grinned and once again seemed on the verge of laughter, relishing his part in the drama. "She did, she did. I have arranged the rendezvous. Meet me tomorrow night and I will take you to her."

"I don't understand. Why can I not go to her directly? Now."

"Patience. All will be revealed tomorrow at the wall of the fountain at the Rue aux Fers. The Church of the Innocent. When the bells ring eleven, she will make herself known. And one more thing that is very important, you must come to the meeting place alone."

****

Back in the dormitory, Madeleine and Jeanne lay on their prized bedsteads, speaking in hushed tones.

"Why meet in the middle of the night? Why at the Rue aux Fers?" Madeleine said.

Jeanne held up the letter, although it had become too dark to make out the words. "She herself feels threatened. That is clear. She's chosen the most obscure, and therefore, the safest place for us to rendezvous."

"But she knows you're in La Salpêtrière. Why not collect you here? Isn't this hellhole an equally unlikely place to meet?"

"She must have her reasons and they must be clear to her even though they elude us. The priest may have powerful friends, and who knows what he is capable of?"

"Murder." Madeleine said the word, and despite the heat of the dormitory, Jeanne shivered. "And you think good old father, what's his name?"

"Dieudonné."

"You think this Dieudonné is the puppet master controlling your aunt? It doesn't make any sense to me. A noble person like her has more pull than a priest. I mean, he's not the Pope, is he?"

Jeanne thought back to the night on the boat. Father Dieudonné could not have presaged her need to be sick. Jeanne said, "He is a man of God, yet still he could not command the skies to storm or the boat to rock."

"No," Madeleine responded. "But if he were sly enough, and on the lookout for the right moment, he could and would take advantage of a situation. Maybe he planned another way of offing you. You know what they say: 'When God closes a door, he opens a window.' Father God's Gift found his window and shoved you through it, making the whole business more convenient and less unsavory for him."

Jeanne considered her friend's words. "What I know for certain is that my aunt is being forced against her will to follow his designs."

Madeleine sat up. "Do you really know that, Jeanne?" In the darkness, Jeanne could not read her friend's expression, but she heard the doubt in her voice clearly enough.

Chapter Twenty-Eight

"There are no secrets that time does not reveal."
~*Jean Racine, Playwright*

La Salpêtrière

Although Monsieur Arnold had instructed her to go alone to meet her aunt, Madeleine insisted on accompanying Jeanne. Knowing first-hand the evil that dwelled in the back alleys of Paris, Jeanne accepted her offer gratefully. They left La Salpêtrière at twilight, and the last rays of sun lit their journey through sinuous streets, across the Seine, and to the appointed meeting place.

By the time they reached the Church of the Innocent and the fountain by which they were instructed by Monsieur Arnold to wait, the darkness of night was absolute. A single streetlamp shone, and they were driven to it like moths to a flame. They stood in the dim circle of light waiting for the sound of eleven bells. On the fountain, built into the wall of the church, bare-breasted nymphs frolicked with cherubs in bas-relief.

"I remember this fountain," Madeleine said. She stepped outside the halo of light and seemed to disappear, her voice coming to Jeanne as if from a specter. "When the king's cortege makes its way to the palace, this fountain is used as a viewing stand for the nobles. When I was a little thing, maybe five or six, I tried to climb it to improve my view. A very fine lady ground her heel into my hand, and I fell and cracked my head on the street. It was the last time I tried to elevate my station in life." She laughed bitterly at the memory.

A shiver ran through Jeanne. "Madeleine?" Silence greeted her call. "Where have you gone? Step back into the light."

"Do you think me a ghost?" Madeleine put on an eerie, high-pitched voice. "Jeanne Denot, I am a visitor from the other side, crawled out of yonder pauper's grave to haunt you!"

"Stop it!" Jeanne stepped out of the light and collided with Madeleine, who had doubled over in a fit of laughter.

Madeleine managed to gasp out, "Oh, but you should have seen your face!"

"How can you cavort like a monkey at a time like this? When my future hangs in the balance? When we stand here, lit like two actors on a stage to be taken advantage of by the nefarious audience of Paris?"

Madeleine straightened herself, adopting a more sober demeanor. "I'm sorry. Truly I am. It's a twist in my nature. At the worst moments, I look for a laugh. Shall we stand under the light again?"

"No. It makes us too conspicuous."

They found a perch on the wall, just outside the ring of light, and waited. The bells of the church began to ring again marking another quarter of an hour. Jeanne stood abruptly, her eyes adjusted to the darkness, and searched the streets for some sign of her aunt.

"The carriage should be here. Why does she make me wait?"

Then she spotted him. Monsieur Arnold. He stood on the opposite end of the Rue aux Fers as still as a post. She called out to him, but he did not move. Was he waiting for her aunt?

"I will go to him," Jeanne said, and without waiting for Madeleine's response, she ran across the darkened street.

"Monsieur Arnold! Did you not hear me?" she yelled.

"Hush. The shrill of your voice attracts too much attention, mademoiselle!"

Jeanne surveyed the street and found it empty. "Attention from whom?" she said. He angled his face, and the murky lighting obscured the ugliness of one side of his flesh. "Where is my aunt?"

"Who are you with? You were instructed to come alone."

"You did not imagine I would come completely alone at this hour."

When Madeleine caught up with them, she had a pronounced limp. "I turned my ankle in the darkness. Who are you?" she asked Monsieur Arnold. "Where is the aunt?"

Jeanne made to respond, but Monsieur Arnold silenced her. "Quiet!" His voice rang out over the empty landscape. He lowered it. "If you had followed instructions, you would be in her arms now. Instead you brought this one," he gestured rudely toward Madeleine, "which has caused her to conceal herself until she can be assured of her safety."

"Her safety?" Madeleine said. "Isn't that rich? We

ventured into the thick of night, two of us alone, kept waiting outside the gates of a cemetery. We're the ones in peril."

"Is she nearby? Does she see us now?" Jeanne peered through the darkness.

Monsieur Arnold sighed in a theatrical manner and Jeanne could smell the fetid odor of his breath. "Yes, and if you can assure me you have no other uninvited friends lurking in the shadows, I will take you to her."

"There is no one save for us," Madeleine said. "Stop playing out these dramas and take us to the good lady."

Monsieur Arnold beckoned them to follow him back to where they first stood outside the walls of the Church of the Innocent. Madeleine, still limping, trailed a few paces behind. Stopping to examine her injured foot, she fell even further back. The man's steps were excruciatingly tentative, as if he were navigating their route arbitrarily. Jeanne wished she could charge ahead and wondered aloud why he couldn't just tell her the location of her aunt, whereupon he hissed, "Patience."

Jeanne felt as if she'd fallen into an unwitting game of cat and mouse and Monsieur Arnold acted the cat. At last they reached a gate, the entrance to the churchyard, and Monsieur Arnold opened it and waited for Jeanne to pass through before him. The high walls veiled the dim source of lamplight outside, but a full moon lit the scene before them. They stood in an ancient churchyard. Jeanne began to call for her aunt. She heard, or rather sensed, a movement behind her. Monsieur Arnold's voice came to her in a rough whisper.

"You'll wake the dead with your shouting, you

mewling bitch."

With that, he shoved her to the ground. Jeanne cried out as Monsieur Arnold knelt on her back, catching hold of her arms, snaring her with such economy she could not move. Madeleine, whose voice came from a considerable distance across the yard, bellowed her name.

Monsieur Arnold rolled her onto her back and sat on her legs. "Do you feel the chill of the blade on your neck, mademoiselle?" Monsieur's voice, so low, so intimate, seemed to emanate from inside her own skull. She nodded. "Make a sound and you will feel it from your insides."

Again, Madeleine called out for Jeanne, and after being met with more silence, she said into the darkness, "I'm tired of this hide-and-seek. If you need me, you'll find me at La Salpêtrière." The gate groaned as it swung shut, and with the sound came the certain knowledge she would be butchered by this two-faced assassin.

"Your friend is wise." Monsieur Arnold's voice had a playful quality.

"There are people who will make you pay for this."

"People have already paid me for this, you silly girl." He laughed, then knelt on her chest, causing her to cry out in pain. "Paid handsomely, in fact. Seems you have become quite an inconvenience to your dear auntie. Not for long though. Not for long."

Terror and pain were now obliterated by her struggle for air. As she hovered on the edge of consciousness, Monsieur Arnold sat back on his heels, and Jeanne managed to fill her lungs. As she did, she saw the glint of the blade in his hand. He raised it above his head, and she rolled away.

"Hold still." Monsieur Arnold landed on top of her, the handsome side of his face deformed by a scowl so fierce, he resembled the Devil himself.

Jeanne thrashed, doing all she could to throw off the aim of his dagger. In the struggle, she became aware of Madeleine who had crept up behind Monsieur Arnold. Jeanne held still, which seemed to surprise him. "There's a good girl," he said, and raised his knife. But before he could lower it, Madeleine made a neat gesture at his throat.

The fiend toppled over, clawing at his neck like someone trying to loosen a cravat. His wound produced a gurgling sound. In the moonlight, his white shirt bloomed black. Jeanne crawled away, her eyes transfixed on the sight of his writhing form as he forfeited his place among the living. After a few moments, he became still.

"I think he's dead," Jeanne said numbly.

"I hope he's dead," Madeleine said, then added, "Get up. Make haste."

They fled the churchyard, making their way through the streets of Paris in the deepest hours of night. Instead of seeking well-traveled routes, as they did on the way to the church, Madeleine sought the most obscure ones. At one turn they happened upon a den of vagrants huddled together, sleeping like a pack of dogs, and were forced to slow their progress, picking their way carefully around the slumbering forms. They arrived at the gates of La Salpêtrière having not exchanged a single word since fleeing the cemetery.

Madeleine spoke: "We must wash before returning. There's a fountain nearby."

A streetlamp illuminated the entrance of the hospital and Jeanne could see Madeleine clearly. She looked no more in need of washing than before they had set out.

"Why?"

Madeleine took hold of Jeanne's hands. "See for yourself."

Her hands, her dress, were covered with Monsieur Arnold's blood.

"God have mercy on us!" Jeanne cried out.

"He did. He gave me a blade and the strength to use it."

"We killed that man."

"I killed him. And he was no man."

"Still, you would not have done it if it weren't for me. We have broken one of the Ten Commandments."

"Stop preaching and collect yourself," Madeleine said, although she too trembled in the heavy night air.

Jeanne sank to her knees on the cobblestones. A palsy of fear passed through her, causing every part of her being to shudder. Her teeth chattered, making it difficult to push words past them. She wrapped her arms around herself and finally managed to say, "I cannot."

"Listen to me, Jeanne Denot." Madeleine knelt beside her. "You must get up. Now. We'll scrub away the mess at yonder fountain. Dispose of your dress. I'll swipe a new one from the laundry. If we do not cover the tracks leading to Monsieur Arnold, we'll find ourselves locked up or swinging from the end of a rope. Do you understand me?"

Jeanne nodded but remained on her knees.

"Forgive me for this, my friend." Madeleine

slapped Jeanne so hard across the face, a ringing of bells sounded in her head. A moment later, nearby church bells tolled two times. "Soon it will be sunrise. Get up."

Madeleine acted as Jeanne's mirror, pointing out spots on her face, neck, and arms that needed scrubbing in the waters of the fountain. Back at La Salpêtrière, Madeleine gained entrance to the laundry as Jeanne waited outside. She emerged moments later with a copy of the light-brown dress to replace the one splattered with blood.

Madeleine took the bloodied garment and hid it under her own dress. "We need to burn this."

Stealing into the dormitory, they found places on the floor and Madeleine fell asleep directly. Jeanne lay with her knees drawn to her chest. She gnawed on her pointer finger, something she had not done since she was a girl. *She paid him to kill me. To make me disappear. What would happen when Aunt Mimi discovered Monsieur Arnold had failed? What, or who, would come next?* The next attempt, for surely there would be a next one, would be easier. *They know where I am.* She had to get out of La Salpêtrière. Leave Paris. Of that she was certain.

Chapter Twenty-Nine

"Pleasure and pain, the good and the bad, are so intermixed that we cannot shun the one without depriving ourselves of the other."
~*Françoise-Athénaïs de Rochechouart de Montespan, Mistress of King Louis XIV*

The *Saint Anne*

A new fever held sway over the passengers of the *Saint Anne*. A delirium that caused the demoiselles to wear rosary beads around their necks and had the mademoiselles arranging their own regular make-shift services when, days before, they could barely tolerate Sunday prayers in the captain's quarters. The madness prompted the sailors to walk wide circles around the female cargo for fear the vaporous form of Madame La Plante would materialize and avenge any impure thought or deed. Madame La Plante, omniscient alive, assumed an even greater influence after her disappearance.

Jeanne tried to ignore the hysteria around her, intent on nursing Jacques back to health. He had gained strength by the hour and on the fourth day of illness he could eat and even converse a little before losing strength and slipping into unconsciousness. When he slept, so did she. She had drifted off and awoke with a startle when Jacques called to her. Jeanne, on the floor next to his bedstead, reached out to hold his hand.

"I'm here," Jeanne said.

"It is so dark," he murmured. Although just after midday, the shuttered portholes allowed only small cracks of sunlight into the cabin.

"Wait." Jeanne opened a porthole to let the sunlight flood Jacques' quarters. He raised a hand to cover his eyes and Jeanne began to close them.

"No. Keep them open. I prefer the light. The living. Seeing you. Except not from so far a distance."

Jeanne returned to his side and knelt next to his bed. She rested her head on his chest and listened to the rhythm of his heart that beat stronger and more steadily now.

"We're nearly there," Jacques said. "I recognize the queer shuddering sensation that happens when sailing in shallow water."

"Captain says we'll be docking by sunup. The land is so close on one side of the ship, if you threw a stone, you'd hit it."

"Well, what do you think of the New World?"

"Nature here seems wilder than in France and somehow bigger. And the air smells gloriously of pine."

He tipped his head back and drew a breath through his nose. "I'm so very happy for you," he said.

"How so?"

"Because now you don't have to bury your nose in my Plutarch."

She laughed then grew serious. "Oh no. Your book. I meant to bring it to you now lest I forget later."

Jacques took hold of her hand. "Keep it and remember me."

She tried to make her voice light. "Do you think I could ever forget you?"

"It is remarkable. I came aboard this ship to go from one point on the map to another. Now I have arrived at an entirely unexpected destination." He kissed her hand.

She smiled at the poetry of his words and wished they could stay like this forever.

Jacques sat up in the bed, wincing as he did so. "Jeanne, the time has come for you to tell me what happened. What road led you to the *Saint Anne*. You must trust me by now to guard your secret."

She got to her feet and paced the cabin as she imparted her story, a narrative with so many turns, she struggled in places to recall details. Francoise and Mimi. Mursay. Her father's death. The journey from Perche and coming upon her aunt and the priest in the woods. Then the voyage on the Seine with Father Dieudonné. Meeting the hermit. Fleeing through the streets of Paris. Her incarceration at La Salpêtrière through the treachery of the sweet-faced Madame Couret. How Madeleine saved her from the false gentleman in the carriage. The night in the cemetery and the killing of the two-faced Monsieur Arnold.

"Now you have it. Everything." She returned to kneel by his bed. "Madeleine has been my guardian angel."

"Yes, a guardian angel of the best sort. One who wields a knife," Jacques said.

"Sometimes I think I'm still here because Papa watches from above and intervenes. He sent Madeleine and then he sent you," she said. "I pray to him the way I used to pray to God. Does that make me a heretic?"

Jacques said, "It makes you a loving daughter to a worthy father. But after hearing your story, I wonder why you can't return to Perche? Your aunt and the priest had the darkest of intentions, there's no doubt of that. But what of your cousin? Surely she'd vouch for you?"

"I don't know if Francoise was caught up in her mother's wicked plans." Jeanne had often wondered about Francoise's sudden case of bedbugs on the day of their departure. "I choose to think not, although I have harbored hateful thoughts for her these months, imagining her occupying a life that is rightfully mine."

"But surely someone within the town or the estate would confirm your identity?"

"They won't stop until I'm dead. Monsieur Arnold made it clear that night in the cemetery. Besides, we killed him, Jacques."

He shook his head. "Madeleine defended you against a murderer intent on taking your life."

"But who would believe a former inmate of the king's madhouse?"

"How did you find your way to the *Saint Anne*?"

"An official came to La Salpêtrière looking for suitable girls as wives. There were certain impediments in the way: I had no proof of baptism. Again, Madeleine saved me, acquiring one from a priest who agreed to falsify my name, changing it from Denot to Davide. Within two days of that night in the churchyard, we were in a carriage and on our way to the harbor at La Rochelle."

"Jeanne, imagine how many ways your story could have ended. Instead, fate threw us together." He opened his arms and again she rested her head on his chest.

Presently, Jacques said, "You know, I've played out a scene many times in my mind since we met. In it I picture a moonlit sky, or a rising sun as backdrop. But here I am, in this diminished state, and can no longer wait for the perfect circumstance to tell you something." His heart began to beat faster, and hers accelerated in kind. "I love you, Jeanne Denot, and the thought of you taking a husband in New France is more than I can bear."

Jeanne held his face in her hands and said, "I love you, too." She climbed into his bed and held him. "I want to stay with you. I want you." She kissed him, then began to cry at the thought of losing him.

He gently caressed away her tears, then their lips met again. Between kisses he moaned, "You're so beautiful."

Jeanne ran her hands over his body, savoring the feel of him, the scent of him. "How will I go on without you?" she whispered.

"You won't," he said. "We'll stay together. You'll tell La Plante you've had a change of heart."

Jeanne sat up abruptly. "Oh, but we cannot," she said.

"We cannot or you will not?"

Jeanne considered how to tell him about what had happened to Madame and decided ignorance would blanket him from any complicity. "Madame La Plante has vanished. Gone."

"From the ship? How?"

"She was found to be missing. The ship has been searched from stem to stern. Nothing else is known of her."

Jacques shook his head as if to clear away the

remnants of a vision. "It's strange. I dreamt of her. It was a nightmare. Teeth was in it, too. Or was it Elisabeth?"

A chill set upon Jeanne and she shivered. "The captain says there will be an inquiry into her disappearance in Quebec."

"You're trembling. Come lie beside me again."

She did so. Holding him in her arms she murmured, "If only we could stay like this forever."

Jacques kissed her softly on the mouth. "But we can. You're not obliged to choose a husband in Quebec straightaway, are you?"

She shook her head. "I heard of one woman who took nearly a year to decide."

"Well then, you need only pretend to consider the candidates and await my return to Quebec in the spring and we will marry."

Jeanne sighed.

"What is it, my love?"

"I feel so foolish saying it aloud."

"I know you to be wise. Considered in everything you do. Say it."

She hesitated again, forming her thoughts into words. "It is only you have never properly proposed to me."

Jacques laughed, then quickly sobered. "Forgive me. We have lived too long without the bounds of propriety." He made to rise, but she put a hand to his chest to stop him.

"What are you doing?" she asked.

Jacques continued to clamber out of the bed, kneeling unsteadily on one knee before her. "Mademoiselle, do you accept my humble offer of matrimony?"

    "Monsieur, I do with all my heart."

Chapter Thirty

"The girls sent to Quebec were housed in the Ursuline Convent, and presented en masse for inspection. The habitants looked them over, 'like cattle'...but the chosen girl, unlike the chosen cow, was free to say, 'no.'"

~*Mother Marie of the Ursulines*

New France

Boarding the *Saint Anne* had been a relatively simple affair. Disembarking required a flurry of activity from every inhabitant onboard. Having caught sight of a crowd of men on shore, the girls primped as best they could. One of the demoiselles had a mirror which she passed from the upper deck to the mademoiselles' quarters below, an act Madame La Plante would have forbidden. There were trunks to be packed and transported topside, causing the passages between decks to clog. All day long, those below heard the thundering of feet from above as the captain and crew readied the *Saint Anne* for her new, albeit temporary, home in the port of Quebec.

With Madame La Plante gone, the captain had asked Jeanne to orchestrate the departure of the girls. She instructed both the mademoiselles and demoiselles to gather on the quarterdeck above, and at the appointed time they stood in the mild autumn sun awaiting the securing of the gangplank. When finally deemed safe for passage, Jeanne saw to it that they disembarked on the shaky bridge with adequate space between them until all gained solid ground.

After they gathered on terra firma, two of the demoiselles fell over directly and had to be helped to their feet, prompting Teeth to comment, "It is dry land. At last the infernal swaying stops and these two ninnies topple over."

Jeanne said, "It is the queerest thing. I, too, feel as if the land is rolling like the sea."

Madeleine, who looked quite pale, held her stomach. "Laurent warned me of this. I think I'm going to be sick."

Teeth stood as straight and as unperturbed as a stone wall. She nodded toward a group of men who had gathered at a polite distance. "Gasp and moan and make fools of yourselves. The men yonder ogle us like a dog ogles a juicy bone." She ran her fingers through her lank hair. "The worse you look, the better I look."

Elisabeth whispered, "Oh how they stare. It is quite rude of them."

"Pay no mind to the distractions around you," Jeanne said, although she too found their gawking impossible to ignore. "We will now proceed on foot to the convent of the Ursulines where we'll be housed until the market is held. We need only await the captain and our escort."

One of the mademoiselles said, "I feel like choice beef that's just been thrown into a lions' cage. They devour us with their eyes."

Teeth laughed. "Liver is more like it in your case."

The mademoiselle responded, "Perhaps I should fetch the hand mirror again. You're not exactly an oil painting yourself."

"Why don't I throw a stick and you can fetch that instead, you scrawny little bitch."

"You have the face of a smacked ass," the girl said and stuck out her tongue for good measure.

"For your sake, I hope the people of New France have poor eyesight," Teeth answered. "If these gentlemen catch sight of the pocks on your complexion, or the lice that frolic in that straw you call hair, you'll be loaded onto the next boat back to France."

"They'll go running at the sight of that black smile of yours. It looks like the pit of Hell."

"Pit of Hell? I will punch every tooth out of your funnel, you crone." Teeth advanced on the girl, tugging her hair sharply. She screamed and returned the injury in kind and in a moment the two of them rolled on the ground, kicking and scratching like a pair of ferine cats. Their commotion caused the men to laugh and jeer, calling out wagers for who would win the fight.

Jeanne clapped her hands and yelled at them to stop, but to no avail. She turned to Madeleine. "What should we do?"

Madeleine shrugged. "Stand well away. They'll either tire themselves out or kill each other."

The mayhem caught the attention of the captain, and with the help of two crewmen, they managed to separate the pugilists. Teeth's nose bled, while her opponent had lost a great chunk of hair and suffered a split lip.

"Ladies! Ladies, please," the captain implored.

After the commotion died down, Jeanne called out

to the assembly, "Come now. Each of you is a Daughter of the King. A representative of France. You need to act accordingly."

When wagons loaded with their possessions were finally ready, Jeanne organized the young women in two rows to make the journey to the convent of the Ursulines on foot. Jeanne led the file alongside the captain. But as they started out, the captain stopped abruptly and signaled for their caravan to halt.

"What is it?" Jeanne asked.

"Madame's record book," he said. "I don't have it. The book is to be registered with the officials of the king. Mademoiselle Davide, do you know where it could be?"

"No, sir. But I'm sure she kept it in the demoiselles' quarters."

"I know where it is, mademoiselle." One of the demoiselles, the girl called Nettie, spoke. "Every night she locked in the drawer of the desk in our quarters."

One of the crewmen was dispatched to search the ship for the missing record book. When he rejoined them, he reported to the captain: the book had vanished.

****

With Madame La Plante and the record book gone, the lines separating mademoiselles from demoiselles faded even further. All five and twenty girls roomed in the same dormitory at the convent of Saint Ursuline, and within the first days of their arrival, a schedule formed. At sunup, they were roused out of bed by one of the nuns. After a breakfast of bread which they ate together, the head of the convent, Mother Marie, instructed them on the day's work, an endless list of chores performed alongside four other nuns: cleaning the stables, feeding the chickens, tending to the milk cows, chopping wood, and moving stones to reinforce a wall surrounding the pasture.

But the day of the marriage market was different. On that gray autumn day, the austere convent bustled with the excited chatter of girls who fluttered about like so many chickens in a henhouse. They had cleaned and refreshed their dresses, sprinkling them with lavender-scented water and Jeanne and Madeleine helped to style their hair. One of the mademoiselles possessed a pot of rouge which she passed through their ranks so by the time they walked the two miles to the harbor, their high color made them look as if they had journeyed a great deal longer.

A group of hopeful suitors had congregated outside the warehouse where the market would be conducted. Mother Marie led them past the men. When they were at last assembled inside, she spoke, "Young women of France, this may seem an unsavory process, made more so by the use of the word 'market,' as if a horse trade will now ensue." A few of them giggled then fell silent as Mother Marie delivered a stern look. "This is no market. It represents the wishes of our king, and therefore the wishes of God himself. It is the beginning of a holy sacrament. A duty to country and a blessing from above. Unions formed today will bear the fruit of the future generations of France. What transpires here is an honor to your sex and to your country."

Someone rapped on the door, but Mother Marie ignored it, continuing her speech. "Your conduct should reflect the solemnity of the proceedings. There shall be no flirtation or affectation around the men. Sobriety will prevail. It is for your own good, girls. You will be choosing a husband. Not a puppy. You will be presented one by one. Say your name, age and where you are from. You may add any additional information you believe significant."

One of the mademoiselles raised her hand and Mother Marie nodded. The girl said, "Is my knowledge of Pope Julius significant?"

A look of confusion crossed Mother Marie's face. "Well, I suppose if you are well versed about the leaders of the Catholic faith, it could be of significance."

"No, Mother. Pope Julius is a card game," she said, and the other girls laughed outright.

Mother Marie paused, weighing the girl's question, then said, "The men of New France need diversion. If you feel it's important, you may mention it." The girl smiled and Mother Marie continued. "After the formal presentations, an interlude will follow where you will get acquainted with the candidates. After that, the men will register preference for no more than five women in ranked order. You will then respond with your preferences. If all goes well, most of you will have wed by sunset tomorrow." A sound somewhere between a gasp and a sigh rose through their numbers and although Jeanne would not be choosing, she felt a stab of anxiety on behalf of the other girls.

Mother Marie organized two rows of eligible mademoiselles, then opened the door to the warehouse and spoke with a representative of the king's army. After a few words, the men filed in. There were twice the number of men than women and soon the chill room became less so. Despite the number of souls crowded under one roof the place was silent save for the occasional nervous cough.

Mother Marie greeted the men and consulted a list, calling out, "First we have one Mademoiselle Andrieu. Will the lady please make her presence known?"

One of the mademoiselles stepped forward, looking peaked under her rouged cheeks. "I am Marguerite. Fifteen years. Born the eighth of May in Paris. In the country of France," she added hastily, and a few of the men laughed. She stepped back quickly to melt into the line of women.

"Thank you, Mademoiselle Andrieu. Next we have Mademoiselle Colin."

Jeanne and several other girls looked up and down the rows of women. Then Teeth stepped forward.

Head held high, chin out, Teeth began, "I am Anne Colin. I was born in Paris on the eleventh day of November. I am newly turned nineteen. I can cook, bake, clean, chop wood, braid rope, sew clothing, tend to animals, draw tallow from suet for candles, make soap, operate a forge, bend horseshoes, mix poultices, and deliver babies."

A man called out, "Is that all?" and a round of laughter rose from the ranks of men. Teeth clenched her fists and appeared ready to find the jokester until Mother Marie stood in her way, propelling her back into the line.

"Look, she can fight, too. You left that off the list," another voice added.

"Gentlemen, I ask you to hold your laughter, please," Mother Marie said. "It is most unseemly given the sanctity of today's proceedings. Most unseemly. Thank you, Mademoiselle Colin. Next we have Mademoiselle Davide."

Jeanne took a half step forward and stumbled over her words. "I am called Jeanne. I am eighteen. From Perche. I am lettered and play the harpsicord. I am also proficient with Arabic and Roman numerals." Although she had no interest in the market, she added, "And I know how to bake bread," then smiled nervously.

So it continued until each girl had presented herself and her accomplishments. When the introductions concluded, Mother Marie welcomed potential suitors to approach the young women. Jeanne hung in the back of the room observing as the others engaged in shy conversation with the motley group of men, some of whom appeared to be younger than herself, while others looked to be in advanced years. As she sized up the most promising candidates, someone tapped her on the shoulder, interrupting her thoughts.

A small man, only barely as tall as Jeanne herself said, "Pardon, mademoiselle. I cannot recall your name."

"I am Mademoiselle Davide."

Although not old, the man's features—his eyes, mustache, shoulders—all drooped, as if burdened by some invisible force. The overall effect called to mind a dog kicked one too many times by his master.

The man performed a courtly bow. "A pleasure to make your acquaintance. I am Monsieur Maximin La Forge."

"Pleased to meet you, Monsieur La Forge." Jeanne curtsied.

"Forgive me for disturbing you. I noted you were separated from the group and dared to capture your attention."

"You have succeeded in capturing it fully,

monsieur."

Jeanne had no intention of engaging in the marriage market, yet still the thought came to her: Of all the prospects in the room, was this little man the only fish she could net?

Monsieur La Forge glanced nervously around the room and said, "I came to make further inquiries following the charming introductions given. You see, I have built my own house with two rooms and a great hearth equipped with a generous spit. The spit can accommodate a pheasant and a duck simultaneously. I venture to guess an entire pig could be roasted there, although without the company of the fowl, naturally."

"Naturally," Jeanne said as enthusiastically as she could, but it sounded more dismissive than enthralled. She scanned the room looking for an excuse to depart the little man's company.

Monsieur La Forge seemed to catch on to Jeanne's waning interest in the particulars of his hearth. He changed tactics. "I am in possession of a generous tract of land awarded me by the local seigneur. There reside five head of cattle, two horses and a number of chickens." He paused and this time Jeanne gave him no encouragement to continue. After a moment of silence he added, "You may wonder why I share this with you."

"No. I do not. I assume this inventory is meant to impress."

"Yes. You are most perspicacious, mademoiselle."

"Monsieur," Jeanne said, "although I am flattered, there are obstacles preventing me from considering any offers of marriage."

Monsieur La Forge's droopy eyes widened. "No,

no! Pardon me, mademoiselle. Your beauty and abilities are great. A woman who can bake bread is surely to be treasured. Yet I share my prospects with you to test them. To discern whether Mademoiselle Anne Colin would find them favorable."

Again, the name confused Jeanne. He spoke of Teeth. She nearly burst out laughing at the prospect of this slip of a man with the rough Parisian. "Then why do you not ask her yourself?"

"Well," Monsieur La Forge searched for the words before finally blurting out, "because I find her absolutely terrifying. I was there at the port, you see. I witnessed her brawling. It was then and there I said to myself, 'That's a woman who could keep the savages at bay. Slaughter a pig. Pluck a goose.'"

"To roast in your generously appointed spit," Jeanne added.

"Precisely. I said to myself, 'Maximin, set your course for her!' Yet the very thought of her terrifies me to the core." Indeed, even considering the prospect of approaching Teeth set his whiskers atremble.

"Her bark is worse than her bite."

Monsieur La Forge's downtrodden mien brightened. "Truly?"

"Yes. If you are good and true to Tee—" Jeanne caught herself, "Mademoiselle Colin, she will, in return, be good and true to you." Jeanne thought of Madame La Plante and added, "Nothing to be frightened of most days."

"Mademoiselle, you who are so gentle of manner, easy to speak with, could you make an introduction on my behalf to the lady?"

Imagining the ferocious lion Teeth paired with this

little mouse was the stuff of farce. Yet Jeanne agreed. It appeared the New World called for a new order.

"I will recommend you highly," Jeanne said, causing the little man's whiskers to quiver anew.

****

Back in the convent after supper, the young women took stock of their harvest of offers. Each of them had received at least a few inquiries. Yet no one's success compared with that of Teeth.

"This new country agrees with me and I with it. Eleven gentlemen asked me to consider their yokes," Teeth said haughtily.

"Twelve," Jeanne said relating the story of Monsieur La Forge.

"That's right. Mr. Droopy Whiskers. With an established house and land. He may be the most promising of the lot," Teeth said.

"Aren't you the belle of the ball?" one of the mademoiselles said, a girl who had only two offers.

"What of it?" Teeth said.

"Nothing." The girl wisely bit back her words.

No one competed for beds at the Ursuline Convent. In the past, other ships had carried twice the number of Daughters, which left the dormitory amply supplied. Regardless, Jeanne and Madeleine chose bedsteads farthest from the door following their habit from La Salpêtrière.

"How many offers did you get, Jeanne?" Madeleine asked. "Or did you manage to hide?"

"I received two. If you had been there, you would have gotten ten times that amount."

"I'm not so sure. By Teeth's success, it appears the currency has changed." One of the nuns extinguished the candles and bid them goodnight. As they settled in, Madeleine whispered, "As for your only true option, Monsieur Suprenant, how will you be able to stand the wait?"

"I won't. I'm already desperate to see him. But am happy to have you in my company."

"How will we manage?" Laurent had changed ships and now travelled to the southern colonies. When he returned, they would marry and stake a land claim.

"Would you love birds shut it?" Teeth growled from across the room. "Some of us need our beauty sleep what with all the gentlemen lining up to pledge their troth."

Chapter Thirty-One

"The one hundred girls sent over by the King this year have only just arrived, and already they are almost all accommodated. He will send another 200 next year, and even more in the years following, in proportion to the need. He will also send men to marry withstanding those who are in the army. Truly, it is an amazing thing to see how the country is becoming populated and multiplying."

~Mother Marie of the Ursulines

New France

In the days after the marriage market, the population of the convent dwindled as one by one the women made their choices. Teeth accepted the offer of Monsieur La Forge. Madeleine and Jeanne attended the ceremony, witnessing as Teeth carefully wrote the "X" on a contract that sealed the agreement next to the signature of the lettered Monsieur La Forge.

Elisabeth made an even better match. Although she had not attended the market, the local miller, whose wife died after the birth of their son, took notice of the girl, and after a good word from Mother Marie, he overlooked the particulars of baby Anne's origins to welcome his new bride to the mill.

After a week's time, Madeleine and Jeanne moved

to a small house used for visitors to the convent. With the absence of the other girls there were fewer mouths to feed, clothes to wash, shoes to repair, yet the burden of chores trebled. Winter approached. The convent required one hundred cords of wood to fuel the four chimneys serving as the only protection against the unrelenting cold. Jeanne and Madeleine chopped wood until their hands bled from the grip of the axe. Their backs ached with every stroke.

Yet the most pronounced pain for Jeanne centered around her heart. Two months had passed, and Jeanne had received no word from Jacques. Her yearning for him made her unbalanced, causing her to see strange visions in her dreams. Of the *Saint Anne*. Madame La Plante. Jacques in his sick bed. It was all she could do to focus on a simple task. A conversation. A thought.

She lived as if on two conflicting planes: Her corporal self in the convent and her fantasy with Jacques, imagining where he was, what occupied his mind, and scripting entire conversations with him. In some ways, physical hardship proved a welcome relief, requiring a level of concentration from both body and mind making her forget for entire moments her awful longing.

One night, as they prepared to sleep, Madeleine said, "You had a nightmare."

Jeanne had a vague recollection of waking up in the dark, her nightgown drenched in sweat. "Oh yes. I'd forgotten. It was about Madame La Plante. We were on the *Saint Anne* and at one point she tried to kill Jacques. Or did he try to kill her? I can't remember exactly."

"Well, someone killed her, that's for sure."

"I worry so much about him. What if he has fallen

ill again? Or killed by savages? There are pirates on the high seas. What if his ship was attacked? Or something worse?"

Madeleine shivered and drew her covers up under her chin. "What could be worse than all that?"

She could think of one thing and the thought of it brought tears to her eyes. "What if he has had a change of heart?" Jeanne said.

****

One morning in late December, Jeanne fetched water from the well in the courtyard of the convent, her feet shod only in her wooden clogs. It seemed more trouble than it was worth to struggle with the clumsy snowshoes. Once outside she regretted it. Although it was a clear day, Jeanne learned that in New France sunshine had a way of making things colder. Clouds, like downy blankets, warmed the air.

In fetching the water, she lowered the bucket several times and each time it returned empty, impeded by a layer of ice. Her feet, exposed in her clogs, burned and itched. Finally, she took hold of one end of the rope and dropped the bucket with such ferocity, the ice cracked, and at last it came up brimming with water.

She had turned to go back into the haven of their quarters when someone shouted her name. Teeth stood outside the gate of the convent. She and Madeleine had seen no other soul, save for the sisters with whom they ate twice daily, for weeks. Her heart bounded at the sight of Teeth and for a moment she forgot the cold permeating her limbs.

Back inside the house, Madeleine cried out in delight, "I never thought I'd say it, but God's nightgown, it is wonderful to see your face!"

"Yours ain't so bad neither," Teeth rejoined.

"How goes it, Madame La Forge?" Madeleine asked, drawing another stool closer to the hearth.

"It goes tolerably well. Maximin heeds my orders well enough. He tends to jabber, more so during morningtide, which vexes me to no end. Yet sometimes I find his chatter comforting enough given the isolation of the farm."

Jeanne pictured the two of them: Teeth with her severe demeanor grunting in response to whisker-faced La Forge. "You paint a picture of matrimonial bliss," Jeanne said.

"It suits me good enough. We have a little one on the way." She patted her stomach. "Summertime, by my count."

They both congratulated her, and Madeleine added, "A bun baking and you two lovebirds barely wed. Monsieur La Forge must be over the moon."

"Monsieur La Forge don't know. I will wait until the quickening to be sure the baby has a firm grip in this world. Hold my confidence for now if you please."

"Not to worry. The sisters aren't exactly gossips. They pray and work and pray and work." Madeleine sighed. "Minus the praying, that's all we do, too."

"So, you've become a nun?" Teeth laughed.

"Never," Madeleine replied.

"Well, I didn't come to tell you about the baby. There are other more pressing matters." Teeth drew a letter from the pocket of her skirt. "I have come to ask if you have received this. It is from the captain, an official of the king, and concerns the *Saint Anne*."

"What news is this?" Jeanne took the letter from Teeth.

"I am not lettered, but Monsieur La Forge gave me the gist of it. There is to be an inquiry concerning Madame La Plante."

"Read it aloud, Jeanne," Madeleine said.

To the household of Monsieur Maximin La Forge concerning a Daughter of the King, Madame Anne La Forge, (née Colin). There is to be held, on the first day of June, on the mark of noon, in the tollhouse of Quebec, an assay concerning the disappearance of Madame Marie-Magdelaine La Plante, the whereabouts of whom is unknown, presumed dead, last seen on His Majesty's ship, the Saint Anne. Madame La Forge, having first-hand knowledge of the particulars surrounding Madame La Plante's last days on Earth is requested to appear at the proceedings. Failure to do so will be viewed unfavorably by the king's authorities.
Signed, Provost Filip de Rohan

"I'm frightened," Teeth said, her hands resting protectively on her belly.

Jeanne folded the letter. "When you barred our entry that day to Monsieur Suprenant's cabin we had our suspicions."

"What?" Teeth's eyebrows shot up in surprise. "You think I killed her?" She glanced around the room as if checking for eavesdroppers and lowered her voice. "But it weren't me."

Madeleine moved her stool closer to Teeth's. "Well then, who did it?"

Teeth covered her eyes. Her hands, cracked and red, testified to the hardships she endured in this new land. After a moment she met their eyes in turn. "Old La Plante entered Monsieur Suprenant's quarters looking for you, Jeanne. Strutted around the room shouting orders. 'It's not suitable for women unchaperoned to care for a man. It's the Devil's work,' and all of her silly nonsense. Elisabeth was there if you'll recall. Madame stared her right in the face and told her she had decided to give baby Anne away. Said Elisabeth could, after all, have an officer since one of the demoiselles died of the pox and she had a shortage, but it meant the baby had to go. Can you imagine?"

Jeanne remembered her conversation with Madame about the officers. "Only too well," she said.

"Elisabeth began to cry and plead with the old witch and said a few choice words about the woman not being truly Christian. She accused La Plante of being jealous because she'd never had a man or a babe, which is when the old crone hauled off and rang her bell but good with a smack to the side of Elisabeth's face. It left a mark and all. Well, Elisabeth popped. She goes and shoves the old bat, sends her flying across the room. Madame hit her head on a chest. Cracked her skull right open like a nut, she did. Blood spilled out all over the floor."

"Dear God."

"Incredible. So, our mild little Elisabeth did her in?" Madeleine said.

"Yes and no," Teeth said. "The old bird lay motionless for an eternity. I figured the girl had finished her right good, so we locked the door to the room, stuffed her body inside the chest, and cleaned up the blood. I feared it would drip through the floorboards and onto the deck below, then we'd have been sunk."

Despite the warmth of the hearth, Jeanne shivered as Teeth fell silent, lost in the recollection. "Poor Elisabeth," Jeanne said. "She must have been frantic."

"You'd think so, wouldn't you? But no. Cool as cream she was. Then you two showed up and wondered why we locked the door."

Jeanne nodded at the memory.

"I sent you both out for more supplies. I needed to get rid of her remains. I hoisted her out of the chest. It was then she made a funny squeaking sound and I realized Elisabeth had not killed her entirely and now I had to finish the job to protect the girl and her small babe. I took hold of the old lady by the scruff." Teeth held out her hands and Jeanne felt the hair rise on the back of her neck at the sight of it. "I twisted the way one does with a chicken. There was only a bit of fight in her. When I was sure she was gone, I lifted her up and shoved her through the porthole, which is when one of the demoiselles saw her as a ghost."

Madeleine whistled. "What a story."

"It ain't no story. It's the truth." Teeth gazed into each of their faces in turn. "Will you betray us?"

"To what end?" Madeleine said. "Time. Distance. They're snow covering the dirt of our past sins. Besides, we have our own tracks to cover."

"What about when the snow melts in springtime? What will be uncovered on the first of June? Why have I been singled out? As passengers on the ship, why not the both of you?"

"When did the letter arrive?" Madeleine asked.

"Just yesterday. Delivered by a young lad. Monsieur La Forge with his poor eyesight mistook him for a savage and nearly shot him."

A jolt of energy coursed through Jeanne's being. Letters were getting through. Perhaps her own would arrive from Jacques.

"You may at last receive word from your Monsieur Suprenant, Jeanne," Madeleine said, reading her thoughts.

Teeth said, "So you believe you will be summoned in due time?"

"Yes. If they seek you as witness then surely they'll seek us as well," Jeanne said.

"You are grinning like a drunkard. As if you look forward to the proceedings," Teeth said to Jeanne.

"It's just I haven't heard from Monsieur Suprenant in such a long time."

Teeth waved a hand. "This is not Paris. There is no order here. The man's heart is tied to your leading strings. Anyone with two eyes could see that. You will hear from him. The only question is when his letter will make its way through happenstance and wilderness to find you." Teeth put her head in her hands and when she spoke, her words were muffled, Madeleine asked her to repeat them. She looked up and said, "That cursed record book."

Jeanne said, "How did you dispose of it?"

Teeth raised an eyebrow. "I didn't. That book has me tossing and turning at night for fear someone will find it." She smoothed her hands over her belly and began to cry. "I shall lose everything! My Monsieur La Forge, my babe. If that cursed book comes to light, all will be taken from me."

Madeleine and Jeanne comforted her as best they could. Later, after she'd gone, Madeleine said, "It appears Madame La Forge has grown a heart as well as a baby. You could have knocked me over with a feather to see tears on that girl's face."

Jeanne remembered the day on the ship when she came

upon Teeth after she thought Madeleine had died.
"She has always had a big heart. It is only now she
dares show it."

Chapter Thirty-Two

"A royal fund was established which gave to every
youth who married before he was twenty-one a bonus
of twenty livres, and to every girl who married before
she was seventeen the same."

~Mother Marie of the Ursulines

New France

As December turned to January, Jeanne's anxiety
produced a constant thrumming in the back of her brain
like a headache: *Where is he? Is he alive? Why has he
not written?* Nothing could fully occupy her thoughts:
not the cold, nor the inquiry, nor the labor of surviving
the winter of New France.

In February, so prodigious an amount of snow fell,
it piled to the rafters of their little house making entry
to the outside world nearly impossible. Like the
dormant flora and fauna around them, Jeanne and
Madeleine hibernated, emerging twice weekly for
services with the nuns. On those days, reaching the
chapel required tunneling a path, making even the
closest destination a voyage too far.

Days crept by with a pattern as unbroken, as
monotonous as the snow-covered gardens surrounding
the convent. Until one morning when they heard a
frightful pounding on the door. On the rare occasion the

nuns called on them, they gave a modest knock.

"God's nightgown!" Madeleine sat up in bed. "Who or what is making that racket?"

After hurriedly dressing, Jeanne clambered down the ladder. Hugging her shawl close to her shoulders, she opened the door to find a young lad standing there. A winter storm brewed on the horizon. Jeanne could read it from the black curtain of clouds hanging over the convent.

A wind blew icy needles through each layer of her clothing, and Jeanne bade the visitor to enter. Madeleine stood by the hearth, preparing a fire. Her magnificent hair, loosely bound in a ribbon, flowed down her back like a rich mantle. The boy stared as if bewitched by the sight of her.

"What is your business, young sir?" Jeanne asked.

The boy's gaze remained fixed on Madeleine. He finally pulled his eyes away to focus on Jeanne. "My name is Stefan, the postman's son." His voice cracked as he spoke. "I seek Mademoiselle Jeanne Davide."

"Have you a letter for me?" Jeanne said, her voice trembling.

"Yes. I do." From his satchel the boy produced a letter and Jeanne snatched it out of his hands. Her heart sank. It was the same notice Teeth had received and was marked with the seal of the *Saint Anne*. She opened it and read it to be sure.

Madeleine asked, "Is it from him?"

"No." Jeanne turned her face to hide her tears. She let the note drop to the floor.

"I am sorry, Jeanne," Madeleine said, retrieving the letter. In doing so she stood in closer proximity to the boy.

"You are very beautiful, mademoiselle," Stefan said, addressing Madeleine in a register teetering between man and boy in squeaky fits.

"And you are very fresh, young man," Madeleine rejoined. "Remove your hat. You're indoors and in the company of ladies. Where are your manners? Has your mother not told you it's rude to stare?"

The boy removed his hat and answered, "No, mademoiselle. Perhaps it is because I have never laid eyes on someone like you before. My gaze seems to gravitate quite on its own, as if I have no hold over it."

Madeleine laughed, looking thoroughly pleased. Male adoration had been part of her daily fare since she was a girl. Starved of it these past months, Madeleine gulped the boy's attention. "Boy. Stefan, was it? How is it that you came across this letter?"

"My father gave it to me. Like I said, he delivers the mail in these parts, except now I'm grown, so I help him. I am thirteen and strong for my age."

Jeanne said, "Who, pray tell, gave it to him?"

"A Monsieur Suprenant."

At the boy's words, Jeanne cried out, "Monsieur Jacques Suprenant?"

"The very same. You are acquainted with him?"

Jeanne tried to control her excitement, but her voice had become as inconstant as that of the boy. "Yes, we know him. It's his correspondence I seek. When did he deliver this letter? Under what circumstances? Do you know of his whereabouts now?"

The boy seemed momentarily bewildered by her rapid-fire questions. Finally, he said, "Monsieur Suprenant is in commerce with my father. We see him once in the spring and once before the winter, although

314

we have yet to see him this season."

"Didn't you just say it was Monsieur Suprenant who gave your father this?" Madeleine held up the letter.

"Did I?" The boy scratched his head.

"Yes, you did," Jeanne said slowly, struggling to control a frustration that made her want to grab the boy by his collar and shake until a sensible response fell out of his mouth.

"I misspoke. My tongue lags my thoughts. I feel quite addled in my brain. It's like this: The letter was from Monsieur Suprenant, but it was delivered to my father by other means."

Jeanne said, "I am thoroughly confused by your narrative. Stefan, this letter is not from Monsieur Suprenant."

"Beg your pardon, mademoiselle. My mother only lately tutored us on our letters. Although my sister is faster than I, I am tolerably able." He took the letter from Madeleine's outstretched hand, blushing as his hand glanced hers and coloring even more when both of them studied him as he read.

Presently he said, "This is not the letter from Monsieur Suprenant."

Jeanne wanted to shout at the boy but forced herself to answer levelly. "Yes. We know that. It is our very point."

"There was more than one. But that letter is addressed to neither of you." He retrieved it from his pouch. "This one is to—" He held it up and squinted. "Mademoiselle Jeanne Denot."

Jeanne grabbed it, and her hands shook as she broke the seal.

My dearest Jeanne,

It has been seven days since I last saw your face. Each has been its own eternity. It is my only hope to hold you in my arms again. Whilst I am trapped bodily, my heart, my soul, my every thought, my happiness, they are anchored with you, my love. Wait for me. I will return when the snow is gone, and the flowers are in bloom. Then we shall never again be parted.

Your faithful,

Jacques

"Well, good letter carrier," Madeleine said, "Do we have your oath that any correspondence forthcoming will be delivered with extra speed to our door?"

Stefan bowed with great ceremony. "You have my sacred promise, mademoiselle. Perhaps it would be wise if I were to occasionally check on your welfare. I don't want to frighten you, but from time to time the savages act out. It could be dangerous."

"We feel safer already, sir." Madeleine curtsied theatrically. "Your gallantry is overwhelming."

When Stefan had at last taken leave, Jeanne reread the letter.

"Madeleine, when do you suppose flowers bloom in New France?" she asked. "The seasons cannot be completely different from France, can they?"

"I don't know. It feels as if everything is dead in this place and will stay that way forever."

Jeanne hugged Madeleine. "I thank God you are here, and fate has once again thrown us together."

"Yes. I long for the day Laurent returns, yet dread the day we will finally be parted, my friend."

"We shan't think of it. We will enjoy each day as if they are something to be treasured, not endured. We shall occupy ourselves thoroughly."

Madeleine laughed. "Why, look at you! You've been as listless as a gravesite flower. Now you're a as fresh as a bud. Tell me, how will we 'treasure' our time in this ice cave?"

"We can perfect our knitting. Neither one of us has any talent in it, but I have an ambition to make a blanket for Teeth's little one."

"Knitting my clumsy loops for months on end. Time will positively fly, I am sure," Madeleine said.

Chapter Thirty-Three

"The girls sent last year are married and almost all of them are with child or have had children already, a sign of the fertility of this country."

~*Jean Talon, Governor, New France*

New France

When the snow subsided in April, and the weak sunlight of winter gained the strength of spring, Jeanne and Madeleine found themselves sleeping heavily from early evening until well after sunup, like heroines in a tale waiting to be revived by true love's kiss. They were thus insensible, wrapped deep inside the cave of an early evening slumber when Jeanne jolted awake from some distant sound like the howling of wolves. At first, she thought it a dream and returned into the abandon of sleep, only to be roused a moment later by the strains of a song.

She listened as the sound grew stronger and a verse emerged from the cool dark air. "A man is for the woman made, woman this man is made for you." Jeanne recognized the voice.

Before a clear thought could form as to the identity of the singer, Madeleine awoke beside her and sat up abruptly. "Laurent!"

She scrambled down the ladder and rushed outside,

dressed only in a nightshift. Jeanne peered out the window to see Laurent lift Madeleine and swing her around as she whooped with giddy laughter.

Back inside the house, Madeleine cried out, "Look who has arrived at last!"

Jeanne dressed and climbed down the ladder to greet Laurent, who hugged her so tightly, her ribs ached. "Laurent," she said, "it is a wonder to see you!"

"A wonder, indeed, to lay eyes on you and on my sweet rose."

Like a newly kindled fire, Madeleine's entire being seemed to radiate light. "I feared I'd never see your face again," she said, and the two joined once again in an embrace, this one even more passionate. Jeanne cleared her throat, reminding them of her presence, and at last they separated.

A knock sounded and Jeanne opened the door to find Mother Marie holding the wood chopping axe, flanked by two sisters. "We observed a man unknown to us entering this place." She spied Madeleine, still clothed in nothing more than a shift. "We came to see if there was anything amiss. It seems you know this gentleman and have welcomed him over your threshold?"

"Truth be told, Mother, he carried me over it," Madeleine said giddily, then changed her tone when she saw the look on the nun's face. "We are, in fact, betrothed."

"Until you are bound in marriage under the eyes of God, it is not seemly for him to be here with you in this," Mother's gaze took in Madeleine's thin nightdress, "state. Monsieur, you may follow us to the main house. We will see you get victuals while your intended readies herself to receive you in a more becoming manner."

****

On a warm summer day Laurent and Madeleine married in the chapel of the convent. As they marked their "Xs" onto the marriage contract, Jeanne cried.

Teeth, heavy with pregnancy, sat in the pew beside her. "Are you not happy for her?"

"Very happy. Only miserable for myself to lose my dearest friend," she sniffed, wiping tears from under her eyes.

"She is not so far removed. Their homestead is a carriage distance."

"Yes. And I have no carriage," she said. The thought prompted a fresh outpouring of tears.

Teeth clapped her on the shoulder. "There, there. At least the weather has turned. There's nothing inhibiting a walk to our estate." Teeth had gained airs since her arrival in New France. Jeanne decided to overlook her pretentions because with them came other, more desirable traits of the new Madame La Forge. Strange how so rough a weed of Paris could blossom into so sweet a country buttercup. "You can while away your time with me and Monsieur La Forge. Isn't that so, husband?" Teeth touched Monsieur La Forge's arm in a way that could only be described as coquettish.

"Whatever you say, my cabbage," Monsieur La Forge said.

No amount of socializing at "the estate" would replace Madeleine's steady companionship. And what of Jacques? Seven months had passed with only a single letter as proof of their attachment. Would she feel the same when, or if, she ever laid eyes on him again? Days, weeks, months now stretched between them, a valley of time she prayed could be bridged upon their reunion. She hiccupped from the effort of swallowing her tears. When Madeleine turned to walk arm-in-arm with Laurent out of the chapel, she found herself smiling.

Chapter Thirty-Four

"God is a sure paymaster. He may not pay at the end of every week, or month, or year, but I charge you to remember: He pays in the end."
~ *Ann of Austria, Sister-in-law to King Louis XIV*

New France

On the first day of June, Jeanne journeyed with Teeth and Monsieur La Forge to the tollhouse where the inquiry into the disappearance of Madame La Plante would take place. Seated in the back of the open carriage, Jeanne adjusted her bonnet to shield her face from any ill effect of the sun which shone directly above them. Given the matter that lay before them, it would be much more fitting if the skies were gray and stormy.

Teeth, riding in the front of the carriage, her girth now considerable with the baby's arrival only a handful of weeks away, harangued Monsieur La Forge with every bump of the journey.

"You are a useless driver, my pet! It is as if you intentionally aim for each pock in the road instead of guiding the horses around them."

Monsieur La Forge's whiskers trembled at his wife's every word. He tugged nervously at his mustache with one hand, while the other held the reigns.

"I promise you, my dear, I am smoothing the way to the extent it is possible. Shall I slow our pace, my little cabbage?"

Teeth clutched her belly and half moaned, half shouted, "No. Just get us there without shaking this child out of my gut!"

When they reached the tollhouse, Monsieur La Forge tied up the horses and offered a hand to his wife. "Careful, my dear. Watch your step," he said as he made to help her down.

"How else would I do it besides with care? I'm not going to jump, you fool!"

Monsieur La Forge offered Jeanne a hand as well and under his breath said, "The hardships of her condition have made my lady rather waspish."

"Beware my sting, monsieur!" Teeth said, and when Monsieur La Forge color blanched, she added, "My hearing is as keen as ever. Mind what you whisper behind my back!"

Monsieur La Forge's reading of his wife's vexation was only partially correct. Teeth's condition served as a cover for what truly ailed her: a gnawing terror that today the truth would come to light. Jeanne's own nerves had grown more skittish as they approached the tollhouse.

A crowd of people had gathered in the foyer. Jeanne recognized many of the mademoiselles and demoiselles from the *Saint Anne* and said to Teeth, "We were hardly the only ones called."

One person who had not been called was Elisabeth. The girl stayed home, safe with her new husband and little Anne. Disorder reigned as the girls circulated, their spouses in tow, catching up on the news of the past eight months. More than half of them had swollen bellies and Jeanne appeared to be the only one without a husband in tow.

Teeth rapped Monsieur La Forge on the shoulder. "I am tired of chitchatting. I need to sit this load. Find us a place at once."

Monsieur La Forge secured seats for them on a bench closest to the dais at the front of the room. As they settled, the captain and two other officials entered. Jeanne scanned the chaos of the room looking for Madeleine and Laurent but couldn't locate them. A bailiff thumped a heavy stick on the hollow floor of the dais, making a sound like the beating of a drum that resounded throughout the hall, sending the crowd scurrying to find seats.

Teeth said, "Heaven help me, Jeanne, I'm so nervous it's all I can do to keep from jumping up and running from this place."

A voice came from the bench behind them. "You best stay in your seat, chubby. I can't imagine you'll get very far." It was Madeleine with Laurent at her side.

Their reunion was cut short by an announcement from the bailiff. "Will the room please come to order!" He paused until the room quieted sufficiently. "We are here, this first day of June, one thousand six hundred and sixty-nine for the assay of an incident on His Majesty's vessel, the *Saint Anne*. The king's servant, Madame Marie-Magdelaine La Plante did disappear on or around the afternoon of the fifteenth of October, one thousand six hundred and sixty-eight. Representing the king's authority, Provost Filip de Rohan will preside investigating any possible malfeasance."

The provost, who had entered with the captain, bowed then seated himself on one of three chairs facing the crowd. The captain and the bailiff assumed flanking seats and Provost de Rohan called out, "The king's authority will call its first attestant, Lady Marie-Louise née de Grancey now Jouvé."

Jeanne had not noticed Marie-Louise when they first arrived. The girl emerged from the back of the room slowly, the mark of pregnancy visible under the folds of her dress. It took Jeanne a few moments to comprehend that this bedraggled figure making her way to the front of the room had once been the beautiful, arrogant demoiselle from the ship. Her porcelain skin was now mottled with red welts, and her crown of golden hair had dulled to the color of a field mouse. Patches of it appeared to have fallen out entirely.

The captain assisted Marie-Louise as she lumbered onto the dais, then produced a chair for her. The provost stood before the girl in silence, sizing her up the way one would an opponent before a duel. Marie-Louise appeared to grow nervous and scratched at a ring of blotchy welts that had bloomed above the neckline of her dress.

At last the provost spoke, and when he did so, his voice sliced through the susurration of the crowd, rendering the room silent. "Madame Jouvé, please tell this gathering of the last sighting you had of Madame Marie-Magdelaine La Plante onboard the *Saint Anne*."

Marie-Louise began to speak but was interrupted by the provost. "Louder, please."

Marie-Louise cleared her throat and sat up straighter. "We had gathered, as was our custom, to say morning prayers in our quarters. We then breakfasted in the company of Madame, and that was the last we saw of her in human form."

"Did Madame say anything of significance during the meal?"

"Significant, monsieur? I am not sure I understand your question."

The provost squared his shoulders and glared at her. "Did she mention anything that would lead you to believe her mental capacity was somehow overburdened?"

She dismissed his question with a wave of her hand. "Absolutely not, monsieur. She was perfectly herself. Righteous and clear of thought and word."

"Were you made privy to her plans for the remainder of that day?"

The girl nodded. "She said she was going to see him." Marie-Louise pointed to the captain. "There was business to discuss. What business it was, I know not. The next time our eyes met, I was looking into the face of Madame's ghost."

The room seemed to gasp in unison and the bailiff pounded on the floor to restore order. The provost asked her to explain.

"We were nearly always in the good lady's presence." As she spoke the words, Marie-Louise began to cry, and the captain produced a kerchief for her. "So when she failed to materialize at lunch, we grew worried. I planned to ask the captain of her whereabouts and search the boat when something drew my eyes to the porthole." She paused and the quiet in the room grew so profound, one could have heard an ant walking. "It was there Madame's face appeared, as white as snow and suspended upside down. Her eyes open, bulging. Her mouth agape as if she were about to speak to me."

A commotion broke out once again amongst the crowd and the bailiff restored order by pounding his staff.

"Did she speak to you, madame?" asked the provost.

"No. She hung there a moment then vanished."

"I ask you once again: Do you have any reason to believe she took her own life? Did you mark her as despondent in any way?"

Louise shook her head. "Never. Madame was a woman of God and self-murder is murder all the same."

After dismissing Marie-Louise, the provost turned to the captain. "According to Madame Jouvé, Madame La Plante sought your company that fateful day. Did you in fact meet with the good lady?"

The captain, who had appeared at ease before, now fidgeted with the buttons on his coat, looking like a nervous schoolboy. "Madame La Plante consulted with me nearly every day of our voyage. That day was no different."

"What was the nature of your consultation with her?"

"Madame provided regular updates as to the comportment of the ladies aboard the *Saint Anne*, sharing observations she recorded in her book."

"Did she share any observation of particular note that day in October?"

The captain gazed out into the crowd to where Jeanne and Teeth sat. Teeth grabbed Jeanne's hand and squeezed it with such intensity, Jeanne nearly cried out. "Yes. She told me she was disqualifying one of the mademoiselles."

"Which mademoiselle in particular?"

"Mademoiselle Anne Colin."

Teeth shouted, "It's not true!" and Monsieur La Forge put an arm around his wife's shoulder and whispered, "Steady."

Provost de Rohan said, "Silence, madame. You will have your turn." He turned his attention toward the captain. "Why did Madame La Plante take you into her confidence? Of what concern was it of yours?"

The captain shrugged. "I know not. The good lady seemed to think it my duty to be abreast of the particulars of the women onboard. She took her responsibilities very seriously and, I suppose, as the most senior figure on the *Saint Anne*, she felt an obligation to report, as it were, to me."

The provost consulted the scroll before him. "Do you know, in fact, whether Madame La Plante disqualified the lady in question? She is, according to official records, married and awarded the king's dowry of fifty livres."

"That is for the record book to determine. But it, like Madame La Plante, seems to have vanished."

"You said she showed you her observations. Do you recall what she wrote in the book that day?" the provost asked.

"I saw nothing. Or I recall nothing. We were readying for our arrival in New France, and more urgent priorities demanded my attention. To speak plainly, I found these discussions to be no more than something to tolerate, to keep the lady placated."

After dismissing the captain, a number of other witnesses were called from the *Saint Anne*. None of their testimony shed further light into Madame's inner state of being or outer actions.

Next, the Provost called Teeth to stand before the gathering.

Monsieur La Forge helped her to her feet, escorting her as she waddled unsteadily to the dais. She ascended it with the help of the captain and her husband. She settled her girth into the witness chair slowly, both hands wrapped around her mid-section.

The provost began: "Madame La Forge, previously Mademoiselle Colin, were you privy to Madame La Plante's plans to dismiss you as a Daughter of the King, stripping you of all rights to the dowry gifted by His Majesty?"

Teeth shifted her weight in the chair. "Yes, sir, I was."

"Can you relate what transpired?"

"She never did take too keen an interest in me nor any of the other girls from steerage. You could say we was beneath her in every sense of the word." She laughed then quickly sobered when the room failed to join in her mirth. "I may have spoken some harsh words to her after receiving an earful in kind. Then she told me I wasn't good enough. She had a way of pushing you down to puff herself up. It's not nice to say, and I mean no disrespect to the dead." Teeth made the sign of the cross.

The provost said, "Yet you are joined now in legal matrimony as your condition clearly indicates?"

Teeth nodded to her husband. "With Monsieur La Forge, who sits yonder biting his nails." A ripple of laughter filled the room.

"Are we to understand you were not, in fact,

extricated from the program?" Seeing the look of confusion on Teeth's face, the provost added, "You were not thrown out?"

"She made the threat any number of times, but never carried it out."

"When did you last see Madame La Plante?"

Teeth's face was as guileless as a child's when she answered: "At prayer services the day before she disappeared."

"Did you mark any tics in her behavior? Any manifestation of inner turmoil?"

Teeth scratched her head and stared up at the ceiling as if in deep contemplation. "She lacked her usual vigor toward the end of the trip. That may have been the fault of her illness. She nearly died, truth be told. At one point, shortly before her death, she told Mademoiselle Davide she was quitting her service."

After Teeth had returned to her seat, the provost called Jeanne's name. He began his questioning where Teeth's left off, asking about Madame's state of mind.

"It's true I cared for Madame when she suffered from the pox and got to know her better than most."

"Did you find her mind to be addled as a result of her illness?"

"No, sir. Madame La Plante was the least addled person I've ever met."

"Did she seem despondent over retiring her service to the king, as Madame La Forge testified?"

"Very much so. She had served as a chaperone on three separate transports to New France. In doing so, I believe she found a calling in life. It's never easy to lose one's vocation."

He nodded. "Do you believe, mademoiselle, that

the lady was despondent enough to take her own life?" The question hung in the air as Jeanne struggled to formulate an answer.

At that moment, a voice rang out from the back of the room. "There is only one person who can answer that, Your Honor."

Jeanne's heart responded before her eyes had the chance to confirm the identity of the speaker.

The provost said, "Who is it who interjects? Present yourself."

Jacques strode toward the dais, and Jeanne found herself thankful to be seated, for were she to stand, she would have collapsed at the sight of him. "I am Jacques Suprenant, passenger aboard the *Saint Anne*."

The tollhouse erupted, and the bailiff once again pounded on the floor demanding silence. "You claim you can answer to Madame La Plante's state of mind?"

"No. But Madame La Plante herself can," he said.

The provost dismissed Jeanne and ordered silence from the crowd. Jacques held out his hand to help her down from the dais, and at the touch of his skin, she felt as if she would faint.

After Jeanne resumed her seat, Teeth patted her knee and whispered, "Be strong." Only then did she realize how much she trembled and had to will her body to stop manifesting the turmoil of her emotions.

Provost de Rohan asked Jacques to provide his name and to state his connection to the disappearance of Madame La Plante. He produced the black record book from his pouch. "I discovered this. I believe it to be the word of Madame La Plante."

The provost arched an eyebrow. He took the book and opened it. "Indeed. How is it that it came into your possession?"

"I found it. Stuffed inside the ticking of my bedding."

A cry of astonishment rose from the crowd and the provost shouted for silence. "How and when did you make this most remarkable discovery?"

"On the voyage from France, I occupied a cabin on the topmost deck. When the *Saint Anne* left Quebec heading for Martinique, I was reassigned to the room where the good lady slept and that is when I made the discovery."

The provost showed the book to the captain and asked him to confirm its authenticity. The captain flipped through the pages and nodded his head.

Jacques continued. "Since then, I've read the book from cover to cover and would point to one particular passage as indicative of the good lady's inner turmoil."

The provost handed the book back to Jacques, who opened it to a passage. "Read here," he said.

At first the provost read silently, his lips moving mutely over Madame's text. "This is most remarkable, indeed." The crowd began to whisper, and one person shouted, "Read it aloud."

Clearing his throat, the provost said, "I shall recite her words written with a neat enough hand on a page at the back of the book. It states, 'The Almighty should have called me home with the pox and nearly did. I wish now to steer a course that takes me closer to His side. To do so, I must first overcome my fear.'" The provost closed the book. "The passage ends there, but the meaning seems clear enough given the circumstances."

Jeanne knew Madame La Plante's words were

about entering the convent. But their misinterpretation would save the lives of Teeth and Elisabeth.

The provost said, "We now conclude this assay with knowledge that Madame Marie-Magdelaine La Plante is, indeed, no longer among us in solid form. There are those who claim to have encountered her ghost, yet she has sent no communication from the other side as to exactly how her physical person came to its demise. Based on the testimony of passengers from the ship who reported a melancholy from Madame La Plante, her own recorded word, and on the histrionics which are the nature of the weaker sex, we can only presume that on or around the afternoon of October 15, the year of our Lord one thousand six hundred and sixty-eight she did cast herself from the *Saint Anne*. The matter is now closed."

Chapter Thirty-Five

"I believe that Canada has never been looked upon as it should be. In fifteen years, there will be enough overabundance to supply the West Indies. I don't say this lightly and I express this opinion after having closely examined the strength of the earth."

~*Jean Talon, Governor, New France*

New France

As Jeanne and Jacques walked back to the convent, she recalled the day two seasons before when she took this same path. Only now, with him at her side, the same road led to a far happier place. Along the way, Jacques told her of how he came in possession of Madame La Plante's record book.

"It took a while for me to notice it. On the voyage to Martinique, my accommodations were switched, and I stayed in the cabin that used to house the demoiselles. We had set sail and were a week into the journey when we hit rough seas. So rough, the mattress on my bed shifted and revealed the black book tucked underneath it. I'm guessing the old lady stuffed it in there. Curious, I read it front to back, then discovered the passage on the last page which pointed clearly to suicide."

Although they were alone on the road, Jeanne lowered her voice. "Madame La Plante did not kill herself. She was murdered." She told him what happened with Elisabeth and Teeth as they tended to him. "It wasn't intentional. But it was murder all the same."

"So, you knew before and didn't tell me."

"I didn't know everything. Or rather, I thought Teeth alone was responsible. And you were so newly recovered. I'm sorry I kept it from you."

"The dream! I had a nightmare about Madame," he said.

Jeanne shuddered. "You must have witnessed what happened."

"What should we do now?"

Jeanne stopped and took hold of his hands. "What can we do? Saying something now puts Elisabeth in grave danger, not to mention little Anne. Or Teeth and her baby. They would both hang for it."

He nodded slowly. "All those lives traded for one. I suppose the inquiry is over. There's nothing to be done."

"What I'm worried about is what will happen when the book is read in full. Madame La Plante rejected both of them as Daughters and I'm sure she recorded their status in her book."

"You don't have to worry about that." He smiled wryly. "I scratched out two damning passages. One concerning Teeth and the other concerning Elisabeth. I also looked for any threats to you, of course. She had written quite a flattering passage concerning your character, and voiced her suspicions about your family, but they were only speculation."

Jeanne made sure they were alone on the path then reached up and kissed him, tears in her eyes. "Thank you," she whispered.

Presently they continued their walk, and Jacques said, "About your family, I've had much time to think about it. When we marry, we must do so under your rightful name, Denot."

"But it's impossible. My records show my family name as Davide."

"You must reclaim it," Jacques said. "Return to Mursay and shine the light of truth into the shadows of your aunt's betrayal."

Mursay. Thoughts she had not entertained in months returned to her. How she would confront her aunt in front of Francoise and the servants and proclaim, "This woman tried to take my life." Her fantasy never carried her beyond this point, for despite her aunt's villainy, the thought of her taken away, imprisoned, was too cruel a notion for Jeanne to imagine.

"Return to France?" The thought filled her with dread. "You know what awaits me there."

"Yes. Your estate, Mursay. All that is rightfully yours bequeathed to you by your father. Not to mention your true identify."

"But if I attempt to reclaim it, my life will once again hang in the balance."

Jacques held her hand as they walked. "Your fingers are icy and your hand trembles so. I understand why you're afraid, but you're no longer a little country girl. You can't be controlled like a marionette with your aunt at the strings. There is too much you know."

"But what am I to do, Jacques? Barge up to the front gates and accuse my aunt of murder? She will deny everything."

"But you have proof. In Madeleine you have a witness to the plot against you and a note in your aunt's own hand acknowledging she knew of your existence at La Salpêtrière and laid a trap for you." He stopped and took her into his arms. "And you have me. Together we will avenge your claim. I swear it. Then we shall marry without fear of our contract being disavowed. I'll marry the right and true Mademoiselle Jeanne Denot."

She closed her eyes, allowing herself to be lost in the sensation of holding him, then stepped back. "It used to be my sole purpose, my reason for living, to return. I burned with the idea of revenge against my aunt and the priest. Then I met you and those fires cooled."

"Then I'm sorry to stir them, I truly am, but if you don't return, we'll live under a falsehood. I want our marriage to be one we can hold up to the light of day before both God and man."

****

Jacques secured passage on the *Saint Jean-Baptiste*, departing for France in the late summer. Until then, he stayed at the La Forge estate. Teeth had extended their hospitality gladly to the man who saved her neck from the hangman's noose, and who possessed knowledge of delivering new life. In early July, with Jacques' help, Teeth gave birth to a robust baby girl, Marie-Thérèse.

Outside the convent chapel where the child had been christened, Jeanne and Jacques, acting as the baby's godparents, gathered with Madeleine and Laurent to admire little Marie-Thérèse in the light of the fine summer morning.

"Named after our own magnificent queen,"

Monsieur La Forge explained. "She is nothing short of a princess. Regard how she holds her nose so high. Regal, is she not?"

Monsieur La Forge held the tiny infant, his arms outstretched, displaying her the way one would a fine pelt of fur or a swatch of the rarest silk. Although Jeanne found nothing extraordinary about the infant, she agreed the baby was splendid, nonetheless.

After they listened to Monsieur La Forge extol the superior attributes of Marie-Thérèse's ears, pronouncing them "exceedingly dainty," her eyes, "brilliant like her mother's" and her general perfection, Teeth steered the conversation in another direction.

"When do you set sail for France?" she asked.

"Two days," Jacques responded. "We will reach La Rochelle in September."

Madeleine sighed and rested her head on Jeanne's shoulder. "Be sure you return, my friend. Promise me."

"I promise," Jeanne said.

"For the life of me I do not understand why," Teeth said. "A grand estate is yours for the claiming and you are coming back here? To the edge of the world? The outskirts of civilization?"

Monsieur La Forge looked crestfallen. "My darling, are you not happy here?"

"Don't be a nincompoop, husband! I am overjoyed with New France. But would I trade chicken plucking, wood splitting, and knit picking for lounging about a chateau with servants at my command? Within a beat of my heart."

Chapter Thirty-Six

"It is not the absence, but the mastery, of our passions which affords happiness."

~*Francoise D'Aubigné, Second Wife of King Louis XIV*

The *Saint Jean-Baptiste*

August 15, 1669
Dear Madeleine and friends,
Here is the first of my reporting, as promised. We have been afloat for some twenty days and time is passing more pleasantly than on my first seafaring adventure. That is partly due to our ship. The Saint Jean Baptiste is a bit more generous in its interior than the Saint Anne, as is the bedding. I have vowed after sleeping in a hammock for sixty-some nights to never look at one again. All five and twenty passengers aboard sleep in a hold. The middle is reserved for families and married couples. Single men have their own area.

Being the only unattached female, I slumber quite alone on a feather mattress situated between two canons in the aft of the ship! My nighttime companions, designed to protect, unnerve me as I often bump into them when moving about in the dark of the hold. Mostly the voyage is improved by the presence of one Jacques

Suprenant. (Perhaps you are not surprised?) We spend our days idly. Well stocked with books, we have made fair headway through our beloved Plutarch (as many times as I travel those pages, I never tire of their narratives). Lest I sound too sober, Jacques has organized a regular game of spillikins with the other passengers that include two families and a retinue of officers from the Carignan-Salieres.

Lively rounds of basset were played last night. The captain of the ship was none too happy to see it and forbade the players from using actual money. He noted that in such close quarters, gambling is ill-advised. So, the group wagered with dried prunes. They have nearly exhausted the ship's supply and I am most curious to see the next currency.

I draft this correspondence from the captain's letter desk, which he has generously offered me. Given the scarcity of paper and ink, I shall end my report here.

August 20

Friends,

Another week has passed since my last missive and so far, the weather has behaved, and we are not too troubled by the churning of the sea. Two nights previously, the Jean Baptiste met with a squall. Nothing to compare to those nights on the Saint Anne where we skittered back and forth across the floor like skimming stones! One of the ladies on board, born in New France and without experience of seafaring, became so nervous at supper that at regular intervals, like a cuckoo clock, as the boat rocked, she let out little nervous peeps that soon grew to gusty shrieking. Although she was entreated to stop by the rest of us passengers, she could not contain herself. The captain doubled the ration of wine, most of it consumed by this lady who was presently as drunk as a bell ringer. Instead of calming her, her imbibing had the effect of doubling her hysteria and her husband was at last obliged to cart her below deck. I saw her the next morning looking much worse for the wear. She avoided meeting my eyes.

August 27

The Jean Baptiste ran into a proper storm yesterday. My hand still shakes at the memory of it. Jacques and I saw the sun first rise from the top deck as we enjoyed our customary stroll. We both remarked how agitated the livestock were in their crates, and Jacques reminded me of the old adage about, "red skies in morning." The horizon was crimson. Over the course of the day, the seas swelled and once again we were stuck dining with Madame Cuckoo Clock, only now she was wound even tighter. Dinner ended abruptly when a cabinet tipped over, nearly falling on Cuckoo's husband. I invite you to imagine what this did to the poor woman's already frayed nerves.

Jacques escorted me to my space in the aft and gallantly refused to leave me alone. So great my terror, I had not a bit of concern about the impropriety of it. Wedged between one of the canons and the wall we clung together, the ship at times listing at angles so sharp, I believed it would turn upside down and plunge us to the bottom of the ocean.

At last, after what seemed an eternity, the water calmed. Today it is as if it never happened. The changeling sea transformed from savage beast to mild lamb. Let us hope it remains so.

August 31

I came across the hysterical wife today. On this beautiful morning I found her crouched near the mizzenmast, her head in her hands. When I greeted her, she pretended not to hear me, so I took pains to crouch down next to her and ask what was the matter and she said, "I do not wish to go to this new country."

"France?" It seemed odd to me to characterize France as "new."

"Yes. My husband has tried to teach me the customs, to tell me of the great towns where the only trees are those rendered into wagons and houses. How will I survive in such a place?"

Raised all her fourteen years in New France, I understand her trepidation. Yet I had to laugh to myself. How mutable is the world around us? There is no one painting or single narrative to capture the true version of life. It is all within the interpretation of the artist.

September 10

Dullness and routine are the greatest blessings of sea travel. God save us from excitement, the unexpected, the exceptional, for they always bring with them torment. Pirates, disease, tempest: all are potential passengers. I think back in horror of the night when this magnificent vessel, one of the largest and finest in the king's fleet, was tossed about like a toy boat in the pond of an angry giant stomping and churning the water. Since then, the days have brought with them no new surprises. The giant is happy and allows us to travel across these waters undisturbed. I have taken to speaking daily with the little wife who fears France so terribly and am now more than a little ashamed at my impatience with her at the beginning of the journey. Now we have lessons where I teach her the niceties of society, working on how she picks up her food at the table so as not to slouch, how to more discreetly pick food from her teeth, and other finer points of dinner table etiquette.

As we are now closer to the end of our journey than to the beginning, my anxieties increase. What shall I encounter upon my return to Mursay? How shall I confront my aunt with the deeds she has done, and will my story be believed? Jacques reminds me of the words of Plutarch: 'Courage is not hazarding without fear, it is pursuing resolutely a just cause.' We shall reach La Rochelle in a number of days which brings to an end dullness, routine, and predictability...

September 20 (or thereabouts, we have disagreements onboard as to the precise date)

We now see land, the distant coast of France! What a queer feeling to know that tomorrow my feet will be on my native soil, although not quite home. Home is a place I have not seen for nearly two years. I left a wide-eyed child, as pampered as a lap dog, and return a woman of the world to face those who conspired to do away with me. Jacques orchestrated a plan requiring me to lay low in the village while he travels to Mursay, seeking my aunt. He will represent himself as a colleague of my father and inform my aunt of a windfall intended for me. With the proverbial bait on the hook, he will enjoin her to sign a contract confirming I am no longer among the living, and in the act, incriminate herself further as I will testify she knew very well of my existence. I still have in my possession the letter from her acknowledging as much.

We will return together to Mursay and confront

her. The thought of it delivers a queer sensation to my stomach. I feel at once sick at the thought, and feverishly excited in anticipation of the look on her face when she catches sight of me! This will be my last letter from the Saint Jean-Baptiste. My next communication should reveal much more about my future. If only I could somehow divine the contents of that letter now.

Your loving friend, Jeanne

Chapter Thirty-Seven

"A voyage of four hundred leagues doesn't scare these heroines at all. I already know two of them whose adventures would furnish the material for a novel."
~*Father Du Poisson, Jesuit Relations, New France*

Mursay

Jeanne sat by the window of her room, observing the children of the innkeeper as they played a game of hide-and-seek in the garden below. The younger child, a boy, wandered about haphazardly, occasionally peering under a bush and yelling, "I'm going to find you!" From her vantage, Jeanne could see the boy's older sister dart in and out behind trees, occasionally mocking him with a whistle which inspired a momentary focus in the child, soon replaced with his lack-a-day manner of searching.

They had been at the inn for two days, during which time Jeanne felt more confined than she had ever been on the *Saint Anne*. The town, a short carriage ride from Mursay, was populated with people Jeanne knew well. Upon arriving, Jeanne encountered Henriette, who now worked at the inn. Henriette, the girl who had cared for her and Francoise as children, the servant who they had abused so casually and so frequently with their dismissive words and, at times, physical blows. Jeanne burned with the shame of it and ducked her veiled head as Jacques secured their rooms with the innkeeper, careful to avoid the curious gaze of Henriette.

On the third day of their stay, Jacques rode out to Mursay to bait the hook with Aunt Mimi and the priest while Jeanne continued to lay low. She ventured into the garden of the inn wearing not only a veil, but a sun mask favored by the women of the court. While strolling the garden, she overhead an exchange between Henriette and the innkeeper from the open door to the kitchen.

"No lock in the world could have held me in that place, I swear to you. It's a wonder the chateau is maintained at all, what with myself, cook, and three of the stable boys leaving on account of the scandal."

The innkeeper responded but Jeanne failed to catch his words.

She leaned closer to the door as Henriette replied, "He was a priest! A man of God. Privy to the darkest secrets of the townspeople. Then from one day to the next he abandons the cloth to marry that harlot, the marquise."

Her companion responded, "I wouldn't darken their door if you paid me."

"Never! Goodbye and good riddance, I told them both," Henriette said. "That woman was no good. And neither was them two snot-nosed girls. Although the drowning of the one was a terrible tragedy, and it is wicked to speak ill of the dead, she that died was the snottiest of the two by far."

The sting of Henriette's words drove Jeanne back into her room where she remained until Jacques returned. From his expression, she could tell something was amiss. He drew a chair next to hers and gently took hold of one of her hands.

Jeanne said, "Did you see my aunt? Was Francoise there? Is it true that she is now married to the priest?"

He raised his eyebrows. "It is true. I often marvel at your ability to know the contents of my head, but this is truly remarkable."

Jeanne told him about Henriette and the conversation she overheard, leaving out Henriette's more damning sentiments about her own character.

"I met your aunt and Monsieur Dieudonné and found them both to be utterly charming and utterly repulsive in equal measure. Knowing what lies behind their false fronts and cultivated manners chilled me to the bone. And it will come as no surprise, but they are very much interested in pursuing the windfall from your demise."

"Did you see Francoise?"

"No. Although we will shortly. They have invited me to a masquerade. A ball to celebrate the pending nuptials of Francoise to one August Loret."

"August Loret? It is not possible!"

Jacques said, "I am quite certain of the name."

"August Loret is a buffoon. A pompous fool who offers nothing but money."

Jacques nodded his head. "I believe you have found the raison d'etre of their union."

"With my inheritance safely in their hands, why would they need the Loret fortune?"

"It appears that your aunt's greed knows no bounds. This is a woman who is capable of murdering for money after all, or condoning murder in any case. A loveless marriage is certainly a peccadillo, one most of this country's finer families are guilty of."

Francoise to marry August Loret! Jeanne could not help but pity her cousin. "How shall I gain entrance to the ball?"

"I asked if I could bring a female companion and Madame Dieudonné was more than eager to extend the additional invitation. Until then we need to procure suitable clothing for both of us and masks."

Since they'd arrived in Perche, Jeanne suffered from nervous anxiety that made it difficult for her to eat or sleep. At the prospect of returning to Mursay, her anxiety trebled.

"You are trembling," Jacques said, gathering her in his arms.

"I don't know if I can do this."

"You would be foolish not to be frightened. They have proved how dangerous they are."

"It is not that, exactly."

"What is it then? You know I'll be by your side every moment." He kissed her cheek. "I would die before I'd let someone harm you."

She started to speak, then fell silent. At last she said, "By confronting my aunt there is no more room for doubt. There is, you see, a small corner of my heart that still loves her and longs for her affection. In that space burns a flame of hope, that all of this will prove to be some disastrous misunderstanding. I dread having the flame extinguished. It's foolish, I suppose."

"To love and want to be loved in return? It's the least foolish thing there is. But, Jeanne, our love will vanquish their deception. Every nook and cranny of your heart will be kindled with it, will blaze with happiness. I promise you."

Jeanne murmured an acknowledgement of his words yet found them naïve. The receipt of love was not like the receipt of goods, or a ledger reconciled by moving sums from one book to another. What her aunt had stolen could never to be restored.

****

A line of carriages snaked its way from far outside the chateau to the entrance of Mursay. "We must arrive in grand style. Make sure they smell the promise of lucre before we even set foot inside," Jacques had said when he went to hire the gaudy carriage.

Among the ostentatious coaches, theirs outshone the rest; drawn by eight white horses adorned with red plumed headdresses, the carriage, lacquered in white on the outside, had an interior of red silk. The stagnant autumn air inside was heavy with moisture. Behind Jeanne's mask, shaped like a butterfly, beads of perspiration gathered. Jeanne brushed them away without fully removing her disguise for fear of revealing her identity.

"I feel a bit light-headed." Jeanne tugged at the heavy silk skirts of her gown, a creation as grandiose as the carriage with yards of bright pink silk embroidered with a white butterfly motif.

Jacques squeezed her hand. "There are only four coaches ahead of us. It is soon our turn."

Alighting from the carriage, Jeanne moved carefully. She struggled to see properly through the slits of her mask, and the silver wig she wore seemed in constant danger of slipping off her head.

She held Jacques' arm as they made their way to the great hall. In the throng of revelers, Jeanne looked for signs of Aunt Mimi and Francoise, hoping to spy them first so she could compose herself before encountering them. At the entrance to the ballroom, Jeanne caught sight of August Loret and his parents greeting each guest in turn.

Jeanne watched as August exchanged pleasantries and observed that his form, portly before, could now more aptly be described as colossal. Sweat streaked the flab of his red-hued skin, and he resembled someone who had been caught in a rain shower.

Their turn for introductions arrived, and Jacques bowed courteously, removing his mask.

August returned the bow, a shallow motion given his girth. "Monsieur Suprenant! You are most welcome here, my good man. Madame Dieudonné told me all about your recent visit. What a pleasure to have you in the embrace of our hospitality at Mursay. And who, pray tell, is this lovely butterfly flitting by your side?"

The way he carried on! As if he were master of Mursay. Jeanne entertained slapping him in response, but instead she curtsied. "Mademoiselle Davide. Pleasure to meet you, monsieur."

"The pleasure is entirely our own." August produced a handkerchief from his waistcoat and mopped his brow with it. "My intended wife arranged my costume for me. She even acquired a horse's head for me to wear, but in this heat, it is out of the question. Will you not remove your own mask, mademoiselle? Many of the other revelers have done so until the night air cools. I am sure we would all be quite enchanted by your beauty."

"You will set eyes on her face soon enough, monsieur, and I promise you will be amazed." Jacques bowed once more before accompanying Jeanne into the ballroom.

They made their way down the staircase. There were no signs of the Dieudonnés or Francoise. Moving through the crowd, Jeanne took inventory of the opulence surrounding them. Damask drapery replaced the plainer linen variety, crystal candleholders now glittered where brass once stood, and an entire wall was outfitted with massive gold-leafed mirrors. A retinue of footmen, none whom Jeanne recognized, stood at attention throughout the ballroom, all of them clad in livery of the finest sky-blue silk.

"So much has changed," Jeanne said. "None of this was here before." She waved her hand, gesturing toward a table laden with silver serving dishes. "No wonder my aunt needs the Loret's money."

At that moment, the music halted. A flourish sounded drawing the attention of the room to the top of the staircase. A footman bellowed, "Madame and Monsieur Dieudonné." At the sound of the name, Jeanne clutched Jacques' arm.

"I have you," he whispered.

The couple swept down the short staircase, Aunt Mimi wearing a white flowing gown with a halo encircling a golden wig. Magnificent wings of gold were fastened to the back of her dress. The former priest wore red breeches from which trailed a tail, and a waistcoat and horned mask in the same color.

Jeanne, transfixed at the sight of them, whispered, "He is the Devil himself," and recalled his face, another mask of evil, as he loomed over her before he pushed her into the Seine.

"She, however, is far from an angel," Jacques said.

Jeanne felt the room begin to spin. "If I don't sit,

I'm afraid I'll fall down." Jacques led her to a seat by one of the open doors leading out to the garden, and Jeanne lifted her mask a little to take in the fresh air.

As Jacques hurried away to fetch a glass of wine, she gazed out over the sweeping lawn of Mursay. It was far more manicured now, dotted with marble statuary lining new stone pathways. In the center of it, a fountain featuring a bare-breasted goddess cavorting with the figure of Neptune spouted water high into the air.

Jacques came back with the wine, and after a few sips, they made their way through the ballroom. Another flourish sounded and the room fell quiet.

"Mademoiselle Francoise Josefine Antonia de Vitré and Monsieur August Jean-Claude Cesar Loret."

All eyes turned again toward the staircase and a shuddering gasp skipped across the room. August had donned his horsehead and made his way clumsily down the steps while Francoise wore black from head-to-toe, her gown rendered from a material that held all the luster of a lump of coal. Francoise's face, partly obscured by a long black veil, had grown more beautiful, her features more refined, womanly.

"What is she meant to resemble? A nun?" Jacques asked.

"A widow." Jeanne's spirits soared. Her cousin's choice of costume could be only interpreted in one way: as a protest against her upcoming nuptials.

"Fascinating choice for a bride-to-be," Jacques said. "Prepare yourself, Jeanne. Your aunt and her devilish husband approach."

Jeanne tightened her mask and braced for the encounter.

"Monsieur Suprenant, there you are! We are so delighted to have you here." Mimi curtsied and glanced at Jeanne. "Who is this lovely butterfly you have netted?"

Seeing her aunt in such close proximity, Jeanne yearned to embrace her, tell her how much she had missed her. At the same moment she longed to flee this house and these people, never to return.

"Allow me to introduce Mademoiselle Davide," he said smoothly.

Pleasantries were exchanged during which Jeanne managed to mumble a few words, afraid her aunt and the priest would recognize her voice.

The priest turned to her, his eyes a vivid blue behind the crimson of his mask. "Are you from Paris, mademoiselle?"

"Mademoiselle Davide is, in fact, from New France," Jacques said.

"How very exciting! We've never met anyone from there before, have we, my love? One imagines such people to be covered by feathers and furs." The priest laughed at his own witticism. "You, however, appear quite tame."

From where she stood, it would be no effort to reach out and slap the blackguard, but she held her impulse in check, if not her tongue. "Beware my teeth and claws. They are savage enough."

"A butterfly with claws. Intriguing." Monsieur Dieudonné swept up the tail of his costume and held it over one arm, the way one would the train of a gown. "My dear wife, we must excuse ourselves from this charming couple. We shall open the dance floor again. I expect to have a spin on the floor with you, mademoiselle." He bowed ceremoniously, removing his mask to kiss Jeanne's hand. She withdrew it abruptly and he looked up, startled.

Jeanne covered her impulse by making a joke. "I do not wish you mauled by my talons, monsieur."

The offense faded from the devil's face replaced by a sly look. "Fear not. I have broken wilder beasts, I am sure."

When they were well away, Jeanne said, "It is all I can do to keep from shuddering around that man. My flesh crawls in his presence."

"He is a most obsequious toad."

Jeanne surveyed the room. "Where has my cousin gone?"

"By all rights, she and her betrothed should have led the dancing." Jacques nodded toward the dancefloor. "Instead, your aunt and the priest have done so."

"This is a strange affair. It feels as if I'm in a dream. A nightmare where everything is familiar yet entirely foreign."

"The nightmare will be over soon. Come. If you are recovered from your spell, we'll carry out our plan."

They took a turn around the room searching for Francoise. From the corner of her eye, Jeanne glimpsed a figure in black darting though one of the open doors leading to the garden. They followed her. The gloaming cast enough light that they could see Francoise as she ran across the lawn toward the mouth of the labyrinth. She paused for a moment, looked back toward the house, then disappeared inside.

As they entered the labyrinth, Jeanne removed her mask. Although the hedges were high and thick, making it impossible to shortcut the maze, the routes within ran at regular right turns without dead ends, and presently they came upon Francoise at the center of it, seated on a bench. Even in the weak evening light Jeanne could see tears glistening on her cheeks.

When Francoise became aware of their presence she wiped at her face with the back of her arm, the way a child would, and covered her face with her veil. "Please go away. I seek solitude in this place, and you are robbing me of it." She ducked her head as she spoke, barely looking at them.

Jeanne stood at a distance from her cousin. She came closer. "I too have been robbed, mademoiselle. But my loss is far greater than a moment of solitude. I have lost my name, all my worldly goods, and what little family I had left."

Francoise lifted her veil to gaze directly at Jeanne, her mouth agape. "Jeanne? Could it be after all this time?" She stood and took a step closer. "Merciful Mary, it is you!" She ran toward Jeanne and hugged her, shouting, "It is a miracle. The answer to my prayers!"

For a moment Jeanne stiffened in her cousin's embrace and then returned it fully, both of them overcome in turn by fits of crying and laughter. Jeanne and Jacques had decided to confront Francoise first, privately, with the news of Jeanne's return and gauge her innocence or culpability by her reaction. Her response revealed the necessary proof.

After more exclamations of surprise and delight Francoise collected herself. "Where have you been all this time, Jeanne? What happened to you? We thought you were dead! Who is this gentleman who accompanies you?"

Jeanne introduced Jacques to her cousin, then sat down with her on the bench and began the tale of her disappearance after the ill-fated trip to Paris.

"My mother told me you fell off the boat and into the Seine on the journey home. We held a funeral for you. Visit the graveyard and you'll see the headstone."

Jeanne shuddered at the length of her aunt's deceit. "She has spun so many lies to cover the truth. What did she tell the court when she turned up without me? Or maybe she told them we were both left behind in Mursay, the victims of an unfortunate case of bedbugs."

"Dearest Jeanne, I do not doubt the dark priest's intentions. But Maman? How could it be? We are both daughters to her, she has said so herself many times and I know it to be true."

Jeanne put an arm around her cousin's shoulders. "Francoise, I have a letter in your mother's hand directing me to meet a man she said would arrange my passage to Mursay. Instead, he tried to cut my throat."

"No." Francoise shook her head violently. "Never. She would never do that. She trusted a scoundrel. It was the false priest who conspired to harm you, not my mother."

Jacques had witnessed their exchange silently but now said, "No one wants to believe that more than your cousin. With the marriage of your mother to the priest, do you not see it only strengthens the motive to be rid of Jeanne?"

"I despise the man! The maggot. It's what I call him under my breath and once to Maman's face. If anyone is behind this, it is him. Perhaps she went along with his schemes, but I promise you, he is the instigator. He orchestrated this marriage with the pig, August Loret."

"Why did you agree, dear cousin?"

Francoise laughed bitterly. "Have you not seen all the finery in the house? Every surface dipped in silk and every bowl in silver. The priest and his avarice have impelled this farcical union, and my dear mother acquiesced because she's in his thrall. I believe they have carried on their love affair for many years before gilding their sin with holy matrimony."

Jeanne recalled how, as a child, she had come upon the two of them in the chapel at Mursay. "But why? It's as if he's bewitched her."

Francoise sighed. "I don't understand it myself. I only know you to be a miracle. When you found me here, I was praying to God to deliver me from August Loret. With you here, alive, everything changes. We must go at once to tell Maman." She rose from the bench.

Jacques held up a hand, stopping Francoise with the gesture. "Regardless of who hatched this plot, both your mother and the priest, or the priest alone, a plot exists. We have proof of it. Let us reveal Jeanne's identity to your mother and Dieudonné in our own fashion, mademoiselle."

Chapter Thirty-Eight

There is little that can withstand a man who can conquer himself.

~*King Louis XIV*

Mursay

As Jeanne, Francoise and Jacques entered the ballroom, Aunt Mimi saw them and said, "There you are, my dearest." Although she kept her voice light, Jeanne could hear an edge underlying her words. "One should never disappear from one's own party, my darling. Although I am happy to see you've met Monsieur Suprenant and his friend."

"Why am I needed?" Francoise said. "Is the fatted calf longing for a dance?"

"Francoise! Do watch yourself." Aunt Mimi laughed. "Forgive my daughter, monsieur. She has a strange sense of humor and suffers the jittery temperament of a bride-to-be." Then, turning to her daughter, Aunt Mimi dropped any pretense of mildness and glared at her. "You and your betrothed are to lead the next minuet. Go find him. Now."

Jacques turned to Aunt Mimi. "Madame, I hate to detract from the celebration, but we wondered if we could have a word with you in private? If now is a convenient time, of course."

"For you, monsieur, I will always find time."

She led them to the library, and upon entering the room, Jeanne nearly fainted. Her father's sanctuary remained intact, his books encircling her as if in an embrace. The smell of leather and the lingering scent of the fires that had warmed this room brought back the memory of her father and the comfort of the place. Tears came, making it difficult for Jeanne to see behind her mask.

Aunt Mimi took notice and said, "Mademoiselle, it appears as if that mask is causing you fits. Surely you can remove it now."

"No. Not quite yet," she said.

Jacques said, "I believe the marquise is right, my love. Show us your face." Standing in front of Jeanne, blocking Aunt Mimi's view, he gently lifted the mask. "Now is as good a time as any. This is, after all, why we sought your confidence, marquise." He stepped back so that Aunt Mimi could see Jeanne's face.

Her aunt drew a sharp breath and staggered away from them. "Jeanne! My God in Heaven. This cannot be."

Jeanne said, "I am so sorry to have disappointed you, Auntie."

The marquise stood as if rooted to the floor, but at Jeanne's words, she rushed toward her, arms open. "Disappointed? How could I be disappointed my dear, dear child. I am overwhelmed with delight!"

As her aunt enveloped her in an embrace, Jeanne's own arms hung limply at her sides. Presently Aunt Mimi took a step back. "Look at you. A woman now. You are so changed."

"I am not the person who left Mursay to journey to

359

Paris more than a year ago. The naïve child. So very trusting. That girl believed in the sanctity of blood ties and could not have imagined the treachery ahead of her."

"Your cold demeanor, Jeanne, the look in your eyes are as good as an accusation. I am overjoyed at your return and know nothing of any betrayal."

"I have a letter, composed by you, leading me to the two-faced villain meant to take my life."

"Two-faced villain? I am lost."

"Monsieur Arnold."

"I know of no such person. Why would I do such a thing, Jeanne? Someone has forged my hand." Aunt Mimi's eyes were wet with tears. She turned to Jacques, her hands clasped, and pleaded, "Monsieur, you must talk sense into her. She is like a daughter to me!"

Her aunt had proclaimed as much on so many occasions, always in the presence of others, like an actress who requires an audience for her words to ring true.

The righteousness of Jeanne's anger vanquished the fear she had felt only moments before. "I am the daughter of Antoine and Agnés Denot. To escape you, I became a Daughter of the King. But when it concerns you, marquise, I am nothing. Because of my love for Francoise, I will show you a degree of mercy. Much more than you would have shown me. But I shall regain my rightful place. Here. Tonight."

Her aunt made to protest, but Jeanne swept past her, nearly running to the ballroom. At the top of the staircase, she bade one of the new footmen to announce her presence.

He hesitated. "Mademoiselle, only the principal

members of the household are announced."

Aunt Mimi caught up with her and ordered the footman to oblige. Jeanne stood at the top of the steps and held out her hand for Jacques to hold.

They awaited their flourish. At its sound, the music ceased, and all eyes were diverted to the staircase. Even before the footman made his announcement, a susurration rippled through the crowd, a noise that grew to a crescendo at the pronouncement of her name.

Madame Loret, who had been dancing with her son, gasped, then wheezed. "August! You must catch me. I am fainting!" August, himself in a state of great confusion, failed to respond and his mother landed in a heap on the ballroom floor.

Jeanne registered some of the pronouncements made: "She lives!" "It is the daughter, is it not?" "Is she a spirit or flesh and blood?"

Francoise came to stand before Jeanne, facing the crowd. "This is my cousin and the rightful heir to Mursay." Francoise pointed at Father Dieudonné, and in her black clothes contrasting with her fair hair and skin, she resembled some beatific interpretation of the Grim Reaper. "The devilish priest must be made to answer." At her words, those standing near the man backed away, forming a circle around him.

The priest had removed his ghoulish mask, yet his face retained its ruddy hue. "I know not of what you speak. Yes, I was with the girl when she fell into the Seine. But it was an accident." He mopped his brow with the back of his hand. "We combed the river day and night to recover her and searched every street in Paris."

Jeanne shook her head. "No, no, no." She

whispered the words at first and then her anger, fired by the audacity of his claims, took hold of her, and her voice rang out across the room. "Liar! The true accident, monsieur, was my surviving two separate attempts at ending my life."

"The priest should be made to pay!" someone shouted.

Father Dieudonné appealed desperately to those around him. "It is not true! The girl lies," he said, his voice breaking. "Where is Mimi? Where is my wife? She will vouch for me." He rushed toward the staircase.

Jacques grabbed hold of him, calling to the footmen for aid in restraining him. Presently, they wrestled the devil to the floor.

The priest cried out, "A storm raged that night. Even a man of God cannot summon a storm!"

Observing his crumpled form, Jeanne wondered how this man had ever inspired such fear in her.

Looking down upon him, she said, "You are no man of God. You only masqueraded as one. Horns and a pitchfork are the truest reflection of the contents of your heart, monsieur."

Great rivulets of tears streamed down the priest's face. "Jeanne, I beg you to have mercy on me." He knelt before her and grabbed the hem of her dress, kissing it. "You are a kind-hearted spirit. A child of God. Judge me not, for you are unaware of the particulars."

Jeanne stepped back, repulsed by his display. "Let me tell you the particulars. I lost my freedom, my name and nearly my life. And you ask me to show you mercy? I refuse, monsieur. You told me yourself that night on the boat, before you pushed me overboard, only God can judge our earthly comportment. I pray he banishes you to the pits of Hell."

Chapter Thirty-Nine

"The future bears down upon each one of us with all the hazards of the unknown. The only way out is through."

~*Plutarch*

The *Saint Anne*

"My name is Jeanne Suprenant," she whispered, the sound of the family name still awkward on her tongue.

She looked around the cabin, the very same one Jacques occupied on their first voyage to New France. Although the portholes were closed, through the dim light, she saw the curl of a smile on Jacques' lips.

"I thought you were sleeping," she said.

"No. I enjoy listening to you practicing your new name too much to sleep." He gathered her in his arms. "Comfortable with it yet, madame?"

"Yes. It helps to rehearse it like a line in a play."

He laughed. "Memorize it thoroughly, because you are not allowed a new role."

"This one suits me rather well. I believe I will keep it for at least a lifetime."

Their lips met, and after a moment, Jeanne said, "We've kissed so much these past days, my lips are bruised."

He put his hands around her waist and drew her

closer, brushing his lips against her neck and across her breasts. "Look how thoughtful your new husband is. I'm giving your lips a rest," he said, as he kissed the length of her body.

They spent the better part of the day in bed, until after a time Jeanne said, "Should we rise and meet the other passengers for supper?"

He lay sprawled across the bed, his head resting on her thigh. "Do we have to? I want to stay like this, just the two of us, forever."

"But what about food? Drink? What about Plutarch?"

He pulled a serious face. "We can't disappoint Plutarch."

She smiled and said, "How very happy I am. Do you think it's right, Jacques? Are we getting more than our fair share of the world's joy?"

"We've both had more than our fair share of its misery." He stretched out next to her, then pulled her into his embrace. "I think we're allowed a few helpings of bliss, matrimonial and otherwise."

"You're right, of course."

"What's this? You're frowning. Are you not happy, wife?"

"Oh, but I am. To be with you. To return to New France to a life of our own making. Yet when I consider poor Francoise—" She couldn't bear to finish the thought.

"You're worried about what will become of her?" Jacques said. Jeanne nodded and lay her head on his chest and he stroked her hair. "Thanks to you, she has Mursay."

"An estate bled to the bone."

The cupidity of Madame and Monsieur Dieudonné had left Mursay close to insolvent. Only after selling off the finery they amassed could Jeanne secure some hope of its survival.

"Perhaps she can revive it," Jacques said.

"Physical needs are easy to satisfy. In truth, Francoise never possessed the desire for the material the way my aunt did. I speak of her spiritual needs. Her mother and the priest imprisoned. The Lorets disavowing her. As much as a union with August would have been its own purgatory, at least she would have been cared for. Who will have her now, wrapped as she is in the shroud of scandal?"

"I don't know. It's terrible she's been made to suffer for the sins of her mother. Yet fortunate to have you as her champion."

"If only the Fates had not been so unkind to her."

"When the Fates are at their cruelest, they impart the greatest gifts. Consider a young woman I once knew. Betrayed by her own blood. Forced to journey to an unknown land to escape certain death. A harrowing story, one unlikely to end well. Yet here you are in my arms back on the very same vessel under very different circumstances."

She raised her eyes to meet his gaze. "Yet here we are."

Jacques kissed her softly and whispered, "Say your name again, my love. I need to hear it to believe it myself."

She bowed her head with mock seriousness, as if she were greeting a stranger. "Allow me to present myself, monsieur. I am Jeanne Denot Davide Suprenant."

A word about the author...

Catherine Pettersson is an author and founder of the Stockholm Writers Festival. Her great, great (and many more) grandmother Jeanne Denot was one of the 800 women known as "Les Filles du Roi," or "Daughters of the King." During the reign of Louis the XIV, the Daughters were shipped to Quebec and matched with husbands, members of the French cavalry. This ancestral fact inspired the historical fiction, *A Daughter of the King*.